Imaginary Crimes

ALSO BY SHEILA BALLANTYNE

Norma Jean the Termite Queen

Imaginary Crimes

Sheila Ballantyne

The Viking Press New York

First published in 1982 by The Viking Press
625 Madison Avenue, New York, N.Y. 10022
Published simultaneously in Canada by
Penguin Books Canada Limited

LIBRARY OF CONGRESS CATALOGING IN PUBLICATION DATA
Ballantyne, Sheila.
Imaginary crimes.
I. Title.
PS3552.A464I5   813'.54   81-65259
ISBN 0-670-48022-3   AACR2

Grateful acknowledgment is made to the following for
permission to reprint copyrighted material:
American Heritage Publishing Company: A selection from *The
Horizon Book of Lost Worlds,* by Leonard Cottrell. Copyright © 1962
by American Heritage Publishing Company.
Curtis Brown Limited, London: Selections from *The Sheik* (1921), by
E. M. Hull.
Harcourt Brace Jovanovich, Inc., and Faber and Faber Ltd.: Three lines
from T. S. Eliot's "The Waste Land" from *Collected Poems
1909–1935,* by T. S. Eliot.
Sir Rupert Hart-Davis: An excerpt from *Fortitude* (1913), by Hugh
Walpole.
Intersong Music: Portions of lyrics from "Anniversary Waltz," by
Al Dubin and Dave Franklin. Copyright © 1941 by Mayfair
Music Corp. Copyright renewed, assigned to Chappell & Co.,
Inc. (Intersong Music, Publisher). International copyright
secured. All rights reserved. Used by permission. Portions of
lyrics from "Sh-boom (Life Could Be a Dream)," by James
Keyes, Claude Feaster, Carl Feaster, Floyd F. McRae, and James
Edwards. Copyright © 1954 by Hill & Range Songs, Inc. All
rights controlled by Unichappell Music, Inc. (Rightsong Music,
Publisher). International copyright secured. All rights reserved.
Used by permission.
Mrs. Ellen C. Masters: The poem "George Gray" from *Spoon River
Anthology,* by Edgar Lee Masters.
Princeton University Press and Diana Ó Hehir: Selections from
"Reprieved" and "Home" from *The Power to Change Geography,* by
Diana Ó Hehir. Copyright © 1979 by Princeton University Press.
Wilson, Sonsini, Goodrich & Rosati: A brief excerpt from a Bing
Crosby song.

Printed in the United States of America
Set in Palatino
Designed by Kathryn Parise

For Borghild and Doreen

My deepest thanks are due the MacDowell Colony, for making it possible for me to complete this book, and my husband, Philip, and my children, Anya and Stefan, for their help in making MacDowell possible.

My crime seemed vague as rumor. It must have happened years ago,
Or not at all, or under water . . .

            I travel
Looking for myself in all the empty rooms
That say, why did you leave us.

                            —Diana Ó Hehir,
                              from "Reprieved" and "House"

Imaginary Crimes

🐾 Faded Photographs 🐾

Here is the picture that haunts me the most: the two of them sitting in her garden, with me between them. I am three, and they are young. Her stone wall stretches the width of the snapshot and beyond, where the forest reaches a limitless, pure dark.

His shirt is white and rolled at the elbows. His hair reflects the midsummer light. His teeth are very white, his arms tanned. He is holding me in his lap as though I were his child. I am pressing a flower against my cheek and staring into the distance.

She is thin and small. A white flower hangs carelessly from her dark hair. She sits by him and smiles directly into the camera. The three of us seem to be growing there, like flowers; rising from the dry summer grass along with the rest of her vegetation. We form a unit which resembles a family, but the truth is that she has left her husband back in their one-room basement apartment in Seattle. She has escaped with me to this familiar Canadian wilderness where she grew up; we don't have to go back until

September. On her left, a lavender bush is in full bloom; her mother, the woman I call Nona, planted it years before the picture was taken. The garden is hers; she built the wall, stone by stone.

There are other snapshots here, whole boxes full. I depend on these artifacts now; there is no one left to ask. I know they are inconclusive, that they yield only partial truths. Studying this particular pose of Valery, for instance, it disturbs me to see her smiling with such abandon; she never did that all those other years she was raising me. And this picture of my father, Ray, taken at some picnic long ago, sitting in the back of someone's rowboat, clutching a beer and flashing that broad smile and steady, open gaze: from the looks of it, you'd think he was the most trustworthy person in the world.

In addition to the snapshots, there is also this aging, black notebook. Within its watery, lined pages, Nona once recorded the evolution of her garden from a thick and absolute wilderness to those carefully cultivated acres, overflowing with flowers, vegetables, shrubbery and trees, between the years 1929 and 1938. I could search this notebook forever and find nothing of what I need to know. Some people keep journals of human events; Nona recorded the history of her vegetation. It's true that people occasionally slipped into her narrative—but only as bystanders to her voracious acquisition of plants—by trade, barter, theft, or, in extreme circumstances, actual purchase.

Mr. Gregson sent me a seedling from his pink hawthorne.
Mrs. Graham traded a forsythia for 1 doz. hyacinths. Planted cuttings of Gloire de Dijon and an unnamed pink rose from Mr. Breeze. Gave Mrs. Pool one of the passion vines. Set out daisies taken from roadside near Mr. Brown's. Found 2 roots of flowering currant on Whaletown Road, half uprooted when the road was widened. Took them home, and on way met Mrs. P. who challenged them, and went running across the chicken yard to get a leaf from her flowering currant to prove mine were respectively maple and salmonberry! She gave in reluctantly after minute comparison.

2

Otherwise, the entire journal reads much the same throughout as the entries on Page 1:

> Transplanted wisteria vine from shack to southeast corner of the veranda-to-be.
>
> Planted jasmine against east wall of cottage.
>
> Planted loganberry vine against old cedar stump at lower gate.
>
> On Christmas day, found Spanish iris, planted in October, two inches up—idiots!

But there is an uncharacteristic entry for September 1938, which, if coupled with the snapshot now in my hand, tells me something after all. It reads:

> Sonya picked big bouquets of Michaelmas daisies and made her own funny little arrangements of flowers in front of her daddy's photograph all summer.

I have a sudden vision of myself at two, learning the arts of funereal arrangement and votive offering. And yet, by the following year, in the summer of 1939, as this next snapshot attests, there I am, perched on the shoulder of Everett MacGregor, sweetly offering *him* a fistful of flowers. He smiles up at me in tanned appreciation, his perfect teeth catching the northern light. Was this an affectionate crime, I wonder, or an adaptive reaction?

I stare again at the three figures in Nona's country garden: there is nothing in their appearance to suggest that great depression which governed their lives at the time the shutter was tripped; not a thing that might betray the chronic poverty which they saw, and would always see, as a temporary inconvenience. In fact, the two of them are smiling as though they haven't a care in the world. The woman is my mother, Valery Weiler. I am the child in the middle. The man is Everett MacGregor, my mother's lover, and it has never occurred to me until this moment that, but for some twist of fate, I might have been his child. That would have changed everything.

3

Sonya Weiler sits on the bare wooden floor of a walk-in closet with a picture album spread across her lap. She is five years old. Her mother, Valery, squats beside her and points to a snapshot of Sonya at the age of two. "That's you," says Valery, unconvincingly.

Valery's knees hurt from bending. If she can get Sonya interested in the album, she can have her coffee and cigarette alone at the kitchen table. She can stare out the window and let her mind wander in peace. It is another rainy day; she has lived in Seattle seven years and should be used to them. It was different before Sonya was born: she could come and go then as the mood struck; she had the freedom to avoid this kind of oppression. It was Valery who had named her firstborn Sonya, after the figure skater Sonja Henie. "She moves through space so smoothly! She has such freedom!" she explained to Ray, the child's father. "Anything you want, honey," he replied, with a half-smile. "You're the mother."

Valery's mother lives on a small island off the coast of British Columbia. She chops her wood, draws water from a well, weeds the rocky soil, and teaches in the one-room island schoolhouse. When a student is "impudent," she always says the same thing: "Don't be cheeky, or I'll box your ears." She has never regretted having been one of the few women in her generation to divorce.

🦢 Kentucky Babe 🦢

Every Christmas, Nona came to Seattle to visit us. Daddy would set up a cot for her in the narrow kitchenette. While he and Mother busied themselves over dinner, Nona would close the swinging door between the kitchen and living room and turn out all the lights so we could play the Dark Game. "Here we go gathering nuts in May, nuts in May, nuts in May!" Nona would sing gaily as we danced around the card table in the middle of the room, bumping into each other, and the table, with increasing frequency. At the end of the song, we collapsed in a heap of giggles on the floor, flushed and exhausted. "You're getting her overexcited," Mother would warn. "Nonsense!" Nona would spit back authoritatively. Daddy smiled and whistled softly as he took the warmed plates out of the tiny oven.

After dinner, Nona would sit on a stool next to my crib in the walk-in closet and sing "Sleep, Kentucky Babe." I lay awake as long as I could in order to keep her there, singing. I twirled the loose bar in the crib softly, inhaling her scent. It was Yardley's English Lavender. She wore it as a kind of bridge between her rugged life on the island and life in the old country as she imagined it to have been. "Where, oh where, has my highland laddie gone?" she would croon wistfully to the tune of "Bluebells of Scotland." I have no idea how "Kentucky Babe" found its way into her repertoire. It wasn't until adulthood that I discovered that Kentucky Babe was a generic term, and did not apply exclusively to me. All those years I thought I was the Kentucky Babe.

Valery sits down at the kitchen table with a sigh; she is about to deal herself a hand of solitaire. Sonya turns the album pages in the walk-in closet. She sleeps in this room, in a crib she is about to outgrow, among the coats and trousers that hang along its north wall. She has slept in this closet for five years, waking from afternoon naps to the *slap, slap, slap* of Valery's cards on the kitchen table. Valery fights her sense of confinement by playing solitaire and reading paperback mysteries. When the weather is clear, she adds walking to her activities. Her one ambition is modest by most standards: she wants a home of her own. Any home will do. Anything but this one-room basement apartment.

She would never have believed, when she and Ray stepped through the door for the first time, that she would still be sitting at this table six years later. It was supposed to have been temporary, until something better came along. It makes her shiver, just remembering, and she pulls her thin sweater more tightly around her. The apartment is damp, being two-thirds underground; she suffers a continual chill. Her eyes sweep her perimeters with growing despair: the 15-by-19-foot living room with its pull-down bed and fading spread; the frayed maroon davenport and reading chair with the stand-up lamp behind it; the modest kitchen table against the south wall; and all of it resting on the faded Oriental with its huge threadbare spots. Behind the pull-down bed is the walk-in closet where Sonya stares at the snapshots. She cannot play, or look at pictures, when the bed is in the up position inside the closet because it takes up all the space. So

Valery leaves the bed down, although that takes up most of the space in the living room. It is a choice she has to weigh each day, and weather is usually the determining factor, although fatigue comes into consideration as well: there are days when Valery does not have the strength to "put up" the bed, whose hinges creak and stick, whose springs have lost their buoyancy, and whose total mass weighs a great deal. Often Ray will put it up himself when he gets home from work, just before dinner; then pull it down again three or four hours later before they go to sleep.

Behind the wall where Valery now sits is the kitchenette—a narrow room, 6 by 13 feet, with cupboards, sink, stove and drainboard. It is in this room that Sonya will sleep in a cot along the south wall when she finally outgrows the crib in the walk-in closet at the age of five and a half. It is in this room, three years from now, that Valery will sit at midnight on a stool in front of the open oven, rocking Greta, her second and final child, named for Garbo in *Camille:* weeping and cursing the landlord for his power to turn off the heat at seven; for their poverty; for Ray's wheeling and dealing; for promises that never come true; for the weight of her own powerlessness. She will rock and hum, in the blind, ancient way of mothers. Every few minutes, the melody line will be broken by spasms of despair as her voice becomes a cough. The colicky Greta wails. Nine-year-old Sonya will lie awake in her cot, watching the mother and child wrapped in a single shaft of invisible heat.

Rain sprays against the three small windows along the south wall; they are the only source of light in the apartment. Valery scans the peeling paint, the chipped molding, the dust balls she hasn't the energy to vacuum. Softly she hums "Amapola," as her cigarette smoke climbs and spreads across the ceiling. On the window sill above her head one pale begonia languishes in a light green pot. On days when there is no rain, it gets a south exposure to the sun. She has kept it alive for five years. It will last another four.

In the walk-in closet, Sonya stares at the photographic images on her lap. There is her mother with Uncle Everett in an old fishing boat that breaks the stillness of Canadian waters. They are embracing. The floor has warmed under her outstretched legs. The family's clothes hang silently on a wooden rack above her head. She wishes her father would come home from work. He represents action and excitement, the lure of the outside world. All Valery does is sit on the maroon davenport, reading mysteries and twirling the red cellophane pull string from her Lucky Strike package back and forth between her thumb and middle finger. Sonya wonders if she will sit and twirl cellophane between her fingers when she grows up. Ray comes and goes at will. He leaves the stifling confines of the apartment early in the morning and doesn't come back until dark. She is awed by, and envies, such freedom. She begs to be taken with him. Let Valery rot on the maroon davenport, lost in her cheap mysteries. The true mystery is what lies out there, beyond this room. Ray knew. She would know, too, someday. It was her destiny.

❧ Bucking the Wind ☙

"Bucking the wind" was Daddy's term for what he did on his way to the store to buy another bottle. The wind would blow in from the south and he would hold his collar around his neck, lower his head, and charge. I came of age when he let me go with him. I was his "buckaroo" (he was stuck on The Sons of the Pioneers; he always listened to them on the wooden table radio. He said they were fine, upstanding Americans), and we bucked the wind together. He often sang their songs as we walked. "Drifting along with the tumbling tumbleweeds," he crooned, leaning into the wind.

He used these walks to the grocery store to draw parallels between our bucking the wind and what people had to do in order to get through life: you bucked. I remember the wind in my face, being scarcely able to breathe, and my hand in his. When we reached the store, he would let me have a ball gum while he played the pinball machines. Mother waited back in the apartment for her loaf of Wonder Bread which, she knew, would come home disguised as a bottle of bourbon.

❧ John ❧

One Saturday Daddy went to the store without me; he left in a hurry. Mother was sitting on the maroon davenport with a faraway look on her face. Shortly after Daddy left, there was a knock on the door. Mother jumped. In came a man whom Mother stiffly introduced as "John." Mother and John sat on the maroon davenport talking. She told him that Daddy was out and that she didn't know where he was. "He's at the store," I said. Mother gave me a strained look; I didn't know what it meant, but I knew it had meaning. It sent a strange current of electricity all the way down my body. She compounded the mystery when she smiled a false kind of smile, and said, "John is a policeman." John smiled thinly in agreement. I was thrilled and confused; he didn't wear a uniform. They must be lying. Daddy could clear this up. No, they said, they didn't want me going all the way up there by myself. "He'll be back in a few minutes, dear. John will wait; he just wants to have a little talk with Daddy. John is Daddy's old friend."

I was really excited about that: here was his old friend sitting right there on the maroon davenport, and he didn't know it. I couldn't wait for him to come back; I secretly hoped I would have to go and get him. An hour later, when Daddy still hadn't come home, Mother reluctantly allowed that I could buck the wind and bring him back.

I jumped up and down beside the pinball machine; I was so excited about John. "Watch it, watch it, you're jiggling it," he said. I told him about John, and it was very strange, he didn't

10

even look up, just kept right on banging the sides of the machine with his palms—PING! POW! DING! Bells rang, lights blinked and flashed. "Yes, dear. Thank you for telling me, honey. But Daddy's busy now, Daddy can't come home just yet." It was the first time I had bucked the wind alone, and I sensed it was going to be that way from then on.

❧

Valery stays in bed late; the day seems to go faster that way. Sonya wakes early, climbing out of the closet crib and tiptoeing around her mother's form under the pale green spread. The windows on the south wall are shut to the morning light by tattered yellow windowshades; they give the room a deep ocher cast. In places where the fabric is worn, little points of pure light show through, forming white tributaries on cracked amber. Once or twice the bedsprings creak as Valery changes position. There are random noises from other apartments echoing through the walls: toilets flushing, radiator pipes cracking, doors slamming as occupants come and go. When Valery gets up, she will not raise the blinds. She will slip an edge between a forefinger and middle finger, and peek through the opening cautiously. This is Sonya's first hint that there is something to fear on the outside. She is confused; the sunlight seems so promising, the air has the unmistakable scent of morning. She jumps up and down and begs to go out. "Be still," Valery whispers. What could she be fearing out there?

Sonya sits on the cold linoleum, blowing dust balls around the molding. She rests her elbows on the sill of the lowest window and peers around the edges of the shade. Shiny black cars pass in the street; people in old overcoats hurry by on their way to work. It is a neighborhood of dark buildings, heavy trees, and wide, pebbled sidewalks. The apartment building rises five stories above the tiny basement unit, and is built with bricks the color of

11

dried blood. Its name curves in flaking gold calligraphy across the foyer door: The Avalon. The neighborhood is known as Capitol Hill. At the end of the street, one mile to the north, is a spacious park, and a sprawling art museum where Sonya and Valery sometimes go when it isn't raining.

There is a war somewhere far away. The people in the apartment across the street were arrested for hoarding sugar. Sonya asks Ray, "What is hoarding?" "It is buying more than your ration book allows and not sharing it with others," Ray answers, as he slips an extra pound of butter into the icebox with a sly smile. He adds: "Those dirty rotten traitors across the street don't deserve to be called Americans. They should be shot. No. Shooting is too good for them; they should also rot in hell."

Once a week, at night, there is an air raid drill. In the spring of 1942 Valery is appointed air raid warden for her block; it is the first time in her life that she has been singled out for anything, and she subdues her flush of exhilaration by thinking: It is wartime. The air raid siren sounds and lights are quickly extinguished; faces peer from darkened apartment windows as Valery slips out the door and walks to the corner to join the other wardens. A black scarf covers her head and her flashlight makes a tiny bobbing circle of light as she walks. She takes her place in the intersection and scans the night sky and the rows of darkened windows. No light must show; the Japs can see it from their planes. They are headed toward the West Coast from Japan, humming over the black ocean on their way to bomb Seattle. Everyone knows it will be by surprise attack, at night. Sonya wakes up screaming. She has seen a Jap. His face looked right in the window. No amount of argument by Ray and Valery can convince her she didn't see what she saw. He was wearing a black coat. She saw his teeth with her own eyes: they were large and white, like rows of porcelain tiles.

The weekly air raid drills give new meaning to Valery's life. Sonya peeks from behind the windowshade, noting the sense of purpose in Valery's walk. She is bursting with pride for her mother. She tells Jenny, her friend across the street, "My mother is an air raid warden." Jenny says, "Oh." It is the first time Sonya has been able to say: I have something that you don't. Jenny has a brother, a house with a porch, a mother who makes taffy on Halloween, who smiles, who does not play solitaire. Jenny sleeps in a bed with a mattress and springs, in a room just for sleeping, called a bedroom. In the autumn, leaves fall from the maple in their yard; they can be swept into high piles and jumped in, rolled in, and thrown. Their smell is a secret so intoxicating Sonya tells no one. Every fall she knocks on the door and asks: Can I play in your leaves?

Between air raid drills, Valery dreams of going to work as a riveter: women are going to work and doing men's jobs. She sees their pictures in the paper: they are wearing their head scarves upside down and tied on top. She begins to wear her scarf upside down. "But honey," Ray asks, "who would take care of Sonya?" Valery agrees; she can think of no one who could take care of Sonya. She lights another cigarette and finds her place in her book. In the evenings, the wooden table radio is tuned to the news; Valery and Ray begin speaking war language. Their voices assume new tones, and a new pitch—somewhere between an animated conversation and a conspiratorial whisper. Sonya's head resounds with the exotic new words whose meanings she doesn't understand: buzz bomb, barrage balloons, the duration, the Allies, the Axis, at the front, victory garden, air raid, war bond, paper drive, collection center.

Valery rises early one morning to announce: "Get all your rubber toys together, they're having a rubber drive. We can take a walk to the collection center." Sonya can't comprehend. Her toys? Squeaky? Porky Pig? "Yes," Valery says briskly. "We have to turn them all in." *Turn them in?* "Do you want Hitler to win the war?" Valery rejoins ominously. Sonya tries, but can't see the connection. Tearfully, she asks again as Valery sweeps all the toys into a paper bag. Valery sighs and attempts an explanation filled with allusions to melted rubber and Jeep tires. The toys rattle, rustle, bump and squeak inside the paper bag as mother and daughter make their way to the collection center. Gradually Sonya understands: Porky is on the first leg of a long journey. He will undergo a transformation by heat. He will become a tire on a

Jeep carrying soldiers across Europe. He will be doing his part for the war effort, as Valery puts it. It seems a lot to ask of a rubber pig. Sonya watches as her toys are added to the heap at the collection center; she has a desperate urge to retrieve just one, just Porky, but Valery is uncharacteristically firm. It would be unpatriotic. On the way home, there is a terrible sensation in Sonya's stomach. This is her first death. She fights to hold back the tears as Valery hums "And the Caissons Go Rolling Along." The war has given Valery a new lease on life. Sonya cannot understand: if it is such a terrible thing that lights are extinguished and people talk in whispers, why does it make her mother so happy?

Every night after dinner Ray takes Sonya out to the back basement hallway for a ride on her tricycle. Their route is to the laundry room at the end of the hall, and back. They repeat this course dozens of times, with Ray whistling a lively tune as he pushes the tricycle. He grips the handlebars and rests one foot on the back wheel bar as the other rhythmically pumps the ground. He accelerates the pace as his whistling quickens; Sonya lifts her feet off the pedals and shrieks as they pick up speed. Their shouts rebound off the flaking plaster walls and echo down the narrow hall. The once lavishly painted cement floor is now peeling off in large, red patches. Sonya has always been afraid of the underground hall and airless laundry room where Valery does the weekly wash and presses Ray's shirts on the huge mangle. Riding the tricycle with Ray is the only time she isn't frightened.

Eventually their noise reaches Mr. Maddox, the landlord, on the first floor. He descends the basement stairway with pained overstatement and makes his way slowly down the rank corridor to reprimand Ray for his lack of judgment. "OK, honey," Ray says loudly as soon as he sees the familiar form at the far end of the hall, "we've had enough excitement for one night." He navigates the tricycle and child skillfully past Mr. Maddox's accusing eyes, and calmly shuts the back door. It is important to him to act as though they were just stopping anyway; it helps him forget that Mr. Maddox controls nearly every other aspect of his life.

After their ride, Sonya will stand on the short-legged stool and

14

lean over the basin to sprinkle Dr. Lyon's tooth powder on her brush. No matter how carefully she taps the light blue can, most of the powder falls into the basin. "Be careful, honey; that's wasting. There's a war on," Valery warns. Ray is having a quick cup of coffee before he settles on the edge of the narrow cot in the kitchenette to tell her a story. It is always Ray who tells the story, never Valery. Sonya doesn't find this strange until many years later, when she continues the bedtime ritual for her own children. She will think to herself as she begins a story for her son: This came from Ray.

✿ *Aunt Mary* ✿

Every night before I went to sleep, Daddy would come in the kitchen, sit on the cot, and tell me an "Aunt Mary" story. He also told "Kitty and Puppy" stories and "Bunny" stories from time to time, but it was clear that these bored him. His favorite was Aunt Mary and, looking back, I suppose if you have to sit on a child's bed every night telling stories, you might as well tell one that has some interest to you.

Aunt Mary lived on a farm. Aunt Mary could look out her kitchen window and see apple trees in blossom. It was always summer at Aunt Mary's, and she was always baking apple pies. The drama focused on the apple pies: she always set them on the sill to cool; she never learned. In story after story, some greedy bastard always came stealing around the side of the barn, side-stepping his way toward Aunt Mary's pie. I wiggled under the covers and bit my nails as Daddy's eyes got larger, and he began wiping his mouth on his sleeve. Would it be Harold, her no-good nephew (thinly disguised)? Or would it be that rotten neighbor boy who was always throwing rocks at her apples, trying to

15

knock them off the trees? The woods were full of potential shirkers of honest labor and spoilers of the American dream. Even old Jess himself, Aunt Mary's hard-working husband, got caught with his finger in it from time to time.

After the resolution, Daddy would stroke my cheek gently with the backs of his fingers before slipping back into the living room to sit with Mother and talk about the war. It didn't take long for him to work himself into a frenzy over all the dirty Japs and Germans who were currently zeroing in on his apple pie.

🐜 Little Uncle Frank 🐜

One of Daddy's favorite stories concerned his uncle Frank. He was called "Little Uncle Frank" because he had gotten the shit beat out of him by his German father, down on the farm, at the age of twelve, and he never grew an inch after that. It had something to do with Little Uncle Frank's father wanting him to do something, and Little Uncle Frank refusing. The father gave him one more chance; Frank declined to take it. So he got beaten until he couldn't move—just lay there, Daddy said, for a very long time. His mother thought he was dead. But he wasn't; only stunted. Daddy really admired Little Uncle Frank. He seemed to want to be like him. But it was as though he knew the price for all that integrity Little Uncle Frank had, and was unwilling to pay it.

🐜 On the Farm 🐜

Daddy's greatest accomplishment as a youth down on the farm in Buffalo, New York, was getting the animals drunk. Whenever someone came to visit us, which was every three or four years, he told how the chickens would stagger, first on one leg, then on the other, and finally fall over, completely drunk. He laughed so hard tears came to his eyes, even after his hair turned gray, whenever he thought of it.

🐿 *Baby Bunting* 🐿

One evening in winter, just as Daddy had settled onto my bed for a story, it started snowing. It wasn't the first time it had snowed in my five years, but it was my first memory of it. The streetlamp outside the kitchenette window illuminated a swirling field of motion; millions of flakes were suddenly spinning out of the depths of the sky. Mother rubbed her hands together anxiously, but Daddy immediately grasped my need to run out to it, to embrace and understand it. He sang as he wrapped me in my blanket and lifted me onto his shoulders:

> Bye baby bunting
> Daddy's gone a-hunting
> Gone to get a rabbit skin
> To wrap his baby bunting in.

Mother stood in the doorway, wrapping her objections around her like a shawl, as Daddy swept me out onto the sidewalk and up the hill into the rain of falling snow; it groaned and squeaked under the soles of his feet. "Bye baby bunting . . ." Daddy sang rhythmically, as we marched through the night. Our breath made clouds that mingled with the swirling flakes; they fell into my face and eyes and didn't hurt at all.

The object of our adventure was the neighborhood delicatessen on 10th Avenue North, four blocks away. Daddy ordered vanilla ice cream cones for the two of us, and an extra pint to bring home to Mother. We forged back through the thickly forming snow, licking our chilly ice cream as the flakes fell all around us.

As we rounded the final corner for home, I savored the special feeling of being his Baby Bunting, riding high on the shoulders of a man who bought ice cream far from home on the first snowy night of the year. When we arrived back at the apartment, Mother's reservations had turned to a kind of sweet acceptance —reinforced no doubt by having her own individual pint of vanilla. It was a night that stood out in my mind for the rest of my childhood as an example of the way things should be done.

❧

Sonya's first memory of what Ray did for a living centers on a gift he brought home for her one evening. "It's a pik-loom," he explained, as he instructed her in its use. "It will revolutionize knitting; from now on, women won't have to do all that work with their bare hands anymore." He and his drinking partner, Eddie Atkins, had formed their own company and called it the PikLoom Company. They were going to become famous for inventing such a clever device; women would be eternally grateful. Sonya stared at the red, foot-long, wooden loom; it was a child's size, whereas Valery's was adult size—about two feet in length. It had an open slot down the center, and rows of small blunt metal pins running down each side of the slot. It came with a pick which, after the wool had been threaded onto the pins, was used to lift the loops over and under one another, up and down the rows of pins. The finished product ran down through the narrow slot, into infinity. Valery wondered what you did after you had achieved this long strip of knitted matter. "Oh, hell, honey, that's no problem!" Ray had responded emphatically; but he didn't explain further, and after an initial flurry of knitting and picking and watching it come out the bottom, both Valery and Sonya quietly abandoned their pik-looms.

Ray and Eddie Atkins struggled on in their one-room shop downtown. This venture had been embarked on after the failure of Ray's Pyroil franchise; he had peddled the motor oil additive on the West Coast in the thirties. Before Pyroil, he had had another short-term business which he called NapRenew, to signify the revolutionary process by which the nap on old and shiny serge suits could be miraculously restored. Customers were asked to leave their suits for two days; the process was a secret. On a shelf near the counter, where customers could see them, Ray kept a dozen or so dark bottles. They were filled with water. They were not for sale. "Oh," he would chuckle when someone would inquire; "those are just the first step in a very intricate process." The customer was to entrust his suit to the "expert." Who, when the customer was gone, would vigorously rub a large pumice stone over the fabric until the shine had disappeared. No, the PikLoom Company is merely a diversion, a filler, a quick-buck enterprise designed to fill in and pay the rent until he and Ed can develop the gold mine.

Ray is vague. The mine is "way up in the mountains." The property "stretches as far as the eye can see." There is so much gold in those hills it will make him "a millionaire twenty times over." Valery will "never have to worry about going broke again." She will "have the little home she has yearned for and deserved all these years." Each night Ray comes home from the PikLoom Company looking more and more subdued. Women just don't seem to realize their need for pik-looms. The gold mine enters into the dinner conversation with increasing regularity.

One weekend he informs Valery that he and Ed are going up to the mountains to inspect the mine. Eddie Atkins is a porcine man with a sallow complexion and thinning hair; there is always a dead cigar hanging from the corner of his mouth. Sonya can't imagine him climbing mountains but Ray seems invigorated by the thought. Valery smokes quietly and says nothing.

While Ray is gone, Valery takes Sonya to her first movie. They walk down the hill to the little theater on Broadway. When she sees Shirley Temple up there on the screen, she thinks she'll just run down the aisle and play with her. The usher asks her to go back to her seat. She is confused that, as she ran down toward the screen, Shirley Temple got bigger and bigger; she wasn't real at all.

The trips to inspect the mine become more frequent. Valery and Sonya spend more time at the movies. Greer Garson and Walter Pidgeon in *Mrs. Miniver* seem like nice people to have as parents. Sonya wants a mother like Greer Garson. She wears pretty dresses, buys frivolous hats, and laughs at herself. She always smiles at her children. She does not sit for hours reading mysteries. Walter Pidgeon doesn't come home drunk and make pik-looms for a living. He looks like a man you could depend on.

No matter what movie they go to, Valery always cries. Sonya watches the war unfold in the newsreels: tanks, guns and planes explode; their noise rocks the theater, it is overpowering. She plugs her ears and looks anxiously at Valery, who says, "It's all right; it's just a moving picture." Planes drone, then dive; hatches mysteriously open in their silver bellies and fat, dart-shaped bombs float out. The checkered earth below sprouts with smoking craters. "What about the people on the ground?" Didn't they care about hurting them? "We have to win the war," Valery explains.

Valery becomes addicted to the movies; along with the Wednesday night air raid drills, they have become her social life outside the apartment. Ray never goes, even when he is home. One night Valery and Sonya walk the mile to the Egyptian Theater; it is raffle night. Valery is excited; she wears her best scarf. After the movie is over, the manager of the theater climbs the little stairs at the side of the stage and announces that the winner of tonight's prize, a complete new set of dishware, is Valery Weiler. Valery's face flushes, her heart turns over. She is stunned; nothing like this has ever happened to her before. One always imagines winning, but never really expects it to happen. She struggles for composure, then slowly makes her way down the aisle to collect her prize. Sonya feels dizzy and confused: Why is there all this excitement over some dishes? People in the audience clap and cheer. It is wartime. No one has money. A complete set of dishes! What a lucky woman. Valery steps bravely down the aisle to claim her prize. She is small and dark, and seems about to slide into the depths of the cavernous theater and disappear. When she reaches the stage, she stares at the box: how will she ever get it home? She will have to go back and get Ray to come and help her with it. It never occurs to her to ask for a ride, or explain her predicament to the manager, who in turn never thinks to inquire.

She tells Sonya to wait; she will run back to the apartment and get Daddy, and together they will get the dishes home. Sonya sits by the large box of dishes in the slowly emptying theater. "Where's your mother?" the manager asks. "Doesn't she want her dishes?" Sonya has been told not to talk to strangers. She stares at the floor and says nothing. The lights begin to flick off, one by one. Sonya feels a rising panic. She is alone in the Egyptian Theater with a box of dishes. How did things ever come to this? It was so nice in the movies until this happened. She sits frozen in the crimson velvet seat. Eventually, Ray and Valery return to take the dishes home. Valery smiles for weeks; the dishes are the only items in the apartment that belong to her. She owns them, even if they are a cheap, distasteful shade of pink. Once, Ray makes the mistake of ridiculing them, and she reacts so immediately, and so fiercely, saying, "Don't make fun of *my* dishes!" that he never says another word. But it is clear by his general manner that he doesn't like his wife winning cheap dishes at movie raffles. Hell, she won't have any need for this crap when he gets the mine operating. He will get her the finest set of china money can buy.

Valery has stopped asking Ray about her other china—the good set—which, along with her Venetian glassware and other items handed down to her by her mother and grandmother, was "put in storage" by Ray when they moved to the basement apartment seven years before. There used to be long fights lasting into the night concerning the whereabouts of her only valuable possessions. Ray hasn't told her, and she has stopped asking; it is as though somewhere, around the sixth year, Valery suddenly "knew" that everything she had once thought safe in storage had been hocked—for exactly what, she isn't sure: to finance the failing PikLoom Company? To buy their daily bread? She tells herself it doesn't matter. Someday soon Ray is going to strike it rich. He is confident and smooth. He cooks the meals and pulls down the folding bed. He takes care of his family. She must swallow her disappointment, contain her sense of loss; she must believe and endure. Times are hard for everyone.

Ray is down at the tavern with Eddie. He is two hours late for dinner. When it becomes clear that he isn't coming, Valery heats up a can of Campbell's tomato soup and watches absently as Sonya eats. When Sonya asks where Ray is, Valery says, "He's working late." In the bath, Valery hangs a little rope of soap around Sonya's neck; she strains to be lighthearted. Sonya laughs, then remains in the tub until all the water has drained. Valery patiently holds out the towel and waits.

After Sonya has been put to bed, Valery takes the pins out of her hair and shakes it loose. She can't go to sleep until Ray gets home; she hasn't the strength to reach up and pull down the bed. She kicks off her shoes and switches the dial on the wooden table radio. It is shaped like a cathedral; its tubes glow from within, casting an orange light into the darkened room. Sonya watches quietly from the cot in the kitchen as her mother begins to dance to the music of Artie Shaw's orchestra. They are playing "Dancing in the Dark." Valery sways and closes her eyes as the tiny apartment fades and the elegant nightclub comes into view. She is a film star now, dancing with Tyrone Power. His bearing is sober and true; he guides her lovingly over the small, exclusive dance floor. She wraps her arms around herself and hums softly as her bare feet slide across the threadbare carpet. A little after midnight, Ray fumbles for the lock. Valery has fallen asleep on the maroon davenport. The radio has gone silent, but the light continues to glow behind the little amber dial.

🐾 *The Sunday Drive* 🐾

Every Sunday Mother would beg Daddy to take her for a ride in our old black Ford. The Sunday drive was her way of letting him know that she was tired of being cooped up in the apartment all the time. It was also the means by which she did her house-hunting. It made no difference to her that he couldn't afford a house. She would direct him to drive by any house that had a FOR SALE sign, pull over to the curb, and go in. There were many arguments over this. Daddy was embarrassed, anyone could see that, even a child in the back seat. But Mother, timid in all else, insisted. It was her way of saying: Enough years have passed; I want my own home. Daddy reluctantly gave in, and faked it very well once we were inside the house and the real estate agent started asking pushy questions. I was filled with admiration and relief. He never let on that he wasn't going to buy. Once back in the car, Mother always withdrew. The viewing never satisfied her, but rather, seemed to intensify her feelings of entrapment and deprivation. Sunday drives were tense and unpredictable. The nicest house could leave her feeling rotten, even a Dutch Colonial, her favorite.

One Sunday we had just come from inspecting a Dutch Colonial and Mother was hunched in the front seat, as far from Daddy as it was possible to get, wrapped inside her dull brown coat and staring out the window. It was raining. As we crossed over a bridge, she suddenly sat up and said, "Turn around and go back." Daddy was testy. "What the hell for?" he wanted to know. "There's a soldier back there, didn't you see him? Leaning against the rail and staring into the water. He's lonely. We should take him home to dinner." Daddy sighed. He turned the car around and pulled over as Mother called to the lonely soldier. You couldn't leave a soldier standing out in the rain in wartime, she's absolutely right, Daddy convinced himself. The soldier smiled incredulously and got into the back seat with me. His overcoat smelled like wet dogs. Mother turned around and faced the back

23

all the way home. I had never seen her so happy. It was the first time in years that there had been a visitor to our apartment. I was so excited, I spilled my milk. Mother glared at me, but said nothing. When the soldier finally left, Daddy kept repeating, "Fine young fellow, fine young fellow." Mother was so flushed with excitement, she dropped one of her new plates; it shattered all over the torn linoleum floor. I caught my breath, and Daddy started to say something comforting, but she just laughed it off. "It doesn't matter!" she said cheerfully as she swept up the pieces and threw them into the garbage pail with a decisive thrust of her arm.

The following Sunday, Ray heads the car back in the direction of the bridge; the soldier is happily waiting, leaning against the railing with a radiant grin on his face. Valery twists open her new tube of Tangee lipstick and pushes the little indicator up the slot with her thumb. She applies the finishing touch just as the car pulls to a stop. The soldier gets in the car and the foursome goes for a ride in the country. Sonya doesn't follow the conversation, but it is a new experience to have someone else in the car; it is a new experience to see her mother talking to someone other than Ray. They have brought a picnic basket filled with things they don't usually buy. In a meadow, they spread a white and red tablecloth on the grass. Ray has brought a bottle of bourbon; Valery looks at it but says nothing. The soldier says, "No thanks." Ray drinks it himself, straight from the bottle.

As they are returning on a road that winds out of the foothills, Valery suddenly asks Ray to stop the car. "What the hell for?" he wants to know. He thinks it's because he's been weaving from one side of the road to the other, but it turns out that isn't the reason. "I want to climb that hill," reports Valery, pointing to a steep incline which is more like a mountainside than a hill. "Aw, honey, what would you want to do that for?" asks Ray, laughing. The more he questions the rightness of this act, the firmer Valery becomes. It will be remembered by Sonya, years later, as one of the few times in her life she saw her mother behave in a firm and decisive manner. Her heart pounds in the back seat; it seems her mother is going to climb a mountain, all by herself, while the rest of them watch from the car. Ray eventually capitulates, and parks by the side of the road. As Valery begins her ascent, it occurs to Sonya for the first time, and in a dim way, that her mother is showing off for the soldier. Showing off is something she has always been told not to do. Bad things come of it, she has found.

Valery gets halfway up the hill and finds she can go no farther. She cannot descend, either; things look so steep and far away from where she stands, clinging to the branch of a tree. She never bargained for this; everything is out of perspective. Her husband, her daughter and the soldier are mere dots standing beside a toy car by the side of the road. Loose gravel escapes from under her foot, sending a small avalanche of stones showering down the mountain. She clutches the branch harder; her heart races. She calls down to Ray, but he's telling the soldier a joke and doesn't hear. Some time passes before the men notice that she hasn't gained any ground, but stands paralyzed midway up the hill. Ray crosses the road and shouts up to her: "What's the matter?" he calls, cupping his hands. Sonya watches from the side window in the back seat. Her mother looks so small, so pathetic, holding on to the pine bough halfway up the mountain. Ray and Valery exchange heated phrases which Sonya can't understand. The soldier leans against the car with his hands in his pockets. Eventually, Ray straddles the drainage ditch along the road and starts up the incline. He finally reaches Valery and guides her laboriously down the steep slope. So deep is her humiliation and defeat, she sits in total silence all the way home. She doesn't even say goodbye to the soldier at the bridge.

🦋 The Visit 🦋

One afternoon, about a week after the ride in the country, the soldier suddenly appeared at our door. Mother acted as though she had been expecting him, but she hadn't told me and I was surprised. The only thing she said was that he had come for a visit. I started to question her but there was something so unusual about her manner that I kept quiet. The two of them sat together on the maroon davenport, smiling and talking. I didn't know what to do. They seemed to take up all the space on the davenport. They didn't look at me, but at each other. I went into the kitchen and got Mother's salad bowl, a gift from Nona, and came hopping into the living room with the bowl on my head. I started to dance, the way I'd seen Carmen Miranda do it in the movies. It didn't matter that the bowl wasn't overflowing with pineapples and bananas and other exotic fruits; this was an improvisation, surely they'd get the idea. It would make them laugh. Then we could all be happy and smile and talk and have a visit together. Mother looked up, then pulled away from the soldier. She stared at me; she was not laughing. I became more animated than ever: frantically, I swung my hips. Slowly, inevitably, the bowl slipped from my head and smashed onto the floor. A large chip bounced away from it across the threadbare rug. I put my fingers in my mouth and giggled nervously. "You've broken my best bowl," Mother said in a quiet voice which was full of rage. The soldier looked embarrassed. I went into the walk-in closet and cried. A few minutes later I heard the door open and close. Mother was silent for the rest of the day. "I was being Carmen Miranda," I said desperately, but she didn't respond. Her silence was terrifying. The soldier never visited again.

🦋

When she is old enough, Sonya is allowed to walk the half mile to the Christian Science Sunday School where she will sit at a little table in the basement and learn about God's perfect love. She will discover an amazing thing: all you have to do is acknowledge it, and it cures everything. There is no evil, hatred, destruction or disease in the world; we only think there is. "Knowing" this truth, and acknowledging God's perfect love, makes all those things disappear. Sonya isn't sure how one goes about "knowing" such a thing and is afraid to ask. The teachers seem so confident; they would think she had let some "error" into her thoughts if she had to ask such a stupid question. She supposes that she hasn't got the hang of it yet, as the war is still on and Ray still comes home drunk from time to time, triggering terrible rows with Valery.

But she likes Sunday School and she feels important walking there by herself. Returning home, she often finds Valery and Ray sitting on the maroon davenport with their arms around each other, smiling contentedly and listening to Bing Crosby on the radio, singing, "When the blue of the night meets the gold of the day, someone waits for me." Valery never misses Bing Crosby; she seems to know that he is waiting for her, there inside the radio. Sometimes, when she is feeling especially warm toward Ray, she pays him the ultimate compliment by letting him know she thinks he looks just like Bing Crosby. "You do, too!" she will tease. "You have the same shape face and same big blue eyes." Ray, who doesn't know whether to feel competitive or flattered, chuckles nervously and murmurs, "Aw shucks, honey!"

Sometimes, if it is hot after Sunday School, instead of looking at houses for sale Valery and Ray will take Sonya to the beach. There she will have fish and chips over Valery's objections. Fish and chips give her the heebie-jeebies. She thinks they are unsafe to eat. Ray tries to reason with her, but she insists: they're covered with grease and wrapped in old newspapers. They're what the riffraff eat, they make her sick. "Bushwa!" Ray will exclaim, as he places the order.

Valery doesn't approve of the other children in the neighborhood, either. Sonya plays with them anyway; they are hard to avoid. To Ray and Valery, the families in the decaying frame houses who are poorer than they are riffraff. "Verna isn't riffraff, she's my friend." "She can't help it, honey," Ray explains, meaning: she's riffraff, whether she likes it or not. Sonya thinks Verna's brother Sidney might be riffraff. Sidney does unbelievable things, like eating dirt. Right out of the ground. Her other brother, Tony, is definitely riffraff: he tortures cats in the basement of the Capitola Apartments, on the corner. Sonya can't tell Valery about Tony; she doesn't know why. She tells about Sidney, instead. He isn't dangerous, just an idiot.

❧ The Capitola ❧

The courtyard of the Capitola was filled with dying ferns and broken beer bottles. It was surrounded on three sides by filthy, cavernous windows. It scared me so much I always stayed away, but one day Tony insisted: "You have to go in with us. I have something to show you."

The basement was dark and humid and smelled of scorched ironing boards. It was also swarming with cats. They produced litter after litter of new victims for Tony. Watching him was my first experience with cruelty. He tied them to stair rails and held lighted matches under their feet. When I tried to stop him, he dropped the cat he was torturing and came angrily toward me. Tony didn't like to be thwarted. I lunged for the stairway and ran all the way home.

Days later, I brought up the subject of Sidney at lunch. Mother sipped her coffee and tried to look interested. "Sidney eats glass

28

and dirt," I told her. I couldn't believe anyone could be so dumb. Sometimes he even put dandelion fuzz in with it and rolled it all around with his tongue. "I told you to stay away from the Capitola," she said firmly, as though it were clear that Sidney ate glass and dirt because of mysterious forces exerted on him by the sinister Capitola.

🦋 Esther 🦋

Esther was Daddy's first wife. She had worked in the same Los Angeles office as Mother, years ago, and had died of tuberculosis. Mother and Daddy met at her funeral. I learned that he had had a "first" wife the day I made him a card for Easter. "Happy Ester," it had read. Mother intercepted it right away, saying it might hurt his feelings. There was nothing she could do after that but explain about Esther. It was hard to imagine Daddy with anyone else; he'd been with us for as long as I could remember. It added a dimension to him that hadn't existed for me before.

🦋

The year she graduated from boarding school, Valery had left the island in search of the father she hadn't seen since her parents' divorce in 1919, when she was thirteen. She traced him to California where she took a job as a clerk, hoping to stay awhile and get to know him. She found it a significant coincidence that her departed office-mate's husband, Ray Weiler, was a Christian Scientist, too. They had so much to discuss after the funeral; they had so much in common. They were married within the year.

The newlyweds moved back north, to the island. It was the

middle of the depression. The only person in the family with a job was Valery's brother, Jack; he supported everyone. Ray became restless on the island; within a few weeks, he announced to the assembled in-laws that he'd figured out just the thing to put the family back on its feet again. No, he couldn't be more specific at this time, he told Jack. It was too complicated. He left for Seattle on a Tuesday, and by the following weekend could write to Valery: I have discovered the most amazing process to renew old, worn suits. Come down on the next boat! We'll all be on easy street by Christmas.

🦋 Sally Rand 🦋

One night when I was six, Daddy came home and presented me with a photograph of Sally Rand. He claimed she was a dear friend of his. It was an 8-by-10 glossy, a standard publicity shot of her posing coyly with nothing on but her fans. At the bottom of the picture she had written: "To Sonya: Grow up as sweet as you are." I stared at Sally Rand and her feathers, wondering what had possessed her to write me such a note. She was unlike anything I had ever seen; there was no one like her in the neighborhood.

When I was older, I concluded that Daddy had gone up to her after a performance and asked her to sign it for me. It seemed like a ridiculous thing for a grown person to do.

✼ Social Security ✼

One of the few legitimate jobs Daddy ever held came directly after the PikLoom misadventure, when he was hired as Personnel Director for Arden Farms Dairy. The work confined him, and he eventually grew so restless that he quit the job two years later, but it netted me a lot of ice cream one birthday.

My friends and I were in the back seat of the Ford, and Mother was up front with Daddy, when he pulled up to the loading platform one Saturday on our way to the woods for a birthday picnic. We spent about an hour at the loading platform, waiting while Daddy argued with one of the men who was loading a truck. "I can't just give you ice cream free; it's against regulations." "Jesus Christ, it's my little girl's birthday! I *work* here! I'm the one who hires and fires all you stiffs!" he screamed. This went on for some time and Mother grew visibly pale. He was finally given some ice cream statues in the shape of animals. Mother unwound and Daddy assumed the manner of generals after wars. When the ices were finally distributed, I remember mine was an eagle.

On the way home in the car, Daddy began his familiar tirade against Roosevelt, the New Deal, and especially Social Security, which he claimed reduced his paycheck to shit. He saw no reason why he should have to kowtow to those petty sons of bitches; he would never grow old and have to live off the rotten government; he wouldn't need their stinking Social Security then. He'd be worth a fortune in gold. He needed it now. "Oh, sweetheart," he sighed to Mother as we pulled up in front of the apartment, "I could be putting that money to good use up in the mountains where it could be doing us all some good."

❧ Mitzi the Butter Wrapper ❧

Daddy came home two hours late the night Mitzi was fired. Mother made toast while we waited, and drummed her fingers tensely on the ring-stained surface of the kitchen table. After the toast was gone, I spread the Chinese Checkers set between us, and she jumped my marbles in a nervous, abstracted way. Finally, the door opened and in he walked—not with his usual brisk step, but with an air of great defeat.

"They let Mitzi the Butter Wrapper go today," he intoned heavily. The little apartment was silent as he lowered himself into the third chair at the kitchen table. He had never mentioned Mitzi before, but he spoke of her now as though she were as familiar as an old family friend. Mother prompted him, and he ran his fingers through his hair, gestured helplessly with his hands, and began to explain.

Mitzi was the fastest butter wrapper in the West. He described the number of separate pounds of butter she could wrap, by hand, in one hour. I can't remember the figure, but it seemed to be in the hundreds, she was that fast. He demonstrated, his hands poised over the table, the art of butter wrapping. "There is a way to do it, an exact way, and Mitzi is a pro. I know, I've watched her. She folds the paper faster than the naked eye can follow." He did it slowly, in the air, so we could follow. "Every dairy has a butter wrapper, and Mitzi was the best. And-then-those-dirty-bastards went and got a *machine*," he caught his breath, "to replace her." He paused a few minutes as this information sank in. My mind was racing to keep up with the details and put them together. Mother lit a cigarette solemnly. I had never seen this particular anguish on his face before. He shook his head back and forth. "They call it *automation*," he informed us, spitting out the word with contempt. "They told her, 'Mitzi, you've been a good butter wrapper, one of the best, but this machine will wrap twice the number of pounds per hour as you can do by hand.' Can you imagine? Replacing a woman like that with a *machine?*" He whistled through his teeth; tears were forming in his eyes. "The poor little thing couldn't believe it; she was crying so hard. The others were crying, too, even some of the men." He kept twisting his fingers in the air, making those precise and rapid tucks at the end of the pound of butter the way he'd seen Mitzi do it. It was a Campbell's soup night; we sat around the little table and bore witness as Mitzi's now useless skills, and Mitzi herself, were invoked, and mourned, and relinquished to history.

*H*ere *are Valery and Sonya on their way to board the steamship that* will take them to Canada. Valery returns each summer to her mother's log house on the island. Ray always stays behind. "Daddy has to stay here to work on the gold mine so we'll all be rich someday," Ray explains to a tearful Sonya as he drives them to the boat at the last minute, running red lights and turning corners on two wheels. Valery presses her lips together and clutches the dashboard; Sonya is thrown from side to side in the back seat. "We'll get there in plenty of time," Ray says when he notices Valery's tension. "Jesus Christ, Ray Weiler always gets his little family to the boat on time!" And it is true; only once does he fail. Sonya remembers standing on a creaking pier in the middle of the night, a blood-orange moon on the rim of a black and terrible sea, and Ray insisting the boat must have left early, and Valery murderously silent.

The journey lasts a night and a day. Mother and daughter will pass the night in a small, airless stateroom whose turn of the century appointments will include bunks with brass rails and a mysterious porcelain chamber pot under the lower bed. When the ship finally docks at the sagging, barnacle-covered wharf, Nona, Valery's brother, Jack, and their old friend Everett MacGregor will be there to greet them. The wooden gangplank is lowered;

it bounces up and down under their weight, but holds firm. As Valery and Sonya descend, familiar voices call. Saltwater tides ripple beneath them. Cedar, pine and fir cast dark shadows across the waters. The hair is moist and humid, as in a dream. Here, in this other world, Valery changes.

Everett MacGregor works in a logging camp outside Vancouver and spends his free days on the island. He and Valery walk for hours through the forest. Sometimes Sonya goes with them, collecting the snails she turns into pets; sometimes she stays behind to help Nona weed the garden. Their lives take on the slow, regular rhythm of the tides. Valery and Sonya gather shells on deserted beaches and bear their bounty home in large Indian baskets. Nona stokes the fire. Friends visit; the night air is soft.

*V*alery and Everett MacGregor are sitting near the shore at the edge of the harbor. A half moon rises over a solitary pine on the end of the rocky spit. His hand is gently cupped on the back of her neck; her chin rests on her knees as she stares into the water. "You were always the smartest," she says quietly. She means that Everett alone, of all the young people who grew up together on the island, stands out in her mind. *You were the one I thought would go on,* she thinks, but doesn't say. Meaning: the special one, among hundreds, who would not be absorbed into the logging industry, who would go on to school in the city. If he is bitter that the long depression has engulfed his dream, he makes no sign; in times like these, he is lucky to have work at all. That he somewhere mourns lost opportunities, she is certain.

"No. You were the smartest," he says gently, and they laugh. Meaning, she thinks, that she got away. "Yes," she joked. "I went looking for a father, and found a husband!" They sit in silence, barely touching. Somewhere a fish leaps in the blackness; pale rings mark its re-entry. Beside them, the old pier sags on its pilings, its moans in the tidal pull a kind of breathing.

"I wish you had never gone away," he suddenly says, in a voice so low it seems indistinguishable from any other night sound: meaning, *it takes time for feelings to grow and find their form. You didn't wait for me.* Valery cannot answer, his words move inside her with the force of blood rushing to the brain. Her heart races and she sighs involuntarily as though to correct its rhythm. He thinks he's hurt her feelings and turns to her, tightening his hold on her shoulder. "I had no right to accuse. Forgive me." She takes his hand. "No, don't, it's not that. Let's walk."

They rise from the dark beach as one form and walk as the forest slowly closes around them. The trail of fallen needles springs under their weight, its leaf mold rising pungent on the night air. Centuries of accumulation hum under their feet. When they reach the meadow, the half moon is visible again, falling to the west above the forest rim. With infinite care they lie in the warm grasses; with sudden, blind unity, reach out. She has waited years for his mouth to cover hers, his rough sweetness to flow into her. She holds his head as they bend together, burning the lost years into the meadow floor, into the island's hard center.

*I*n September, when mother and daughter board the boat for the return to Seattle, Valery starts staring into space again. She sits in the stateroom as the ship rocks gently from side to side, and has nothing to say. Sonya asks what's wrong, but her mother remains silent. She feels her chest tighten and finds it hard to breathe: she is alone at sea with her mother, but her mother isn't there! She dashes outside and is reprimanded by the captain for running on the deck.

Back in Seattle, Valery eventually rouses herself to take the child for a walk in the park; leaves are turning crisp on the trees. Sonya climbs the stone statues in front of the museum while Valery snaps her picture with the Kodak box camera. Then she escorts Sonya through the galleries, pointing out the paintings that

35

have become her favorites over the years. Afterwards, Sonya gathers chestnuts under the giant trees while Valery stands nearby with her hands in her pockets, quietly humming "I'll Be Seeing You."

*I*t *is nine o'clock in the little basement apartment. Valery and Sonya have* eaten dinner alone; it seems that Ray has important business to take care of and will not be able to join them for the evening meal. Sonya does not know how Ray has conveyed this information to Valery—by leaving her a note in the morning, or by waking her before he left. They do not have a telephone. Valery isn't saying how she knows Ray won't be home until late; she just reports it in a soft voice as she sets the dinner before them: Campbell's tomato soup and slices of Wonder Bread spread with butter. Ray is the family cook—when he is home. "Honey, I should have been a chef," he often says to Valery as he whips up one of his specialties, German meatballs, potatoes and gravy. Valery agrees. She hates to cook, as does her mother. "Nona couldn't cook *toast* without burning it," Ray has insisted on numerous occasions, and Sonya always corrects him: "Yes, she can! She puts it on a fork and holds it over the fire. It tastes good!"

Valery lingers at the table after dinner. She tears the red cellophane strip off another package of Lucky Strikes, lights a cigarette, and stares across the room as her fingers begin to rotate the cellophane cylinder back and forth. Sonya plays with the new red and white package; Lucky Strike Green has gone to war. She knows; she heard it on the radio. She doesn't understand how a cigarette package can go to war, and knows she won't get a satisfactory explanation, so doesn't ask. She offers to play Valery a game of Chinese Checkers. Valery declines. She seems to be listening for something.

Eventually, she hears what she has been waiting for: Ray's key, trying to find its place in the lock. Sonya's eyes widen; she watches her mother watching the apartment door. It is just across the room, but Valery makes no effort to rise. "I'll let him in!" says Sonya, glad that her father has returned at last. "No," Valery says sternly. "Stay where you are." Sonya is stunned; something very strange is going on, but she can't imagine what it is. There is a terrible tension in the room. Valery's eyes are glued to the door as Ray's key fumbles and scrapes away on the other side. Sonya experiences unbearable sensations in her chest. If a person needs help opening a door, you go and help him; anyone knows that, even a six-year-old child. The picking and scraping continue. Finally, there is the unmistakable sound of a fist banging the door and then a foot kicking it from the bottom. Valery still doesn't move! Eventually, Ray Weiler lunges into the room; his face is red, his eyes watery. The look on Valery's face is one of skillfully contained violence. "Hi, honey," Ray says thickly in a sing-song voice. Sonya is appalled: this man isn't her father! He is someone who looks like her father. She doesn't run to hug him. His speech is thick and its tone is high; she has never heard these cadences before. She watches Valery to see what she will do.

In his depths, where reason and perception faintly stir, Ray Weiler knows he's in the doghouse. Abruptly, he defends himself. Valery remains silent. His voice grows louder; within minutes, he is throwing a chair. Sonya runs upstairs and knocks on the landlord's door. "My mother and father are having a row," she whispers breathlessly. "So I hear," sighs Mr. Maddox as he accompanies her downstairs. When they enter the basement apartment, Valery is lying on the floor holding her face; tears run from her eyes. Ray turns and stares in disbelief. "Why, honey," he says to Sonya, "what did you do that for?" She doesn't know; it seemed right at the time, but now she feels she has betrayed the person who loves her the most. Solemnly, Mr. Maddox remonstrates with Ray. Ray is contrite in the presence of the man who has the power to throw him out in the street. Sonya feels he will never forgive her for what she has done. He will be right not to. It was a terrible mistake. She sees his humiliation, and knows that she is to blame.

In September 1942, three weeks before her thirty-sixth birthday, Val-
ery Weiler takes a streetcar downtown to have all her teeth pulled
out. They have ached for years. False teeth have been advised as
the modern solution. Ray has promised to pick her up at the dentist's and drive her home. Sonya this day is sitting in the corner of
the first-grade room of the Edgemont School for Girls, staring at
the portrait of George Washington which hangs in the back of the
room and can only be viewed when facing the corner. She has
committed an infraction of the rules, but she doesn't know what
it was or what the phrase means. She will become familiar with
the portrait of George Washington; she is the dumbest in the
class, she just doesn't catch on to anything. Among the things she
can't understand is how a great artist could present an unfinished
canvas of a famous president to a private school and not finish the
bottom. George Washington floats on messy white fumes, on vaporous clouds of thin white paint. From his filmy height he looks
down and judges her with arrogant eyes.

She has been enrolled at Edgemont despite the fact that Ray
can't afford the tuition. Valery insists that the neighborhood
school is "rough." Her own mother never allowed her to attend a
rough school; neither will she allow Sonya. Ray accepts this edict
with a sigh. Nothing is too good for his little girl, he says with a
strained smile. Valery smiles, too, in triumph. The family will regain its true status, everything takes time. After dinner, Ray announces he is going for a little walk around the block. Hours
later, Sonya hears Valery say, "You were at the tavern, weren't
you?" and Ray, thickly, protest: "Hell, honey, I *told* you: I just
took a little walk around the block!"

When Sonya arrives home, she sees a weeping woman curled
on the maroon davenport, holding her face. It is her mother, and
all her teeth are gone. Ray lowers the pull-down bed and Valery
climbs in. "Let her sleep, honey," he says to Sonya. "She'll get

her new teeth next week; she's feeling kind of punk right now."
Valery refuses to talk for a week. Sonya goes cold from the shock
of seeing her mother so transformed; without her teeth, she
doesn't look like Mother at all. Sonya tells the girl in the seat behind her: "My mother's going to be a riveter and win the war."
"You're getting your germs on my desk," says the girl. Sonya
doesn't know what germs are, but they must be bad judging from
the girl's expression. The teacher instructs her to "face the front."
Her cheeks are hot as she stares at the blackboard. She understands nothing that is written on it.

One week later, Valery comes home from the dentist crying
again; Ray says, "Aw, honey, that's ridiculous; you do *not* look
like a horse!" Sonya peeks into the bathroom, where Valery
stands before the mirror baring the new false teeth. She does look
like a horse. Sonya holds her breath: this just can't be, that her
mother is losing her parts like this, and changing form and shape.

🐚 *Like Mother, Like Daughter* 🐚

After weeks of sudden outbursts of uncontrollable crying, Daddy
gave Mother some money to take her mind off losing her teeth.
She hadn't been out of the apartment for two weeks, not even for
a walk around the block; she was sure people on the street would
laugh.

"Here, sweetheart, here's some moola, go downtown and buy
whatever your heart desires." She didn't pick up right away, but
it was such an unaccustomed event, being handed money like
that, that you could sense a subtle shift in mood taking over. By
morning she was almost a new person, having for the first time in
years a tangible goal, and some tangible cash in hand with which
to pursue it.

39

What she did was to spend it on two identical dresses—one in her size, and one in mine. She explained that they were called mother-daughter dresses, and that they were the new style; presumably every mother and daughter in America were now wearing identical clothes. They were made of cotton and had light blue vertical stripes, with flowers in between. She helped me on with mine and put a ribbon in my hair, and then put her own on and dabbed some cologne behind her ear. When Daddy's key turned in the lock that evening, she hastily posed the two of us before the door, side by side, with our arms around each other. Looking up at her for some explanation for this behavior, I noticed the grotesquely unnatural smile on her face; her teeth were in place, but they still didn't fit. They were all wrong—for her mouth itself, and for her fragile features. "Surprise!" she exclaimed when Daddy walked into the apartment.

"Well, well, well, what have we got here?" he queried cooperatively, picking up his cue.

"Mother-daughter dresses!" Mother sang happily. She beamed down on me, waiting for some corresponding enthusiasm. "Like mother, like daughter!" she prompted gaily, but I refused the message in a stubborn way that surprised even me. I didn't want to be like her, but I didn't let on in so many words. It would have hurt her feelings and sent her back to the davenport for months.

"This calls for a little celebration," Daddy said expansively, ignoring my sulk and acting as though he'd never before noticed the fact that Mother and I were related. The whole scene had an artificial tone to it that made me jump up and down, dislodging the ribbon in my hair. Daddy went out to the corner store for some beer, his idea of a celebration, while Mother retied my sash and replaced the ribbon. It was nice to see her happy, but the price seemed too high for me to pay. I became provocative and pulled the ribbon out again. By the time Daddy returned with the beer, Mother had removed her dress and retired to the bathroom in her old chenille robe. Daddy rapped lightly on the door, but she wouldn't come out. She stayed in there for over an hour while Daddy drank all the beer and blamed me for upsetting her. I blamed myself too, but was unaccountably mad at her as well. I

40

wished I had Verna's mother, down the street; she was always smiling and relaxed. She might have been riffraff, but at least she had all her teeth.

❧ *The Opal Ring* ❧

The circumstances surrounding this birthday demanded a special effort to compensate for Mother's grief, and Daddy rose to the occasion by buying her an opal ring.

She had spotted it a month before, in the window of a little neighborhood jewelry store, as we took an after-dinner walk. She wouldn't leave the window, she loved that ring so much. It was her birthstone and it was obvious that she envisioned it on her finger; clear that she regarded the ring as hers. Daddy looked at it politely, but left the general impression that the ring was beyond his means and out of the question. He admired it with her in a resigned way that seemed to say: You deserve it, honey, it's a beauty; what a damned shame these rotten circumstances prevent me from buying it for you now. When I'm a millionaire, you can have twenty opal rings. By the time we returned to the apartment, it was clear from her expression that in her mind she'd given up the ring.

I was let in on the secret the day before her birthday: what Daddy had been doing all these weeks was gathering boxes of varying sizes that would fit into each other; he collected dozens. The idea was to put the ring and its tiny box in the smallest, innermost box; then repeat the process until the largest box contained them all. When he handed her this giant gift, she would never guess. He had been hiding the boxes in the laundry room, behind the mangle. Somehow, he had managed to purchase the ring.

On her birthday night, he took me out in the back hall for our tricycle run as usual, and we detoured into the laundry room where all the boxes were. With his forefinger to his lip, he

41

showed me the ring. He opened all the boxes within boxes within boxes, one by one, until we were down to the rare gem itself. I could hardly contain myself; I thought he was the cleverest man in the world.

Mother's surprise was genuine and absolute. For a few special hours, the opal ring made up for losing all her teeth. She asked Daddy to slip it on her finger, and as he obliged she said, "I will wear it as long as I live"; and she did.

❦

*I*t is the spring of 1944. Here is Valery, lying on the maroon davenport; but this time she is happy. And here is Ray, sitting beside her, with his hands on her stomach—which, Sonya notices for the first time, has swelled to the size of a melon. Sonya has just come in from playing in the vacant lot; she is invited to join her parents on the maroon davenport. Together they announce that there is a baby in there; it is to be her new brother or sister. She is invited to put her hands on Valery's belly in order to feel the baby kick. She is stunned; she never knew such a thing was possible— babies inside the stomach! She reaches out and lightly touches the mound. There is a faint rippling underneath her palm. In the months to come, her friend Verna asks: "When is your mother going to have her baby?" and Sonya always says, "Tomorrow." After a while Verna grows bored and stops asking, and Sonya feels betrayed. They talk about having a new baby, but it never comes. It's all talk, just like the gold mine. Ray starts referring to the mound as "Gus." He wants a son. Valery reminds him that it might be a girl. He says, "Then we'll have to call her 'Gussie.' " He laughs hard at his own joke. Valery seems happy except for the fact that they are still living in the one-room basement apartment. Her dream home has not materialized. Ray says to trust him, the gold mine will be producing soon; their little family will be on easy street. A baby buggy appears and is placed along the east wall of the living room, next to the reading chair and stand-up lamp. "Hell," says Ray; "a baby doesn't take up much room!"

❧ Chef Boy-ar-dee ❧

When Mother went to the nursing home to give birth to Gus, Daddy and I were left to, as he put it, "shift for ourselves." It was a challenge to him, and he met it with ten cans of Chef Boy-ar-dee spaghetti. Mother was in the nursing home for five days, and for five nights we had Chef Boy-ar-dee for dinner. "When the cat's away, the mice will play!" said Daddy, winking. I don't know what he thought Mother would do to him, if she knew, be-yond saying something like, "You can't have spaghetti five nights in a row, Ray." If he had been stronger, he could have looked her in the eye and said, "Why not? We love spaghetti and we're going to have it every night until we get tired of it."

Instead, each dinner became a ritual of disobedience. One can for him, and one for me. We giggled and slopped it up, for you never knew with babies: they could come at any time and then it would be all over for us. We had to make every minute count. I stared at him lovingly across the table, thinking: here is someone who knows how to live! I had never seen him so spontaneous. It was thrilling to sit there, night after night, indulging our greed. I even made up a little song, which Daddy thought was as good as anything Shirley Temple had done: "Just you and me and Chef Boy-ar-dee!" I sang.

❧

*R*ay and Sonya drive in the old Ford to the little wood frame Christian Science nursing home to see her new sister. Ray has lost his little Gus, but hides his disappointment. He tickles the baby under the chin and whispers, "Our little Gussie!" but Valery corrects him: "You'll have to get used to calling her Greta now; that's her real name." They bring Greta home to the new buggy against the east wall. The tiny apartment swells with new products and new smells: fluffy blankets, mountains of diapers; strange powders and the musty smell of milk. Greta gets a set of shiny sterilized Evenflo bottles; Sonya wants one too, but Valery says, "They're just for babies."

Sonya watches from the depths of night as Valery tries to warm the crying baby. Ray complains to Mr. Maddox, but the heat continues to be turned off abruptly at seven o'clock. It is the middle of January. Valery sits in the kitchenette by the open oven, rocking; she walks the borders of the living room rug with Greta in her arms, singing Irish lullabies she's heard Bing Crosby sing on the radio. In the mornings, when it is warmer, Greta is bathed in the kitchen sink. Sonya is allowed to rub oil on her feet; she anoints her sister. A new spirit has entered the apartment: Valery gets out of bed in the mornings, there are things to be done. After lunch, Sonya takes the new baby for a walk in the buggy. She can sense the neighbors watching from behind their stained curtains as she navigates the heavy wheels over the cracks in the sidewalk.

⚕ Home on the Range ⚕

When Greta was five months old, we finally left the one-room basement apartment and moved into a little five-room wood frame house that seemed like a palace by comparison. It was on the outskirts of Seattle, at the end of a dirt road, surrounded by evergreens and open space as far as the eye could see. Daddy was quick to warn Mother that this was *not* the dream house, but a temporary rental; the owners would be reclaiming it in six months.

The warning fell on deaf ears: she spent hours in the yard, spading the hard earth and inserting bulbs and tubers of all descriptions which she would never see bloom. She took long walks and even made friends with the few, scattered neighbors. I was allowed to roam free. One day a stray cat came by and we kept it. It was the first pet I had ever had and, in time, it produced a litter of kittens next to the furnace in the basement. There was an apple orchard in back and Mother said that when summer came, Daddy could string a hammock between the apple trees and "live the life of Riley" on weekends. He kept reminding her that the owners would be back in summer, but she didn't seem to hear. She seemed to undergo a transformation in that house; she even started cooking in its modern kitchen. She smiled and laughed a lot, especially watching Greta grow. She never stayed in bed in the mornings, and she stopped smoking cigarettes and reading murder mysteries. Every evening at five-thirty, the three of us would line up on the small couch by the living room window which overlooked the road, and watch for Daddy to come home. As the Ford rattled into view, Greta would pound on the glass with her tiny palm and squeal with delight. Mother and I would be laughing so hard that when Daddy walked in the door, he would start laughing, too. "What are all my girls laughing at?" he would say in disbelief. In a dim way, which I couldn't articulate, we seemed to be just like other families now.

Daddy changed, too; his fights with Mother stopped and I can't remember him drinking while we were in that house. Because we were outside the city limits, and my bus ride was long, he began to drive me to school in the mornings. Mother would stand with Greta on the small, sagging porch and wave goodbye as we bumped and jerked down the dirt road. "Home, home on the range," he sang softly to himself as he eased the Ford onto the main road. He had a sweet smile on his face: a new life had begun, and it was good.

One evening, shortly before the owners are due back, Ray announces that the mysterious mine is about to pay off; Valery is just a technicality away from her dream house. When she asks when they will be moving, Ray grows vague: "Honey, would I tell you things were going to be all right if I didn't mean it?" When summer arrives, and the dream house has failed to materialize, Valery takes Sonya and Greta to Canada; Ray stays behind to "wind up the deal." He puts their few remaining possessions into storage. Valery will never see them again.

They settle on Vancouver Island, in the home of Valery's brother, Jack. Greta has learned to toddle; she makes everyone happy. Valery moves purposefully around the large old house, running after Greta and helping Jack's wife, Edith, in the kitchen. For the first time, Sonya perceives her mother as an ordinary, active person. She has, at the age of nine, her first experience of imagining a future: she sees them all returning to Seattle in the fall to begin life in the new house; she imagines that it has a porch and that she and Greta will sleep in bedrooms. Valery will have a garden in the yard; she will be happy, as she is now. When Greta gets older, she and Sonya will be friends. Ray will not come home drunk. He will come home and mow the lawn. Sonya will offer to do it for him, but he will refuse. She will make lemonade instead, and serve it to the family in a large frosted pitcher. They will all sit around in their back yard and laugh.

Sonya and her cousin, Andrew, play in the graveyard across the road. It is a country graveyard with a small church in the center; it is choked with brambles and weeds. The children's graves have white stone lambs sculpted on the headstones, the adult graves have stone pillows. Sonya and Andrew lie side by side on their backs, their heads on the stone pillows, pretending they are dead. From this position she can watch the humid clouds passing over the rim of the forest where the graveyard ends. Later, they sneak into the church and insert a dead grasshopper between the pages of the Bible at the altar. Won't the minister be surprised! They think they are very clever; Sonya thinks she has seen some-one do this in a movie, but can't remember for sure. It seems as though her life is a movie, she does such unaccustomed things: they climb trees and steal the neighbor's plums; they throw apples at the mean boy down the road. They feed the chickens and gather their eggs. They hide in the hay in the creaking barn. Sonya learns to ride a bicycle; it wobbles down the country road, but she keeps it upright. Greta learns to say "Mammy" and "up." Valery learns that she has advanced cancer of the breast from the doctor in town, to whom she has gone with the complaint of pain. She is told she has a fifty-fifty chance to survive if she has imme-diate treatment. Her brother Jack is with her. They stand inside a phone booth together while they try to reach Ray in Seattle. When he comes on the long-distance wire, Jack says, "It seems that Valery has a touch of cancer."

Strange days follow. Sonya's confusion is greater than any-one's because the others know what has happened, but they haven't told her. Greta is too young to know anything, at least in words. Perhaps she senses a change in her mother as she ner-vously waits for Ray to arrive. Together, they will make a de-cision on what to do. Jack, who does not embrace the Christian Science faith, advises immediate surgery; this is to be expected. Valery says she will wait: she and Ray will decide. Sonya will not remember this week later in life. She remembers the events which followed: Ray arriving with a strained look; then Ray and Valery departing with Greta and leaving her behind.

Her aunt Edith explains that Ray and Valery and Greta are going back to Seattle in order to locate, then settle into, just the right new house. It is suggested that this task can best be accomplished if Sonya remains in Canada. Just think, she can attend school with Andrew in the fall! Ray and Valery will be in touch as soon as they locate the perfect house. Sonya doesn't understand, and is not excited, and does not ask. She undergoes a profound inner change. She forgets her own school in Seattle, forgets that she is, for the moment, homeless. She becomes an actor in a movie. The movie's title is *Left Behind in Courtenay, B.C.* The opening scene finds her sleeping between cotton flannel sheets upstairs in her aunt and uncle's house. Someone is shaking her awake. The sheets are winter sheets that hold the warmth in. She doesn't want to get up. It is the first day of school. It is still dark. Her aunt has built a fire in the fireplace downstairs and hung the children's clothes over the screen to warm. Sonya dresses in the dark; the clothes are hot against her skin. This is the most exciting adventure in her life. Her stomach is light and shifts easily; she is sure the other children will tease her. Aunt Edith says, "Nonsense!" Nona says, "Rubbish!" They don't know that the boy across the road calls her "Yankee." Even his mother does it. "Here comes the Yankee," they say whenever she plays in their barn. She doesn't know what a Yankee is, and is afraid to ask. It couldn't be good.

A lunch is packed for her to take to school. She and Andrew walk the two miles in the early morning chill. It is so foreign there, among strangers who all know each other, but not her, that she can hear nothing the teacher is saying. She takes notice of small things, insignificant details: the smell of a history book; the ocher texture of a pull-down map of Canada; the rough, grooved surface of her wooden desk. On the playground a strange girl offers her half a lime popsicle. She has no idea where it could have come from. She will remember its taste the rest of her life. On the way home she eats large chunks of tar from the freshly rolled roadside. At night she falls exhausted between the cotton flannel sheets. It takes all her energy to keep certain things out of her mind. She hears a new word, and it is applied to her: "scatterbrain." She remembers thinking of Valery and Ray only once during the months in Canada; their images swam in her mind and she thought: I am an orphan. She loses interest in her movie; she doesn't think she will like the ending.

When it finally does end, it is shot in sepia tone and stars Nona and Sonya stepping off the boat onto a sagging wharf and racing in Ray's old Ford to the dream house containing the stricken Valery and the exuberant Greta. Neighborhoods flash by; avenues brim with fallen leaves. When the car finally pulls up to the new house, Sonya sees there is a maple tree in the front yard. It also has a wooden porch; her excitement rises. As she walks through the front door, she sees Valery standing there in a green chenille robe, reaching out to her with little stick arms and a frail smile. There must be some mistake; where is her mother? Who is this person in the green chenille robe? A bird, an apparition. Greta dances and giggles, Nona starts to cry, Ray claps his hands together with forced vigor and says, "We need a round of drinks!" Sonya is distracted and forewarned. This movie will be the kind you wish you'd stayed home from. She is taken through the house; it seems too good to be true. She is shown her bedroom— a whole room, just for her. Greta sleeps in Sonya's old crib, along the west wall of Valery and Ray's bedroom. There is an empty bedroom which Nona will sleep in while she is here. She must return to Canada by the end of the month in order to collect her pension check. But she'll be back.

By Christmas, Valery is weaker. Throughout November she sat by the fireplace, chain smoking and smiling weakly at Greta as she bounced and played on the floor. Years later, Sonya will learn what is obvious to everyone else: that Valery and Ray have decided to fight her cancer with God's perfect love. That would explain her smile, in the face of her obvious decline—a decline which everyone, including Valery herself, denies. "What's the matter, Mother?" Sonya will ask over and over. "Nothing, dear," Valery will answer, forcing a thin smile, picking a loose piece of tobacco from her lip. Ray has bought her her dream home at last. He was right; everything works out in the end, if one has faith. She is not too weak to string the newest fad on the Christmas tree: bubbling lights. They are hollow glass candles filled with colored water, which bubble when they're plugged in. Bubbles rise endlessly within the new lights; Greta laughs, Sonya stares at them in a trance. Finally Valery says: "Sonya, you will go blind if you stare at the bubbling lights any longer." The smell of fir is pungent in the room. Valery sits down at the old upright piano and awkwardly plays "Beautiful Dreamer." She learned it at boarding school in Victoria, many years ago. It is the only piece she knows and she plays it over and over again.

The day after Christmas, Mr. Percy, the former owner of the new house, comes to pay a visit. He and Ray retire to the living room. Their voices grow louder, and Valery begins twitching the cellophane back and forth between her middle finger and thumb. Putting her finger to her lips as a signal to Sonya, she edges closer to the living room and listens intently. It seems that Ray has lied to her; not only has he not bought the dream house, he hasn't even paid the rent! Valery crawls slowly back into her bed; huge sobs rack her small body. Sonya withdraws into her own bedroom and pretends not to listen, but leaves the door open a crack. "Aw, honey, Jesus Christ, you don't understand!" Ray screams defensively, after Mr. Percy leaves. "I wanted to make you happy!" he cries, his voice breaking. It takes three days, but eventually Valery speaks to him again. She has no choice; she is having trouble moving. She can no longer push the vacuum, or lift Greta. A housekeeper will have to be hired.

❧ Big Mae ❧

Big Mae was the first. We had never had a housekeeper, and no one wanted one now. She was hired because Mother was dying. On the day she arrived, Mother sat anxiously by the window in her green chenille robe, peering through the curtains and tensely pushing back loose strands of hair. Eventually, an enormous figure heaved itself around the corner; it was draped in black and listing from side to side, like a boat. "That couldn't be . . ." she whispered, and we both laughed. It was.

Mae was kind and we never called her Big Mae except behind her back (in the same way that Daddy later referred to Mavis, whose last name was Parris, as Mavis Pear-Ass). Big Mae kept Cliquot Club ginger ale on the top shelf of the closet in the extra bedroom. It didn't make any difference to her that we had a kitchen and a refrigerator. The Cliquot Club was hers; it stayed with her. She was that way about everything she owned. But Big Mae was generous. The night Mother died, she took me into her room and poured me a glass of her very own Cliquot Club ginger ale. It was warm and flat, but other than that it seemed to be just what I needed. We sat in her room waiting for the undertaker to arrive and killed the whole bottle of Cliquot Club. Big Mae didn't seem to mind. She just kept shaking her head and saying, "Terrible thing," over and over. "Terrible thing, the missus going like that." I don't know what Daddy was doing while we were drinking away; I didn't want to look.

Big Mae left shortly after that. She seemed to feel her duty was discharged: she had been hired to help Mother through her illness; now that the illness was over, so was her work. I think children made her uneasy, but she was never unkind—although fat, and strange in many ways. I was sorry to see her go.

❧

*I*t is April; Easter is only two weeks away. Sonya comes home on the bus from the Edgemont School for Girls just in time to see Ray wheel Valery from the bathroom to the bedroom in a wheelchair—a distance of approximately twenty feet. Her heart seems to stop beating. "What's that for?" she asks them in a whisper. "Oh, nothing, honey; it's just a little temporary assistance until Mother feels strong again!" There is not a single person in the household who will acknowledge, and say in words, that Valery Weiler is dying: neither Ray nor Big Mae, nor Valery herself.

Valery calls Sonya into her bedroom. She is so pale; her skin looks like paper. She is sitting in the wheelchair in front of her dresser mirror; there is a hairbrush in her hand. She extends it to Sonya and whispers, "Brush my hair." Sonya wants to go outside and play. She doesn't want to look at Valery ever again. What a terrible thing! Only a truly rotten person would not want to look at her own mother. Slowly she takes the hairbrush from Valery's dry hand. Her hair hangs down around her shoulders in tangled, greasy clumps; it hasn't been washed in a long time. Slowly Sonya starts to brush. Valery stares straight into the mirror, her face full of hollows and strange shadows. Sonya moves the brush up and down, up and down, in shallow, tentative strokes. She is repulsed by the tangled, lifeless hair and by the odor that emanates from Valery's body. There is no way out of this labor of love and revulsion. She brushes faster and faster. At last Valery says, "Thank you." "You're welcome," Sonya calls, as she runs out of the house. She runs to the playground five blocks away, and pumps the swing so high it threatens to loop over the bar from which it hangs and spill her to the ground.

On Easter Sunday, Valery sits propped in the wing chair in the living room as Greta is paraded into the room. She has been specially dressed for the occasion by Big Mae and Ray in a little pink pleated skirt, a pink blouse and sweater, and new white shoes. They bring her over to Valery as a kind of Easter surprise. Valery

52

kisses the back of her neck and exclaims feebly, "My little pink marshmallow!" "That's not all, folks!" announces Ray, as he brings a cardboard box into the living room. Out jumps a white Easter rabbit. Greta squeals and grabs the rabbit around the middle; its eyes bulge. Ray takes the rabbit away. Greta screams, "No! No! No!" She is two years old. Valery shows her how to pat the rabbit and she calms down. Ray hides some Easter baskets behind the furniture which Sonya and Greta quickly find. Ray wonders if Valery could manage to come out on the front lawn for a family Easter snapshot. Valery whispers, "No." Ray puts the rabbit on the lawn, and Greta kneels down beside it. Ray snaps the picture just as Greta looks up. "That should be a good one," he comments proudly. Valery doesn't live to see it. Ray begins to prepare the Easter dinner while Valery sits in the wing chair watching Greta eat candy eggs on the floor. An overflowing basket rests between her baby legs. The bunny is put in the basement, where it litters the floor with its droppings and eventually turns gray from the dirt. One day, it will mysteriously disappear and never be seen again.

A week after Easter, Valery calls again to Sonya as she arrives home from school. Big Mae has taken Greta to the park; Valery is alone in the house. Sonya walks slowly into the bedroom, holding her breath. She has held her breath every day after school since the wheelchair. She has developed new feelings about her mother which she can hardly contain, much less comprehend. All she knows, and she knows it absolutely now, is that Valery is different. She is not pretty and cool and perfumed, like the mothers at the Edgemont teas. She doesn't smile. She just sits there in a moldy chenille robe, smoking Luckies and waiting to die.

Valery looks up weakly from the wheelchair; it is positioned next to the dresser. She explains in a thin voice that there is an item in the bottom drawer which she needs, and which she can't get for herself as she can neither stand up, bend over, nor reach. As Sonya opens the drawer, Valery instructs her to reach into the blue box. She withdraws a sanitary napkin, something she has never seen before. Valery takes the napkin and, opening the folds of her green chenille robe, places it across her diseased breasts. In that instant, Sonya sees for the first time what is the matter with her mother. There are no breasts; just acres of bleeding, oozing craters, as far as the eye can see. *Planes drone overhead, their hatches open and dart-shaped bombs float out of their silver bellies and plunge into the ground. The earth below is pocked with fiery, smoking craters. It is ravaged and torn to pieces, just like her mother.* Valery clumsily fastens the sanitary napkin to herself with pathetic strips of white adhesive tape. Her eyes meet Sonya's for a second; they are blank.

The night of April 22, 1947, sees unaccustomed visitors to the dream house on 51st Avenue South. First, there is the Christian Science nurse, who is called to the home around seven o'clock—just after dinner. Christian Science nurses are only called in extreme situations. The Christian Science practitioner, Mrs. Hoyt, is present in slightly attenuated form via the telephone receiver, which has been left off the hook. Mrs. Hoyt is understood to be there on the other end of the line "working" for Valery. Sonya knows that "working" means concentrating very hard and having no evil thoughts. If she can do it, too, maybe their combined efforts will make Valery well. She has been taught in Sunday School that having evil thoughts about someone can actually bring about the evil. She uses a lot of energy keeping those thoughts out of her head; she doesn't want to hurt anyone. She works so hard at this, she doesn't hear what the teachers say and can't understand words on the printed page.

Sonya spends the evening of April 22 sitting on the edge of her bed; she leaves the door open just enough to catch what is going on but avoid its undiluted force. Sometimes she squints through the crack and sees Ray rushing from Valery's bedroom to the phone in the hall, where he whispers a description of her condition to Mrs. Hoyt: what she says, how she looks, what she has or has not taken by mouth. The Christian Science nurse rushes back and forth between the bedroom and the bathroom with cool cloths. By eight-thirty, Sonya can no longer stand her helplessness; she goes into the kitchen and pours a small amount of orange juice into a flowered glass and takes it in to Valery. She walks carefully, watching the edges of the rug to make sure it doesn't spill. She doesn't look up until she gets right to the edge of the bed. Valery is propped against three pillows; there are deep hollows under her eyes. Sonya whispers, "Would you like a drink of juice?" Valery smiles faintly and whispers, "Yes." Sonya holds the glass out to her mother but before her hand can take it, the Christian Science nurse swoops in and intercepts it. "She doesn't need that now," the nurse commands as she ushers Sonya out of the room. Ray doesn't protest; Valery can't. Sonya makes no struggle to return. She goes back to the edge of her bed and lies down. She stuffs all her fingers in her mouth and rocks back and forth. At nine o'clock, she hears the Christian Science nurse pick up the waiting receiver and whisper to Mrs. Hoyt, "I think she's gone."

The nurse replaces the receiver and goes into the bathroom and shuts the door. Sonya gets up from the bed and looks around the door frame into Valery's bedroom. Greta still sleeps peacefully in the crib against the west wall. Over on the double bed a man is holding a corpse in a green chenille bathrobe. His head is bent, so she can't see the expression on his face, but the corpse in his arms has its face toward the door. Sonya has never seen skin so white. She is jolted by the sight; it means something so significant that it is beyond comprehension. She stares at the face, hoping to see something there—she doesn't know if it is a sign of life, or an indication that her mother is finally at peace. Her parents are locked in each other's arms, stuck together, frozen in a mute tableau on the bed against the north wall. Greta sleeps on through the death of her mother, whom she will not remember. The Christian Science nurse dials the undertaker. Sonya backs out of the room and finds Big Mae standing behind her in the hall. Big Mae holds out a glass of ginger ale and guides Sonya into her room. They sit on opposite sides of the bed, a tray with the bottles of ginger ale between them. Sonya never hears the undertaker come and never hears him go. After Big Mae retires for the night, Sonya finds Ray sitting alone in the living room; he stares straight ahead, his hands gripping the arms of the wing chair like a stone pharaoh. She climbs into his lap and they sit together in the wing chair,

55

saying nothing. Down in the basement, the Easter rabbit quivers on the hard cement. Somewhere, Valery evaporates and is no more.

In the morning, Greta runs from room to room, calling "Mammy!" Her new white shoes echo over the hardwood floors. Freshly picked flowers are clutched in her hand. Someone says, "Mammy's gone." Sonya doesn't remember who it is. She thinks she's seen this scene in a movie before, but can't remember where.

🥀 *The New Dress* 🥀

It was raining, as usual, the day Daddy and I went to the old Bon Marché department store to buy Mother a new dress. He forced me to go with him; I didn't want to. The funeral was in two days, and Mother deserved a new dress to be buried in. It was the least he could do for her, he had said, looking away.

We went up the wooden escalators to the second floor. Two saleswomen descended on us right away, but the taller one made it first so the short one just faded back behind the racks of dresses. "Yes, sir. May I be of assistance today?" she said. Daddy cleared his throat. "Yes," he said, "thank you. I am looking for a dress for my wife." She beamed. "Right this way, sir!" I started to inch away, pretending interest in the dresses farthest from the scene. "Come here, darling, stay with Daddy; don't get lost," Daddy said loudly. "I *won't* get lost," I hissed, but he insisted that I stick to his side—like a leech, or an appendage. In a dim way, I sensed he needed me to play this scene.

The clerk guided us to the dresses which were on a special rack: set off by themselves, inserted in a niche in the wall, under special lights. Almost as an afterthought, she said brightly,

"What size is she?" Daddy didn't seem to hear. He was examining, in the vaguest way, a red and yellow paisley dress. His eyes were clouded. She repeated the question: "Sir?" "I beg your pardon? Oh. Well . . ." And here is where everything shifted; I had been expecting it. "My wife has passed away. Just this week. We need something special for the burial . . ."

The brightness faded immediately from her face; all traces of it vanished. She blinked a couple of times, but other than that you could see she was doing a good job controlling herself. She was beginning to wish that the other clerk had gotten to us first. I had almost begun to feel sorry for her when she did a terrible, unforgivable thing: she turned it all around. She put her hand on my head! She began to murmur things: "Oh, I *see*; I'm so sorry . . . yes, I understand . . . is this your daughter?" I wanted to fade away into the endless racks of dresses. There was nothing to do except stare at the floor and stick it out. It was clear from that moment on she knew she had him where she wanted him. A man whose wife had just died wouldn't lower himself to discuss price.

"Wait here a moment, sir; I will be right back." She bustled into a back room. I knew what was coming, and so did he. He was powerless to reverse it. He let his hand run listlessly down the aisle of dresses, in the manner of one who finds himself hopelessly trapped in hostile territory.

She emerged with one dress, holding it up so the light could shine directly on it. It was the most horrible dress I have ever seen. Green, with black diagonal stripes. Or black, with green diagonal stripes. The memory blurs; but it was black and green. A total disaster. It would have given Mother the heebie-jeebies. The saleslady looked from the dress to Daddy, from Daddy back to the dress. Her hands shook slightly. I had to concede it wasn't the most pleasant sale of her life.

"Yes, that's a nice dress. A very nice dress," he said helplessly.

We left the store, going out through the revolving door into the rain, with Daddy holding the unspeakable dress in a box under his arm. He carried it as though it were a bomb about to explode. I kept thinking: It wasn't fair. Mother had wanted a new dress for years, and he hadn't done a thing about it. Now he's trying to pass himself off as a big spender, a man of infinite sacrifice. Too late, too late. Where was it written that the dead need new clothes?

🐝 *The Casket* 🐝

He did it again at the funeral home: dragged me along to pick out just the right casket. The carpets were deep maroon and the lights were very dim. Mr. Glover, the undertaker, had come down from his office on the second floor to help us choose. Soundlessly, he led us to the casket room which was sealed from view by long velvet drapes.

Securing the drapes to one side with a little cord, Mr. Glover explained the different choices and their respective prices. His voice was in the lower register, soft as velvet. It was understood that the two lower-priced pine models were beneath consideration. Daddy eyed them from time to time, with quiet desperation, but in the end took his cue from Mr. Glover and selected the second most expensive model. I secreted myself behind the velvet drapes. "What the hell are you doing in there," Daddy whispered furiously to me as Mr. Glover went to attend to the paperwork. "This is a respectable place."

🐝 *The Service* 🐝

The following day we were all dressed up in our best clothes, back at Glover's Funeral Home. The service took place in a special room the size of a small auditorium. Rows of folding chairs had been set up to accommodate the mourners, but there were only three people there: the lady who lived next door to the

58

south; the lady next door to the north; and the lady directly across the street. They sat some distance apart, as though they had sprinkled themselves across the auditorium deliberately in order to make it appear there were more of them. They bobbed conspicuously in that vast, embarrassing sea of chairs. "Who told them Mother died?" I asked Daddy; I felt so exposed. "They read the papers," he said. It was in the *paper?* Now everyone would know! And stare at me.

The family gathered around the casket: Nona, Uncle Jack, Daddy and I. Nona and Uncle Jack had hurried down from Canada when they heard the news. There lay Mother, fresh as a peach; there was even a trace of a smile on her face! She looked so healthy, I wanted to reach out and touch her; there must have been some mistake! She had recovered in the funeral home! God's perfect love came through! It wasn't until I got up close that I saw that the peach color owed itself to a fine layer of tinted netting that had been stretched across the top of the casket. Still, its implications did not get completely through. I stared and stared, watching for a sign of life. After a long time, it was suggested that I move on so the others could have a look. I stood off to the side, holding my breath and trying to figure out what to do. I knew that my mother was about to be buried alive, but I was unable to speak. Couldn't they see she had revived? Maybe one of the grownups would discover it before it was too late. If I told them, there would be chaos; they would know it had been a mistake to let a child attend a funeral.

I tried to cry; I felt it was expected of me. But somehow, with the three neighbors looking on, it wasn't possible. I knew they must think me a terrible person not to cry at my own mother's funeral. But there are some things you just can't do, even when it counts the most. I stood on the sidelines for the rest of the service, trying to reconcile the way Mother looked here at her last showing, and the way she had looked the night she died, lying in Daddy's arms in the old brass bed.

At the cemetery, as they lowered her into the ground, I found myself thinking of Esther, wondering who would be the "third" wife, and whether funerals were where you usually met them. As the first shovel of dirt was tossed on top of the casket, Nona began wailing and tried to throw herself into the grave. Daddy and Uncle Jack had to restrain her, and I have no memory of anything that happened after that.

⚘ Roxie ⚘

It's hard to say whether Roxie was our third housekeeper or the fourth or fifth; there were so many of them over the years after Mother died. I think she was in there around second or third. She wasn't the thirteenth. That was Sybil. And she wasn't the first, that was Big Mae.

It was a warm evening when Daddy brought Roxie home for an "interview." She kicked off her black spike-heeled shoes right away, on account of the heat. I thought it was rude the way she tucked her legs under her on the sofa, but Daddy just smiled in a sickening way and said, "Play something for Roxie, honey." I played "Clair de Lune" and she said, "Oh gosh, that's purdy, real purdy." Something in her manner bothered me, so I started banging out "Chopsticks" and Daddy's face turned red. "That's enough of that, honey," he said, controlling himself. What did he think I was, a trained monkey?

About a month after Roxie came to stay with us, the rabbit disappeared. I went all through the house trying to find it. The last place I looked was Daddy's bedroom. The door was closed. I couldn't understand that; it was still daylight. When I opened it, there he was on the bed, curled up with Roxie. They pulled apart the minute they saw me standing there. Other than that, they continued to lie there, staring at me. "Hi, honey; I didn't hear you come in," he said lamely. They just kept staring, as though I were the freak. I showed my contempt for them by walking out. I couldn't believe the way he had lowered himself, lying on Mother's bed with that slutty Roxie.

60

I spent a long time staring at the moon that night; it was large and full and veined with strange geography. I began to see it as a symbol—of somewhere else to go when the time came.

⚘ Fainting ⚘

Every day, that first summer after Mother died, I went up to the playground to faint. Five other girls and I met in front of the swings after lunch; I have no memory of how it began, or whose idea it was. The point was to breathe in and out as fast as you could, then—while someone grabbed you from behind, squeezed you around the chest, and lifted you off the ground—hold your breath. If you had panted deeply enough and fast enough, you fainted and promptly dropped unconscious to the ground.

I remember the otherworldly sensation of "coming to," lying on my back in the grass: at first everything was black; then lighter, with black spots; then I saw the sky—impossibly high and far away—and then, gradually, the faces of my friends came into view, their features blurred at the edges. They stood in a circle over me, peering down excitedly. "She's coming to!" they would whisper, nudging each other with their elbows. It was a game no one ever grew bored with, no matter how many times it was repeated. Everyone seemed awed and amazed at the coming-to. It was my favorite moment: you were no longer panting and going black; no longer numb, dead, gone, but tingling all over with new life.

For hours we died and were reborn until the day one of the mothers across the street looked out her window and noticed the wide circle of boys at one end of the playground, playing baseball, and the tighter circle of girls at the other, fainting. She grabbed her telephone and brought our fainting sessions to an abrupt end. The others accepted the loss with equanimity, but I was frantic; fainting had become an obsession. It proved I could come back from the dead.

61

🦋 Hazel 🦋

Hazel came sometime before Roxie. Hazel read the Bible to us every evening after dinner. She was not subtle about it, and caused no end of embarrassment. The neighbors could see right in the kitchen window where we sat around the table: Greta, Daddy and I, our heads bowed like naughty children, while she stood at the head of the table, holding the black book aloft in her bony hands; they were raw and large and always smelled like celery. Why Daddy let her do it, I will never understand; he must have been desperate. He did get a childish satisfaction from poking us in the ribs while Hazel was preoccupied with the Scripture, and making derisive little faces behind his hands. It was ridiculous, her standing there at the head of the table, and him making faces like a schoolboy. Whose house did she think it was? She forced us to take piano lessons from her, too, once a week, just as if she were a legitimate teacher.

Her son, Anthony, came to visit her once before she left us to marry some man she had met on the Seward Park bus. He went to Salvation Army school and dressed completely in black. He had the pinkest face and the fattest hands of any boy I had ever seen. His eyes shone vacantly behind clear plastic frames and no matter how much you tried to talk to him, he never had anything to say.

🦋 Gerald 🦋

I liked Loretta's son better. He was evil, like me. We used to hide behind the garage after dinner, eating Twinkies. Gerald could never get enough Twinkies. It may have crossed Daddy's mind, and Loretta's too, that we were having orgies out back every evening. We were, in a way. It was very ritualized. We would bite off the ends, then break them in half and run our tongues down the whipped cream centers slowly, dragging it out, neither of us wanting to be the first one to have no more Twinkie left. You could make it last a long time the way we did it. Daddy could be heard screaming on hot summer nights from deep inside the house, "Where in the name of Christ are all the Twinkies going?"

Daddy said it was good riddance when Gerald ran off to join the circus. He kept referring to him as "that no-good roustabout." For a long time after that I had dreams about Gerald, doing whatever roustabouts do: hanging by one leg from a trapeze, in a white satin suit, with a Twinkie in his mouth.

❧ Wilma ❧

Wilma was decidedly short-term. She was there one day and gone the next.

Daddy eventually got Wilma on the big brass bed too; but she was smarter than Roxie. He had to change tactics with her, so he cried a little. "Crocodile tears," she would say. She even said it to me: "Do you know what crocodile tears are?" "No," I said. I had no idea, couldn't imagine crocodiles crying or, if they did, why. "They're what your Dad cries when he wants something from me," she said. "Oh." Wilma made me uncomfortable, from the day she came until the day she left.

The day she left came without warning. I came home from school and there were all her bags lined up on the porch, and a taxi waiting in the driveway. "I asked the cab to wait," Wilma explained. "I didn't want to go off and leave Greta here alone. I wanted to do the decent thing and wait until you got home from school." She went on to explain that the reason she was leaving us like that was because she couldn't stand the tension in the house any longer. Or the way Daddy ranted around, screaming at everyone. And, presumably, his crocodile tears had been the last straw. We stood there in the driveway, watching Wilma drive off in the cab. Greta started to cry, not so much because of Wilma herself, but because someone else was leaving. It made me mad that she was crying; I didn't want Wilma to interpret that as meaning that we had any feelings about her whatsoever. "We don't need her," I said to Greta; "we're lucky that she's gone. Stop crying those crocodile tears."

❦ *Flo* ❦

Flo was "a dear old friend" of Daddy's. She had red hair. Mother used to joke about her when she was alive, teasing Daddy and saying, "Is that a *red* hair I see on your shoulder?" It used to catch him off guard, and he always jumped a little before laughing.

We were left without a housekeeper for the remainder of the month when Wilma left. Things were chaotic and Daddy spent a lot of time slipping out of the house at night, saying he had urgent business in the mountains. He was always there the next day, though, which made me think of mountains lined up just across the street. He spent a lot of time on the phone that month, pouring out his troubles to Flo. I heard snatches of their conversations and was startled to hear my own name come up in connection with the word "incorrigible."

One evening Daddy came up to me soberly and said, "There is a very understanding woman on the phone and she would like to say something to you." She had a seductive voice and the gist of what she had to say to me was that Daddy was working his heart out for me. It sounded as though he had planted the words in her mouth. I thought it was a cheap trick, getting her to tell me to behave, "because he is such a wonderful man." Who was she to tell me about him? She may think he's wonderful, but I know how he really is. We have different points of view concerning him. I hung up, thinking: The next time he wants me to behave, he can tell me himself.

❦ Yohimbine ❦

Whenever I needed clothes, I had to ask Daddy for the money. Since this always provoked extensive monologues on the subject of uranium, lasting well into the night, I began to skip this step and simply tiptoe into his closet while he sat in the living room reading *Reader's Digest*, and look in his wallet. If there was more than twenty dollars there, I would ask him. If there was less, I would skip it.

One evening, while feeling in his pocket for the wallet, my hand touched a little bottle. I felt I had no choice but to investigate it since, as a Christian Scientist, he would have been cheating to have had pills. The little bottle simply said YOHIMBINE the label. That was all. I had vague suspicions right there, but it wasn't until I looked it up in the dictionary that I learned Daddy was carrying around Spanish fly. That explained his one-night trips to the mountains. From then on, I felt decidedly superior to Flo.

❦ Fay ❦

Fay came to live with us two weeks after Wilma's departure. Fay had just left her husband, Roger, and thought that ours was a perfect little home for her daughter, Mary Lou. In fact, she couldn't have been more pleased with things, as Mary Lou and Greta were the same age. It didn't seem to matter that they fought all the time; being the same age made everything perfect. Fay thought Daddy was "a wonderful man" too; working his heart out the way he did to keep a home together for his girls. She couldn't have been more shocked when, a week after she came to live with us, two enormous policewomen appeared at the front door.

"Why, of course," she said to them, after they had sat down on the sofa. She would be more than happy to tell them whatever it was they wanted to know about Mr. Weiler. There had to be some mistake. He was a devoted father and a wonderful man.

Well, no, that wasn't quite the story we heard, the policewomen related. We have it all here in the report. It seems a woman by the name of Wilma Acheson claims he beat his children and endangered her own life while she was working in Mr. Weiler's home as a housekeeper.

Fay was a star, I had to admit, as I sat out of sight on the floor in the hall, listening to them talk. She might not know the whole truth, being a recent arrival; but she was not about to let Wilma Acheson, or any policewoman, cast aspersions on her employer. "Just come and see for yourselves," she said, leading them into Greta's room. The shades were drawn; she was still napping. "I will pull up the shades and you'll see there isn't a bruise on her body." Greta woke up—there was star material there, too, as she smiled and did a little dance for the visiting ladies—and sure enough, there was not, praise the Lord, a bruise on her body. I had to credit the policewomen: they seemed genuinely pleased to see it—not disappointed, as I had expected. But if I thought the inquisition was over and I was to be spared, I was wrong. One of them turned to me and began asking questions.

"Does your father ever beat you?"

"No."

"Does he ever strike you when he's angry?"

"No."

"Are you happy here?"

"Yes."

I was brief because I was certain that they were warming up to ask me to show them if I had bruises on my body. It turned out, though, that if one had the gift of speech, and said the right things in a convincing way, one was not obliged to relinquish one's body to the Seattle Police Department. They left with apologies, saying that things seemed to be in order. Fay was quite upset, but her faith remained unshaken, right up to the day she returned to her husband, Roger. Fay was referred to ever after by

Daddy as "the only good one in the lot." It was one of the few things on which we did not disagree.

The Monroe Pool

In the winter, my friend Margaret and I always swam at the Monroe Pool on Saturdays. It was located in the basement of the old Monroe Hotel on 2nd Avenue, in an area called "niggertown" by those who didn't have to live there. We usually came home on the bus afterwards, waiting in the rain outside the pool hall on the corner. For some reason, on the last Saturday that I was to see the Monroe Pool, Daddy decided he would pick us up. I protested, but he seemed determined: "I will *be* there at five o'clock," he said.

I didn't think anymore about it—we bellyflopped for two hours—until, surfacing from a spectacular plunge, I saw his pinched face swim into view. "Get out of that pool this minute," he said. I stood dripping on the chlorine-stained tiles and demanded to know why; it was only ten to five. During the scene that followed, I tried to inhale as little as possible; it was like breathing the vapors of hell. He ranted for a full ten minutes (but it was a peculiar, self-contained ranting; it wouldn't do to have the niggers see him lose control).

Going home in the car, he made it clear that that was to be the end of the Monroe Pool. No daughter of his was going to swim in that cesspool. I wept and argued: what did he mean, cesspool! But he was rigid. He insisted he had seen a turd floating somewhere in those murky depths. I was horrified. "What do you mean, a turd?!" After all, I was the one who had spent the afternoon there, and I hadn't run across any turds.

It was only years later, around the time when the papers carried the news that the Monroe Hotel was to be torn down (and its dirty cesspool with it), that I began to suspect that the whole turd business had had more to do with the lithe black bodies who churned those muddy wastes with us every Saturday than it did with turds. He had invented the turd; it was the only way he could think of to prevent me from swimming with niggers. He knew I wouldn't buy it if he put it that directly; he figured I'd buy the turd, though. I must confess I came close. It was a hard image to put out of your mind. In the months that followed, I gradually began to accept as a fact that the Monroe Pool had turds. Or at least had had *a* turd, at one time. It took the spirit out of me, just as he had planned.

🎔 *Anniversary Waltz* 🎔

I was ten the first time I heard the "Anniversary Waltz." I had been visiting at the home of a wealthy classmate from the Edgemont School and Daddy had come to pick me up. It was a silent house, with forty-two rooms and acres of carpets. He parked the old Ford a block away, from shame.

Gigi Rucklehaus and I were sitting at her piano, imitating the music teacher at school. We were doubled over; we were that funny. Her father and a friend of his were in the room. They were putting records on his new phonograph. Their cocktails made the sound of little bells across the plush pile carpets.

—Why did he have to come, I am thinking.

"Do come in. So good to meet you."

—The industrialist is shaking a con man's hand! I am stuck to the piano bench. Gigi is still convulsed, but I know something terrible is about to happen.

"Like you to meet . . . Just in from Palm Beach . . . And what did you say your profession was?"

—Lies.

"Hi, honey."

—Don't look at me. Disappear.

"We have to be getting home now."

"Won't you join us for a cocktail?"

"Oh, no, thank you so much. That's very kind of you to offer, but no, thank you all the same."

—Trying to pretend he doesn't drink! All those empty whiskey bottles under the sink!

"We're just trying out our new record player."

"Beautiful machine. Wonderful grain in the wood. I know. I like to think I know my woods."

"Please. Are you sure you won't join us?"

"Well, if you insist." Nervous laughter, hands up, protesting.

—Grab it. You know you want to grab it, swill it, numb the pain.

". . . if you insist. But only a small one please."

—Two fingers, indicating.

Gigi's father pushed the button and the record dropped with a smooth *splat* onto the new turntable and the "Anniversary Waltz" began to play. It took up all the air in the room. Daddy stood there with them, balancing the drink like an acrobat about to fall, poised rigid, as though something very fragile were bound to break with one wrong move.

—Don't stand so stiff! This house is full of *carpets!* And his eyes began to glaze—just slightly, he has it in control, at least for the moment—and they stood around the phonograph, the three of them, listening politely, with nothing to say, to the "Anniversary Waltz."

> *Ohhhhhhhh, how we danced*
> *On the niiiiiight we were wed . . .*

—Oh, turn it off. Can't you see. He's just lost his wife. He can't tell you that—but he might. Please hurry. Finish the drink and take me home.

❦ The New Coat ❧

Daddy has asked Ingeborg to take me shopping for a new coat. The sleeves on my old one are halfway to my elbows; the hem dangles threadbare, inches above my knees. Ingeborg Johansson has been in this country four months; her brother, John, saw Daddy's ad for a housekeeper and got her this job. She has tight little blond curls all over her head and weighs nearly three hundred pounds. She has taught Greta to say, "Tack för maten" at the dinner table, to which Ingeborg always replies, "Var så god!" She blushes whenever Daddy speaks to her, and also when she is angry. I don't think she understands what she is supposed to be doing at our house besides the cooking and cleaning. Once, when I was on the phone with Margaret, she came bursting into the hall and wrenched the receiver out of my hand with one violent twist, and when I protested, she pulled my hair with such ferocity, I lost my balance and fell against the wall. I screamed and wailed and locked myself in my room, but I knew even then that I couldn't tell Daddy. I knew right away what he'd say: "Housekeepers don't grow on trees." She pulled Greta's hair, too, under the guise of combing it, but not as violently as mine: Greta was little and cute and was busting her gut to learn Swedish. She didn't sass back, like me.

I heard Daddy rapping lightly on Ingeborg's door after dinner. He whispered that his motherless darling, the one who ties up the phone for hours, needed a new coat, and he wondered if Ingeborg would mind taking me downtown one evening when the stores were open and helping me pick one out. As he handed her the money, he hinted that this same darling was also in need of something a bit more substantive than a coat—a mother, for instance—and that he would be forever in Ingeborg's debt if she could find it in her heart to take his little daughter out to dinner, too, and perhaps offer her—words failed him at this point, but he spread his hands wide, before the blushing face of Ingeborg Johansson, indicating the impossible smorgasbord of attention, guidance, love and concern he wished for his little girl. Ingeborg nodded and blushed and giggled and grunted; she kept nodding her head and muttering little sounds of assent as she carefully put the money into her purse. Daddy backed out of her room, smiling sadly, with one hand raised in a gesture of gratitude and relief.

I would rather go without a new coat than be seen downtown with Ingeborg. I pray no one from school sees us together. As we move down the racks, turning the new coats this way and that, a new fear strikes: The clerk will think she's my mother! My mother was small and dark, I want to say; not gigantic and blond! I feel such a sudden despair for having lost her, and such anger at her for dying, it takes me by surprise. I feel helpless, wanting her back, and ashamed to need Ingeborg to help me shop. I feel sorry for myself, and pity for Ingeborg for having to spend her evening with me. By the time she finally chose the shocking pink coat for me, I was sweating from the effort required to keep all these feelings in check. I was exhausted and on the verge of tears, and didn't have the strength to protest. She suggested I wear the new coat to the restaurant for dinner. I thought: If anyone sees me, I will die. I will throw myself under the wheels of the Seward Park bus the first thing in the morning.

Ingeborg picked a place on 3rd Avenue called Little Bit O'Sweden. We sat down at a small table and were served an assortment of strange, but good, things which I'd never had before. I felt like something from outer space, wrapped in the shocking pink coat and listening to this strange woman speak a foreign language to the waitress. No one spoke to me at all. I was glad when the food arrived; it gave me something to concentrate on instead of sitting there waiting for Ingeborg to try to be a mother to me. She never did attempt it. She smiled at me occasionally, though, making happy little noises with her mouth full of food. When the dinner was over, I thanked her in Swedish even though I didn't have to because Daddy had paid for it. "Var så god!" she said with a giggle, as her face flushed. I was dimly aware that the evening had been as awkward for her as it had for me. She was so relieved it was over, she hummed Swedish songs all the way home on the bus. I was beyond caring if anyone thought she was my mother; I was trying to figure out how to get through the winter without having to wear the new coat.

A Regular Job

It drove Daddy crazy that there were so many valuable things in the ground which Mother Earth jealously guarded for herself. He became more tormented as each day passed without his having claimed them. At various times in his life, every member of the family, on both sides, had suggested that he get "a regular job." "Aw, shit, Jack," he would say; "you don't understand. That's for the ordinary *working* stiffs!" And back he would go for another two or three years, to the little 8-by-10-foot office on 2nd Avenue, to prop his feet on the desk top, whistle softly to himself, and forge on. Together, he and Ed would sit with their feet on the desk, drinking bourbon and planning new deals. When the gold mine failed, they began to speak of timber. There were so many possibilities for striking it rich! Anyone could see that, but they usually didn't, because they were all horses' asses.

Emptying the Garbage

The first Easter after Mother died, Daddy and Eddie Atkins took us for a drive to the woods to see what new things the Easter Bunny had been up to. Eddie was waiting on the sidewalk outside his transient hotel with his three children—nicknamed Dinty, Sis and Sport—from his former marriage. They piled in the car and we all headed for the woods.

While we waited in the Ford, Daddy and Ed tiptoed into the ferns with a bag of "garbage" in one hand and a bag of bourbon

72

in the other. This was known as "checking out the spot." When questioned, they said, "We're looking for a good spot to dump the garbage." I wondered what was wrong with our garbage can back home, but there was something about the situation that suggested you would blow something important if you asked.

What seemed like hours later, they emerged, wiping their mouths on their hands, saying, "This looks like a good spot." That was our cue to get out of the car and begin our foray into the woods to see if the Easter Bunny had in fact been about. We found lots of eggs, but no trace of garbage anywhere.

🐰 *An Evening with Eddie* 🐰

One night, just after dinner, Daddy received a phone call from Eddie. It was Ingeborg's night off, so he bundled Greta and me into the Ford and drove downtown to Ed's hotel, just on the edge of skid row. He found it convenient that there was a tavern on the corner where he and Ed could discuss their urgent business, but he explained to us that there was some ridiculous law which prohibited children from accompanying their fathers in taverns. So, although it broke his heart to do it, he would have to leave us outside, locked in the car.

"Thirsty! Thirsty!" sang Greta, no doubts clouding her mind that this would gain her admission.

"Precious darling," whispered Daddy sincerely, stroking her hair. "She's too young to understand," he said to me, as an aside. I was too young to understand, too, but didn't let on.

Wrapped in our blankets, we sat and watched the night life from the steamy confines of the Ford. Every now and then a drunk would drum his fingers on the windows and smile toothlessly at Greta. An hour or more went by while Daddy and Ed downed their business. At last he came out and slid unevenly into the driver's seat and started toward home. He was driving fast, but I found that if I burrowed down in the back where Greta was sleeping, I lost all sense of fast and slow, and was spared seeing all the objects he narrowly missed hitting.

Just as I was falling asleep, I became aware of a siren in back of us. Daddy was flagged down and pulled over to the curb with an expression of utter disbelief on his face.

"Do you have any idea how fast you were going, sir?" the officer asked, flashing his light into the back seat, right into our eyes.

"Wha? Oh, well, Officer, there must be some mistake."

"No mistake, sir. I was behind you for six blocks; I clocked you at fifty-five. This is a twenty-five-mile-an-hour zone, you know," he added.

"Officer, I admit I may have lost track of my speed for a while there. You see, I was trying to get my two motherless babies home to bed."

The flashlight came our way again; I guess he was trying to make sure there was no mother hiding back there. Daddy started to wipe a few tears on his sleeve. "Just trying to get my little motherless babies home," he whispered. The policeman began to back away from the car. "Well, sir, you may proceed; just try to watch it in the future, if you will."

"Thank you, Officer; you're a real credit to the force. I won't forget this, you can be sure of that."

Daddy started up the engine and got back on the road, clearing his throat and wiping his nose on the back of his hand. By this time I was crying.

"What the hell are you crying about?" he wanted to know. "That pip-squeak scare you with his flashlight?"

"Yes."

"Aw, hell, honey; you don't have to worry about things like that when you're with Daddy. Hell, if any pip-squeak cop ever gave your daddy any trouble, I would knock his block off, you know that. Now lie down and go back to sleep. We'll be home before you know what happened."

🏵 Sunday School 🏵

It was important to Daddy that we go to Sunday School. Every Sunday morning at eleven he would drive us to the Third Church of Christ, Scientist, explaining why we needed religious instruction: "You goddamned rotters, you're not worth the powder it takes to blow you to hell. You aggravate the living bejesus out of me." Then he would drop us off and go back home to crack open a fresh bottle of Heaven Hill bourbon.

Sunday School was held in the basement. It was cool down there. We sat at little tables and read the Bible and Mary Baker Eddy. We took turns telling of "demonstrations": those little skirmishes with Adversity which we had had during the week, which somehow always managed to be mastered with the winning combination of God's love and "perfect understanding." I could never manage to bring myself to discuss Daddy, though, whom I secretly felt to be my biggest adversity. I was near crazy to have a demonstration over him.

🏵

Ray is changing. He can sense the shifts, the great upheavals, taking place inside him, and guesses they are visible to others, too, but has no power of his own to reverse them. On the road, wrapped in the private confines of the tattered Ford, he cries softly to himself. This makes him feel ashamed, but at the same time provides some measure of relief. As he wipes his eyes on his sleeve, strange incidents flash before him; he can discern no order, sequence, or explanation for their appearance. His slight frame shakes with sobs as he sees himself long ago, on the screened porch of the small wood frame house in Buffalo. His mother is unhappy, he can't remember why but he knows he is the cause. He thinks he can make out the contours of an old icebox in the background, just outside the kitchen door. The wide porch sags. Is her finger raised? Did he steal, or is he telling her a tall tale? She was stern, she planted both feet firmly on the ground and simply took root. He can never make her smile! But he'll find some way to make them proud; all it takes is ingenuity and a little luck. Little Ray, the charmer of the family, the one with the big imagination. Who called him that? His brother Frederik works in their father's candy store, but Ray is undependable; his mind is always somewhere else.

Suddenly, images of Esther swim before his eyes; he sees her apparition through the old divided windshield. He pulls the car off the road and breaks down. All his women dead, all his deals fallen through! And back at home, his babies: he is all they have. The weight of their future settles on his chest and tightens. He turns the engine off as his sobs rack the frayed interior. Then suddenly he is back in Buffalo again; he remembers wetting his bed. What shame! And the recriminations, the punishments. It always happened after the nightmares: he would wake just as the milk wagon clattered down the street; all around him spread the icy wetness that nothing could hide, nothing could explain away. Yet he has managed all these years since then, he tells himself firmly. He has taken care of his babies. He has made deal after deal and when those fell through, he borrowed, it wasn't stealing, hell, they'll get their investment back a hundredfold! He has kept a roof over their heads and food on the table. He has even managed some culture and refinement. Valery would be proud. He imagines her expression if she could hear the girls play the piano. That would be something to see! He bursts into tears again at the thought.

Thank God for Marian Linden, taking Sonya as a pupil at a reduced rate! She knows talent when she sees it. He'll make it up to her someday, bless her heart. He always knew his daughter would be a concert pianist, if someone just had faith in her. Why, a few years from now, when she's performing with symphony orchestras, when she's famous, she'll be able to repay Miss Linden a thousand times over. And her daddy will be there, you can be sure of that, right in the front row. When the deals come through, there'll be enough money to switch little Greta to Miss Linden, too. Poor old Hazel, she tries her best, he can't deny that; and Greta works hard for her, practicing her scales and doing her written work. But Hazel hasn't got real training. Real training is what counts. Hell, anyone can sit in their living room playing the piano! Hazel was all right, though. She did her best, he can't fault her for that: continuing the girls' lessons even after she quit, even after she left them to marry that jackass, and moved to Genesee Street. She understood the hell he was going through, trying to keep a home together for his babies. She made allowances when the payments fell behind. He can't understand why Sonya was so ungrateful: refusing to practice, skipping her lessons. Hazel gave her the basics, can't she see that? Well, Marian Linden will make her rich and famous—if she practices.

He blows his nose hard and replaces the handkerchief in his back pocket. Clearing his throat, he starts up the car; the engine hums as he pulls it smoothly back on the road. You can't afford to lose control, no siree. You can't let the big guys get you down; you have to keep your chin up, you have to keep bucking the wind. What would become of his little girls if he ever let them down? It has often been suggested that he give himself a break; it's hard on a man trying to raise two children by himself without a wife and mother. Some people (Ed, the guys down at the tavern) think that when the wife goes on you, the kids have to learn to shift for themselves. Look at Dinty and Sport, Ed points out; they're doing all right at the Longview Home for Boys. All he has to do is find some way to get out there on Sundays to visit, and no one makes him do that if he doesn't feel like it. They get taken care of, they've got no complaints. Why is Ray driving himself into an early grave trying to be a father and a mother too?

Sometimes, after a few rounds with the boys in the tavern, Ray will come home stoked up and embracing the new philosophy. "I should have left you two rotters to shift for yourselves!" he will scream as he tries to get the dinner on the table. Laverne, the housekeeper of two weeks, has just run off with her boyfriend.

"Put the meatloaf in the oven at five o'clock and 350 degrees, hon, and tell your dad that me and Billy are just goin for a little ride." Never has a man less equipped for parenthood tried so hard! When Sonya had the flu, he sat on her bed with an unfamiliar Bible held in uncertain hands, and faked it so well she recovered in no time. There is something deep inside him, which he doesn't understand, that will not let him desert his children. No matter how much they demand of him—help with homework, money for clothes, nightmares, illness—even when they aggravate the living Jesus out of him, he hangs in. Hell, it's not their fault that bitch ran off, he tells himself as he arranges three little salads on separate plates. He whistles desperately under his breath as he carefully lines up the sliced tomato wedges on the sides.

He recalls the time when Ingeborg accused poor little Greta of stealing a bracelet from her room; he was a model of patience. He sat on Greta's bed and told her the story of George Washington. "And when his father said, 'Who chopped down the cherry tree,' George Washington replied, 'Father, I cannot tell a lie. I am the one who chopped down the cherry tree.' Do you understand, sweetheart? You must always tell the truth, even if you've done something you shouldn't have. George Washington grew up to be the first president of the United States because he had an honest character, even as a young boy." "I didn't do it," Greta maintained stubbornly. No, from the very minute he gets home at night he tries to teach his daughters right from wrong. "If I can just instill in them the right values," he tells Glenda, the new housekeeper whose knee lies under his hand, "they will grow up to be fine, upstanding Americans and my life will not have been in vain."

✄ Going to Victoria ✄

Every summer, Daddy took us on the boat to visit Nona in Victoria. She had moved downtown to the Ritz Hotel when the island life became too hard for her. The Ritz was rundown and filled with watery-eyed old ladies, and Nona pretended she was just staying there temporarily.

Daddy would reserve space on the ship for the Ford and book a stateroom so he could pass out in comfort with the newspaper over his face, while Greta and I ran loose around the ship. It was a four-hour trip and when he wasn't passed out in the stateroom, he would take Greta into the lounge where there was a grand piano, and make her play for all the elderly men and women who were sitting around just waiting for some five-year-old prodigy to play for them.

"Play something nice for the people, honey," he would whisper to Greta, who obediently climbed up on the piano bench and flexed her fingers just as Hazel had taught her. Greta played "Für Elise," and everyone applauded. An old man came over to her and gave her a nickel. This scene was repeated every crossing. I couldn't see the difference between what Daddy was doing with Greta and what a circus barker would do with a trained seal. I always edged away before the old man got up with his nickel; I usually went out on deck and thought of jumping overboard.

✄ Driving to School ✄

The Edgemont School was Daddy's Waterloo, but he never directly protested Mother's decision, not even after her death. It was a promise he felt he couldn't go back on, indefensible as it had become. The only emotional outlet available to him were the times when he drove me to school in the mornings; it all came out then. He went through every stop sign and drove at unbearably high speeds. He ranted all the way, getting more whipped up as the miles rolled by. He screamed and gesticulated, often taking both hands off the wheel to let me know he was serious. I sat frozen beside him, staring out the window, my face burning and my head pounding. This was his way of telling me that Edgemont was busting his balls. I was too cowardly to open the car door and fall out, but I kept the possibility alive in my mind. By the time he pulled up to the back entrance of the school, my mind had hardened into the paralysis which was to become my chronic state during my years at Edgemont.

Humiliation was the foundation on which the Edgemont School was built, and served for decades as its guiding principle. It was the one device which, over the generations, the faculty and staff had found to be most effective in maintaining discipline and order. You were humiliated every time you turned around: for not curtseying promptly when an adult entered the room; for talking in class; for having to "go to the lavatory"; for wearing jewelry of any kind; for "speaking out of turn."

❧ Tea ❧

Teas were designed to train Edgemont girls in comportment. They were held in the library. The only people who were ever invited to these teas were the mothers of Edgemont girls, and since I had no mother to invite, I didn't see why I should have to attend. The headmistress didn't see it that way; according to her, that was all the more reason why I was in need of polishing my social graces.

It was rigorous training, making it across the lush Persian rug with a cup of bone china filled to the brim, and facing that sea of formidable mothers, swathed in fur and panting delicately for their cups of tea. I usually spilled it, and was told that the library could be used between teas to balance books on my head so that I could achieve "grace and balance." I went to the library between teas, but instead of putting books on my head I read Howard Fast. This lasted until the librarian discovered that we had Howard Fast in the library, and all his books were removed.

❦ *Abigail Irons* ❧

Miss Abigail Irons was the headmistress of the Edgemont School. She was tall and imposing and had the eyes of a hawk. They flashed like minerals; they were capable of spotting the smallest infraction of behavior; they could see through walls. They were particularly responsive to the glimmer of jewelry.

"Is that a ring I see on your finger?" she would command as she appeared in some dim hallway, out of nowhere.

"Yes, Miss Irons," I would answer, barely remembering to curtsey; "it's my birthstone . . ."

"You are aware that jewelry is not permitted at Edgemont?"

"Yes, Miss Irons."

"Yet you flagrantly flaunt the rules and regulations by adorning yourself with this . . ." She couldn't even speak the word, it was beneath contempt. She reached out and, twisting my arm, led me into the office. The office was where Edgemont girls sat to repent their infractions. It was also the place where they confiscated your jewelry.

Each year, when my Edgemont bill became embarrassingly overdue, Daddy would make his pilgrimage to Miss Irons' office to rub his palms sincerely over the edges of her massive desk, searching for just the right words.

"Mr. Weiler," she would begin very slowly, regally. "It is quite distasteful for me to have to broach this subject . . ." and before she could finish, he would be into the windup, pouring out his heart to her with just the right proportions of humility and charm.

"Yes, yes, Miss Irons; you can't imagine the pain it causes me to be here, sitting before you like this. What can I say? Except that I know you, with your culture and refinement, will appreciate the burden—a burden of love, of course, but a burden nonetheless—of trying to raise two motherless children; to keep a little home together for them; and to inculcate them with the values that you so steadfastly uphold here at Edgemont. If you but knew my gratitude for your patience, your understanding, your firm but loving guidance of my little daughters. If you knew what it meant for a widower like myself to be able to entrust his children to your care. Well, Miss Irons, I am completely beyond words . . ."

She was his, for another year.

⚜ *Reform School* ⚜

Dear Mr. Weiler,

We wish to bring to your attention that your daughter, Sonya, was discovered wearing a ring on her finger in class today. This is the second time this semester that Sonya has come to school with jewelry on her person. We understand your very difficult position with respect to there being no mother in the home. But we feel we must call your attention again to the fact that Edgemont permits no personal adornment of any kind, with the exception of the school emblem—in 14 Karat gold Old English lettering—which may be purchased through this office for $14.95 at the beginning of each school year.

Sincerely yours,
(Miss) Maude Pitts
Executive Secretary
The Edgemont School

Daddy came up to me, waving the letter in front of my face, in what would pass—to the uninitiated observer—as a calm and reasoned attempt to discuss my latest infraction. He had even waited until after dinner, in order that the confrontation have the appearance of civility. Did I take my cue from all of this and humbly murmur something like, "Yes, Daddy, it's true. In a moment of weakness I forgot the rules and wore the ruby birthstone ring that Mother gave me . . ."? Had I had the foresight to have said that, he would have been completely disarmed; might even have fired off a few mild "screw Edgemonts" (for their ridiculous rules, for their blind insensitivity to the sentiments of a motherless child).

Instead, in the throes of immediate panic, and referring to the second incident instead of the first, I shouted: "It wasn't *jewelry!* It was my Tom Mix whistling ring! They had no right to take it away; it wasn't adornment, it was necessary! Shelley and I signal each other on the playground with it!"

He was very slow to respond, which was a bad sign since the most explosive responses have the most prolonged overtures. He looked like someone had hit him between the eyes; they were squinting open and shut in little spasms, as though he couldn't quite make up his mind which would have the more dramatic effect: an open-eyed scene, or one played with the eyes completely sealed.

"Where is this goddamned frigging whistling ring? Where did you get such a piece of crap?" he finally got out.

"They advertised it on the radio; you send in ten box tops of Ralston Shredded Wheat . . ."

"Tom MIX! Good God Almighty, to think a daughter of mine would wear a Tom MIX whistling *ring* to a place as cultured and refined as the Edgemont School. Here I am working my heart out to send you to the finest school in the country, and you pull a stunt like that. Do you know where they send incorrigibles? *Reform* school, that's where. You can sit there in *reform* school and whistle your fucking brains out. Tom MIX. By-de-Jesus-Christ-Almighty," he sighed, tapering off. It was my cue to slink away, and his cue to limp into the kitchen in pursuit of the bourbon, a broken man. It was culture and refinement, after all, which justified the gigantic pile of unpaid bills accumulated during my years at the Edgemont School.

Shelley Kaplan

Shelley Kaplan attended Edgemont from the first through sixth grades, when she was expelled for wetting her pants in the course of an uncontrollable giggling fit in class. She was my best friend. Her father owned a chain of movie theaters where he held private screenings for his friends. All of Shelley's birthday parties were screenings. Mr. Kaplan previewed the worst crime and horror films the late forties had to offer, and I always came home from the parties in a state of emotional turmoil. Finally, Daddy exploded. "That's the last goddamned lousy kike movie you're ever going to see!" he ranted late one Saturday afternoon. "Shelley Kaplan is not a kike!" I screamed at him. "Not a *kike*?" he spat. "With a name like *Kaplan*? You're goddamned right she's a kike! And so are her mother and father! They're all rotten lousy kikes, with no culture and refinement!" I loved Shelley more than ever after that. It became a lifelong pattern: whoever Daddy called a kike, I made my best friend.

My Summer Vacation

Every fall they asked us to write a composition entitled "How I Spent My Summer Vacation." I dreaded this ritual; it filled me with uncontrollable panic since there were only two choices open to me: to make up a terrific summer vacation like the ones my classmates had; or to tell the truth. In the end, I always made up a terrific summer vacation, just like my friend Margaret's. I tried it the right way first, but somehow I could never bring myself to hand it in. Who would believe it?

How I Spent My Summer Vacation,
by Sonya Weiler

This summer I spent a lot of time swimming down at the lake with my sister Greta. I spent a lot of time down at the lake because our housekeeper, Laverne, ran off with her boyfriend and my father said the agency told him summer was a bad time for replacements. So every day Greta and I went swimming at the lake. I tried to teach her how to swim, but she kept going under so I told her she was stupid and sent her back to the shallow water with her inner tube while I read my movie magazine. She got a terrible sunburn and when we got home Daddy said, "You haven't got the brains of a louse, letting your baby sister get all sunburned like that."

After that, I had to stay indoors with Greta until her skin stopped peeling, so we listened to soap operas on the radio and I modeled a very sad-looking face out of Greta's modeling clay. Even after it was finished, I couldn't bear to mess it up. It had haunting eyes, and I couldn't believe I had created it. It is the only thing I ever created.

On Sundays, Daddy sometimes took us for a picnic to a little resort lake an hour's drive from where we lived. He had the best of intentions, I am sure, but he always ended up drunk, lying on the grass under some tree—usually a weeping willow. I saw no particular significance in that, at the time. Greta and I would go swimming until we turned blue and all the other people started going home. Daddy usually woke up just in time to say, "What the hell is going on here? What time is it? What the hell is the matter with your lips? They're blue. Haven't you got any brains, staying in the water when you're turning blue?"

One time we went to a lake where they had boats for rent. "Let's go boating!" I said, and for some reason Daddy said, "You want to go boating? All right, all right, if I can find the piss-ant who's in charge around here, we'll go boating." We went boating. Out in the middle of the lake, Greta stood up in the boat and Daddy went to pieces. He swung at her with one of the oars, but missed. His voice could be heard all the way across the lake. I thought we would all capsize and drown, but somehow we made it to shore. Then we all got in the Ford and drove home at high speed.

In the evenings, I locked myself in my room and cried.

Sometimes I would listen to Rachmaninoff's "Isle of the Dead," and sometimes to Nat King Cole singing "They Tried to Tell Us We're Too Young." The people down the street had Mario Lanza's recording of "Because," and whenever I babysat for them I played it over and over, right up to the time they came home, no matter how late it was. That record got me through the summer. It was my first love song, and I would imagine someone handsome, in a white shirt rolled up at the sleeves, and kind, driving with one arm on the wheel and the other around me as we coasted down the highway toward California.

In the end, I turned in the following; no one ever questioned it, only corrected the spelling and punctuation:

How I Spent My Summer Vacation,
by Sonya Weiler

Mom and Dad, my brother Nick and my Aunt Viv and I all went to Palm Springs. We got terrific tans and liked Palm Springs very much. Then everyone got bored with Palm Springs and Aunt Viv said, "There's not much going on here, let's all go to Hawaii instead." So we went to Hawaii on the Lurline. That's the same boat Jane Powell went to Hawaii on in the movie *Luxury Liner*. We got terrific tans in Hawaii. Then we got bored in Hawaii so Mom and Dad and Nick and Aunt Viv said, "Let's go to a guest ranch in Arizona so Sonya can ride horseback every day." So we all flew to the guest ranch in Arizona where I went riding every day. I got a terrific tan in Arizona. It was a wonderful summer.

❧ The Listening Room ❧

Although Edgemont provided an adequate escape from Daddy, there was no institution, per se, that provided an adequate escape from Edgemont. You had to invent your own. Mine became the listening room in the Record Department of Frederick & Nelson's department store. Hermetically sealed and absolutely unassailable, it offered two crucial things that I felt were lacking in my life: peace and privacy.

I would go there every afternoon after school with my friend Margaret, and we would listen to Russian music. This was one of the rottenest things you could do in the early fifties, and my sense of betraying all that Daddy valued gave me the courage to endure both him and Edgemont. These afternoons often ended the same way, with our doing pantomimes to Tchaikovsky's "Marche Slave" (backs hunched, eyes crossed, limping across the record room with Siberian snow on our shoulders), and the manager of the Record Department opening the door a crack and saying, "Are you young ladies seriously interested in buying this record?"

❧ Mr. Leavitt ❧

Besides the listening room in the Record Department, Frederick's had two other sanctuaries to offer: the Photography Department on the main floor, and Books on 3rd. Mr. Leavitt was one of the salesmen in Photography. Margaret and I dabbled in photography and had crushes on Mr. Leavitt. Two or three times a week we would lean heavily on the counter and ask him to describe a certain lens. He never seemed to tire of twirling, clicking and polishing all those cameras for us. As he bent over the instruments, we would gaze at his soft brown hair and his tanned fingers as they manipulated the delicate equipment. Our hearts were pounding and we were always afraid he might look up suddenly to see us with our faces flushed and eyes rolling across the ceiling.

Every night we retired to our beds on opposite sides of town, there to dream of Mr. Leavitt. Back at Edgemont the following morning, we would meet secretly in the lavatory and sit on the radiator, comparing Mr. Leavitts:

"What did you do with him last night?" Margaret would whisper.

"We went riding in the desert, and when my stallion ran away with me he . . ."

"*We* went riding too!"

"Oh, Margaret, we have so much in common!"

One day I caught the late bus and there in the back, on the aisle seat, sat none other than Mr. Leavitt. I wished that Margaret were with me, as I thought I would faint. I recovered on the grounds that I had to be conscious in order to observe WHERE MR. LEAVITT GOT OFF. Someone had to survive to witness it and tell. It was the chance of a lifetime.

When the actual moment came, he bounded lightly down the steps, right into the waiting arms of the drabbest little woman I had ever seen; she was fat and her hair was beginning to gray. Together they walked right into the drab little house in front of the bus stop. I couldn't believe my eyes. Mr. Leavitt, lord of the lenses; Mr. Leavitt of the pounding plain. There had to be some mistake.

"What the hell are you looking so sour about?" Daddy wanted to know as I walked in the door. "And what are you doing coming home two hours late?" It took great maturity to walk into my room and close the door without a word. I played "Scheherazade" and wept.

🦋 *Mr. Strathmore* 🦋

With the demise of Mr. Leavitt, there was nothing to do but move up to Books on 3rd. I stopped taking pictures and started to read. Margaret's mother had begun insisting that she come home right after school, so I was left by myself in Books. After a couple of weeks of browsing, I noticed one clerk in particular; he really stood out: tall, with broad shoulders and gently graying hair. His suits were a bit shabby, which made it perfect. There was a quality in his eyes that seemed to mourn that he should be waiting on customers in Frederick's. I knew right away that he represented distinction: an author whose time had not yet come and who endured the rabble with exquisite forbearance.

I wanted him to notice me—not me as I was, standing there

blushing, but me sensitively leafing through a volume of poetry. The question was, Which one? Would he be more impressed by my leafing through Millay, or my leafing through Whitman? He looked like a Frost man himself. I would have preferred the encounter to take place over Robinson Jeffers—in particular, *Roan Stallion*—but it didn't fit: there was an urbanity, a melancholy, about him that was better suited to Eliot. Or maybe Auden. As I continued my search for just the right volume, I noticed him move out of the corner of my eye. Slowly I turned and looked at him. He was on the far side of Books and he was speaking to another woman! She was waving a cookbook in front of his face. I knew the pain he must have felt as he rang up the sale.

Then, before I could make a choice, before I could even leaf, he was beside me in all his commanding grayness, close enough to see his nameplate: Mr. Strathmore.

"May I help you?" he asked. My mind raced. It was too late to fake things out in Poetry. The choices were too confusing. Cunningly, I moved over to Fiction, where one table was completely covered with copies of Mikhail Sholokhov's *And Quiet Flows the Don*. You couldn't go wrong with that. Something that massive, containing what must be enormous depth and scope, couldn't fail to impress him.

"I want to buy this," I whispered breathlessly, lifting the book off the table. I noticed there was no wedding ring on his finger as he took it from me and headed for the sales counter. My heart was pounding as I offered him my tightly wadded babysitting money.

"I'm sure you will enjoy this," said Mr. Strathmore, as he handed me my jewel in a green paper bag with FREDERICK'S stamped on it.

"Oh, thank you, Mr. Strathmore; Russian literature is my favorite."

Going home on the bus, I sat perfectly still in the sharpness of early Russian spring, on the banks of the quietly flowing Don, Mr. Strathmore burning at my side.

"What do you mean bringing this commie crap into the house?" Daddy roared, grabbing for the book.

"It belongs to a friend at school!" I screamed. He wouldn't dare throw out someone else's property.

"Well, you give it back tomorrow on the double; if I see it in this house again, it's going in the furnace."

That night I smoldered with shame at the thought that Mr. Strathmore would ever find out what kind of father I had: a book-burner. I imagined telling him, and imagined his response: "My dear, I live alone; you are welcome any time he gets out of hand." Before bed, I played the Tchaikovsky Fifth Symphony out of love, out of loss. I knew I could never return to Books on 3rd.

❧ Mr. Wendell ☙

Mr. Wendell was the director of the choir at the Episcopal church across the street from Edgemont. Whenever they ran short of boy sopranos, Edgemont girls were asked to fill in. He had curly blond hair, filmy eyes and delicate fingers. It was rumored that he was "queer." Margaret and I knew he wasn't queer; he was merely waiting for the right one. We were the right one.

As often as we could, we would slip into the chapel in the hope of catching Mr. Wendell sitting there killing time playing the Bach Toccata and Fugue in D Minor. We hung around after school, sometimes staying until dark, in the hope that he just might feel like an evening run-through at the organ. We sat near the darkened altar; the air was chilled and smelled of damp stone. If someone had come upon us we would have appeared to be deep in prayer, not erotic fantasies. In my mind, I was running away from home and seeking sanctuary in the chapel. It was a moonlit night. I would surprise Mr. Wendell in the act of playing the "Arioso" from the Bach Concerto in D Major. He would be playing the "Arioso" in order to keep from going mad from lack of love. Just as he finished, I would appear behind him and say, "Mr. Wendell, I have never heard anything so beautiful; I know exactly how you feel. I am yours."

One evening we sat for nearly two hours and he didn't make an appearance. We boarded the bus with deep resignation and as it rolled past the neighborhood tavern three blocks later, whom should we see through the open door, downing a huge mug of beer and laughing it up with his buddies? It brought our Episcopal period to a crushing end. When I got home, three hours late, Daddy demanded to know where I had been. "In church," I answered. He scratched his head and reheated my dinner, and hadn't, for once, a single thing to say.

🔸 *The Sheik* 🔹

One Saturday while I was out swimming, Daddy found my copy of *The Sheik*. I had hidden it under my bed in the beginning, but as time went by I became sloppy and left it lying around in plain view.

When I came in the door, dripping stale lake water onto the peeling linoleum, he was standing in the kitchen with *The Sheik* on the counter, whipping himself up for what promised to be at least a three-quarter-of-an-hour job. "I want an explanation for THIS," he said, flicking his nails on the cover.

> *"Come," he whispered, his passionate eyes devouring her.*
> *She fought against the fascination with which they dominated her, resisting him dumbly with tight-locked lips till he held her palpitating in his arms.*
> *"Little fool," he said with a deepening smile. "Better me than my men."*
> *"Oh, you brute! You brute!" she wailed, until his kisses silenced her.*

"Did you hear what I said? I want an explanation why this cheap crap was in your room."

> *She became aware that night had fallen, and that they were still steadily galloping southward. In a few moments she was wide awake,*

91

and found that she was lying across the saddle in front of the Sheik, and that he was holding her in the crook of his arm. Her head was resting just over his heart, and she could feel the regular beat beneath her cheek. . . . With a start of recollection she realised fully whose arm was round her, and whose breast her head was resting on. Her heart beat with sudden violence. What was the matter with her? Why did she

"Look at me, you numbskull! Where the hell are your brains? Did you hear what I said?"

"No. What? What are you talking about?"

"Don't play dumb with me! I know trash when I see it, and this is trash! I try to teach you culture and refinement, and you . . ."

not shrink from the pressure of his arm and the contact of his warm, strong body? What had happened to her? Quite suddenly she knew— knew that she loved him, that she had loved him for a long time, even when she thought she hated him and when she had fled from him. She knew now why his face had haunted her in the little oasis at mid-day—that it was love calling to her subconsciously.

"God damn it all to hell!" He was screaming now. I wrapped my towel more tightly around me. There was a huge puddle of water on the dark linoleum floor. My mind wasn't working at all; instead of racing wildly to manufacture some explanation, it simply dripped, like the water on the floor—aimless and liquid, a blank.

His dark, passionate eyes burnt into her like a hot flame. His encir-cling arms were like bands of fire, scorching her. His touch was tor-ture. Helpless, like a trapped wild thing, she lay against him, panting, trembling, her wide eyes fixed on him, held against their will.

"It says right here, 'Seattle Public Library, due . . .' Jesus Christ Almighty, you've had this piece of shit out for over five months! Do you know what this is going to cost me in fines? Why, this is just like taking the food out of your little sister's mouth! Do you have any idea what opinion the librarian will have of you?"

But she knew herself at last and knew the love that filled her, an over-
whelming, passionate love that almost frightened her with its immen-
sity and with the sudden hold it had laid upon her. Love had come to
her at last who had scorned it so fiercely. The men who had loved her
had not had the power to touch her, she had given love to no one, she
had thought that she could not love, that she was devoid of all natural
affection and that she would never know what love meant. But she
knew now—a love of such complete surrender that she had never con-
ceived. Her heart was given for all time to the fierce desert man who
was so different from all other men whom she had met . . .

"I have forbidden you to read this trash. I have tried to bring
you up to appreciate the finer things of life, but all you read is
cheap crap! *The Black Stallion! The Black Stallion Returns! The Son of*
the Black Stallion! The Island Stallion! The Roan Stallion! Jesus P.
Christ Almighty, and now, *The Sheik!*" He leaned on the counter
and wiped his forehead with the back of his sleeve.

The Sheik was my turning point; it marked that place where I
entered the world of adult passion, however removed, and self-
assertion, however undignified. I grabbed the book off the
counter and ran out of the house, shouting, "If you take *The Sheik*
away you'll never see me again!" The neighbors turned off their
hoses and stared. *The Sheik* was never mentioned again.

❧

*E*aster has a way of coming back, year after year. It has the power to
arouse Sonya's carefully suppressed memories of Valery. She has
tried to forget that she had a mother. Once, on the bus, a student
in another grade said in a loud voice, "Someone told me you
didn't have a mother," and Sonya had felt hot and dizzy, and had
stared out the bus window, seeing nothing, and missed her stop.
But other than that—and the inevitable stress produced by

Christmas without Valery and their birthdays without Valery—she has, she thinks, managed to drive all thoughts of her mother underground. Since Valery has abandoned her, she has worked to master the art of abandoning Valery. This requires most of the energy which would otherwise have been spent learning things in school.

Sonya leans on her desk and stares out the large gothic windows of the Edgemont School. She is entering a home where a dream family awaits her. *"Here she is!" they chorus happily as she steps into a cozy, well-lit room. A fire is burning in the fireplace. The mother and father smile; they are so happy to see her. "What took you so long?" they inquire. "We were so worried about you." The father sets his pipe aside and rises; the mother smoothes her skirt; she is careful about her appearance. Their arms reach out to her; she lets herself be taken in.* She imagines the homecoming many times, varying the intensity of the mood, changing details here and there. Sometimes the teacher will interrupt before she can even stage the scene. Then there is the picture drawing; she does everything in her power to stop herself, but there are some days when the pencil just seems to move of its own accord. It always creates the same picture: a mother with her arms around a daughter. She renders this scene over and over, and the warmth it makes her feel has to be compensated for by destroying the picture as soon as it is finished. She pencils it over in thick black strokes before tearing it to shreds. It would be disastrous if anyone were to see it and know the depth of her need, the extent of her loss. To have to draw the picture is like a crime, a thing that sets her irreversibly apart; no one else in the class needs to do it. The magnitude of that desire makes her hide her head in shame.

It requires such energy to create and destroy, to screen out the teacher's voice and enter these private worlds, to guard against discovery, to cover her tracks. Sonya is reprimanded for not listening. She becomes even more unlike the others. She becomes thick, slow, stupid. Some housekeepers confirm her assessment: Mavis says, "You're stupid! And you stink. Why don't you take a bath?" She does take baths; it must be that certain people are born intelligent and sweet, and others are not. She thinks it might have something to do with being blond and enjoying social position: Gigi, Trish and Wendy have their own horses, their own ski lodges, and maids who iron their blouses. They all have blond hair. Mavis says, "I'm not paid to iron your clothes." Sonya hates Mavis, but she knows Mavis is right: she *is* a misfit. Ray called her that one night at dinner, and Mavis picked it up right away, whispering to Sonya under her breath the next day, "What a *misfit!*"

The housekeepers always go away for Easter, leaving Sonya to absorb its impact alone, with Greta underfoot. Greta is still not old enough to be a friend; she needs too much and Sonya has to do it for her: pick up her room, read her stories, comb her hair, select her clothes in the children's department of Sears, give her baths. Ray no longer helps with these things. Not a young man when he married Valery, he is now growing visibly older. A fifty-four-year-old man deserves some peace and quiet. Making deals is hard work; keeping a roof over their heads is enough to drive a saint crazy. He is bushed.

Easters are always the same, beginning with the high-speed drive to the Christian Science Sunday School, and the late pickup and high-speed drive home. Then Ray passes out on the living room couch, leaving the basket-filling and hiding to Sonya. She doesn't like doing this alone, but appearances have to be kept up; Greta is still young. She carefully fills the baskets with the straw and the candy eggs she has bought at the drugstore the day before. She wraps colored cellophane around the baskets, the way they do in the department stores. Then she hides them and calls for Greta to help her find them. She feels so lonely doing this; something is missing, it isn't exciting anymore. Her stomach feels light and apprehensive. She wants to wake Ray so he can share this with her, but she knows if she does, he will find some fault, some excuse, to vent his anger; she knows he is drunk, and that his personality has undergone a profound change since Valery's death. Now he is almost continuously yelling, cursing, or staring into space; having him passed out on the couch is the better alternative. After the basket ritual, Sonya takes Greta down to the lake. As Greta skips before her, throwing bread to the ducks,

Sonya remembers a line from a poem she discovered in Frederick's: *April is the cruellest month, breeding/Lilacs out of the dead land, mixing/Memory and desire* ... He sure hit it on the head, she thinks.

Here is Greta posing for Sonya. Sonya copes with the emptiness of weekends and holidays by taking snapshots of Greta with the old box camera. Greta is tired of being ordered around—this pose, that pose—but doesn't protest because Sonya is all she has. Over the years, Sonya will amass hundreds of snapshots of Greta; any event will serve as an excuse to take her picture. She becomes obsessed; Greta is memorialized on all occasions, great and small: Christmas, birthdays, walking in snow, picking flowers, riding a tricycle, feeding the ducks. Greta multiplies and abounds. The more Ray drinks, the more he screams and calls her a misfit, the more frequently Sonya leaves the house with Greta and the camera in tow. As Ray's despair increases, new names of derogation are added to his vocabulary and directed at Sonya: Ingrate. Cocksucker. Blockhead. The worse she feels, the more pictures she has Greta pose for. Greta always complies; she has no choice. Years later, when she discovers the hundreds of snapshots stuffed in manila envelopes, Sonya will wonder: Why did I take so many pictures of Greta?

Here is Greta, sitting on the front lawn of the dream house on 51st Avenue South. She is four and a half years old. She has a woolen scarf on her head. She is staring mutely at a branch of heather in her lap. Sonya must have picked it off a bush for Greta to hold in the picture. Greta's lips are slack and her eyes are dull. Sonya will stare at this snapshot on a rainy day far in the future and remember for the first time the context surrounding it, which is invisible to the naked eye. One had to have been there at the time it was taken. One had to have lived in the house, whose yard now forms the backdrop for Greta's strange pose. She is an obedient little robot, doing what she is told: posing with a sprig of heather so her sister can record her on film. No one, looking at this picture, would ever know that she has been deaf for three months. She has also stopped talking. It is something both Ray and Sonya have noticed, but neither will discuss it, it scares them so much. They pretend it isn't true. Privately they invoke God's perfect love, but they both know that God's perfect love doesn't work. They do not take Greta to a doctor—less because of Christian Science, whose influence is waning, than because neither wants to hear a doctor say it: "Your daughter/sister is deaf and dumb." Once or twice, they each individually attempt to disprove the terrible truth by sneaking up in back of Greta when she doesn't know they are there and clapping their hands loudly right next to her head. She never moves, or turns around, or changes expression. She doesn't respond in any way. To Sonya, it is as though something familiar is starting all over again; she fights it by pretending she doesn't notice. Dunce. Misfit. Numbskull. Click. Click. Click. Something familiar, beginning again: someone she loves has been damaged and is losing her parts; is shrinking, receding, and growing dim.

Months later, the deafness disappears as silently as it began. Sonya notices the change and says, "Greta can hear again!" and Ray smiles. It is never mentioned again. Years later, Sonya will read of the phenomenon called hysterical deafness and wonder if that is what Greta had. It would make sense; who wouldn't want not to hear Ray ranting and yelling, especially a four-year-old.

Sometimes Sonya goes alone to the basement. There is a ritual she performs there, in a tiny storage closet, which she doesn't understand but which she is compelled to repeat. It isn't a thing she plans; weeks can pass without her going downstairs. At other times, she finds herself removing the padlock from its hook and stepping inside the closet. Originally a canning pantry, it overflowed, no doubt, with Mrs. Percy's canned preserves. Now the shelves are empty, except for a few strange objects, lying in a row. Closer inspection reveals them to be the carcass of a mouse, its tiny teeth exposed; various dead insects; a withered bird.

Sonya doesn't understand it; whenever she finds something dead in the yard, she is compelled to recover it and place it on the closet shelf. She concentrates on it very hard: it isn't really dead, only appearing to be. It is up to her to reveal its true state of being and return it to its living self. The mouse was the first. She puts it on the shelf, closes the closet door and sits down on the stool. She

97

pulls the light string and the closet is thrown into darkness; not even a crack of light shows through. She holds her breath and is terrified; she knows she must imagine very hard. The invocation begins. All her energy goes into concentrating on the mouse: in her mind, she sees it running across a field; its little feet move swiftly, its brown fur ripples in the wind. If she can remain in the closet long enough; if she can invoke God's perfect love expertly enough; if she can "know the truth" about the mouse—that it lives—strongly enough, *then it will be so.* A resurrection will have taken place in the storage closet in the basement of the dream house on 51st Avenue South. Sonya Weiler will have the power to restore life to the dead.

*O*n *a rainy weekend in the middle of winter, Sonya takes Greta to see* the Ice Follies. While they are there, Sonya experiences strange sensations low down in her stomach. When she gets back home, she sees the blood. She is thirteen. For three years she has been pretending that she will never menstruate. Since the year after Valery's death, from the first time she learned (in a magazine? from her friends at school?) that women menstruate, she has been in a quiet, chronic state of panic: whom should she tell, if and when it should happen to her? Ray? or Mavis? She can't think of anything worse than telling her father, unless it is telling the housekeeper, Mavis. You have to tell someone, so they can show you what to do. Thinking about this is so taxing, and the conflict about whom to confide in so overwhelming, that she puts it completely out of her mind. Maybe she will be that one in a million to whom it won't occur.

It is all the more disturbing, then, to suddenly find herself faced with the real, instead of the imaginary, dilemma. She solves the problem by no action of her own, but because she has sat in the bathroom for so long (one hour? two?) trying to decide, that eventually Mavis beats on the door, demanding to know what's going on in there. Did she fall down the toilet? Mavis laughs at

98

her own joke. Sonya doesn't know where she gets the strength, but such things, she knows, often come from desperation: she yells through the door to Mavis that she has her period. She is not Sonya Weiler. She is some girl in Nebraska, calling through the door to her mother. There is nothing out of the ordinary going on here at all. She floats in space, two feet above the toilet. Mavis recovers from her shock and takes command, throwing a sanitary belt, two pins, and a napkin into the room through a crack in the door. She does not come into the room. She says: "You can use these until you can get your own. You'll have to go to the drugstore tomorrow. You pin it to the ends." Mavis' face is flaming; her head begins to ache. She does not want to be reminded of her first period. She has more contempt for Sonya than ever.

Before Sonya goes to the drugstore, she has to ask Ray for money. "What do you need it for?" he asks. "I have to get some things," she says, evasively. Ray continues to interrogate; money doesn't grow on trees, doesn't she know that? In tears, she blurts out that she needs the money for Kotex. She has never said the word before, although she has seen the ads. If she can say it to her father, maybe she can say it to the man behind the counter at the drugstore. Ray flushes. Of course, he says rapidly; he thinks he's got it right here. He fishes in his pocket and comes up with more money than she will need. His eyes meet hers for an instant; they are proud. They are sad. They are despairing.

Sonya has never known such pain. She knows it's called cramps; she reads *Mademoiselle*. She has read that you can take Midol for cramps. She uses the extra money to buy a tin of Midol. She has never taken a pill, and doesn't know how to get it down. She sits on the floor in the corner of her room with her knees drawn up and rocks. She doesn't know what to do with the used napkins; they are bloody and foul. She rolls each one up and puts it in a paper bag, then puts the paper bags on the shelf in her closet. Mavis hadn't told her what she's supposed to do with them and she is not going to ask. She imagines they get thrown out, but she doesn't know if it is all right to put them in the garbage can; it seems wrong to mix them with food. She has heard somewhere that you can't flush them down the toilet; she

99

wouldn't have tried it anyway, because it might clog the toilet and then everyone would know she had done it. They'd know for sure she was stupid. She can't ask her friend Margaret because Margaret hasn't gotten her period yet. Her mother hasn't told her anything, either; Sonya wonders what good it is having a mother if she can't tell you the facts of life. She assumes Margaret's mother will tell her some information about disposal when the times comes, but until then she'll just have to go on storing them in the closet. In a short time, the closet smells so bad she has to hold her breath to go in. Even later in life, when she has a daughter of her own, she cannot remember how those napkins—eventually grown to thousands—ever got out of the closet. Maybe they were left there when the Weilers moved from the house; maybe the new occupants had to call an exterminator to fumigate her room.

Sonya's thirteenth year is also the year the family leaves Valery's dream house. The move is sudden and many things have to be left behind for Goodwill. It is the first of many such moves, all of which leave Sonya feeling the same sense of loss. Losing her few possessions in small increments with each move is like losing parts of herself. She feels as though she's in a row boat on a violent sea and her things, like ballast, are being thrown overboard. She gets lighter and lighter with each passing year. By the time she passes through the decaying doors of the King Street Station to board the train to go to college, she feels herself to be without weight or substance altogether. A leaf is going to college.

🦋 Looking for Houses 🦋

Three years after Mother died, Daddy was told by Mr. Percy—with finality this time—that we would have to leave. He had not paid the rent for so long that it was beyond further discussion.

Even the milkman had joined in the talks; there was nothing to do but go somewhere else. Daddy hurriedly located another house on Cascadia Street whose occupants would be away for the summer; we would only be there three months. Moving was the hardest thing I had done in a long time; so many of my things were thrown out or left behind. Daddy said we would be making do for a while and couldn't be dragging all that stuff around. It was easy throwing out Greta's things, but it wasn't easy getting rid of mine. I'd start crying and then Daddy would come into the room and yell, "Stop bellyaching, and get that stuff out of here. We've got to move, pronto!"

The new house was in a better neighborhood; it was owned by a family named Rundquist. Their two children were rich and blond. Their portraits, done in oil, hung prominently in the living room; they took up the entire west wall. Once, when Daddy invited a prospective investor in his gold mine over to discuss a deal, he had the nerve to pass them off as us. "Well, thank you," he chuckled, feigning modesty, in answer to the man's remark: "Handsome children." The two Nordic Rundquists looked on in horror. I spoiled everything by walking into the room seconds later, my conspicuously dark hair spilling over my shoulders, and my dark eyes sending Daddy a mean challenge. I imagined the investor thinking of me as an adopted third wheel—a kind of cross between a savage found in the forest and an apprentice hired hand. I could see that Daddy was trapped and I felt a mixture of pity for him and fury. I already felt like an intruder in this perfect home: a dark misfit, out of place among the flowered wallpaper, French doors, and Persian rugs. The sense of placelessness intensified with every move and I always tried to beg off when the time rolled around for us to go house hunting again. "I'll just stay here and finish my homework," I would say.

"No, dear. You and Greta will come with Daddy. The three little Weilers have to stick together." I never understood the "little" business; did he regard himself as being as small as Greta and I? Three Little Weilers, Three Little Kittens, Three Little Pigs. It made me sick when he referred to us like this. I liked it better in the days when we were a different Three Little Weilers: just him,

Mother, and me, before Greta. I would freeze when trying to make sense of this new constellation and my part in it. A lot of my anxiety would be discharged in the form of sadism toward Greta: burning her dainty, trusting finger with the cigarette lighter in the Ford one day when Daddy left us waiting while he plotted one of his deals; pulling her hair in frustration while trying to get out a tangle as she danced and jumped around the room. When she was older and could understand plain speech, I even told her, "You killed Mother." It haunted her into her adult life, when she finally challenged me: "Is it true what you said about my killing Mother? I have to know." "I never said that," I told her. "You must have imagined it."

Whenever we accompanied him to inspect the homes for rent the scenario was always the same. We approached the door and he would ring the bell. I twisted Greta's arm out of sight and told her to be good. My stomach was a black pit where demons slid and crawled. I wanted to cry, but always smiled instead. After the brief exchange of pleasantries with the owner, he always came right to the point. "My precious darlings have lost their beloved mother just recently," he would intone. It was his standard introduction, and he used it five, even six, years after the fact. The lady of the house never differed in her response. I got so I could anticipate her look of surprise and the expressions of pity that followed. I found it hard to breathe; I was mud and blackness. I stared at the ground. I can remember the lint in every house, I became that small. I went into myself so far, I passed through the other side. His lilting voice droned on as Greta and I stared at the floor, or stroked the family pets. He always explained our circumstances in a way that would capture the general tragedy but delete the sordid detail. The lady of the house would offer coffee, a cocktail, a piece of cake. Within minutes, she would offer her home.

❦ *Marian Linden* ❧

Marian Linden taught piano in a small, immaculate studio apartment on 9th Avenue North. For some reason which I will never understand, she agreed to take me as a pupil at a reduced rate the summer I turned twelve. I had fought with Daddy for months over my lessons with Hazel. Even when I told him that she hit my fingers with a ruler when I made mistakes, he was curiously undisturbed; I guess the price was right. He continued sending Greta to her, free of charge, but I finally refused. After a standoff of many months, he started to throw Marian Linden's name around as though he'd known her all his life.

Some prodigy who lived in the north end of town had given a recital which was covered by the local papers, and Miss Linden's picture had been featured as his teacher. Maybe she reminded Daddy of his sister, Mabel. Maybe he was just desperate to find someone more impressive than Hazel who could keep me at the keyboard with a minimum of strife, and thus fulfill another one of Mother's dreams. By the time he'd begun alluding to my Carnegie Hall debut, he must have realized it would help to start with lessons. He didn't phone Miss Linden because he had learned from experience that nothing beat a face-to-face encounter; he simply forced me into the car one Saturday and brazened it out at her door five miles later.

I was too awed by her to sulk. She was very gracious, inviting us into her living room and even offering tea. I sat stiffly in a straight-backed chair and listened as Daddy calmly cited Mother's death, my nonexistent talent, his great dreams for me and, incidentally, the multimillion-dollar property in his name, the timber rights to which at this very moment no less than five major lumber companies were turning purple competing for. Marian Linden listened politely, drew in her breath at the appropriate moments, and said, "I see." It was hard to interpret her reactions; she had an innate dignity that made her seem very well-contained. She was not an old woman, but she carried herself with a certain respect and treated others that way, too. Her amber hair was thick, and just beginning to gray. She wore it in an upswept style, held in place with a large tortoise-shell comb.

As Daddy's voice droned on, I let my eyes wander around the apartment. The walls were a stark white and the Steinway glistened richly at the far end of the room, by the window. There was a small Oriental rug in the middle of the room, and well-chosen prints hung at balanced intervals along the white walls. By the end of our visit, she had agreed to take me on provisionally, at the reduced fee. I don't know whether it was kindness or pity which motivated her and I have trouble making that distinction even to this day. The interview felt no different from renting the homes, or being enrolled in the Edgemont School: after watching him operate, I always felt I had gained admission by fraudulent means. I would argue this point with myself, saying: Well, most of what he said was true, wasn't it? And I'd answer, yes, it was true, but there are certain uses to which the truth can be put, certain ways of manipulating it, that come dangerously close to lying. The gold mines and properties weren't true; those were just figments of his imagination. But then I'd get confused; because if those weren't true, then how would we survive? I ended up believing in them, while at the same time retaining my skepticism about them— which amounted to a form of nonbelief, without the risk.

Once a week I took the bus after school to the dark brick building with leaded windows and climbed the stairs to Miss Linden's apartment. She had no delusions about my future, only a steady belief in the perfectibility of present skills. It took her about three weeks to see that something was standing in my way of achieving that goal. She tried, in a gentle and respectful way, to find out what was wrong. I was torn between the wish to confess the chaos at home and its effects on my concentration, and the fear of more Police Department matrons if I did. Investigating a second complaint, they would be sure to notice Daddy's growing disintegration and remove us from the home. I couldn't explain that, for me, the lessons had become less a goal than an emotional oasis. I was terrified that she would terminate them because of my lack of progress, yet could think of no way to overcome the turmoil inside that kept me from progressing. It was enough just to be in her presence each week, to slide onto the piano bench and feel her there at my side, concerned, and knowing what she was doing. It was enough to see the evidence of art and truth and civilization there on her walls, and in her gestures. I groped for some way to get this across to her, but failed.

🐾 The Kreach Apartment-Hotel 🐾

The Rundquists returned from Europe in the fall to reclaim their charming home, and the Three Little Weilers bailed out more of their detritus in preparation for the move. The leaves were turning on the trees; there was a pungent smell in the air. Either no one was renting at this time of year, or Daddy ran out of steam and money, because on September 3, 1950, we moved downtown to the Kreach Apartment-Hotel on 5th Avenue, across from the Public Library and the USO. I felt very fortunate having both culture and cheap crap so close at hand, but it was a low point for Daddy; he had always managed to rent houses before.

It was crowded, with just two small rooms and a kitchenette; and it was intimate, in an uncomfortable way. It lacked something, but I didn't know just what it was. Greta and I shared the one bedroom, and Daddy slept in a pull-down bed in the living room. Every night I could hear him moaning to himself under the sheets; I imagined it was his way of mourning all that was lost to him: Mother, the dream house, his string of uncompleted deals. The deals were what he lived for; he was only half-alive when he wasn't negotiating one. He always said that he was living for us, and we really wanted to believe that—and did, for some time. But it was the deals that brought the blood to his heart and the light to his eyes.

I spent a lot of time at the library, since Daddy had pulled his Monroe Pool routine concerning the USO. I watched from a dis-

105

tance on hot nights, with the traffic blaring in the street below. I leaned out the open window of our little home on the 4th floor and listened to the saxophones across the street and watched the servicemen dancing with their girls. It occurred to me for the first time, there in the Kreach Apartment-Hotel, that my time would come.

🦋 *Trip to the Mountains* 🦋

Whenever Daddy and Ed went to the mountains looking for gold, they would be gone for two or three days and Daddy always came back agitated and drinking heavily. His explanation was always the same: someone had tried to do him in. The stories he told had the same theme, with minor variations: someone had tried to push him off a cliff. He twisted his ankle and they left him for dead. A snowstorm came up and he and Ed became separated. He struggled for hours to make his way back to civilization but the others in the expedition didn't send for help.

When he was young, he pursued a dream of silver in Mexico. Later, the lure became gold. After Hiroshima, it was uranium. By the time I was in my teens and the space age was upon us, he had moved on to the rare earth metals: plutonium, beryllium, titanium; ytterbium. His eyes assumed a faraway look as he spoke of them. The words rolled off his tongue, the way they did when he was negotiating a deal with the big shots at Anaconda Copper. "Ana-con-da, Ana-con-da . . ." Over and over he caressed the name.

If there was one lesson he wanted us to learn from his trips to the mountains it was what to do if we ever got lost up there. It was a standard refrain and he launched into it after each of his trips. We didn't pay much attention; it seemed unlikely that when we grew up we would be making trips to the mountains looking for treasure that had eluded him all these years. He emphasized three things: 1. Always carry matches. 2. Always look

106

for Forest Service markers (and learn to interpret them *before* going to the mountains). 3. Always follow rivers downstream, on the assumption that people always need water and where water is, so are people. "Rivers always lead somewhere," he would say, pouring himself another drink.

He leaned back wearily in his chair and wiped at his brow with a carefully folded handkerchief. His pockets overflowed with arrowheads and minerals. After a while, when he ran out of steam, he would reach in and pull them out and hand them over to us. "See those flecks of gold?" he would ask, rotating a small rock sample between his thumb and forefinger. "Those will make us all rich someday." He emptied his glass and sighed. Vistas of indescribable promise stretched before him in the distance behind his eyes. I knew it even then, because he never quite focused on us but always just beyond us, and in that space it was possible to see what he was seeing there himself. But it would be years before I understood that he sought those gulfs, and courted the isolation in that space. He hungered for an immensity large as his fear.

Only once did a trip to the mountains include us. His restlessness grew so large one Sunday, not even the bourbon could subdue it, and he herded us into the car and headed northeast. Within two hours we were standing at the base of a vast, remote waterfall—drenched in its whiteness, deaf with its power. Greta and I jumped on the boulders at its base and began to climb; the rocks were slippery with mist and Daddy called up to us to stop. We could hear nothing over the roar, but eventually his gesturing caught our eye. He looked so small down there, standing by the Ford at the end of the old service road. We climbed back down and when we reached the bottom, he was leaning against a giant Douglas fir with his hands in his pockets, whistling "Cool Water."

He took me aside and pointed across the valley that lay beyond the road; he stretched out his arms as though to take it all inside him: the whole of the forest, its forgotten thickness; the perilous sweep of space between mountains. His eyes began to water as he spoke of the land: its richness a promise made to him long ago, in darkness. It was clear he wanted me by his side in some way, wanted us to enter his dream together. I knew that was impossible; knew that my own love for this geography was a separate thing from his vision of it. I could see that he was alone in this quest, as in all the others: heading out once more under that western sky, watching for signs, forgiving the landscape its silence.

❦ *The Big Deal* ❦

Once Daddy negotiated a big deal. He had staked some claims, he said, and the big shots had given him an advance on the mining rights. *These* big shots were from Alaska-Canadian Mines. You couldn't roll their name off your tongue, but you could roll your hands through their money: he had it spread all over the living room floor. It was the first time I had ever seen a five-hundred-dollar-bill. "Boy oh boy oh boy oh boy," he said, over and over. "Honey, now do you believe all the things I've been telling you all these years? Here it is. Oh boyohboyohboy. Our ship has come in." He scooped the bills into his hands and tossed them in the air.

"Your daddy," he continued (he often spoke of himself in the third person—the effect it had on me was that I was always on the verge of turning my head around to see who else was there), "has staked four claims up there in the mountains, and I've named them after you and Greta. They are called Sonya I and Sonya II; Greta I and Greta II." That struck me as unoriginal, but I said nothing. "Someday," he said, waving his hands over the money, "all of it will be yours." I don't want it, I thought. And by then I really didn't. But I didn't say it; it was making him delirious, and there was no telling what he would have done if he had thought I was not delirious too. In the night, though, I couldn't resist thinking: *Somewhere there is land named for me.*

❦ Shorty ❧

One evening, shortly after our ship had come in, the phone rang and Daddy said, "I'm not in." I answered it to hear a voice say, "Ray in?"

"No, he's not here right now; can I have him call you?" I was a dutiful daughter.

"Now, listen. You tell him Shorty wants to see him." (He pronounced it Shawty.) "Ya got that? Shorty. Tell him I ain't waitin' no longer for what he owes me. You tell him that. Say, 'Shorty ain't waitin' no longer.' " Then he hung up.

"Shorty says he ain't waitin' no longer for what you owe him," I reported. Daddy looked up in mock surprise from *Reader's Digest*, his thumb marking his place in an article entitled "Great American Tycoons."

"What the hell are you talking about?" he said. "It must have been some asshole with the wrong number."

❦ Vernon Stone ❧

One day in winter, Margaret and I stayed downtown after school to read movie magazines. By the time we had digested Stewart Granger's life history in *Silver Screen*, it was four-thirty and my bus transfer had expired. Margaret had just enough money for a fresh fare to get herself home; I had none. There was nothing to do but to run over to 2nd Avenue and see if Daddy was at the office, and get a ride home with him.

Just as the elevator doors began to close, a tall, balding, dark-skinned man dashed in. We were the only people in the elevator. As I studied the back of his neck, I thought: At last I know the full meaning of the word "swarthy"! He stood very still and carried the filthy remains of what had once been a briefcase in his hands.

The elevator moved slowly toward the 10th floor. He was going to the 10th floor, too. There was something strange about him; I felt uneasy, as though I were just beginning to understand the word "sinister." Daddy was right; Nancy Drew mysteries were poisoning my mind. I tried to concentrate on worse things, such as what I would do if Daddy had already left the office.

At the 10th floor the doors opened and the swarthy, sinister man began walking down the long corridor, at the very end of which was Daddy's tiny office. I walked behind him, feeling ridiculous, pretending I was on my way to another office. It crossed my mind, but I rejected it as totally out of the question, that he was on his way to see Daddy. Countless steps later, that's just where he went: right up to the frosted glass door with the inscription

General Minerals Co.
Raymond Weiler   Eddie Atkins
Mining Engineers

I stood helplessly by as he knocked.

"Dr. Stone, come in . . . oh, honey, what are you doing here?" Daddy ushered "Dr. Stone" into the cramped one-room office, and I sidled in behind him. "My transfer expired," I said heavily. It was only then that the man turned and looked at me. His eyes were dark and piercing. I went over to the one window to lean out and watch the people swarming like ants ten stories below.

The office was very crowded, what with Daddy, Ed, and now Dr. Stone with their feet on the desk, talking business. I think Daddy was embarrassed that I was there, hanging out the window with an expired transfer, just when he was prepared to do important business with Dr. Stone. But he was a gentleman about it, introducing us just as though I mattered: "Dr. Stone, this is my daughter Sonya; honey, this is Dr. Vernon Stone, the eminent geologist. He and your daddy"—who? what? where is he? oh— "are going to make a deal."

Dr. Stone didn't speak, just inclined his head slightly toward me and smiled in a sinister way. Eminence didn't drink bourbon with his feet on the desk with Ray and Ed; I was young and without means, but I knew that much. Eminence wore a pith helmet and made love to Deborah Kerr in the African bush. I leaned out the open window waiting for them to finish the bottle and consummate their deal. At one point, I pondered how it would feel to hit the pavement ten stories below. Daddy paused once, to say, "Honey, I've told you before—don't lean out so far."

Many weeks later, Daddy returned from one of his trips to the mountains with a terrible story; it had an edge to it that the others had lacked. Vernon Stone had tried to kill him. Even Nancy Drew would be on guard with a statement like that. He sat down heavily at the kitchen table and didn't even bother to pour himself a drink; he took it straight from the bottle. "Oh, honey, you don't know what I've been through, but I won't trouble your young mind with such terrible things," he groaned, then went right on and spilled out a tale of terror and betrayal, the nucleus of which was that Vernon Stone had tried to push him off a cliff. When I asked where Ed had been at the time, how he had managed to escape, what had become of Vernon Stone, he grew vague and started pacing the floor. "I trusted him. He came to me with the finest credentials. I let him in on our mine. Oh, your daddy has made a terrible mistake. I admit it. A Judas Iscariot, that's what he is. Judas, Judas." I wanted to hear what happened next, but by then Daddy was drunk. No matter how hard I pressed for details, all he did was mutter "Judas."

The only thing Daddy would say about Vernon Stone in the weeks that followed was that he had managed to discover that Stone was an impostor. He was really an eastern European peasant who had come upon the crashed plane of the real Vernon Stone, stolen his credentials, and come to America to impersonate him. That was how he explained why Dr. Stone tried to kill him. I suppose it was the only possible explanation; eminent geologists don't go around doing things like that.

❦ Douglas MacArthur ❦

Every time Daddy left on another trip to the mountains, I began doing strange things—like writing letters to General MacArthur. I wrote them in study hall while everyone else was studying. When the three o'clock bell rang, I crumpled them up and threw them in the waste basket. It wouldn't do to be discovered with letters to General MacArthur in your possession. My worst fear was that when I took my seat on the bus, one of my classmates would reach down into the aisle and pick up a letter I had just dropped and read it to the whole bus:

> My Dear Douglas,
>   I will never forget the way you looked at me from your open car during the parade. My girlfriend and I waited on the curb for two hours, and we never dreamed that you would actually notice us, considering the number of people there. It thrilled me, just as it did the last time we saw each other—remember? It was during the storm on the P.T. boat when you took me in your arms and whispered, "I shall return."

❦ Biology ❦

In Sunday School (where they welcomed "children through the age of twenty"; it was a strange sight to see those hulking forms at the little tables), we were told: If they try to teach you science in school, it is your right to refuse to learn it. To avoid any course in Hygiene, Biology, Chemistry or Physiology, have your parents write a letter stating that your religious beliefs are opposed to such instruction. It is against the law for them to teach you things that conflict with your religion.

Such thinking derived from a central tenet of Christian Science—what they called The Scientific Statement of Being, which begins: *There is no life, truth, intelligence, or substance in matter.* Everything was "infinite mind"; the physical was an illusion, a lie. It always puzzled me that a religion which reviled science would name itself after science. Still, I repeated the words from memory Sunday after Sunday and year after year, along with everyone else. Ninth-grade Biology was my moment of truth.

Miss Higgins rubbed her thin hands together soundlessly; an exaggerated smile stretched her sagging face as she prepared the slide for our first lesson. The natural sciences were her great and only love. Strands of white hair escaped from the bun at the nape of her neck and fell over her rimless glasses as she peered intently down. We stood around nervously, suppressing giggles and scratching our elbows. It was hard to understand a woman her age getting this excited over smears and blobs. Slide in place, microscope focused, she finally beckoned us with one hand, saying, "All right girls, line up single file and tell me what you see."

Nothing prepared me for what I saw: living things moving around, sliding, swimming, passing each other, crossing over one another, going about their business, living their invisible, independent lives. I pulled back my eye in disbelief and looked skeptically at the slide: there was nothing between the two glass strips but a drop of water, just as Miss Higgins had said. I looked again, I hogged the microscope. I could hear throats being cleared, broad hints that I move on and let someone else have a crack at it, but I continued to stare in amazement; I could not give it up: this water was alive! These forms were moving; they had energy and sensitivity. They must have intelligence, too, even if it might seem "blind" to us. The Scientific Statement of Being echoed urgently in my head as I stared unblinking at the little diatoms crossing and recrossing one another, as in a dance. *There is no life, truth, intelligence, or substance in matter.* I considered the actual words for the first time, and grasped their meaning. There was no way I could reconcile it with what I saw: this was *matter*—and it was jumping with life. Here were the hard facts, the concrete reality. You could see it with your own eyes, microscopic as it was,

113

and others could see it, too. It meant that all of the natural world, even that part that was invisible, was teeming with energy and life.

I finally relinquished the microscope to the girl behind me, and stood by the laboratory window looking out, knowing that a turning point had just been reached. It was one thing to pray, instead of seeing a doctor—that could be seen as a choice between separate authorities; but it was altogether different to deny visible reality. There had to be a system that would allow for matter and mind at the same time. Weren't we examples of that unity ourselves? I knew I could never go back to Sunday School, soothing as it once had been. I knew the people there were kind, even loving; but in the face of the miraculous diatoms that was not enough.

🦋 Sybil 🦋

In 1952 we moved for the sixth time. It was red brick. Daddy talked his way into that house the way he had the others, by using Greta and me as the motherless pawns. Shortly afterward, Sybil was hired. She was tight and brittle, an all-time bitch; I hated her from the start. Sometimes after dinner she and Daddy would stand and look out the window at the shimmering lake and the Cascade Mountains beyond, and Daddy would hoist his arm up awkwardly around her shoulder as he whispered of investments in mining properties. It didn't matter that the properties lay deep in the crevices of his mind; he knew avarice when he saw it. She would invest. It was simply a matter of playing your cards right and biding your time. Sybil claimed she had become a housekeeper only to provide a ready-made home for her eight-year-old twins, Ernestine and Geraldine. Tucked away somewhere, Daddy was certain, was the large settlement she had hit her ex-husband for after their divorce. Sybil had class, I had to admit: a hard, vicious kind of class. She kept Seagram's Crown Royal in her closet.

She could decimate us without lifting a hand; I knew there was real skill involved—being so vicious, yet using only your mind and your mouth as weapons. Mavis used to bash Greta's head against the bathroom wall until her nosebleeds drew attention to this practice, but Sybil could cut you to pieces with one look. Even if I had known then the full extent of her capacity for vengeance and how it would affect me even into the future, there still wouldn't have been a single thing I could have done.

The owners of the red brick house were abroad for two years but before they left, Mrs. Ramsey, the lady of the house, had insisted that their record collection was for us to enjoy—so long as we were careful. It was there, after a fight with Sybil, that I first discovered Shostakovich.

Sybil had left in an icy rage, taking the twins and slamming the door behind her. Greta was at a friend's house, and Daddy was still at the office. As I thumbed through the Ramseys' records, I jumped with surprise when I came to the Shostakovich Concerto for Piano and Trumpet. I felt a thrill of secret pleasure to have discovered Communist music right in our "own" home; only the year before, I'd made the mistake of mentioning the Red Army Chorus record I'd seen while babysitting for the people down the street, and Daddy had refused to let me sit for them again. With a twisted sense of adventure, I slid the record out of its jacket and put the needle in the groove. The sounds that leaped into the room were bombastic, agitated and grim; I felt their discord in waves, like small shocks. The piece was anarchy; it frightened me to be alone in the house with it.

I can't explain why I didn't turn it off and put the record back; there was a perverse, inexplicable satisfaction in letting it go on. I played it a second time, awed to be a firsthand witness to such corruption. By the third play, I began to notice harmonic sequences of rare, majestic beauty, and dark, elegant passages born of a staggering melancholy. It was hard to believe that less than an hour before I'd found it revolting. It now seemed a rich and complex statement, a message from an underground voice who spoke in code in order to be heard.

I played it over and over, marveling at my discovery. It was all the sweeter for being a secret I couldn't share. The bombast was a front; underneath was delicacy, knowledge, unspeakable longing. I didn't know it then, but what had started as an act of rebellion was becoming a form of love.

⚓ Sailing ⚓

One morning during the summer, while I was practicing Beethoven's "Pathétique" Sonata on the piano, the doorbell rang. It was the boy next door. "Hi, would you like to go sailing with me?" he said. I had seen him out the window but I didn't know his name. I just stood there wondering what he was asking me sailing for. There had to be some mistake. I was fourteen and had split ends and went to Edgemont, where talking to boys was the only offense considered worse than speaking out of turn.

"I'm taking my boat out on the lake and my mother thought it would be nice if I asked you to go with me," he tried again. "Well, I guess so," I said. What else could I have said? "I have to stay here and play Beethoven's 'Pathétique' "?

The lake was very calm; we got all the way out to the middle before I asked his name. It was Bill. He decided we should go swimming right there, off the boat. I thought the water was too cold. " 'The time has come, the Walrus said,' " he quoted, as he pulled me into the water. I saw no significance in that at the time. It wasn't bad once you got in and there was a special freedom swimming around in the middle of the lake early in the morning.

We were drying ourselves off when Bill said, "What does your father do?" It could have been the most innocent question in the world, I suppose, but I began to shake, and the whole scene—Bill, the boat, the lake—began to blur. "Well, he works in the mountains a lot," was all I could get out. I had never known how to answer that question, and coming as it did, out there in the middle of the lake, it seemed doubly unanswerable.

"What does he do in the mountains? I mean, what's his line of work?" Bill persisted. The only choices open to me were to fall overboard and sink quietly to the bottom, or ask him why he had to know.

"Why do you want to know so much?" I asked him. It was his turn to squirm. "Uh, well, my parents were wondering, you know. Just curious, I guess."

We sailed back in silence. It was clear now why a good-looking boy like Bill would ask a fourteen-year-old with split ends to go sailing with him. I knew he would never ask me again, and he never did.

❦ *Stripping the Gears* ❦

Daddy taught me to drive the day I turned fifteen. We would all get in the Ford, Greta in the back seat and Daddy beside me, and head for the relative calm of Lake Washington Boulevard. It was hard learning to drive with Daddy screaming in the front seat and Greta screaming in the back. "Oh, Daddy, she's going in the lake! She's going in the lake! We're all going to die!"

"Take it easy, Greta; she's not going to do any such thing. No daughter of mine goes in the lake."

His confidence would carry me a few blocks until he, too, started screaming. "Look out! Look out! Watch it, watch it; Jesus Christ, you're stripping the gears!" It didn't take me long to learn that, to him, nothing was worse: cutting in front of another car; slicing into someone's neatly trimmed parking strip; going too near the edge of the lake—these were trivial, compared with stripping the gears.

"Let the clutch out *slowly!*" he would shout as we jerked along. I was sweating and frantic. I hated the lessons, but was determined to learn. I knew instinctively that driving would be my salvation in years to come.

It finally came together in spite of Daddy's efforts. If there was anything I learned from him that summer, it was how to strip the gears. When I finally got my license and was driving along the lake at midnight with my head out the window, singing along with the Top Ten, I stripped and stripped away at his shitty old gears. Nothing gave me greater pleasure; I was able to go to sleep without any trouble at all.

In the fall, Sonya is required to write a short story for English class. She doesn't know where it comes from, but an amazing tale unfolds the minute she puts her pen to the lined paper: A young girl goes out riding in the wilderness one day. After a long journey, she comes to a log cabin in the mountains where she discovers a fugitive hiding out. They talk for a long time, and she discovers he is her long-lost father who had been in prison many years. He says he's dying of wounds he received while escaping. As she rides off desperately for help, a sudden snowstorm intervenes. She struggles on, blinded by snow and tears at the story's end, knowing her efforts are hopeless and that he will die. The teacher chooses this story to read aloud to the class. Sonya is embarrassed; she doesn't want anyone to think it came from real life, because it didn't. Just as the teacher is reading the last sentence, the bell rings and everyone bolts for the door. The teacher hands her the story; it is the first "A" she has ever received. She wonders if the humiliation of being exposed as someone who writes dumb melodrama is worth an "A."

⚱ Cruising ⚱

Once I had my driver's license, I asked Daddy for the keys to the car almost every night after dinner. I would drive across town and head for the churches. I felt such an emptiness since leaving Christian Science; I knew I could never again accept those beliefs, but I seemed to need others to replace them. One didn't *believe* in science; one observed and accepted it. Sometimes I picked up Margaret and we would cruise for churches together; her parents were agnostics, and retired at nine each night in separate bedrooms.

Almost everyone at Edgemont was High Episcopalian; it was simply a part of their lives—like the stables and the country club; they went every Sunday and took it for granted. I found Episcopal hard; they didn't lock their doors at night like the Methodists, but it was always dark inside, cold and forbidding. Being inside their church, you felt an icy beauty—the kind that had the highest approval, and couldn't be touched. I always felt badly dressed in the Episcopal church—as though, if it weren't night and deserted, but filled instead with Sunday's congregation, the regulars would stare politely and wonder, *Who is she?*

One night we made an unusually promising find. It was almost eleven o'clock and time to be getting home; our luck had been bad: either locked doors, or cavernous, forbidding places you wouldn't want to enter. "Let's try just one more," I pleaded and Margaret agreed. I swerved down a deserted street in an unfamiliar neighborhood and there on the corner stood a Catholic church. Not only were its lights on, but the door was open; I pulled over to the curb and parked. Quietly, almost tiptoeing, we climbed the hard stone steps with beating hearts. I imagined a priest inside, waiting for a miracle. His highest goal was the saving of souls, but no one had presented himself as a candidate tonight. He would be disappointed—after all, that's why he left the door open—but he wouldn't lose faith. He would just putter around the altar, straightening things, biding his time before closing up at eleven. When we walked in, he would be shocked to see us. I imagined him shaking his finger: "What are you girls doing roaming around alone at this hour?" he would admonish sternly. "Father," I'd say, "we're looking for something to believe in." "Ah," he'd answer, "that's different. You've come to the right place, my child."

A bank of little candles flickered by the altar, casting a warm light over the pictures of saints on the wall and the painted plaster statues lining the aisle. Jesus hung sadly on the cross in the middle of everything, but there wasn't a human being in sight. I held my breath in a mixture of excitement and fear; it had been thrilling to step over that foreign threshold, to enter forbidden territory. I knew the door wouldn't be open if they didn't welcome people, and yet I had the feeling we shouldn't be there, that only Catholics should—the door had been left open for them. As we sidled down to the altar, it felt more like trespassing with each step. The wavering light cast eerie shadows over the walls, the atmosphere was tense with the expectation of ritual and mystery. I wanted so much to embrace it, but it wasn't mine. With each passing minute I was more and more convinced that there was a Father in there somewhere, behind the folds of drapes, around a plaster archway, waiting silently behind paneled wood, watching. And because we were outcasts, desecrators, he wouldn't show himself to us.

Suddenly a gust of wind blew in the open door, setting the candles sputtering. The faces of the statues and saints no longer looked benign, but cheap and harsh and menacing. You could see the paint flaking off them in little chips. They had no power. The church no longer seemed awesome, but deserted. "This is creepy," whispered Margaret. "Let's get out of here." Together we turned from the altar and ran. As our footsteps echoed through the hollow alcoves, I imagined the Father in pursuit. I wasn't sure if he was angrily chasing us out, or trying to offer us something before we got away. We took the front steps two and three at a time, jumped into the Ford, and roared away. Late that night, as I lay in bed, I tried to understand my sense of loss; there had been nothing in there but gaudy statues and empty space.

There didn't seem to be a denomination anywhere that could offer what you needed at night—when you needed it the most. I didn't cruise for churches anymore after that.

🦋 *Typing* 🦋

Each spring brought a conference with Abigail Irons, the purpose of which was for each student to discuss her course of work for the following year. Each May, with dread, I entered the inner sanctum of Miss Irons' suite of offices. She would scan me contemptuously from the other side of her massive desk, taking in with one sweep of her dictatorial eyes my chewed off fingernails (hidden unsuccessfully in my lap), stringy hair, wrinkled and spotted uniform—all glaring evidence of my general unsuitability for the Edgemont School, and pointed reminders of my unpaid tuition.

"Speak up," she would say at last. "You want to take *what?* instead of Latin next fall?"

"Typing," I whispered.

"*Typing?*" she repeated with revulsion. Virginia (Gigi) Rucklehaus, Katherine (Cricket) Spaulding, Priscilla (Puckie) Pruitt and the others would all be taking Latin. Abigail Irons knew I didn't have the mind for Latin, the inclination toward Latin, or the social standing for Latin ("Aw, shit, honey, Latin is a dead language, everybody knows that! You don't need a dead language to clutter up your mind; it would be a complete waste of time. Latin!" Daddy would sputter, then, as if to objectify his contempt, would break into an exuberant volley of Pig Latin: "Oh-nay aughter-day of ine-may eeds-nay oo-tay other-bay ith-way atin-lay!").

"Why do you want to take typing," she queried coldly, watching for my response and enjoying the wait.

"Because I want to be a writer," I whispered unconvincingly. As though in response to the word "writer," my fingers twitched involuntarily from their sweaty nest in my lap.

"A writer," she hissed dreamily. I knew what she was thinking. It was bad enough that Typing had slipped by the board of directors as an acceptable course of instruction; even worse that, for some reason which had momentarily escaped her, she had neglected to expel me. She stared at me as I dug my thumbnail into my opposite palm to keep my emotions in check. Surely by now she had noticed my wrinkled skirt and the fact that the rain had long ago obliterated its pleats. By now she was thinking: What else could she hope to amount to, with a family like that.

✦

Raymond Weiler is speaking in tongues. He stands at the head of the table in the dimly lit dining room of the red brick house and strains to carve the roast he has just removed from the oven. Sybil sits down at the table with slow deliberation; the twins lean on their elbows, whispering to one another. Greta hunches miserably over her plate; her hair is uncombed and she has been crying. "You look like something the cat dragged in," comments Sybil, a mean smile playing over her thin, freshly glossed lips. "Leave her alone," says Sonya, desperately. The twins giggle, their eyes darting up and down the table, sensing trouble not directed at them and therefore fun. "I wouldn't talk," Sybil retaliates quickly; "you look worse than she does, with your hair like that. You look like a whore."

"By-de-Jesus-Christ-Almighty, hn-hn-hn-hn," chants Ray as the meat keeps slipping off the carving knife, splattering blood onto the tablecloth. He knows the meat isn't all that's slipping, but has no margins left to regain control. He knows his children are targets for Sybil's cruelty; he sees her striking out at them, he's not blind. Hell, she doesn't even cook anymore! He has to come home after a grueling day of wheeling and dealing with those bastards downtown and get the goddamned dinner started; that's why they eat so late. She doesn't do the washing, either.

122

She doesn't do anything anymore, except stir up trouble. She's not fooling anyone, the bitch; he'll see that she rots in hell just as soon as his big deal comes through. He can't do a goddamned thing about it now, however, because the capital that went to launch this deal came from her. She folds her arms across her bony chest, stroking the sleeves of her cashmere cardigan, and watches him struggle. "You're stupid!" Geraldine whispers to Greta. Sybil pretends she doesn't hear. Sonya stares across the table at Sybil; she has heard that in some cultures—or is it some cults?—if you stare directly at a person and wish them harm, it will happen. She has given up Christian Science because it doesn't work, but maybe the evil thoughts part is worth another try. Her stomach is in knots; she has no appetite for this dinner, but if she doesn't make a pretense of it, Ray will go crazy. She offers to help him serve, which he interprets as criticism, setting off another round of unintelligible expletives and grunts. Greta starts to cry again and he turns his frustration on her. "Stop that goddamned sniveling this instant or go straight to your room!" he explodes, the carving knife poised in midair. Greta runs from the table, knocking over her chair. "Clumsy!" Sybil hisses at her fleeing form. "You all leave her alone!" Sonya shouts, near tears. "Holy-Jesus-Christ-Almighty-you-goddamned-rotten-sons-of-bitches, if this doesn't stop you can all go straight to hell!" Ray screams. The twins are watching him now; their mouths hang open. There is no way to rescue this meal, no way out of the storm that is building to a swift and ugly conclusion. Sonya sits frozen under the sixty-watt bulbs—a bomb that can't afford to explode, a statue with a stone mind, a zero. Ray is out of control now; he throws the carving knife down the table, where it stops just short of Ernestine's lap. "What are you doing!" cries Sybil in alarm. "You must be out of your mind!"

"Go to hell, the whole damned lot of you!" Ray screams. "I work my heart out and this is all I get, nothing but bickering and sniveling!" He paces the hardwood floor, gesticulating wildly as Sybil retrieves the roast and ushers the twins into the kitchen. She pulls the swinging door shut behind her as Ray storms out the front door. Its slam echoes through the rented house. Sonya rises from her chair in the empty dining room and goes upstairs to Greta's room where Greta lies sprawled on her bed. She picks up a hairbrush and absently begins to brush her sister's tangled hair; she recites a variety of imaginative possibilities for Sybil's demise, and eventually Greta's tears subside.

❧ *La Bohème* ❧

I knew I would be all right if I could make it to Wednesday. That was the day I went to Marian Linden's and struggled through my unpracticed scales in order to soak up an hour's worth of tranquility, discipline and attention. Sometime around the second year, she had begun interrupting the lesson at the halfway point, saying it was perhaps time we had a little break and that she would take that opportunity to play a record she was anxious for me to hear. Graciously, she would produce a snack of toast and juice and we would sit in the little alcove by the window while the record played. Sometimes it would be Chopin, sometimes Bach. On days when it rained, she substituted hot chocolate for the juice. As the music filled the room it seemed to cast a visual glow over everything, even on cloudy days. We often talked while the music played; Miss Linden didn't expect either of us to sit in rapt attention, but every now and then she would suddenly interrupt herself, or me, at the beginning of a particularly stunning passage, raise her finger in the air, and say "Listen!" in a breathless whisper. Her face was in love with the music. When the moment had passed, she would come back from wherever she'd just been transported and resume our conversation, radiant and refreshed. Sometimes I didn't even hear what she said; it would pass right through my paralyzed mind unrecorded, like everything else. It was enough that she spoke, that she took the time to show this special interest in me. I wanted to tell her of my dream to be a writer, but I knew it would hurt her feelings so I didn't.

I'd always begin the hour by doing a quick run-through of the scales, and maybe play a passage or two from one of my old pieces; and sometimes she couldn't help herself, she'd slide over onto the bench and show me how it should be done, and then I'd repeat it after her the best I could. But by then the records and the conversations took up most of the Wednesday hour. Every now and then she would mention the phrase "musical education" in connection with these sessions, but they were clearly for pleasure and not instruction. She would pause from time to time, as she always did, to ask about things at school. At the end of the hour, she would give me a record to take home and play during the week in exchange for the one she had loaned me the week before. I carried the record home on the bus in a kind of trance. It was the first time I had ever been entrusted with something valuable which belonged to someone else. I began to feel I must be special for her to do that.

I put it on the turntable in the living room as soon as I got home, while Greta and the twins screamed and fought, and Daddy cursed and dropped things in the kitchen. I would put my ear against the speaker and screen them all out until they no longer existed. The time Miss Linden loaned me one of Bach's Brandenburgs I was reluctant to give it up. When she opened her door the following week and I handed the record back, I said, "My life will never be the same after this." She seemed startled at first, but quickly recovered and then seemed pleased. I was startled myself, saying a thing like that. I knew she must think I was being melodramatic, but she never said anything to make me ashamed, and as a result I grew even bolder. At the end of that hour, as I was going out the door, I said, "I will never forget you." Miss Linden looked at me sadly for a minute, then said, "Oh, yes, you will, someday." That surprised me, so I said, with even more conviction, "No. I won't," and I never did.

The Saturday Daddy took Greta to the Barnum & Bailey Circus, I had the entire house to myself; Sybil and the twins were downtown shopping. Miss Linden had loaned me Puccini's *La*

Bohème—the whole opera, not just the highlights—and I spent the day on the floor, with nothing to screen out, my eyes closed, listening. A week later, after my lesson, she said, "I happen to have an extra ticket to *La Bohème*; I'd like very much to take you, if you'd like to go." I said I would love to go; I had never been out to an opera. "Wonderful," she said. She wrote down the date on a piece of paper and added, "Be sure to tell your father that I will drive you there and bring you home."

It should have occurred to me a long time ago; there were so many indications, even a blind man would have caught on: Daddy hadn't paid for my lessons in over a year, and having the truth come out the way it did, in the middle of a drunken argument over going to *La Bohème*, made it seem all the more of a shock I would never be able to absorb, much less live down. I was filled with such shame, I had no idea how I was going to get through my next hour with Miss Linden. When I arrived at her apartment I couldn't sit down on the piano bench, but just stood there dumbly, my arms frozen at my sides. "Come on," Miss Linden said lightly, "let's begin." She started to take her place on the chair beside the bench, but I turned away from the piano and from her, and stared out the large leaded window. How could I tell her that I knew? And whether I told her or not, nothing would ever be the same again. It was clear now why she had cut the lessons short; it was clear that she, too, was embarrassed and ashamed and that's why she had said nothing; that's why she just continued as though nothing had changed. I saw, with a terrible clarity, that her interest in me—all the exchanges which had so enriched my life and which had kept me going through the worst of times—stemmed from pity. It hadn't just happened naturally, the way love does when you feel you belong somewhere. She hadn't been generous because she had liked me, but because she felt sorry for me and didn't know how to handle turning me away. It proved that I was pitiful. And it meant I could never come here again.

Miss Linden came over to the window and stood beside me. "Something's wrong," she said, waiting for me to volunteer. I imagined opening my mouth, and no sounds coming out, the way

126

it happens in dreams. It would have been the easiest thing in the world for Gigi Rucklehaus to handle; she'd probably say something clever like, "My pa forgot to pay the bill again," and laugh. I could sense Miss Linden waiting, and eventually she prompted, "What is it?" I tried to formulate a response but my mind was like a nest of mice, scattering; thoughts tumbled, then disappeared. My heart turned over and over as my breathing grew irregular from the effort of holding back tears. "Sit down," Miss Linden said, motioning to the window seat and sitting there herself. I sat beside her, but turned my head away. The rain was falling at a diagonal, in thin little streaks, across the leaded windows. Even with my mind locked in the deep freeze, I always took note of unusual detail. "Sonya, you must tell me what's the matter." I heard her voice down a long tunnel, and it was impossible for me to travel the distance between my end and hers. "Does it concern coming here?" she finally asked, wising up.

I took a deep breath, as though to speak, but my mouth wouldn't open. The question seemed so simple, but to answer it would require the opening of a door within a door within a door, into infinity. It was a relief to hear it voiced; but I could never explain that it involved more than just shame over nonpayment. There were no words in my vocabulary that could ever get to the depths of it. "Does it?" she repeated, more firmly this time. I stared at the hardwood floor as the little clock on the wall ticked nonchalantly on. When I finally managed to nod my head, Marian Linden released a great sigh. There was silence for some minutes, and then she seemed to straighten, to gather herself up as though preparing to face something she had been avoiding for a long time.

"I should have taken that up with you directly, in the beginning," she finally said. "I think I can see how you must feel. It puts you in a very difficult position now. I'm very sorry." She seemed to falter here, and since I couldn't speak, I just stared at the floor and waited for her to go on. It was just a matter of time anyway; it would all be over soon. She'd say that she'd been wrong to keep me on under those circumstances, something to that effect, and wouldn't make it more difficult for me by compounding that mistake now. And then I would gather up my books and maybe even say something dumb like, "Oh, that's all right," so her feelings wouldn't be hurt, and maybe even thank her, and then walk out her door forever. I was about to lose someone I needed and I couldn't do a thing to stop it. I kept seeing myself in my mind's eye, opening my mouth and speaking on my behalf: I would say, "My father throws knives and calls me a misfit. Sybil says I look like a whore. I am responsible for my sister, Greta, but I can't even take care of myself. Coming to you on Wednesdays is the only good thing in my life." And then I imagined her hearing what I would say, and either she wouldn't believe me, or she would be so ashamed, hearing those things, she wouldn't want me to visit her ever again. And then I saw Daddy's face, twisted and despairing, and I didn't know which was worse: to betray him by telling, or betray myself by keeping still. So I continued to sit, doing nothing, paralyzed and drifting in space.

"You see," she resumed in a halting voice, "by the time the matter became clear . . . it was hard for me to let you go. I thought the conversations and the records would be a way of . . . not losing each other." Those weren't the words I'd been bracing for. Her hand reached out and rested lightly on my arm. "Sonya, please look at me," she said. There was a jade ring on her finger. I had seen it many times but never noticed it before. My arm burned where her hand was; no one touched me anymore, no one had touched me for a long time. I couldn't bear its weight; I had mastered name-calling and being screamed at without crying, but her gentleness overwhelmed me. My mouth opened at last, and my voice caught. "My father . . ." I started, and buried my head in my hands. Miss Linden's arms went around me; it was the strangest feeling, being held after all those years. She just said, "Oh," and held me closer. I let myself be drawn into her. I can still see the weave of the sweater she wore that day. I could even hear her heart, keeping time as steady as a metronome. As the minutes passed, I slowly understood: there was no longer any need for her to demonstrate her love; her gesture spoke for her. And I didn't have to agonize for explanations anymore. She knew without knowing.

"Well," she finally said, "what's done is done. It's good to have it explicit. We will stop the pretense of the lessons." She sighed decisively and kept an arm around me. I rummaged in my pocket for a Kleenex. "You will continue to visit me, as before," she said hesitantly, almost as an afterthought. Then quickly added, "I count on seeing you; our time together has come to mean a great deal to me." I nodded yes; I was speechless and exhausted, but curiously triumphant: now that Miss Linden and I had negotiated our own arrangement, now that things were on our terms, Daddy would have no say. It was even possible that, with her help, he couldn't prevent me from going to *La Bohème*. Over hot chocolate, I was able to clarify things without dwelling on the details of my fight with Daddy. "I will call your father," she said resolutely, as though that would settle everything. I knew if she managed to reach him when he was sober, things might work out, but I couldn't tell her that.

I don't know what she finally said to him, or what he said to her, but one week later she took me to see *La Bohème*, as planned. It was strange to watch the figures on stage enacting the events I had previously experienced only in sound. There was just one bad moment, when Mimi lay dying. It was so protracted, so beautiful, so terrible a scene; it brought back with such force the night Mother died, I had to dig my nails into my palms and hold my breath to keep from crying. Except for that, I felt a great sense of privilege to be attending such an event, with Miss Linden at my side, just as though I belonged there.

✤ *Running Away* ✤

Dwayne lived directly across from the red brick house. He was about my age, fifteen, and had close-cropped sandy hair. He wore large black horn-rimmed glasses which obscured what few features he had. I had seen him going in and out of his house, and he

no doubt saw me going in and out of mine, but we never acknowledged each other until the day we were thrown together on
the Number 10 bus. He was coming home from a dentist's appointment, and I was returning from Miss Linden's with a stack
of commie records in my arms.

"The FBI would take a dim view of what you're doing," he
observed, shortly after taking the seat next to me. The bus was
filling up; it was late in the afternoon, and getting dark. The windows were all steamed up.

"You sound like my father," I said, on guard. "This is actually
very good music. You should listen to it and see for yourself."

"Their music is ideological propaganda," he replied authoritatively. I could sense Shostakovich, Khachaturian, Prokofiev and
Kabalevsky stirring on my lap, and imagined them sighing, "Sad,
but true."

"That doesn't really matter, even if it is true," I said, defensively. "What matters is how the music makes you feel."

"Ah ha! Ah ha!" he hissed, cracking his knuckles. "That's just
it! It works on you in subtle ways, and pretty soon you end up a
Communist. You don't even know what hit you! That's why they
call such influences 'insidious.' "

"That's not true," I said. "I used to think the Shostakovich
Concerto for Piano and Trumpet was the ugliest thing I ever
heard, but I've listened to it over and over and now I think it's
beautiful, and I'm still not a Communist." He tipped his head
back and squinted at me with great suspicion. I felt a little thrill of
fear run through my body. Maybe he would report me to Senator
McCarthy and I'd have to sit in front of a microphone, facing
those formidable men behind the giant interrogation table, and
convince them I wasn't a Communist. "Why do you persist in
listening to Shostakovich, then, if you're not a Communist?" they
would demand.

"Because I like the sounds," I would answer innocently.

"If you like the sounds, that means the influence has already
had its effect on you; that's the whole point of propaganda. We
have no alternative but to declare you a Communist."

"Wait a minute! Point of order! Let me play it for you, just

130

once—well, maybe three times. Are you afraid of *sounds*? Do you think listening to sounds will make *you* Communists?"

"*Play* it? For *us*? Outrageous! Take away her records! Take away her Tom Mix whistling ring! A degenerate Communist has no right to wear the ring of a fine, upstanding American cowboy like Tom Mix! Take *her* away, lock her up!"

The bus jolted along, stopping and starting up again every few blocks. We bumped against each other with every change in speed, and argued all the way home. I couldn't understand why it was so exhilarating; I couldn't understand why I didn't just ignore him, and stare out the window as I usually did. He was just like Daddy, anyone could see that. Just before Dwayne went into his house and I went into mine, he pulled a pen from his shirt pocket and withdrew a little notebook from his jacket. "Let's exchange phone numbers," he said, "in case a new idea strikes me in the night."

I ran into the kitchen with unaccustomed buoyancy. Sybil was sitting on a wooden stool in her beige cashmere sweater set, slowly peeling carrots. "You can't have any of these," she said right away; "your father's going to be late tonight and he asked me to help him out; otherwise I wouldn't be in here." I took some bread and jam instead and as I was leaving the kitchen, she said, "Don't you have enough pimples? Or are you trying to win a contest?" I was proud of myself; I walked out very calmly and completely ignored her. I went into the living room and turned on the record player. As it was warming up, I had an inspiration. Pulling the telephone from its place in the hall, I was able to stretch it to within three feet of the record player. Slowly, my heart pounding, I dialed Dwayne's number. As his phone began to ring, I slipped the needle into the groove.

"Hello?"

"Is this Dwayne?"

"Yes, it is he." God. Didn't he know how kids talked? I thought of hanging up quickly, before I got more deeply involved, but the music had started and that might give me away.

"This is the girl across the street. That you met on the bus this afternoon. Sonya."

131

"Oh. Have you changed your attitudes yet?"

"No. In fact, the reason I'm calling is I had another idea. I thought . . ."

"You listening to music? I hear music in the background. Do you like the classics?" he interrupted.

"Yes, very much. I go to the opera. Do you like classical music?"

"Of course. It is the only music worth listening to," he answered arrogantly.

"I think so, too, mostly," I said; "but I also listen to the Top Ten. I think 'Glow-Worm' is a nice song."

" 'Glow-Worm'!" he spat. "That is a degenerate song, with idiotic lyrics, sung by *Negroes* . . ."

"Oh, you know it," I said. It threw him off guard, but only for a minute.

"I've listened to it only enough to be qualified to have an opinion, and to criticize it," he said in measured tones.

"Can you hold on a minute? I hear my sister calling me," I lied. "I'll be right back."

"Uh, sure," said old Dwayne, unsuspecting. I laid the receiver down on the rug as the Khachaturian *Gayane* Ballet Suite revolved melodically.

I went out on the back patio of the red brick house and stared east at the darkening lake in the distance. He was pretty square and also ugly, but at least he had a mind. I thought how thrilling it would be if he could open himself up to other cultures, and how important it made me feel to think I might be the instrument of his enlightenment. After about ten minutes, I went back to see how he was doing; to my surprise, he was still on the phone.

"Hi, this is Sonya. I'm back. Are you still there?"

"I'm still here. How come you were gone so long?"

"Well, my sister got in this fight with the housekeeper's twins so I had to go and break it up."

"Oh."

"I'm sorry it took so long," I said.

"Oh, that's all right. Actually, it was quite pleasant listening to the music you had on. I don't think I'm familiar with that piece. Who is the composer?"

"Did you like it?" I said, my voice rising.

"Yes, very much. What is it?"

"Oh, it's ballet music. Let's see, let me check, hmmmm, it's one of those long names, I can't pronounce it. Actually, I've never heard of him, but he composes very good classical music. The lady who owns this house has lots of records in her collection by obscure composers. Maybe I can play another one for you some-time, if you'd like."

"Uh, yes, that would be very nice. I could play you some of mine over the phone, too. I have quite an extensive collection myself."

"OK," I said, in a triumphant flush. At just that moment, the front door slammed and Daddy came storming down the hall. "Turn that goddamned thing off this instant!" he shouted. "I have to go," I told Dwayne hurriedly and hung up, quickly sliding Miss Linden's hot albums under the carpet.

Dinner that evening came to stand out in my mind as one of those times in everyone's life when certain limits are exceeded for the first time, and where one discovers through one's reactions just what those limits were. Daddy had simmered the veal shanks he got from the butcher on credit that evening; Sybil contributed her narrow carrot sticks and six underbaked potatoes. We all sat stiffly, as though waiting for something innocent to set off some-thing terrible, as it usually did. I remember noticing the dark cir-cles under Daddy's eyes as he lifted the meat from the pot and carefully set it out on the plates. And then everything happened very rapidly, things just began slipping, until the whole room seemed to be poised and about to slide off the edge of the world.

It began and ended with Sybil; Daddy was too far gone that night to rise to any bait, but Sybil was wired for action. Her eyes moved restlessly up and down the table, rejecting him, sweeping past Greta and the twins, and finally coming to rest on me. I could sense her warming up for trouble and moving in for the kill. "Who was that boy you were talking to?" she opened, sweetly.

"What boy?" I answered, cautiously. "You mean there's more than one?" she said, incredulously, in a high false voice. "I wouldn't have thought that possible!" I stared down at my plate and picked at my food as nonchalantly as I could, to give the impression I was unconcerned. I could sense Greta and the twins hunched expectantly over their plates, eyes darting, picking up signals. Finally Sybil turned to Daddy. "She doesn't seem to want to answer me," she said. It wasn't hard to imagine the look on his face as he said, "Answer Sybil's question, honey," in a quiet, defeated voice.

"It was the boy across the street, as you could plainly see since you were looking out the window," I said slowly. "We were on the same bus coming home."

"Sonya's got a boyfriend! Sonya's got a boyfriend!" the twins chorused in sing-song whines.

"We were discussing classical music," I said evenly, my face heating up, my other systems alerted.

"You mean those Communist records you've been playing in the living room?" Sybil said, teasingly. Daddy's fork stopped on its path between the plate and his mouth. "Are you listening to Communist records?" he demanded, in a voice that lacked its usual force.

"They're not Communist records!" I said, angering. "They're classical music! Leave me alone!"

"He must be even uglier close up than he looks from a distance," Sybil said quickly, changing ground. I was caught off guard and found myself leaping to his defense on the matter of looks, when in fact he did look pretty bad up close. "He is not!" I said. "How would you know if he's ugly, you haven't even seen him, except from the window." It was a mistake to discuss him, it was a mistake to answer at all. It was as though I had no mind or will of my own, but was being carried along by some force generated by the power of Sybil's malice; it was as though she had orchestrated everything in advance, and I, all of us, were just responding automatically to her direction. It gave her the opening she was waiting for, and she responded triumphantly.

134

"Well, he must be pretty bad if he has to waste his time with you."

There probably was a lapse of some seconds, but I don't remember it. I remember burning with a kind of black heat which affected my vision; I could only see out the sides. I don't remember leaving the table, only retrieving Miss Linden's records from under the carpet. I don't remember putting on a coat, only lifting Daddy's car keys off the table in the hall and running out the front door. I remember nothing after that until I came to, somewhere on Route 10, traveling east. I remember knowing then that I was going to cross the mountains and keep going on the other side. I remember knowing then that if I had come that far, I must be running away. It seemed like such an awesome commitment, I began to cry. The old Ford trembled and shook as it plowed on through the night. By the time I reached Ellensburg, Washington, nearly three hours later, I also knew I had no money. I knew I would have to go back home.

Crossing the mountains again was hard. I had never experienced enormous trucks bearing down on me suddenly out of the blackness; never before felt the urgency of their weight, or the terrors of the open road. It was close to midnight. I knew that I had solved nothing by leaving, and that returning would bring not only more of the same kind of pain, but probably also a new sense of shame—for having run off and made the pain explicit. I felt I couldn't live another day with Sybil in the house; and yet I knew, in some unclarified way, of Daddy's financial dependence on her. It didn't seem to matter if I drove east or west, there was no direction that offered a way out. On the descent, just after crossing the summit, I deliberately let the car coast. I remember imagining what it would be like when it finally went out of control: it would leave the road entirely and plunge into space. It would sail through the blackness and disappear. It seemed all right, painless even, because I was, myself, blackness. The falling would be quiet; everything would merge, and nothing would ever hurt again. But as the car picked up speed, the records suddenly starting sliding off the seat beside me and when I reached out a hand to stop them, it was like touching Miss Linden—not her, exactly, but some recollection of her. The thought went through my mind: *Miss Linden cares,* and that knowledge brought my foot onto the brake, and slowed the car to a normal speed. When I finally pulled up in front of the red brick house, all the lights were out. But in one of the upstairs windows I saw a hand holding the curtain back; and behind the hand, Daddy's face straining out, as though keeping a vigil there in the dark.

*I*n the autumn there is a new English teacher at the Edgemont School whose manner and example inspire Sonya to write poetry for the first time. Berta Nordstrom is very clear about her favorite poets; she doesn't mince around. At every opportunity, each of which is self-created, she reads aloud from her worn collections: Whitman, Frost, Millay, Robinson, Dickinson, Emerson, even Poe. Her silver bracelets jingle as she lowers the book from time to time for emphasis, and looks around the room. Her gray, upswept braids stand atop her head like a kind of halo—solid, even imposing, but something one could believe in. The class is divided: some fidget, others doze. But the sonorous tones of her voice penetrate Sonya's long sleep. Startled by the familiarity of works she already knows but has never heard aloud, her mind begins to stir. There is something in the spoken voice that releases rhythms, depths and meanings that have escaped her on the printed page; something in those resounding overtones that haunt the ear long after the recitation ends.

At home, she finds that if she eats dinner quickly and locks herself in her room, she can avoid most of the chaos which attends the evening meal. Night after night she locks herself in and writes poems. When Greta knocks on her door, wanting an ally or seeking escape herself, Sonya says firmly, "I'm studying."

When Ray responds to Greta's tears and raps on Sonya's door with his knuckles asking why she shut her sister out, she repeats that she is studying. This change so takes him by surprise, there is a momentary silence; then she hears him through the locked door, whispering earnestly to the sniveling Greta that Sonya has big things on her mind and mustn't be disturbed. It is one of her most important discoveries, and she is so impressed with the sense of autonomy which accompanies it that she rearranges all the rented furniture in her room in a bold attempt to stake out some claim of her own. Late at night she copies by hand a poem from a book that Berta Nordstrom has loaned her. She sees it as a warning, with implications for her. She promises herself that she will put its message into practice, just as soon as she escapes from Ray.

George Gray

> I have studied many times
> The marble which was chiseled for me—
> A boat with a furled sail at rest in a harbor.
> In truth it pictures not my destination
> But my life.
> For love was offered me and I shrank from its
>   disillusionment;
> Sorrow knocked at my door, but I was afraid;
> Ambition called to me, but I dreaded the chances.
> Yet all the while I hungered for meaning in my life.
> And now I know that we must lift the sail
> And catch the winds of destiny
> Wherever they drive the boat.
> To put meaning in one's life may end in madness,
> But life without meaning is the torture
> Of restlessness and vague desire—
> It is a boat longing for the sea and yet afraid.

In time, Sonya finds the courage to show Miss Nordstrom the poems she has labored on at night. They all have a single theme, death, but she doesn't see this at first, and Berta Nordstrom doesn't point it out. She simply praises where it is due, and makes suggestions when she thinks they are in order. By Christmas vacation Sonya has completed enough poems to fill a small notebook, which she gives to Miss Nordstrom on the last day before the holidays. "This is for you, for Christmas," she explains, catching Miss Nordstrom just as she is tucking her many volumes inside a well-worn briefcase and slipping her arms into the sleeves of her coat. She looks up in surprise; it takes her a few minutes to understand. She reaches inside her purse and withdraws her glasses. Carefully, she holds the notebook open across the palm of one hand while turning its pages slowly with the other. "My dear child," she finally says, looking up, "this is a magnificent gift. I shall treasure it always, you may be sure."

ᛉ *Berta Nordstrom* ᛉ

A week before Christmas, Miss Nordstrom invited Margaret and me to her house for dinner. I felt very privileged having a legitimate reason to turn my back on Daddy, Sybil, Greta and the twins and walk out of the house. At first I thought Miss Nordstrom might favor us because we were the only ones who didn't sleep or twitch when she read poetry in class; later it occurred to me that she might find us special because we were able to use what she had to give. Margaret's poems were exclusively about horses, and mine were all about things dying before their time. Our writing had to be done in the strictest secrecy because if Cricket, Puckie, and the others ever knew, it would be all over the school in fifteen minutes and we would be worse outcasts than we already were. But aside from those hazards, it was exhilarating to feel the thrill of creation, to know that it was possible to turn the misery of life into some form of art. And strangely enough, being able to do that also became a means of enduring life itself.

As I drove the Ford across town, I had my first intimation of a destiny outside my present time.

Miss Nordstrom met us at the door and ushered us into her warmly lit living room as though we were honored guests. I suppose, in a way, we were. A fire burned brightly in the fireplace, and everywhere was loving evidence of her native Norway: painted chests, candlesticks, pictures on the wall. Two entire walls were lined with books, and the smell of pine and fir and spruce boughs filled the air. As we admired the framed etching of Brahms which hung above her small piano, she said, "I would love to offer you a glass of sherry, but you understand why I can't." We assured her that we did, indeed, understand the absurd restrictions on her generosity, and accepted apple cider instead.

Over a carefully prepared dinner, we discussed topics which were impossible to explore with anyone else, either at home or among our classmates. We compared poets and styles; we admired the art that covered her dining room walls; we exchanged favorite composers and favorite compositions. The most daring point in the evening came when Margaret described how her mother had cried over Nixon's Checkers speech. "Oh, that dreadful man!" Miss Nordstrom burst out, in spite of herself. "Imagine manipulating people's emotions like that!" She was taking a big risk talking politics with two students from Edgemont; teachers elsewhere had been fired for less—for just being suspected of holding dangerous opinions. I listened quietly and never let on that Nixon had manipulated my emotions, too. I had been out driving in the Ford, twisting the dial and trying to get the Top Ten, when all of a sudden there he was in the middle of the speech, and before I could change the station, his voice was breaking. I drove on transfixed.

It was after eleven when I got back home and I was so stimulated I couldn't sleep. What did Daddy know about culture and refinement? All he did was rant and rave and tell us to be honest while he told whopping lies to everyone. Miss Nordstrom was the real thing. I locked my door and pulled my copy of Millay's poems from under the bed. Daddy had told me to get rid of it

139

weeks ago, saying, "She had a terrible reputation! There was nothing refined about her in the least. She burned her candle at both ends."

"What do you mean, she burned her candle at both ends?"

"Never mind, it means she was a tramp. You take that book back to wherever you got it or I'll throw it in the gutter where it belongs."

I sat there on the floor, searching for the poem where she does it. Around midnight, I felt an enormous restlessness come over me, intense longings, all unfocused, demanding a dramatic conclusion. I tiptoed down to the kitchen and withdrew a white candle from one of the bottom drawers. Returning, I locked myself in again and switched off the light. I went over to the window and threw it open. The moon was riding high in the sky. Dark clouds raced across its face so that its pale light alternately shone, then was rubbed out. The curtains fluttered dramatically in the wind. I sat down at my little desk and picked the wax off the end of the candle so the wick there could be lit, then ritualistically lit both ends. My heart was racing; what a wonderful, unusual thing to do! Only someone imaginative, like a poet or a rebel, would have conceived of it. Then suddenly a gust of wind invaded the room, fanning the flames at both ends and splattering hot wax all over my hand. I dropped the candle unesthetically on the floor. This natural disaster brought an abrupt end to my attempt to emulate Millay, but I continued to sit at the little desk each night, with the moon over my shoulder, seeking written form for my feelings and trying to validate Miss Nordstrom's prediction that I would be a poet someday.

🦋 *The Summons* 🦋

It was a Saturday afternoon and Sybil was downtown again shopping with the twins. Greta had an overnight at Missy Dugan's house on the other side of town. Daddy was hunched over the dining room table, under the sixty-watt bulbs, making minute notations with a ballpoint pen on half a dozen maps he had spread out before him, and I was curled up on the living room couch with all the doors shut, listening to the Shostakovich Fifth Symphony and reading *Silver Screen* magazine. Doris Day was having love problems, but on the other hand, she'd gotten her big break. I read with interest that she was still a Christian Scientist; maybe being on the road all the time singing in those bands prevented you from achieving the kind of quiet contemplation you needed in order to see through deceptions and come to your own conclusions. I was just tearing open the wrapper on another Mounds bar when the doorbell rang. Within seconds Daddy was opening the living room doors and motioning for me with his index finger.

"Honey," he whispered urgently, "there is someone at the door for Daddy, and I can't talk to him now. You go and answer it and tell him your daddy isn't home. Say he's up in the mountains and you don't know when he'll be back. Go on, honey, do what Daddy asks you. Don't give me that look! Daddy wouldn't ask you to do something unless it was necessary. There are some papers that this man needs and Daddy hasn't had time to prepare them, that's all. Come on, for Christ's sake! Get off that goddamned couch and answer the door. Tell him I'm up in the mountains. And act natural."

The doorbell pealed for the third time. Giving Daddy my most contemptuous look, I struggled to rise. If he didn't have the papers ready, why couldn't he tell him himself?

"I'll be down in the basement; you let me know when he's gone," Daddy whispered as he slithered down the hall, beating a fast retreat.

I opened the door and a large, heavyset man asked, "Is this the residence of Raymond Weiler?" I swallowed and said, "Yes."

"I'd like to talk with him a minute," he said politely. He was dressed very neatly in a business suit and tie.

"He's not here," I said, barely audible.

"Oh, I am sorry . . . I was hoping to find him here. I'm very anxious to give him these papers."

141

"I could give them to him when he comes back from the mountains," I offered.

"I'm sorry, we can't do that. I have to serve, ah, ahem, ahem, I have to give these to him personally, but it's kind of you to offer. You say he's in the mountains? When do you expect him back?"

"Oh, maybe in a few days, maybe in a week," I said, my mind drifting. I could tell he didn't believe a word I said. I was afraid he would say, "I'm sorry, miss, but we have to break down the door and search the house." I was afraid he was going to pull something out of his vest and flash it in my face like they did in the movies, elbow past me, and find Daddy cowering in the basement like a cornered rat.

He finally left, and Daddy crawled out of the basement. I went back to my movie magazines but I couldn't concentrate anymore. Not even James Dean helped this time. As I ran my fingers over his brooding profile, trying to stimulate my interest, I heard the sound of breaking glassware in the kitchen. By evening, when Sybil, the twins and Greta had all returned, Daddy was so drunk he was misjudging doorways and walking into the walls. I knew that something was wrong, but I wasn't sure if it was their fault or his. I suspected, from the circumstances, that it was his but I couldn't stand to think of him in that larger sense of being bad. It was one thing for me to have my personal differences with him; another thing for him to be guilty of wrongdoing in the world at large. I felt ashamed of him, then felt it was wrong to feel ashamed when I had no concrete evidence. I felt the fear one feels toward outside authority, but he kept telling me there was nothing to fear. "Aw, shit, honey! You don't have to be afraid of those goddamned sons of bitches! They couldn't hurt anyone if they tried." My feelings were so confused I couldn't even put them in a poem.

Daddy continued drinking all day Sunday and by five o'clock had completely passed out in the wing chair in the living room, where he listed in a half-slouch, snoring loudly. I tried to wake him around ten to get him to bed but he swung his arm out wildly, as though waving away an insect, and fell back into a stupor. He was still slouched there the next morning when I came downstairs to make my lunch for school. I thought he had died; his face had no color, and his mouth hung open lifelessly. It was such a shock to see him like that, I turned cold all over, even though my heart was beating fast. I was afraid to shake him because if it was true that he was dead, I didn't want to be the first to know. I felt very cowardly about that. I decided to go into the kitchen and make as much noise as possible while getting breakfast for Greta and the twins; and if that didn't rouse him, then I'd wake Sybil and let her deal with the body. I worked hard not to think about what would happen to us if he were dead.

I rattled and banged, and soon it had its desired effect: Daddy came weaving into the kitchen, a look of utter confusion on his face; he didn't even have the energy to scream at us, but staggered out again and climbed the stairs to his room. I put the twins on their bus, and Greta and I had to run for ours and just barely made it.

In class, it was just like fifth grade again: I stared out the window and didn't hear a thing the teachers said, not even Miss Nordstrom. For the first time, I failed to hear her words, although I was aware of the beat of her voice in the background—an undertone, barely perceived, like the rhythm section of a band. I didn't even hear the bell when it rang, or the chairs being scraped back or the thundering stampede of everyone leaving the room. I sat in my chair, looking out the window but not seeing. My first awareness was when Miss Nordstrom came over and placed herself directly in my line of vision. She took my face between her hands and said, "There is an old saying, and I want you to remember it: 'This, too, shall pass.' " Her hands were like silk, and her voice was rich and clear, her eyes steady. It seemed amazing to me that she, too, could know things without actually having all the details; that she could understand my feelings, if not my life, without my having to spell them out. It was the second time that year that I had an intimation of a time beyond the present, and a life beyond the red brick house. The things Miss Nordstrom and Miss Linden taught me, their belief in me, their particular love, made it possible to imagine myself transcendent: creating new worlds and surviving alone. When the day arrived that I had to

143

think specifically about my future, it was Miss Nordstrom who insisted I apply to college; alone, I would never have thought it possible. When the time actually came to apply, I picked one college—as far away as I could imagine at the time—in California, and Miss Nordstrom and Miss Linden wrote letters of recommendation. I was relieved the application required only two, because there was no one else I could have asked.

Miss Nordstrom brought a book to school the next day which she passed on to me, saying, "I want you to read this." It was by Hugh Walpole and its title was *Fortitude.* Its first sentence read, " 'Tisn't life that matters. 'Tis the courage you bring to it." I knew that it was a message that was being passed to me, not just a book; it was a code, which she expected me to decipher in my own time and in my own way.

Every evening Raymond Weiler paces the floor, his hands behind his back, chanting of conspiracies. When the pitch of his voice becomes too high, or the tone too threatening, Sonya slips out the back door and takes refuge in the Ford. Greta Weiler spends more and more time at Missy Dugan's on the other side of town. Missy's mother is just like the mother she has never known: she is always there when the girls come home from school, whipping up something good for them to eat. She welcomes Greta warmly and always invites her to spend the night. She treats Greta just like one of her own daughters. It is peaceful and civilized at the Dugans'; they have white wall-to-wall carpets in every room in the house. Missy is just like the sister Greta always wanted and never had; Sonya is too old, too bossy. In time, Greta spends more of her days at the Dugans' than at the red brick house. Once, Ray phoned to ask, "What's going on here?" Mrs. Dugan assured him it was no trouble having Greta; the girls are inseparable, she told him; you'd think they were twins! "Well," he concedes, "that's just wonderful. If my little Greta wants to be with your little Missy, who am I to stop her?"

⚘ Mt. Rainier ⚘

The setting sun was casting its last light on the eastern peaks as I steered the Ford out of the driveway. I could see the long shadows that defined their ridges and breaks, even from this distance. They were a deep purple, almost black, and the snow on top was the lightest shade of pink. The atmosphere was hazy, as always—as though a wall of particles, illuminated by the dying sun, surrounded and guarded these mountains, setting them apart from everything else on earth. Rising far above the others was Mt. Rainier. It hung suspended in those strange mists that ring this city like a border, or an embrace. I could see it riding that sea of blue air, hovering like an astral body: sacred, constant, a thing to trust. It had been there for me since my first memories of landscape; it dominated and blessed this place like a parent or a god, its divinity an unquestioned thing. It could be dangerous, driving, because there was about that mountain something that compelled worship; its presence was hypnotic, it had that power. I could lean out the window in the south bedroom of Mrs. Ramsey's red brick house and stare at it for hours.

When the light faded, and the mountain gradually disappeared and was absorbed back into its surroundings, I turned the Ford around and headed in the opposite direction. The car was like some hungry thing as it lunged through the blue-black night. The moon hung half-eaten in the west. I flipped on the radio and twisted the dial, but nothing held my interest, nothing seemed to satisfy. I knew I had to stay out until Daddy had chanted himself to sleep, and that would be another two or three hours. I drove

145

past Miss Nordstrom's wood frame house, past Miss Linden's brick apartment, even Mr. Wendell's crummy old chapel, but all their places were dark. I began to wonder strange things, in particular whether happiness would ever be a possibility for me, or whether it was reserved for people with living parents, paid-for houses, and, possibly, more deserving hearts.

🐦 Waiting on the Corner 🐦

When Daddy asked me to meet him downtown after school, I should have been suspicious; sometimes I think I'll never learn. "Honey," he said, "Daddy has an appointment today in that area; I might as well give you a ride home. If you can avoid taking the bus, why not?" "That area" was the corner of Frederick's; everyone waited for someone there. "Meet me at the corner of Frederick's" meant one corner only, the one in front, near the main entrance.

I had been waiting there in the rain for an hour and a half, and he hadn't shown yet. I kept squinting through the sleet, my eyes peeled for the Ford. All the kids from school had come and gone. They always met their mothers there, for a quick soda, or a quick cashmere sweater, before running back to the underground garage where their Cadillacs purred silently, waiting to take them home. I passed through every emotion, from that first inkling that someone hasn't come, moving quickly to the fear that they won't come, and finally the terror that they may never come again—with its attendant ruminating about where that leaves you. I was angry, then worried, then frightened to death. Sometimes these feelings repeated themselves, and sometimes they merged into one. I don't know why I didn't just give up and go home on the bus. There was something about his instructions that kept me rooted to the spot. "I'll pick you up at three-thirty sharp. You *be* there," he had said. It wasn't the first time he had said he'd be somewhere or do something and had failed, but it was the longest and the most upsetting.

I stood first on one foot, then on the other. There seemed to be something about me then which was incapable of standing on both feet at once, with my weight evenly balanced. I carried a stack of books which I rested on alternate hips. I was shivering after the first half hour but was afraid to go inside for fear I'd miss the car. There were so many people going in and out the doors, I couldn't see the road from the inside. My coat and hair were soaked and by the end of the first hour, I was sure that something had happened to him; yet, in some magical way, I believed that if I stayed right where I was he would eventually come through. He always had. As I was debating this in my mind, Miss Nordstrom came bustling out through the swinging doors and stopped to say hello. "What are you doing outside in this rain?" she asked. It was after five by now, and already dark. I tried to be as nonchalant as I could when I said I was waiting for my father. It seemed very important to speak naturally and to stand in an unpathetic way. It was as though if I acknowledged—to her, or to myself— that anything unusual was happening or that I was afraid, that admission would make my worst fears come true and I would never see Daddy again. And that would make me an orphan, and everyone knew what happened to them. As I stood there talking with Miss Nordstrom, everything depended on holding myself in check. One false move and the dam would break; and I would cry out that I wanted to go home with her, where it was quiet and warm and civilized. One false move and I might say, "I want to be your child," and that was unthinkable, even though it was true.

At six o'clock Daddy came weaving up the rain-slicked sidewalk and took my arm just under the elbow. By then I had frozen into a permanent form and was rooted to the pavement outside Frederick's now closed main entrance. "Oh, honey," he murmured, his whiskey breath making little clouds in the chill night air. "Your daddy is sorry to have kept his precious darling waiting for so long, but when he tells you what he's been through, you'll understand." Together we walked the six or eight blocks to

147

the gas station where the Ford rested in battered innocence. On the way home I tried to listen as he droned on, but it just wasn't possible. I found that if I concentrated on the patterns the lights made through the steam on the windows, it transported me into another world—one where his voice was just one more line of sound in a background of swirling color and undifferentiated noise. Dimly, I remember concluding that he'd been in a tavern somewhere, drinking; it was the logical assumption to make. His explanations made no sense at all, filled as they were with conspiracies that simply couldn't have taken place in downtown Seattle on a weekday afternoon. He kept repeating that he would never leave his baby out in the cold, meaning me, and while his tone was soothing, the evidence said otherwise. I turned the car heater to HI and leaned against the door and fell asleep.

🐞 *Glandular Fever* 🐞

It seemed like just a cold at first; but by the fourth day my fever was still high, so Daddy concluded it was flu. He brought home seven movie magazines to get me through the siege. At the end of the week my glands were so swollen it was an effort to breathe. For the first time in my life I thought I was going to die—just like Mother, wasting away in bed while he dashed around trying to be useful. I couldn't tell him that because I was still governed by magical taboos, the worst of which was that to *think* something was to make it happen. To speak of it would seal your fate for sure.

When my skin turned yellow and I began to fight for every breath, Daddy finally mobilized himself to face the crisis. Now that Mrs. Hoyt was dead, it fell to him to plow through reams of Scripture by himself and hope for the best. It took him a while to locate the Bible, but he finally settled on my bed and began to read aloud. At one point I was certain my throat was closing for good, and I begged him to call a doctor. That's what Cricket

Spaulding's mother did when she had glandular fever, and she was back in school in five days, I pleaded in a terrified whisper.

No, Daddy insisted; this was not "glandular fever" and I didn't need a shot. It was a touch of evil and would respond to positive thought, if not God's perfect love. He cleared his throat and continued reading. As I lay there, I tried to let the tone of his voice comfort me, the way it had when I was small. It isn't hard to banish reason from your mind when you're burning up inside and not much air is getting in. I drifted in and out of consciousness as he droned on and, as he was my last and only hope, believed in him again.

When his voice gave out, he simply sat there stroking my face, as though—if he kept watch long enough—the thing in me would give up. He brought me water, helped me sit, wrung cool cloths and stayed by me all night. In the morning, his face was gray with strain but his hand was still holding mine. I saw that I was still alive and that the swelling had gone down, although my skin was still yellow. "That will go away in time, honey," he assured me, and in time it did.

❧ *The Letter* ❧

The day I received the letter informing me of my acceptance to college, it was as though my own ship had come in. It was after school and I was so excited I showed it to Sybil because she was the only one around; I was that desperate to tell someone the news. She read it quickly with her mouth twisted in a sneer, and said, "What kind of college would want you?" I told Daddy about it as soon as he came in the door two hours later. That was a mistake, too. He immediately launched into one of his frequent states, in which he would rant, first on the subject at hand, then on all manner of wild, disconnected things, often for hours. His basic style was to pace the floor and rant against all the wops, kikes, dagos, niggers, sheenies, spics and pinkos who always

149

lurked in the poorly lit corners of his mind. They were all cock-suckers to him. They had never heard of culture and refinement.

"Oh, Jesus Christ, honey. You don't know what you're talking about. You're too *young* to know. Your daddy knows about *college*." He spit the word out, as though ridding himself of some poison. "Your daddy knows about *professors*. Those nincompoops will try to teach you all kinds of Communist ideology and warp your mind. I know, don't think I don't know; I've been around. Those pinko intellectuals will distort your values and do everything in their power to turn your head around and ruin everything that I, and all decent, upstanding Americans like your daddy, hold precious . . ."

"The only way you can stop me from going is to kill me," I shouted in desperation, tears streaming down my face. They were the first words spoken as a free person. Their effect on him was instantaneous: he stopped cold. You could see the wheels turning in his mind, calculating how he was going to handle this unexpected obstruction. He ran his fingers back and forth over his evening stubble, and finally said, "Well, precious darling, since you feel that strongly about it, who is Daddy to try to stop you?" His capitulation went to my head. I was openly defiant from then on, saying things like, "How dare you accuse me of smoking?" and leaving the car ashtray heaped with butts.

✦

*J*une brings the Senior Prom. Sonya knows she won't go; the reason is simple: misfits don't go to proms. She doesn't even mourn this loss, but accepts it as natural. However, it turns out that someone, she never does find out who, feels it is important that the senior class turn out for this event 100 percent. Therefore it is suggested that she buy a formal. It is not suggested, but implicitly understood, that she will just have to go crazy trying to figure out someone to ask to accompany her to the Senior Prom. In desperation she calls Dwayne; they haven't seen much of each other in the past year or two, but they have continued to play occasional records back and forth over the phone. Under her indoctrination, he has been exposed to Kabalevsky and Rachmaninoff, in addition to the Khachaturian; she is saving Shostakovich for last because he will be the acid test. "The Senior *Prom*? How can you even *think* of asking me to suffer through four hours of *band* music?" Dwayne asks incredulously. "I wouldn't do it if I didn't have to go myself," Sonya explains. "No *thanks*. Call me again when you've come to your senses." Because she attends a girls' school, and because she has lived in six different neighborhoods since coming of age, Sonya doesn't know any other boys she could ask. She finally confides her dilemma to Margaret, whose brother, Nick, is pressed into service at the last minute.

The dance floor has been sprinkled with Ivory Flakes to make their feet slide. Her new strapless formal (the purchase of which has cost her a three-day marathon with Ray, who after a last-minute phone call from Margaret's mother finally relented and forked over the "asinine" sum of $27.98) won't stay up. Her palms sweat; she thinks Margaret's brother's attitude is unnecessarily self-sacrificing. For the obligatory four hours, she wraps her arm around Nick's self-sacrificing shoulder and holds his self-sacrificing hand as they bump into her classmates and their partners on the Ivory-flaked floor. Around nine o'clock, a strange boy cuts in while Sonya and Nick are attempting to dance. Sonya's immediate reaction is shock: why would anyone want to cut in for her? It's probably someone doing it on a dare; afterwards, they will all huddle in the corner and laugh their guts out. It is hard to believe, but he stays with her for two dances. He says he's with her classmate, Della, who, if such a thing is possible, is one split hair less popular than Sonya. Not only does he stay with her for two dances, he holds her close and has an erection. It will take her years to understand her mixed reaction: shock, fear, triumph, desire. She wants to hold on to him, to bury herself in him, but doesn't; he belongs to someone else. When the second dance ends he even thanks her, then plunges back through the

151

tulle and satin mass of Edgemont girls to reclaim Della in a far corner of the rented hall. They did not exchange names; only "morons" would do that.

When the prom is over, Nick and Sonya drive to the Rucklehaus mansion in Windermere, where a post-prom, pre-breakfast party is supposed to be in progress. Sonya is tired; her feet hurt. Nick guns his father's Cadillac up the Rucklehaus drive, then swings it around and pulls it over in the trees. He switches off the ignition with a dramatic flick of his wrist and reaches under the seat, pulling out a long brown paper bag. He unscrews the cap on the bottle inside, throws back his head, and gulps. Coming up for air, he wipes his dripping mouth on the back of his arm and releases a dramatic "Aaaaah!" Sonya stares in fear: he is going to get drunk and then he will get violent; or if he doesn't get violent, he will make advances, which she doesn't want. Or maybe he will throw up, or if he doesn't throw up, he will pass out, like Ray. Drunks are unpredictable and frightening; nothing you think of to do ever works. Nick becomes aware that she is staring at him and shyly sticks the bottle in her face. "Sorry; want some?" he asks, thickly. "Uh, no, thanks. Let's go in to the party." "Nah, we got lots of time, lots of time." Nick settles down in the driver's seat and takes another long pull on the bottle. The fumes are making Sonya sick. She wants to go home but she can't ask Nick to take her before he's ready; she owes him a lot for just agreeing to be her escort to the prom. Other cars begin to clog the drive, and finally she gets up the courage to join a group of classmates heading for the house. "I have to go to the bathroom," she tells Nick, shutting the car door. He nods his head in an exaggerated way; "Yeh, sure, yeh, sure," he says, unconcerned.

Sonya opens the big oak door and steps over the threshold. Everywhere, as far as the eye can see, are classmates and strangers, sprawled the length and breadth of the Rucklehauses' champagne wall-to-wall carpeting: smoking, drinking, making out, and sleeping. It is three in the morning; the giant house is cold and quiet. No one raises a voice above a whisper; there is no music. Sonya wades through the sea of sluglike **under**water

152

bodies, looking for Margaret. Icy crystal shards gleam harshly from the ceiling chandeliers. The vast circular stairway is aswarm with twisted flesh. The girls whose dates have passed out are poised there on the lower steps, staring into space. She takes her place beside the blank starers and waits for Nick to come in and offer to take her home. At four o'clock he staggers in the door and trips his way over the fallen bodies. "Hey. Where ya been? Ya wanna go home, already?" "Oh, that's really nice of you to offer, Nick. That's just what I want to do."

Driving back to the other side of town, Sonya holds her breath as the car weaves from side to side. The roads are deserted: the worst thing that could happen is that they would plunge into the lake, and it is shallow around the edges. That is the worst that could happen, as long as they don't plow into a tree. For the first time she is relieved to be returning to the familiarity of the red brick house. As he pulls up in front she thanks Nick profusely for whatever pain and inconvenience his forced service has caused him. He sits with his left arm draped over the steering wheel and says "Yeh" about five or six times, while nodding his head. He doesn't get out of the car to escort her to the door, which is just as well because, as she shuts the car door and starts up the steps, her attention is caught by a quick motion in the upstairs window: Ray, again, watching to make sure no wop son-of-a-bitch takes advantage of his daughter. As she unlocks the front door, she turns to wave at Nick but he has already blasted off in a cloud of upper-class exhaust. As she climbs the stairs to her room she hears Ray's bedroom door quietly snap shut. She suppresses the urge to scream: Why were you watching me? What were you afraid of?

❦ *Raunchy Riffs* ❧

The week before graduation, Puckie Pruitt threw a slumber party for the senior class. It was held at her grandmother's Windermere estate on Lake Washington. The children's two-story outdoor playhouse on the north lawn was larger than the apartment where I spent my first eight years of life.

"What kind of horse manure is this—a *slumber* party?" Daddy had inquired the week before. I stared at my loafers with the coins in the slots as Bill Haley and the Comets blasted out "Rock Around the Clock" from the console radio. I bent over and rerolled the cuffs of my jeans three or four times in order to maintain control. I knew it was just a matter of time before he threatened to destroy the radio. "Turn that goddamned boogie-woogie off this minute before I tear the radio out of the wall!" he yelled, biding his time as he tried to decide whether to go for the slumber party directly, or to detour for another attack on my listening habits. He must have been bushed that night because he launched into the slumber party the minute the radio went dead. He didn't say it in so many words, but it was clear that this represented something that had been cute at one time: camping out on the living room rug with someone's parents telling us when the giggling had to stop. But now it was out of control; this time, he knew, we would rock around the clock, and there was nothing he could do.

When Mrs. Pruitt patiently explained the genteel nature of this particular slumber party, he relented. The party *was* genteel the first three or four hours. The Pruitt wisteria was in full bloom and dripping from the balconies; sixteen Hudson Bay blankets warmed the scattered mattresses erupting the length of the polished recreation room floor. The giant room in the mansion's depths resonated with nothing more disturbing than the strains of the Top Ten—to which some Edgemont seniors listlessly sang along ("Sh-Boom, Sh-Boom, ya dada-dadada-dadada-da") between drags on their Viceroy cigarettes. But around one in the morning, after the Pruitts had retired three floors above us, someone unlatched the French doors and ushered in four boyfriends, a fifth of Scotch, and an Earl Bostic album.

The boyfriends put the needle in the groove and settled in with Wendy, Trish, Puckie and Cricket to share the Scotch; the rest of us lingered on the periphery, squinting through the smoke. "That's the ugliest music I've ever heard," I whispered to Margaret, who was leaning against the knotty pine wall rolling her hair in pink plastic curlers. It seemed there was no middle ground between noise like this and the banalities of Patti Page singing "How Much Is That Doggie in the Window?" They drove me back to the classics, time after time.

"Yeah," she nodded weakly; it was two in the morning. We dragged our blankets into the butler's pantry on the floor above, but Earl Bostic's saxophone followed through the ceiling. By the album's third or fourth play, I reluctantly began to embrace in it something that I saw was also in me. It seemed so foreign and abrasive, as Shostakovich had before it; but as the strains of "Harlem Nocturne" pierced the silence of the Pruitt estate, I recognized those moments in the music where it, and I, corresponded. I fell asleep with those raunchy riffs reaching places in me I'd never known were there.

ᛉ Graduation ᛉ

My graduation from Edgemont had a profound effect on Daddy. After all his years of sacrifice and hasty shuffling, here I was at last: wobbling down the auditorium aisle in three-inch heels and a white robe, with one dozen red roses eating into my hands and a white tassel blinding my vision—one of the chosen. It was the only time I had ever seen him speechless. He sat silently next to Nona and stared straight ahead, sober in every vein for this incredible achievement: twenty-seven reprimands in eleven years; the bottom third of my class; and Mother's dream fulfilled—an Edgemont Girl.

After the ceremonies, the graduating class gathered in a receiving line to endure the best wishes of the assembled parents and friends. They descended on us in an endless procession of sharkskin, perfume, mink and pearls, then floated past. There were no tears; tears would have been an impropriety. There was hysterical gaiety on the part of the highly polished mothers, and sober pride on the part of the distinguished fathers. Until Daddy and Nona came down the line. Nona, in her old cloth coat, smelling of Yardley's English Lavender, fresh off the island. There is no way a successful commingling of Yardley's English Lavender and Chanel No. 5 can be achieved. All the women in the line knew this instinctively. I had just learned, and it came as a shock. They were too cultured and refined to look down on anyone, but it was written in a hundred invisible messages; it bounced off sleek hairdos and filtered into every corner of the room. I grappled with my love for Nona, and my wish to see her disappear.

Daddy committed the unforgivable act: his eyes filled with tears just as he reached my place in the line. They weren't even crocodile tears; they were real. He was thinking of Mother and wishing she could see me standing there with my red roses. I looked everywhere, and at everyone but him. I smiled at the person to his left; I smiled at the person who came after him. He would not move on. He just stood there facing me, holding up the whole line, drenching me in his terrible tears. I knew what he wanted from me, I knew his terms. Acknowledge me! said his eyes. Show your gratitude and cry! Let me know it was worth the price! I held my smile in place, right to the end.

❧

*T*he summer Sonya graduates from high school is hard for Greta. Sybil has packed her bags and moved the twins to the other side of town, and Ray doesn't have the energy to hire another house-keeper for the summer; why should he, as long as Sonya has nothing to do. Let her earn her keep, since she's abandoning them in the fall. The Three Little Weilers will be no more, he says to her one evening at dinner. What will little Greta do without her big sister to take care of her? Sonya stares at her fork and says nothing. This too shall pass. *We must lift the sail/And catch the winds of destiny/Wherever they drive the boat.*

"Did you hear what I said? I said: 'How will little Greta manage without her big sister to take care of her?' Her little heart will break!" Ray hisses. Greta eats quietly across the table; she says nothing. *It isn't life that matters, but the courage we bring to it.* Sonya struggles to keep her feelings under control; later she will drive around the lake with the radio on and the window down. Frank Sinatra is singing "Don't Blame Me." By midnight she knows she can go home. Ray will have passed out and she, too, will sleep: certain in the knowledge that she has made the right decision, Greta's broken heart notwithstanding. She cannot afford to think of Greta or she will not survive. She will take her swimming every day, though, and buy her new clothes for school in the fall, although they won't look right on her: Greta's hair is stringy and untended, and giant unhealed scabs fester on her knees. Sonya feels responsible; then sorry; then finally refuses to look at all. This is not her child; just some stranger who has grown into something unexpected and overwhelming. She shuts the door to her room and counts the days until September.

❧ The Roomette ❧

There was a big scene in the train station the morning I left. Daddy had purchased me a "roomette." "I don't want it!" I screamed. "My friends are in coach!" Did I think he was crazy, he said, that he would let *his* daughter go off to college sitting up all night in coach like some bum? "The issue is settled; you will sleep in the roomette." Did I think he was on welfare, like those other slob fathers, letting their daughters sit up all night, in chairs, on a filthy train? I tried to explain that I wanted to sit up all night, with the others in coach, to watch strange things flashing in the night, on the way to somewhere. He calls me an ingrate.

In order to drive his point home he insisted on accompanying me on the train, car by car, back to my roomette. I guess he wanted to see what his fifty dollars had purchased. "Ah, see, honey; this is so much nicer than those stinking coach seats," he said. I sat down, sullen but obedient, waiting for him to get off the train so I could join the others in coach and sit up all night, thinking: Who needs his corrupt old roomette. "I think the train is going to start," I said. I wanted to avoid the inevitable emotional scene. I also had a momentary flash that the train might start, and he would end up at college with me.

"No dear, we still have three minutes left," he said, pulling a little package out of his pocket and holding it out to me. It contained a pair of earrings with artificial stones. He had bought them at the magazine stand while I stood in line. I didn't want the earrings either. They lay there heavily in my lap like something precious that I should be touched by. A terrible wave of sadness came over me; I hadn't wanted to be touched by anything he did.

"They're beautiful, Daddy. They're just what I needed." Two more minutes.

"You're welcome, sweetheart; it was Daddy's pleasure." Now it was time for the fumbling, the promises to write, the kisses. There were tears in his eyes as he turned to leave. I don't know if I was patting him on the back or pushing him out of the roomette

158

as the conductor called "All aboard." We didn't wave because the roomette was on the opposite side of the train from the station. I was grateful for that.

❧ *Letters Home* ❧

Dear Daddy,
The controller called me into his office today to say my tuition hasn't been paid and he has had no answer from you. Did you get his letters? I am working as a waitress; it's not like in a truck stop, just serving meals in the dorm. I have to buy books and supplies. Please answer soon.

Dear Miss Nordstrom,
College is everything you said it would be, and more. I carried your volume of Whitman with me on the train; it was an overwhelming experience to look out the window and realize: there was America rolling by, right before my eyes! There is even a class here which is devoted entirely to writing poetry! I am earning my own money working a number of odd jobs because my father hasn't paid my tuition and is too proud to admit it. I make 25¢ per page typing people's papers; I'm so glad I talked Miss Irons into letting me take typing! I also get a quarter a dress ironing, but I like the typing better. I love it here so much, I would do anything to stay.

Dear Miss Linden,
You will not believe this, but there was a concert in the concert hall this evening, and one of the music teachers, who is also the pianist, played *the* Chopin etude—remember, the last piece I worked on when I was taking lessons from you? It brought that year back so clearly, I had everything I could do to keep from crying. It isn't that I'm not happy here, but sometimes I think of you and remember all the things you gave me that were important and good and I wish those days weren't over.

There are people here who are very nice, though, and the music programs are wonderful. At first I was so homesick, I played the Brandenburgs on my roommate's record player every day. All my new friends are music majors, isn't that funny? I sometimes feel left out, and regret that I couldn't be one, too; but I know there is no substitute for early training and lots of practice. I know that writing is important, too; I still have the bookmark you gave me when I first confessed my wish to write, and will try always to keep in mind its inscription: *To thine own self be true.*

Dear Margaret,

My poetry class here is as stimulating as Miss Nordstrom's. That, and the concerts, almost make up for the lack of interesting males. I did have a terrible shock a week ago, though, when I spotted someone in the orchestra who was an *exact replica* of Mr. Leavitt! I nearly fainted, which would have been fatal as I was sitting in the balcony. However, on closer inspection, the resemblance faded to a mere hint. I hope you are keeping your poetry up, too. Would you believe there are actually *other people* here who write it? It would be exaggerating to say the whole campus is beating down the door to Poetry I, but you aren't considered a freak if you like it. I nearly died of shock.

Dear Daddy,

The controller called me in again today to discuss the unpaid tuition. We talked about a loan, which I would like to apply for, but he says you have to sign the papers as my legal guardian. Would you *please* sign the papers when he sends them? It is very important to me to be able to stay here. Your not answering is putting me in a difficult position, and I am finding it hard to study.

❧ The House on Harvard North ❧

When I went home for Christmas vacation, it was to yet another house and yet another housekeeper. This house was dark gray stone, and was located on Harvard Avenue North. Viola had three children of her own, two of whom were living in foster homes, and while I was staying with Daddy and Greta for the holidays, she claimed she was expecting another one, by Daddy. He vehemently denied it, but didn't ask her to leave. A bizarre kind of truce followed, with Viola preparing the meals and shooting everyone meaningful glances, and Daddy spending more and more time away from the house.

On the evenings when he was home, I tried to convince him that there was nothing shameful in applying for a student loan.

"A lot of students have loans, Daddy, and I need to apply for one, too."

"Oh, Jesus Christ, honey; your daddy will be worth a fortune someday. You don't need any goddamn loan. You'll see; I'll have enough money to donate a building to the college, if that's what you want. They'll name it after me: Weiler Hall. Now isn't that better than a piddling loan? Hell, loans are just another form of welfare. Those dirty Communist bastards; you'll see me dead in my grave before any daughter of mine goes on welfare!"

"It's not welfare! You pay it back!"

"Bushwa! Those pinkos have already distorted your thinking; don't think I can't see it."

"They're not Communists! They're wonderful people, and they help students get an education!"

"Bushwa!"

Viola appeared about this time, leaning around the door frame, saying, "Ray? Would you mind coming up to my room when you've finished with her? There's something we gotta discuss."

I floated alone from room to room, watching an early snowfall from strange windows. For the first time, I realized: I was eighteen

161

years old and completely on my own. I was packed and ready to return to college two days early.

❦

*H*ere is Greta Weiler, age nine, hopping on a pogo stick in front of the rundown stone house on Harvard Avenue North. This is not a snapshot, but a moment in time. Raymond Weiler has not gone to his office this day. He is in an upstairs bedroom having an argument of a personal nature with his housekeeper, Viola Potts. A police car cruises down Harvard Avenue North, slowing down as it passes the gray stone house. Presumably the driver witnesses Greta Weiler on her stick. At the corner the car makes a U-turn and passes the house again, traveling in the opposite direction. It slows to a halt shortly thereafter, and parks. Within minutes another police car cruises by, and parks on the opposite side of the street from the first. Together the officers watch the gray stone house. Greta Weiler hops faster and faster. From the upstairs bedroom window, Raymond Weiler parts the curtains with two fingers and sees the police cars waiting below. Greta hops and hops. Raymond calls to Greta: "Honey, you're going to fall down and skin your knees if you hop that fast." A few minutes later, Ray comes out the front door and walks confidently over to the nearest patrol car. He leans in the window and talks for what seems to Greta a very long time. She hops and hops and hops. Eventually, she loses her balance and falls. "I told you that would happen," says Ray with mounting fury in his voice, as the police cars drive away.

Sonya has many jobs. She feels exhausted and exhilarated at the same time. She stays with faculty and friends during vacation; she house-sits and works as a waitress during the summer. She opens her first savings account so she will have the money to pay her tuition in the fall. Climbing the stairs to the roof of her friend's apartment, she adds her laundry to the other clothes on the lines and, surveying the hot, dry California hills, she starts to cry. She is in exile; she cannot go home again. She is a survivor in a strange land.

A month after the start of her second year in college, she receives a message that the Dean of Students wants to see her in her office. The Dean begins by clearing her throat; it is hard for her to get out what she has to say. There has been a letter. It is from a woman by the name of Viola Potts, but she refuses to let Sonya see it. Sonya tries to listen, tries to take it in as her mind fogs over, then begins to freeze. *What has he done now to ruin my life?*

The Dean paraphrases its contents succinctly: "It seems your father is in jail." Why couldn't he have just said he couldn't afford college, Sonya thinks. Why did he have to go into the pinko routine? The Dean is vague about the reasons behind Raymond Weiler's incarceration, but clear about Sonya's staying in school: Sonya is not to feel this news has any bearing on her status at the college, she insists firmly; she promises that she, and the rest of the college community, will do everything they can to see that Sonya gets work and financial aid to see her through to graduation. They are making a mistake, Sonya thinks to herself, keeping on the daughter of a criminal. Now she feels like a criminal, too.

🐝 Hazel's Letter 🐝

Imagine my surprise when I received a letter from Hazel. She wrote that she was still teaching piano, and had converted to Christian Science in the years since leaving our employ. She had heard the news about Daddy and she wished to give me whatever information she could so I would not worry. She had come by this news via Viola. Was there ever a mouth, in the entire Pacific Northwest, that worked with such unfailing dispatch? I imagined a network of ex-housekeepers, extending the entire length and breadth of the State of Washington, keeping the wires and mails humming with news of their former employer, Raymond D. Weiler. Viola had phoned her, Hazel said, to report that her daughter would no longer be taking piano lessons, as she planned to remarry and move to Santa Fe. "To a decent man, with a regular income," she had added pointedly. In addition, she was sure that Hazel would want to know that their former employer, Mr. Weiler, was in jail, and that the charges against him went by the names of Grand Larceny, Bunco, and Fraud. Hazel went right into action, collecting what information she could for my sake.

... your grandmother has temporary custody of Greta, who is now in Canada. I called the District Attorney yesterday. The office is not sure what it is all about, but among the charges lodged against your father is that of "bunco" (whatever they mean by that—the secretary herself couldn't say for sure).

Evil punishes itself but it can never touch the perfect child of God and it is this PERFECT man that we must hold in thought if we would truly help and sustain Mr. Weiler and I am sure your understanding of the Truth will guide and direct you.

🐝 The Lawyer 🐝

With a great deal of effort, and many discreet inquiries on the part of two of my professors, I was able to learn the name of Daddy's lawyer. I took the train to Seattle to talk with him; I had still heard nothing directly from Daddy. I wore a very mature-looking outfit borrowed from my roommate, and sat in the lawyer's office with my legs crossed, smoking a cigarette. He had taken the case, he said candidly, but he didn't relish it. I said I just wanted the facts. I saw myself as Joan Crawford, saying this. She would be hard and to the point. Seeing myself as Joan Crawford kept me from crying. The lawyer patiently related the facts: it seemed Daddy had persuaded a number of people to invest in nonexistent mining properties. I made it clear that he was not to let Daddy know that I knew. That would destroy him, I told myself. The lawyer said he understood.

Not long afterwards, he wrote that Daddy had so impressed the judge with his sincere manner, and rhetoric, that he had been given a three-year suspended sentence, on condition that he remain in the State of Washington and pay everything back to the plaintiffs within that time.

🐝 The Explanation 🐝

After a three-month silence, Daddy finally wrote. The return address was that of the decaying Nash Hotel on 2nd Avenue.

Daddy owes you an explanation for the long delay in writing. I wanted to write you many times, so you wouldn't worry, but because I was in the wilderness, it was impossible.

Your daddy has happened on the biggest deal of his entire life. I will not bore you with the details here, which your young mind will understandably not be able to fully appreciate. But

165

you can believe me, dear Sonya, the pot of gold at the end of the rainbow is here at last. These past months your daddy has put in excruciating long hours and weeks, negotiating with one of America's biggest—hell, *the* biggest—mining companies. The task has been so arduous in fact that—although it broke my heart—it was necessary to send Greta up to Canada to live with Nona until I can complete this deal. That should give you some idea of its importance. Although it grieves me to be separated so long from my little family, you will soon see that it has been worth it.

I have to leave soon for another trip to the properties, but the next time we speak—I know it would seem an exaggeration—your Daddy will be worth millions.

🐝 *The Meeting* 🐝

The Dean of Students set up a special meeting with herself, the controller and me, wherein it was agreed that I could receive a student loan without Daddy's signature and continue with my part-time jobs. It was suggested that the amount of the loan could be increased at any time I felt my studies suffering. I was so overwhelmed with gratitude and shame, I didn't know what would be the right thing to say, so I said, "I don't know how to thank you."

At night I began to sink into strange hypnagogic states in which wild birds beat their wings against the walls of the room, and whole string quartets played themselves out in my brain, although the record player was off. I began staying up all night, listening to Gustav Holst's "The Planets," to stave off the hallucinations. I felt detached from everything, severed from all foundations; a satellite suspended in unfamiliar space forever.

I fell asleep every morning as soon as the lights were dimmed for the slides in my eight o'clock Ancient Civilizations class. I slept for three weeks, beginning with "Sumer: The Dawn of Civilization," and ending with "The Lost Worlds of Anatolia," where I dropped out with an Incomplete.

Some things penetrate to the core, even in sleep: from the depths of the darkened auditorium came the professor's voice as he read, the lectern light casting a faint glow over the text:

No one knows who the Sumerians were . . . but virtually everyone agrees that these brown-skinned, dark-haired people who came down from the mountains of Iran to settle the marshy lands of the Tigris-Euphrates Valley were the first people in history to develop the arts and practices that constitute civilized life. During the course of the fourth millennium B.C. they had already raised proud cities with monumental temples. . . .

At a very early date Semitic tribesmen had intermingled with the nations of the Nile Valley to prepare the way for the development of Egyptian civilization. . . .

Another wave of Semites had rolled eastward into the Tigris-Euphrates Valley and by 2300 B.C. usurped the control of its city-states from the native Sumerians. They assimilated the indigenous culture of Sumer and . . . reinvigorated a civilization that survived almost two thousand years more through the leadership of Babylonia and Assyria.

Oh, beautiful Semites! Roll eastward, intermingle, reinvigorate. Don't let anyone call you kikes or commie bastards. Raise proud cities . . .

❧

*S*onya goes to Canada for Christmas this year. Aunt Edith and Uncle Jack are raising Greta; they have no choice. Nona lives in a small cottage on the same property; things are hard. Jack lost his job with the logging company and has finally found work as a salesman in the local hardware store; it does not agree with him. By Christmas he has ulcers.

Ray meets Sonya at the train station in Seattle; he has taken a

167

bus from the Nash Hotel on 2nd Avenue. Together they walk to the pier and board the boat for Vancouver Island. It is the first time Sonya has seen her father in a year. He is pale; he doesn't seem to hear what she says. His eyes move rapidly from one object to another; he rubs his palms together with a swishing sound, then cracks his knuckles. "The big interests are out to crush the little guy," he says in anguish. He hints at plots and counterplots, his voice rising. Sonya tries to read a magazine during the crossing; she tries to develop hysterical deafness, but for some reason this only succeeds in classrooms. Ray doesn't seem to notice; he is talking to the wall, to the ship's ceiling.

When they arrive Edith serves everyone large glasses of grapefruit juice and they sit around a big table. Jack is tense and withdrawn; the cousins have grown; Greta is shy. Sonya notes how remote she seems from the warm, bright baby she once held and washed and took for walks. She realizes here, for the first time, that Greta thinks of her as her mother. This knowledge comes as such a shock, she throws up her grapefruit juice in the bathroom. She can't imagine being a mother, to Greta or anyone else. It seems too much to ask.

Ray feels uneasy being there; he goes out and buys a large bag of groceries to try to make amends. As he spreads them on the table with great ceremony, Jack takes offense. He resents Ray's coming up here acting like a big shot when it is Jack who is raising his kid and paying the bills. Ray's face flushes. He says,"Aw shit, Jack, don't be so touchy." Jack snaps back, " 'Who pays the piper, calls the tune!' " Ray slams the door and stalks down the country road. "He meant well," says Edith cautiously. "Never trust a lone wolf," recites Jack in a fury. Sonya tries to talk with Nona, but she has changed, too. She seems old, and tired, and wary; she's as jumpy as Ray. "Mind you don't say anything to make matters worse!" she warns emphatically.

It rains the day Sonya and Ray leave to go back. Greta runs after them and cries. "Take me with you!" she pleads. "I can't do that, I have to go back to college," Sonya says, forcing a smile. When she arrives, there will be a letter already waiting for her. It has a squirrel in the upper right-hand corner, and reads:

It's so nice to have you here this Christmas. I hope you will be with me every Christmas from now on. You're the nicest sister anyone could have.

Love from Greta

*S*onya takes on three additional jobs; it leaves her little time to think, and she is grateful for that. She takes a psychology course and learns names for Ray's behavior. "Paranoid," "delusional," "psychopathic," she murmurs under her breath each time she discovers one of his rambling letters in her post office box. The terms become an invocation against whatever threat is lurking within the letter. It helps to categorize him in this way. It names her terror and reduces him to a bearable size. She decides to major in psychology and become a psychologist—then she can apply the terms to any and all who threaten her, and their power to terrorize will fade; she will acquire the power herself. She gradually relinquishes the "stupid" and "numbskull" masks and begins to hear things in class. She pushes Raymond Weiler to the darkest corner of her mind.

There are mixers, dances, parties on weekends. Her friends try to persuade her to participate; only squares and brains don't go to parties. They stay in the library, studying. Sonya doesn't stay in the library weekends; she babysits. She explains that it's because she's now self-supporting and has to take the job instead of going to the party, which is true, but not the whole truth. In fact, she prefers to babysit because it makes her feel like part of a family, even if it is only for four or five hours. She carries the babies in her arms and sings; she reads the older children stories. Later, after they are asleep, she walks around the house and imagines that she, too, lives there. It always disappoints her when the parents come home and she has to go back to the dorm. It is as though she had expected them to tuck her into bed, too; as though she had expected them to invite her to stay and live with them until she grows up.

❧ *Arthur Stedman* ☙

If Arthur Stedman ever regretted his reputation as a minor poet, he made his peace with that fact long ago. He seemed to accept his limitations along with his skills, and this gave him the kind of calm authority you could trust. He was not distracted by his own ambition. His focus was sure and uncontaminated by either personal vanity or envy of the young. He was not rivalrous, but challenged what he took to be the best in all his students. There were times when his challenges were taken for provocation, and students with low thresholds for criticism often dropped out of his class. But for those who remained, the writing of poetry was regarded as a serious pursuit, and on them he lavished his absolute attention.

In the early weeks of his class I considered dropping out. Where Miss Nordstrom had rarely criticized and mostly praised, Dr. Stedman mostly criticized and only rarely praised. It was some time before I realized that his criticism was the highest form of praise, and the going those first months was rough. I would place my chair against the far wall and lean there for support as he stood behind his desk and held the sheets of paper that contained my recent work under the crooked lamp, scrutinizing them in silence. He always chose to stand, rather than sit, and it lent a special vigor to his consideration of your work. I leaned and waited, knowing that at some point soon he would brush back the graying shock of hair that fell across his forehead, remove his horn-rimmed glasses in one rapid stroke, and say, "Now don't you think this line is trivial?" He would then proceed to read aloud the offending image or line which fell short of his expectations for good poetry. "Always choose the *dangerous* word!" he would say.

For those brave enough to stay with him, his rare praise came to represent an achievement you could believe in. It was hard to defend poetry as an important pursuit in the mid-fifties, but Arthur Stedman made it seem exceptional. He didn't fret about outside indifference. His fidelity to his students and to his work was complete. I stayed in his class for the rest of my college years, and he gradually fostered in me an allegiance to my own vision and a respect for my power to express it. In years to come I would drift far, far from even the memory of that vision: it retreated to the darkest center of me, and lay low. It burrowed there like a lone cicada waiting out its cycle, invisibly coiled for rebirth.

🐝 *Jonathan* 🐝

Jonathan's father was the pharmacist at the drugstore across from the college. His mother managed the soda fountain. I got a summer job working behind the counter with Jonathan. He had just been accepted to law school and felt jerking sodas was beneath his dignity, and doing it with a sophomore was doubly beneath his dignity, but his parents liked college-age jerkers behind the counter. They thought it gave the drugstore class.

On the Fourth of July, Jonathan took me to the beach in his red convertible. He asked me in the kitchen the day before: "You got any plans for the holiday tomorrow?" He asked it so quickly, so deftly, the same way he threw the sodas together, that I didn't have time to think. I said, "No." "Good," he said smugly. "We'll go to the beach in my new convertible." It had been his present for getting into law school.

The trip to the beach took two hours in holiday traffic, over miles of steep, winding roads along the cliffs overlooking the ocean. I was sunburned and nauseated by the time we spread the blanket down. Jonathan whipped out a giant-sized thermos of martinis. He thought he was very sophisticated. He had even brought along little paper cups. The sand burned my legs and the waves crashed in front of us as I downed the first cup of martini. It tasted like gasoline. "No, I'm just fine," I said lightly, when he offered the second cup. I smiled convincingly. I was relieved when he didn't criticize me for being a poor sport. He finished the whole thermos himself. The sun beat down. My lips were chapped from the salt air. I lay on the blanket stiffly as Jonathan leaned over me and strained to be sophisticated while he fumbled and groped in a drunken attempt to make love. I tried to strike a balance between being a good-time, good-natured, fun date— which I knew was expected—and being a drag, dog date who wished she were home reading W. H. Auden. Above all, I tried to avoid being a cock tease. I wasn't sure how that could be achieved without risking being considered a dog, but I knew it was second in importance to not getting knocked up. Girls had been known to have been not taken home from dates because they were cock teases. They were just let out of the car and abandoned. That's why it was advised you always carry a dime, just in case you crossed over that elusive line that separated the cock tease from the good-time date.

Jonathan staggered back to the convertible and managed to steer it onto the road. He kept removing his horn-rimmed glasses, squinting, then putting them back on. We started climbing the cliffs just as the sun was sinking into the ocean. The car was weaving all over the narrow road, and I was on the ocean side. I held my breath and gripped the door handle in a futile attempt to hold the car on course. Jonathan's face was flushed and set; his jaw was as tight as if it had been cemented shut. His fingers curled tightly around the wheel. I wanted to suggest we pull over, but didn't dare break his concentration. I could imagine that any sudden distraction would shatter his effort, as well as his pride, and send us plunging onto the foaming rocks hundreds of feet below. I knew I was going to die; as we climbed the steep coast road it was clear he would never make it to the top. No one could drink an entire thermos of gin and negotiate all these turns; the first three had been luck. I felt it was a fitting punishment for having not only made out in broad daylight, but for having done it with a drunk.

When he made it not only up the cliffs, but also to the restaurant parking lot, it went to his head; he ordered two more martinis with dinner and spilled his entire salad down the front of his button-down shirt. When he drove me back to the apartment I was house-sitting, he seemed genuinely hurt when I wouldn't invite him in.

Back at the soda fountain on Monday, we worked side by side as though the Fourth of July had never taken place. At one point in the day, when I was scooping ice cream cones for a family of four, he said loudly, "You're giving them too much, those scoops are too large." He thought he could order me around like that because he was the boss's son. I don't know what got into me; I certainly wasn't a cheerful coworker, much less a good-time date: I threw the scooper into his pristine white chest, sending chocolate ice cream coursing down his spotless apron. "If you don't like the way I do it, do it yourself," I said, and stormed out of the drugstore as the family of four looked on in horror. His mother sent my final paycheck through the mail. I wasn't even worried about being without work with the summer not half over. I knew now that I could do anything. I would survive. That had been my first public defiance. I daydreamed about it for the rest of the summer.

🐝 *Prudence and Avery ("Chuckles") Fletcher* 🐝

I hadn't bargained for Prudence Fletcher. After job-hunting for a week and finding every summer job already filled, I phoned the Dean of Students in desperation. Well, yes, she said; she could understand—being single by choice—the frustration of being hounded by the boss's son while trying to scoop ice cream for a living. On the other hand, things did not come easily in life, and one could ill afford to throw tantrums in early July if one wished to make a down payment on one's tuition in September. Still, having come from the school of hard knocks herself, she could sympathize. She would make some calls and get back to me. Within the half hour, she had called back. By a lucky coinci-

173

dence, she related, the very wealthy alumna Prudence Fletcher just happened to need a maid for the rest of the summer. She had no objection whatever, the Dean said, to an inexperienced, non-professional college girl filling the bill—at least until she could get a permanent replacement from the agency. No, in fact, she had rather liked the idea. It pleased her, the Dean seemed to think, to be helping out a poor student from her old alma mater.

The job wouldn't be too demanding: a little laundry, general housecleaning, plus serving at Mrs. Fletcher's weekly bridge luncheons. In return, she offered a room in her showcase home, meals, and fifteen dollars a week. As I hung up the phone I looked around the little apartment whose owners would be returning shortly, and knew that I'd made the right decision by accepting Mrs. Fletcher's offer. Nights and weekends were lonely with all my friends back in their home states—camping out, shopping with their mothers, lying in the sun—whatever it was normal people did during summer vacation. As I went into the kitchen to make a sandwich for dinner, I noted the small garbage pail overflowing with empty tuna fish cans and had a sudden vision of what life could be like at the Fletchers'. I saw the three of us sitting at the dinner table, laughing and exchanging warm glances, listening with rapt attention to one another's accounts of the day.

The first thing Prudence Fletcher did on my arrival was point out the ten-thousand-dollar beige wall-to-wall carpeting that premeated every room in the house. Under no circumstances was anything to be spilled on it. She stressed, a second time, its cost: "Ten thousand dollars," she said with great pride. As I admired the carpet she kept a thin smile in place. It seemed glued to her face, held there by sheer force of will. She showed me the utility room and how to work the washing machine. She couldn't resist lifting the lid to a giant freezer that stretched the length of one entire wall. Within its depths were thousands of pounds of frozen prime beef, in every conceivable form and shape. The message was clear: Prudence, who—she pointedly confessed—had been poor in her youth, would never want again. After the tour she led me into the maid's room off the kitchen. "Make yourself at

174

home," she said, shutting the door and disappearing. There was a small bed against one wall, a bureau in the corner, and a small table by the window. I unpacked my clothes and began the first of a long series of letters to my friends that were to be my only social contacts for the remainder of the summer. Whatever dreams I had had of hitting it off with the Fletchers began to erode that first day; by the end of the week, they had evaporated forever.

Every morning before setting off for her charity work, Prudence Fletcher wrote out a list of the chores I was to do for that day. She had already spelled out my general duties, but there was something about making the lists that seemed to give her a strange satisfaction. Dusting the patio furniture was the only job I refused to do. It seemed insane to dust something that sat outdoors and that they never used. She didn't notice for about two weeks, then one day she said, "Did you get to the patio furniture?" She never used my name. "Yes," I lied. "Well, I must say, it looks very grimy," she sniffed, running her finger in a black streak across the surface of a white enamel table. "It must be the smog," I said, unconvincingly.

One evening she came home late and in a foul mood. I was in the kitchen broiling steaks. She wanted to know why I hadn't begun the potatoes yet. I didn't know how to cook potatoes, but I couldn't admit this. She stood there with her hands on her hips, glaring at me. I knew exactly what was in her mind. She wanted to fire me, but her social conscience was giving her trouble. As it turned out, Chuckles arrived just in the nick of time and did something whose ultimate effect was to infuriate her all the more: seeing my dilemma, he quickly set aside his jacket and briefcase and, rolling up his sleeves, began peeling potatoes over the sink. He stood beside me and showed me how it was done, in a way that preserved my dignity and also made a game of it. He joked about the Army; he began to sing. His thinning silver hair fell rakishly over his forehead. Prudence retired to her bedroom. It passed through my mind for the first time that Chuckles was a lonely man. The Fletchers had no children; the formidable Prudence was a humorless companion.

On one other occasion he defied her by forming a small alli-

175

ance with me. On their anniversary he came home with a large box of fancy assorted chocolates for Prudence. "You know I'm trying to lose weight," she chided as she drifted across the ten-thousand-dollar beige wall-to-wall carpeting on her way to the bedroom. As she dressed for their evening out, Chuckles came tiptoeing into the maid's room where I sat writing letters. His finger to his lip, he brought forth a small box of chocolates from behind his back. "Here, this one is for you," he whispered. "Don't tell, now." Then he quickly backed out of the room, smiling a sad, sweet smile and closing the door behind him so that she wouldn't see. I hid the chocolates on the windowsill and cried. The next morning, when I overslept, Prudence stuck her head into my room to inform me she was leaving for the day and there was work to be done; and just before she shut the door, the shiny red box caught her eye. She gave me a look that made me feel like a criminal inside, even though I knew I hadn't done anything wrong. That night they ate dinner on trays in their bedroom; I could hear them arguing through the closed door. Chuckles Fletcher didn't joke, or sing, or peel potatoes again. I did my jobs and retired to the maid's room after helping Prudence prepare dinner. They ate on trays in their bedroom. I wanted to run away but there was nowhere to go. I knew the Fletchers were doing me a favor and, in their eyes, being kind. I realized then for the first time that it is better to be alone, and to be lonely, than to live with people who are not your parents, not your friends, not in any way a family. That is the worst kind of loneliness there is.

On the morning of my last day at the Fletchers', Prudence rapped her knuckles lightly on my door, opened it just enough to put her head into the room, and whispered in her throaty manner, "You may join us for Sunday brunch in the living room, if you'd like." She wore a navy blue monogrammed bathrobe. I didn't know if I should dress to join them, or if they were having brunch in their robes. I was afraid to go after her and ask. To be safe, I dressed. It was a mistake. Chuckles had set up a card table by the picture window next to the hi-fi set, and they were in their robes. Awkwardly, I took the third seat which they had conspicuously set up for me. Chuckles put a record on the turntable. Prudence sat back, admiring the view from her hilltop home, and smiled charitably as she stirred her coffee. The living room filled with sounds of the musical *My Fair Lady*. Every now and then, at mysterious intervals, the Fletchers would look at each other and laugh discreetly. At one point Prudence said directly to me, "Isn't that amusing?" I didn't know what she was referring to, I couldn't understand anything on the record, but I knew enough to flash a smile and say gratefully, "It really is!" I knew they thought this was what families probably did on Sunday mornings or on special occasions. I knew they considered this brunch a generous offering, and a special treat for me, and I knew further that they were pleased with themselves for having offered to share it, and themselves, with me; after all, I wasn't a real maid. It was their goodbye gesture to me. I tried to seem happy, and bit the inside of my mouth hard whenever it felt like I might cry. The record finally ended, and I went back to college. I never saw Prudence or Chuckles Fletcher again.

❧ *Desmond Webster* ❧

The following summer I apartment-sat for vacationing professors, feeding their cats and watering their plants, and traveled by bus to my job as a researcher at a nearby university. I sat in the library copying information and bringing it back to the little office where the professor I worked for labored on his latest book. He was remote, though not inconsiderate, and it wasn't until I heard a coworker refer to him as "a lone wolf" that I fell in love with him. I don't know why that phrase seemed to seal my fate, but it did. From then on I saw him in a completely new light: gentle, reserved, handsome, and obviously suppressing his love for me. But it wasn't until we ran into each other at the same foreign film one night, and he invited me to join him for coffee, that I blurted out, "I love you." He looked at me for a minute, then escorted me to his car, where we sat quietly kissing for the next hour. It was wonderful to be in love with someone who was not only a thinker, but who appreciated foreign films. It didn't even matter when he said he was married; this kind of man came along once in a lifetime in 1957. For the rest of the summer we sat in his car after work, exchanging favorite poets and making out; then went to various exotic restaurants to eat. We had to patronize out-of-the-way places, but I never felt degraded. It wasn't until he began to talk about leaving his wife that I suddenly found myself looking forward to returning to college in the fall. He phoned me at the dorm throughout September, but I always said I was too busy, with all my classes and part-time jobs, to see him. For the rest of that autumn, whenever I thought of Desmond, I told myself: You got away just in time.

I knew my judgment was right, and yet I was flooded with a sense of loss. My roommates stepped cautiously around my prostrate form as I lay in the middle of the room, with the Shostakovich Fifth Symphony grinding out its special pathos on the portable record player. Even though the break had been my doing, the emptiness seemed overwhelming. We would never exchange looks again, or literature; never again touch. We would no longer hold each other, or eat together, or laugh. It was like losing a parent. All the time I was thinking I would never recover, I knew somewhere that I would. And I did.

※

In the spring, when Sonya is awarded the annual poetry prize, she writes a special note of thanks to both Miss Nordstrom and Miss Linden. She has finally achieved something that seems to justify the faith they had in her. She no longer writes to Ray; she writes her former teachers as though they were her parents, describing her loves, discoveries, hard times and hopes. Their responses confirm that there is someone at the other end of the void between her and a past she can never return to.

Near the end of her final year at college, Sonya receives a letter from Ray's lawyer, informing her that repeated attempts to locate Ray have been in vain. For this reason he has no choice but to dissociate himself from the case. If at any time she should hear from her father, or require his assistance, she should let him know.

🐟 *Daddy's Letters* 🐟

For graduation Daddy sent me three letters, postmarked Reno, Nevada, and written three days apart. In the first, he apologized for his long silence and described his newly adopted home as an ideal place for a man of vision to convert his intimate knowledge of Mother Earth into a fortune. He has something of great importance to tell me, he hints, which he subsequently unveils in his next letter:

> Sometime, if you and Daddy ever have a quiet hour or two together, I'm going to unburden an idea about a book that a famous-to-be college graduate is going to write! Two facts will make it a seller. One: the youth of the author; Two: its title!
> The author is 21 years of age . . .
> The title: "My Father Remembers . . ."
> Now if someone like the late Dorothy Thompson (who was a famous author and writer—as well as having been a classmate of my sister Mabel) had written a book with that title in her late years it would not, perhaps, have created any special interest. But when an author of 21 years can use that title on a book, and record the wealth of facts and memories that *your* book will contain, it will really be something new in the book-publishing world!
> Just four of the items: 1. "My Father Remembers" shaking

179

the hand of President McKinley, at the Pan American Exposition in Buffalo, N.Y., in 1901! Two hours later President McKinley, still in the Temple of Music shaking hands with a long line of people, was shot by an anarchist named Leon Czolgosz, who had his hand bandaged in a white handkerchief to hide the pistol. President McKinley died four days later—just a short distance from our home. Czolgosz was electrocuted. This is a part of our country's history which "My Father Remembers."

2. In 1898 Cuba was owned by Spain. Our battleship *Maine* was anchored in Havana Harbor. One night it was blown up and sunk. More anarchists of that day. Our future President, Theodore (Teddy) Roosevelt immediately embarked with his Rough Riders and stormed up San Juan Hill and we won the war over Spain. Cuba was then freed from Spanish rule. Now—what is there here that "My Father Remembers"? Well, my Uncle Robert (my mother's brother) was one of Roosevelt's Rough Riders, and your father remembers that each night in his prayers he asked God to protect his Uncle Rob and bring him back home. This, too, is American history "My Father Remembers."

3. "My Father Remembers"—the famous murder case in New York City—when Harry Kendall Thaw shot and killed Stanford White. And "My Father Remembers" reading the newspapers every day during the infamous trial of Sacco and Vanzetti!

4. "My Father Remembers" when homes were lighted either by gas mantles or oil lamps—electric bulbs came later. And my father remembers, as a child, seeing the great inventor of the incandescent bulb—Thomas Alva Edison!

5. "My Father Remembers" *his* father's *father*, who died in Buffalo, N.Y., when my father was 14 years old. My Grandfather Otto (your great-grandfather Otto) was born in the Bavarian Alps in 1820!

These are but five items to be found in your first book—"My Father Remembers"—by Sonya Weiler, age 21 years.

And now, a short time after the crack of dawn tomorrow, Daddy will be on his way, with more miles to traverse, more rough country and high mountains to pit the human carcass against, more deeds in need of accomplishment. There is a certain sense of achievement in winning physical tests against the ruggedness of Nature that, for me, no other efforts seem to achieve.

I was unable to read the letter without remembering the way he was always going to make me into something. These moments were especially intense after he had lost some deal, which meant that I was going to be a lot of things a lot of the time. I imagine he figured you had to play all your cards, and a daughter's achieving something would be better than nothing achieved at all: in 1948 I would be a famous concert pianist—if I would only practice; in 1949 I would prepare early to swim the English Channel, with him as my trainer; in 1952 I would win the Kentucky Derby. The list was as long as my interests were then. It seemed that whatever I enjoyed doing, Daddy knew of a way to turn it into a profit.

Greetings from Nevada!

Re: the clipping from the *Examiner.* The "Brain Game" is published daily, and like all good puzzles, covers a great diversity of subjects. In this one I blush to report I got them all correct except No. 5—I didn't know the assassin of President Garfield. However, No. 8 will tell you my reason for clipping and mailing it to you. If you recall, Daddy even remembered the correct spelling of that Russian anarchist's name! (Now read the clipping).

Which brings me back to our recent thoughts concerning the book my precious daughter is going to write.

So now I'll contribute the substance of another chapter! "My Father Remembers"—when there were no automobiles in the world! When Henry Ford finally got his first one to run the year was 1903. Hell, Daddy was ten years old then! How many other young authors at the tender age of 21 can write this? Now—if you were to use the title "My Grandmother Remembers," the title and contents would have no value, for thousands of writers 21 years old could write of many interesting occurrences.

It might be interesting if you wrote to Nona and asked her opinion. I'm sure she would very quickly see the value in the title of the book—"My Father Remembers."

And now I must be on my way again. I will be loving you,

dear Sonya, every moment I have life; in the lovely midnight hours and in the iridescent splendor of the dawn; in the brilliant light of noon-time and when the evening shadows steal across the valley, and the sun is setting in the purple hills.

When I failed to respond to my graduation present after two months, Daddy made one final effort to immortalize himself through me. Did he see me as his last ore-rich vein?

Somehow, we haven't had the time to chat over an idea of Daddy's—we didn't plant the first little acorn that could grow into the mighty oak of ideas that my daughter would gather together in book form. I feel that Daddy could be the father of the author whose first book would be so fine a success as to make any future efforts superfluous. I have never been more serious about anything in my life—nor as certain of its success.

Here is another item that should help to alert you to the gold mine you have in your hands.

We find recorded, in any encyclopedia—Elbert Hubbard; American editor, writer and printer; born Bloomington, Ill., June 19, 1856—died at sea, May 7, 1915. In 1895 he settled in East Aurora, N.Y., where he established the Roycroft Shop, so-called after the 17th century printer, Thos. Roycroft. From his press came a series of "Little Journeys to the Homes of Great Men."

Now: "My Father Remembers"—in 1909, while playing shortstop on our high school baseball team, we journeyed to East Aurora, N.Y., to play the East Aurora high school team: meeting—after the game—the great Elbert Hubbard, at the Roycroft Inn; and conversing with him—as a team—for more than an hour!

Pause: for change of scene—and now sweet darling, here is another anecdote (look up that word) that will be of interest. "My Father Remembers"—when the New York Giants won 26 straight games! Yes, that's right—26 straight! This was in 1916 when the Giants had, as one of their pitchers, the great left-hander, Rube Marquard, who won that year 19 straight games. When the season was over, Marquard made several appearances on the vaudeville stage in N.Y. State and "My Father Remembers" seeing him at Shea's Theater in Buffalo, N.Y.

And this: "My Father Remembers" *his* father (who was an ardent baseball fan) telling him when he was only ten years old, that the great Joe "Iron Man" McGinnity had just pitched and won his *third double-header* in the month of August—in 1903 for the New York Giants! (Where are the real men of yesteryear?).

Now can you see, Dear Sonya, the intense interest that would be generated by one after another of these very human events and bits of our country's history that were witnessed, and lived through, by the father of a young 21-year-old girl?

And now sweet darling I must end this lovely visit with you.

❦ *Graduation* ❦

Daddy and Nona arrived in time to see me receive my diploma. They stayed at a cheap motel near the college. It surprised me when they came; they had been out of my life for so long. Daddy never referred to his book idea again and I was relieved. But my biggest surprise was the telegram from Jack: it said that Greta would be arriving the following day. Many weeks were to pass before I realized the true significance of this event: that they had sent her to me as a graduation present. Daddy and Nona returned to Reno and Victoria, respectively, the day after graduation. With no explanation or warning, I became the guardian and sole support of Greta Weiler, age thirteen. I was the last to know.

My little sister had grown; she had entered adolescence with all the hallmarks of that phase: erupted skin, stooped shoulders, and low self-esteem. Beneath these flaws, a fragile beauty made its first appearance. Because it was June I assumed that she had been sent to spend the summer with me, and would return to Canada in the fall. There was just enough room for her in the summer sublet apartment I shared with three classmates. It was the middle of a recession; we all spent endless weeks looking for jobs. We took part-time work wherever it could be found: selling purses in department store basements, filling in for secretaries who were on vacation. Interview after interview, we were told we

183

were "overqualified." We couldn't imagine what that meant; we didn't feel qualified for anything. Once, in July, Daddy sent a hundred dollars in cash in an envelope. One night I asked Greta if she was anxious to get back to her friends in Canada. She stared at me for a long time, then said, "I'm staying here with you. I'm living with you from now on." I thought there was some mistake; I had plans to join my roommates in New York in the fall, where we would work and save money for graduate school.

I told Greta that that would be nice, it really would, but I had other plans. They did not include raising a thirteen-year-old child. Greta started to cry. She said that Uncle Jack and Aunt Edith had told her they would love to have her, but they couldn't afford another mouth to feed and Ray was no help on that score at all. I was the only one left. Well, no, I said in desperation; there was a very nice family on the campus who took in stray people. At this very moment, three teenagers whose parents—for one reason or another—couldn't care for them were living in their home. I was sure that Greta would feel comfortable there. Greta cried harder. She screamed and wailed. She buried herself in the pillows on the couch and said, "You are the only family I have!" I thought of Daddy; I thought of Nona; I thought of Edith and Jack. I even thought of Valery. I felt betrayed by them all.

But as I watched Greta it became clear there was only one thing I could do. I said, "I didn't know it meant so much to you to be with your own family. I love you. I will take care of you." That very evening my roommates said, "Let's go to the foreign films." They did not mean Greta. As we started out the door Greta ran out of the bedroom crying, "Take me with you!" I felt bad that I hadn't thought to include her, and equally bad that she was afraid to stay alone. I wondered if she would be tagging after me on dates, or when I married, and after she became an adult. By the end of the summer I had accepted that Greta would be my responsibility for the next five years, and after that things went better. I threw myself into the role just as if I had been her real mother.

❧ *Leo Slade* ❧

I saw Leo Slade's ad in the paper: *Temp secy sml dentl offc dntn. Temp* meant three weeks, I discovered later; but by that time it didn't matter. I had applied for four jobs already that week, and lost them all to overqualification. The minute they found out about the college degree, they put the application form back on the shelf. "Oh, you're overqualified for this job, honey," they'd say without even looking up from their desks. Rutland Paper Products Corporation, down by the railroad tracks, had been my latest rejection. I had cried at that one. "Please consider me," I whispered urgently. "I have a dependent to raise. I *have* to find a permanent job." "Aw, gee, hon, I understand, I really do, but see, my boss—if he ever found out—well, ya know what I mean?" She drew the side of her flattened hand dramatically across her throat. "I know what you mean," I said, and stumbled back across the tracks in my three-inch heels from Leeds to wait for the bus home.

Leo Slade's office was on the seventh floor of an old medical-dental building in downtown San Francisco. He needed a three-week replacement for his regular secretary, who was on vacation. "She's been with me eleven years," he said significantly, as he half sat on the empty secretarial desk during the interview. "That's wonderful," I nodded. "Any previous job experience?" he asked. "I put myself through college doing typing and other jobs," I said, before biting my tongue. I swore that if it cost me this job, I would follow my friend Angie's advice: "Tell them you were a waitress in a drive-in; that will qualify as past job experience, but won't ruin you the way mentioning college does." Angie had landed her present job in the scarf department that way, and planned to leave it just as soon as she could break into advertising.

"Oh." Leo Slade said. "You worked your way through college? That's very impressive. So did I. And dental school, too. You're hired." He flashed a perfect smile; his capped teeth shone under

185

the fluorescent lights. I had to hold on to the arm of the chair; the speed with which I had just been hired made me dizzy. He stared at me in a benign way, absently smoothing the bald patch on the top of his head. I felt so triumphant at having landed my first job, I wandered all over town for the rest of the day, stepping lightly as though not really touching the pavement, and seeing everything in a totally new way. As soon as Angie got off work we headed straight for the Bottoms Up bar in Lester Alley to celebrate. By the second drink I saw the handwriting on the wall and called Greta to tell her I'd be home late. We had to wait in the Trans-Bay Terminal until the 9:25 bus.

"What do you want to be someday, when all this is over?" Angie said thickly, as we joined the derelicts on the benches in the nearly deserted terminal.

"As soon as I have Greta raised I'm going to be a writer," I answered dreamily.

"Oh, you'll be married by then," said Angie with resignation. "That's four or five years away," she continued thoughtfully. "Christ, if I'm not married by then, I'm going to be a nun."

🕸 *Home in the Hills* 🕸

With Daddy hiding out in Reno and Nona on her pension in Canada, I set out to find a steady job and an apartment in which to raise Greta. It was important to me that she not be embarrassed by having to live with a sister. I imagined her bringing home friends from junior high, and my asking them, "Would you like some hot chocolate?" I spent most of my first month's salary decorating our barren three-room flat in flaming color from India Imports so she wouldn't be bringing her friends home to some drab walk-up, but to a stylish working girl's apartment with all the touches a home might have, except for a mother and father.

Daddy honored us with a visit that Christmas. The first thing he said when he came in the door was, "Oh, honey, you don't know what it does to Daddy to see you and precious little Greta having to live in a place like this." "What's wrong with our place?" I demanded. *You have anything better to offer her?*

He wouldn't leave it alone. "You don't understand, honey. A growing child needs something better than this. I have a dream which is soon to become a reality: When I get through with my heartbreaking work in the mountains, I'm going to buy a real home, a *redwood* home, high up in the hills, where Greta and I and my sister Mabel can all live together in harmony. It won't be one of these cheap pink plaster apartments in a rundown area. It will have hand-carved wood inside, and maybe a pool, too. Hell, yes—a pool. Our little family deserves the best."

I had hoped he would be proud that I was working my heart out to provide a little home right here for Greta and myself. I thought: If he pushes this any further I'm going to finish him. It was the ace up my sleeve, and I pictured it mentally as the Big Scene. It would go like this: "I *know* about the larceny. I *know* about the bunco. I *know* about the jail. I know! I know!" There would be nothing he could say to it. It would shut him up for good. That was why I couldn't use it. There is no irritant as painful as an ace up your sleeve that you can never use; it's the kind of thing that causes oysters to produce pearls.

"Yes," he was whispering, "a home in the hills ..." Greta's eyes were beginning to light up; what was I to her, or our little apartment for that matter, compared to a home in the hills with Daddy and a pool? I could see I was losing her; it was clear that something had to be done. It was hard finding something, on the spur of the moment, which would be as effective as the Big Scene. In the end I pulled a Daddy on him. I ranted, I screamed, I threw things:

"Here I am working my heart out for *your* daughter, and you don't even have the decency to be grateful!" I yelled. "Every morning I ride three stinking buses to work and sit in front of a typewriter all day just so Greta can live near her school and have a decent place to invite her friends!" I threw one of the new pillows into the bookcase for emphasis. Some of the books fell out. To make sure he got the point, and to scare him just enough without devastating him, I alluded to it: "I know some things, and if you force me I will go to court and we'll see who is more qualified to have custody of Greta!" It was a calculated risk, and it worked.

"Honey," he said, looking very sincere, "I had no idea you felt so strongly about providing a little home for your baby sister. Daddy has misjudged you. You were right; what you're doing for Greta is a fine thing, a brave thing, a valuable thing. Daddy never should have doubted your courage. If this is what you fine girls want, then who is Daddy to interfere?"

It was like winning the battle and losing the war; somehow he had managed to make it my consuming desire to take on his responsibility, when in fact I didn't want it at all. But when faced with the home in the hills, the only thing open to me was to defend our little apartment to the end. Greta behaved with more respect after that, and Daddy never criticized it again. Suddenly our little place looked very beautiful to me—I had created it for us, and defended it against its enemies. Greta became mine after that; I had staked my claim on her, whether I'd intended to or not.

🐾 Lola Kovaks 🐾

After months of temporary and part-time jobs, I finally decided I would have to be willing to pay an agency fee for a permanent job. Things were that desperate, and so was I.

Early on a Monday morning I entered the waiting room of the employment agency and waited my turn for an interview. The little room was packed; every chair was taken, and people who couldn't sit were leaning against the walls. Eventually, a woman in her fifties, with platinum hair, came out from behind a frosted glass partition and called my name. I followed her into the little cubicle with her name on the door: LOLA KOVAKS. Her heels were at least four inches high.

"Mmmmm, now, let's see," she mused as she scanned my application. Her thumb nervously clicked the push-top of her ball-point pen in and out, in and out. Her false eyelashes swept up and down my application like brooms. "I think I've got just the job for you, since you're a college grad," she said suddenly, reaching for her file. "This man just called yesterday. He's a law-yer and he needs a new secretary. Think you can handle it?" "Yes," I said at once, without thinking. "Good. Now, I'm sorry to say, this one is *not* a no-fee job. That means the employer isn't willing to pay the fee, so the employee has to do it. Let's see now," she mused as she calculated the fee, which was based on a percentage of the monthly salary. It came to a third of my first month's salary and I didn't know how I would ever pay it, but I didn't say a word. This was my big moment, my big chance, my first full-time permanent job. I knew that masses of other women were sweating anxiously out in the tiny waiting room. I knew enough not to question the fee, the job, Lola Kovaks, or anything else. The important thing was to get hired and to pay the rent.

Lola Kovaks gave me the address and wished me good luck. I took the streetcar down Market Street to Geary, then walked over to Mission and finally located the office; it was seamier than I had expected from her description. The little elevator jerked to a stop at the second floor, and I walked down a dark, lonely hallway with an octagon tile floor. At the far end I saw the sign: MICKEY MALONE, ESQ. I gathered my courage and went in.

🦎 *Mickey Malone* 🦎

The outer office contained one metal file cabinet, one office desk with typewriter, and a single straight-back chair. Behind the desk, a harried woman with circles under her eyes strained to make an erasure without spilling crumbs into the machine. She looked up as I shut the door behind me. "Oh, you must be the new girl. The agency just called saying you'd be over. Have a seat and I'll tell

189

Mr. Malone you're here." With that, she got up wearily and knocked on the door which led to the inner office, saying, "The new girl is here." Someone deep inside the inner office grunted, and the secretary ushered me in.

Mickey Malone's corpulent frame was propped behind a giant mahogany desk. He must have weighed close to three hundred pounds. He wore his white shirt open at the collar and rolled up at the sleeves. His cheeks and nose were an unnatural shade of red. The butt of a dead cigar hung from fleshy lips. He was the most revolting human being I had ever seen. The thought of working for him made me physically ill, so I compensated by being unnaturally polite. "Sit down," he grunted, waving his puffy hand in the direction of a chair. He continued reading some papers before him, however, so I used the opportunity to scan the room. Although the desk was impressive, the rest of the room was in appalling taste: two large television sets dominated the space behind his desk; a brass spittoon was anchored by its side. The bookcases contained vases, bookends, ashtrays, statues—everything but books. Badly rendered oil paintings in gilded frames competed for space on the walls, and the carpet underfoot was a bilious shade of green and about two inches plusher than an office warranted. Two enormous couches had been shoved against the south and east walls. "I said, 'Can you type?'"

"Oh, I didn't know you were ready. Yes. I can type. The agency tested me at eighty words per minute. That includes accuracy."

"OK. OK. OK. I got a lotta letters need to go out; Shirley is leaving tomorrow. She'll show you what to do. You'll work at her desk." He waved me away with his heavy arm. Two oversized diamond rings flashed from the flaccid hand. His thick black eyebrows made an almost theatrical contrast with his crimson face. Looking beyond him, I noticed for the first time a young woman in a small room in back of his, hunched over a typewriter with what looked like long legal papers coming out of the carriage. He looked up in annoyance to see that I was still there. He followed my eyes into the next room and said impatiently, "She does my legal work; you won't be doing any of that." I walked shakily back to the outer office and asked Shirley, "Does this mean I'm hired?" and she said, "If he sent you out here to me to find out what you're supposed to do, I guess it does."

The month that followed was like living in hell. My sole job was to sit all day, typing the same threat letter over and over again. There were hundreds of names and addresses on a long list to whom these were to be sent. It seemed that Mickey Malone had an arrangement with the collection agency down the hall; when people failed to meet a debt, their accounts would be turned over to him. Most of these accounts were with cut-rate bargain stores which sold inferior quality merchandise, mostly furniture, and required the customer's signature on a small-print contract at the time of purchase. When the merchandise failed to arrive, or arrived damaged, and the customers failed to meet their payments, their accounts were turned over to Mickey Malone. It gave me a headache typing this letter over and over, day after day, threatening people with lawsuits and attachment of their wages. Once, during my lunch hour, I tried to discuss it with the other secretary: didn't she think it was awful, threatening people this way when they'd obviously been sold a lot of crap? Shouldn't we find some way to inform them of their rights?

No, the other secretary said; it was none of our business. We were paid to work for Mr. Malone; our loyalties should be with him. It didn't bother her at all that his office was furnished entirely with reclaimed goods. Riding home on the bus, I wondered if I could possibly take on Mickey Malone by myself. I imagined appealing to some perfect higher authority on behalf of all the people being exploited; and the authority would shake its finger in outrage, sending Malone to prison and releasing all the stereos and TVs back to their original owners. But deep inside I knew that no one could touch him, and I knew that Malone also knew this. It would take collective effort and overwhelming evidence. I lay awake nights trying to figure out a way to restore justice and keep my job, too. Before I could come to the right decision, Mickey Malone took everything out of my hands.

It was five o'clock on the last day of the month and I had just finished typing the latest batch of threat letters. As I placed the last letter on top of the pile of others awaiting his signature,

191

Mickey Malone left the office with his overcoat on his arm. He never said goodbye; he rarely spoke to me at all. As I put the cover on the typewriter I noticed his shadow through the frosted glass; he was standing in the hall talking to the racketeer who ran the collection agency.

I straightened up the desk and put on my coat. As I turned out the light and came out in the hall he wheeled around and shoved a paycheck in my face. "I won't be needing you anymore," he said. I opened my mouth and stared, trying to think of what to say. He was nervous and impatient; he slapped a rolled-up newspaper repeatedly against his thigh. He had expected me to just take the check and evaporate down the elevator shaft. I felt outnumbered, standing there in the deserted hallway with the two of them. I finally managed to ask him why. "The job is finished, I don't need you anymore," he said. "It's simple." My heart was beating wildly and I worried that I would start crying. "I was told the job was permanent," I persisted; "I just paid nearly a hundred dollars to the agency for it." "That's your problem, not mine," Malone snapped, thrusting his arms into his overcoat. He turned and locked the office door with a decisive twist of his key, then turned back to the collection agent and resumed their conversation as they made their way down the hall toward the elevators. I didn't want to be alone in the empty building, but I also didn't want to ride down in the same elevator with them, so I ran down the stair exit, and cried all the way to the bus stop.

In the morning, I phoned Lola Kovaks and explained what happened. Now that I would be job-hunting again, I desperately needed the fee back. I didn't even know the term "misrepresentation" then, but I tried to get that point across as best I could. She seemed to understand what I said, and agreed that Mickey Malone hadn't been aboveboard with her. She was even sympathetic to my plight. But no, she said, there was no way the agency could be held liable for the fee. No, she said, it really was a shame but there wasn't any way the agency could refund me; they had acted in good faith. She said I'd have to take that matter up with Mr. Malone. I had neither the energy nor the courage for that, and never did.

🐾 Elvis Presley and Marvin Levine 🐾

Marvin Levine lived in the apartment next door, along with the dark-eyed Oscar, from Cairo; stocky Ibash, the Turk; and blue-eyed Bill, a sandy-haired ex-Episcopalian from Marin County. They were graduate students at the university. I felt safe living next door to graduate students. I felt that living in Berkeley was the only compensation for being on my own and having to raise a teenager; and that having thinking, cosmopolitan neighbors would make a lasting impression on her and give her some respect for the world at large. Having neighbors in graduate school almost compensated for not being there myself.

When Daddy first learned who lived next door he reacted predictably. "Holy Jesus Christ, say that again? You're living next door to a dirty Jew kike, a no-good rotten Turk, *and* a filthy Arab?" "We sometimes have them over for dinner, too," I said, relishing my new power as head of the household. Now that he knew I knew, he was completely at my mercy. There wasn't anything I couldn't say or do. The realization was exhilarating, for about five minutes; after that, it was lonely and frightening. Heads of households have to watch their step every inch of the way. "Well, just so long as you don't buy any pitted dates." He narrowed the focus of his revulsion the minute he sensed my power. "They pick their noses, then they remove the pits."

"What are you talking about?"

"The dirty Arabs, that's what I'm talking about!"

"They have modern factories. Machines remove the pits. Where did you hear such a ridiculous thing?"

"Aw, Jesus Christ, they do *not* have modern factories! They're a dirty, backward country. They pick their noses and remove the pits by hand! I read it in the *National Geographic!*"

I met Marvin indirectly. It was his roommate Bill who had knocked on the door one evening, leaned cleverly against the frame, and, holding out a metal measuring cup, whispered, "Could I borrow a cup of whiskey?" "I'm sorry, I don't have any,"

I answered. "I don't drink." I had no sense of humor. I barely refrained from adding, "I have to set an example for my little sister, whom I'm raising." "Well, come over for a glass of milk, then, so we can get acquainted." I went over for a few minutes, shaking hands with everyone as Bill made the introductions. Oscar's eyes alone stood out at that meeting; I barely remembered Marvin at all. Just Oscar's black eyes, serious and direct, the kind that go right to your soul. I kept my distance from Oscar and hated myself for it in years to come. I was not ready then to have anyone see into my soul.

The second time Marvin and I met was when he knocked on my door himself to ask if I had any paper plates. He explained, with some embarrassment, that the four of them had lost track of whose turn it was to do the dishes and an argument had ensued, and grown; the result was that all four now refused to touch the dishes. The standoff had lasted a week and every dish, glass, piece of silverware, and pot and pan in the apartment now lay heaped and rotting in the kitchen sink. The smell had gotten so bad that Bill was sleeping at a friend's. I invited Marvin to eat with us, and he happily accepted. He said the siege had only one more day to run, then it was his turn for the dishes. He didn't mind doing them when it was his week to do them—that was how four ethnically diverse students managed to live together; but he didn't think it was fair that he should have to do all the past week's accumulation, too. What did I think? Greta excused herself and retired to her bedroom. Marvin and I discussed strategies of communal living and apartment maintenance over coffee. From Greta's bedroom came the bombastic chords of Elvis Presley's guitar. THUMP-THUMP-A-THUMP! BOOM-BAM-BOOM! Then his voice joined in—wailing, growling, hurling itself into every corner of the room. Suddenly Marvin leaned forward and asked, "Would you like to go to the foreign films on Saturday night?" My heart skipped a beat, and I accepted immediately.

On Saturday night Marvin knocked on the door and we walked the mile and a half to the little theater that showed foreign films. When I saw the marquee I couldn't believe my eyes.

W. C. Fields wasn't a foreign film! I turned to Marvin in despair. "Don't you like W. C. Fields?" he said, and before I could respond, added, "I love him, I just adore him, I can't get enough of him. He's my favorite comedian of all time." How could I say I couldn't stand W. C. Fields, on a first date, after a declaration like that? I sat watching Marvin laugh for two hours. I couldn't see anything funny about being a drunk. I couldn't decide if Marvin was an idiot, or if I was being overly rigid. I couldn't come to a conclusion about that at all.

On the way home, we walked side by side without touching. Marvin was still chortling away over W.C. I wondered about his capacity for romance. Just as we turned the corner and the apartment house came into sight, a dog barked suddenly from across the street. It startled me; involuntarily, or so I told myself at the time, I linked my arm through Marvin's. His posture seemed to improve after that and he stopped laughing. Just as we got to the apartment, he said, "Do you mind if we walk around the block once?" I couldn't imagine why, we'd just come a mile and a half, but I agreed. We walked around the block in silence. As we approached the entrance once more, he said heavily, "I have something to tell you." Jesus, I thought. He can't say he loves me; we just met. Tightening his grip on my arm, he finally whispered thickly, "I'm Jewish." It struck me as so funny, so ludicrous, that I burst out laughing, doubling up right there on the sidewalk at midnight. "What's wrong?" he asked, frantic by now; you could see the perspiration forming on his forehead. "Is that *all*?" I managed to gasp. Marvin couldn't believe it. He started French kissing me, right there in the street; his mouth, like a tender mollusk, attached itself and settled over mine. I closed my eyes and drifted in those depths until a car sped by with its horn blaring and interrupted us. I shocked him further by inviting him in for hot chocolate. I thought that was the kind of thing that older sisters raising thirteen-year-olds did.

Marvin and I dated for the rest of the year. We finally broke up because I wouldn't sleep with him. On our last evening together he came over for dinner holding a dozen red roses; he held them out to me with both hands. I had set the small, low coffee table for dinner so we could sit on the floor, on pillows. I offered to include Greta but she smartly read the handwriting on the wall and made herself a sandwich and retired to her room. He tried one last time, valiantly, over dessert. "We could wait until she's asleep. Or we could go up on the roof with a blanket. I have a rubber. What would be the harm?" I got up to reheat the coffee. Marvin stared with tears in his eyes at the red roses in the center of the table. THUMP-THUMP-A-THUMP! BOOM-BAM-BOOM! "God damn it! Turn that degenerate music off this minute, or I'll tear all his pictures off your wall!" I screamed, directing all my pent-up feelings at Greta. Elvis was the last straw. Elvis the Pelvis was a threat. I couldn't afford to let myself go, that was the issue. Not with those rhythms. It was my job to keep her intact and safe until she grew up. That was my destiny now, to set an example. It was my destiny not to hear the rhythm, so that there would be someone in the responsible position when she heard the rhythm.

Every year on my birthday, for the next three years, a box of red roses arrived at the door. There was always a little card saying that I was thought of often, and remembered with great fondness. I could never decide whether Marvin was demanding and pushy, or whether I had made a terrible mistake. I could come to no conclusion on that, not even after three years.

❧ Telegraph Nights ❧

Daniel and I are smoking marijuana. It is early for this, 1959; we are ahead of our time. I am free for the moment because it is Christmas, and Daddy and Nona are here. They are there, with Greta, back at the apartment—the way they should be, the way they always should have been. There is something about their presence within those walls, their odd coupling, that has let me off the hook.

We are sitting in his pickup, curled in each other's arms, tight as a cocoon, passing the joint back and forth. I am barefoot, even though it is raining. Telegraph Avenue glistens under the streetlights, dark as a river. We are out here because it's his roommate's turn to have his girlfriend spend the night, and my apartment is full of relatives. Daniel lives in the downstairs apartment of the new brown-shingled house we moved to in the fall. His beard glows with an eerie warmth as the rain sifts slowly down under the streetlight. We kiss between drags. His mouth is a tunnel of feeling where I dissolve, liquid as the night. It is warm in the pickup; the small AM radio hums with the Platters singing "Smoke Gets in Your Eyes."

We have been exchanging our poetry for three months. He works as a carpenter during the day, and is due to be shipped somewhere far from here by the Army next month; we spend evenings reading each other's work. Outside North Beach, it's rare to find another poet; Telegraph Avenue doesn't count, they're all on welfare, sitting around the coffeehouse all day pretending to scribble something of importance. The same depressive themes run through all Daniel's poems that do through mine; in fact, he's more depressed than I am, which is the rarest find of all. I think this sadness is the main reason he takes so many drugs; but there is so much sweetness there, I don't dwell on his problems, or the future, just trust the special bond between us now. Somehow, losing myself in him is not a loss. I know how it is to feel like an old woman at twenty-one, tied to the needs of another. Our Telegraph nights are excursions into unknown territories, made familiar by touch. We always end up in The Mediterraneum coffeehouse for our espresso nightcap. Our wet poems leave imprints on the marble tables.

I've never been high before; I'm not even me, and for once I don't mind. I float now in his arms, sailing over the detritus of Telegraph Avenue; my feet don't even touch the sidewalk. We sense a new time coming, when what we value will be valued by many; we feel a community taking shape, but Daniel won't be here to see it. When he goes away I make Telegraph Avenue a shrine: it will never mean anything to me again except the nights I spent there with him.

❦

*S*onya *has been supporting Greta for two years. She commutes to San* Francisco on the 8:11 bus to her new job as a secretary in a medical office, and returns home on the 6:15 bus. Greta is fifteen. Sonya prepares dinner after work while Greta does her homework in her room, and after dinner Sonya always receives a phone call from the man she is dating, a resident at the hospital across the street from her office. Sometimes when the phone rings it will be Greta's boyfriend, Jim, the high-school student-body president. If Jim calls before Alex, Sonya exercises her prerogative as head of the household, telling Greta: "Please get off the phone; I'm expecting a call." Greta has become beautiful and popular, all the things Sonya was not. Their development almost seems to be coinciding, right here in this small apartment. Eight years apart in actual age, they are not far apart in social development. Sonya has just begun to explore life; always in the background was that silent injunction: take care of your sister. It has governed her every move and decision.

Sonya's friends from college have all married. Two have had babies. Her best friend at work has just had a Mexican abortion. It is the third Mexican abortion among her office friends. She will do anything to avoid a Mexican abortion, at least until Greta is eighteen and can take care of herself.

🎋 Linus Pauling and
Alexander Greenberg 🎋

I had just left the hospital coffee shop and was walking down the hall on my way back to the office when I heard footsteps behind me. I knew without looking that it was one of the interns; he was trying to appear casual, while walking as fast as he could to catch up with me. He was about to ask for a date. They usually did it in the coffee shop, if it was empty; but if there was a crowd, they approached you in the hall outside. (One morning at the counter, a bleary-eyed intern had slid onto the stool next to mine, leaned toward me and said, straight out, "Are you starved for affection?" His hair fell into his eyes in dark, greasy shards. I said, "Of course not," and left quickly. Anyone so desperate that he could read your own desperation at ten in the morning had to be avoided at all costs. If you gave someone like that an inch, the next thing you knew he'd want to sleep with you, and I couldn't do that because I had to set a perfect example for Greta.)

"Ahem." He cleared his throat, hoping I'd turn around, but I didn't. If I kept up a steady pace, I could make it to the door, then the street, and then I could run across against the light and he'd give up. These pursuits always made me feel like prey. I tried to imagine a situation where you could meet people naturally and get to know them gradually; where friendship and intimacy could develop as a result of long association.

He caught up with me just before I reached the exit door. With no subtlety whatever he pulled out a little black book and asked me if I was free to have dinner on Wednesday night. He had interesting eyes; they were green. I felt that all the people going in and out of the lobby were drawing only one conclusion seeing me standing there being confronted by this intern with his little black book. I retaliated by saying, "No, I'm not free; I have a poetry class on Wednesday nights." "What about Saturday, then?" He didn't hesitate a minute. Ordinarily, I would have felt trapped by such a maneuver, but this was my big week. "I have a Ban the Bomb protest march on Saturday." He scratched his head. That slowed him down a bit, but he was clever; he came up with a compromise: he could meet me after the demonstration and we could go somewhere for dinner. Was that all he was interested in, eating? Didn't he care that without a test-ban treaty we could be blown up in a matter of seconds? Why would I want to go out with someone whose priorities were so twisted? What could we possibly have in common?

Linus Pauling ran his fingers through his snowy hair and spoke with urgency about nuclear disarmament as pigeons rattled the palm trees in Union Square. The crowd attended closely, with a mixture of righteousness, awe, and a ubiquitous sense of doom. A well-dressed man on a cable car gave us the finger; some hecklers on the sidewalk yelled, "Go live in Russia!" Alex Greenberg, uncommitted, picked me out of a crowd of four thousand and his first words were, "They won't let us in the restaurant with you dressed like that."

"What's wrong with what I'm wearing?" He looked genuinely offended. He scratched his head. I had on what I always wore when I wasn't dressed like an impostor masquerading as a secretary: tunic, long black stockings and sandals, and a large wicker basket over my arm to carry my political material. "You look like a mailman with that thing over your arm." He took my elbow and escorted me away from the throng, most of whom also wore sandals; these weren't his kind of people. "Why do you dress that way?" he persisted. "Because I'm a beatnik! I also write poetry, drink wine, and hang out at the Co-Existence Bagel Shop, with all the crazies . . ."

"Yeah? I live just around the corner from the Co-Existence Bagel Shop!"

"How interesting."

"I'm sorry . . . I've offended you."

"Don't give it a second thought," I said, brushing up on my

sarcasm. "You interns just seem naturally offensive. Is it because you're all New York Jews?"

"I'm not an intern," he said, bristling; "I'm a resident. In psychiatry," he added pointedly.

We found an Italian restaurant in North Beach that admitted me, subversive garb and all, and where I let Alex Greenberg know we had something in common, after all: his training in psychiatry and my paranoid, psychopathic father. In the ensuing months it began to seem that going with a behavioral scientist was almost the same as if I had gone to graduate school and become one myself.

Sonya has taken an extra job typing in the evenings to pay for Greta's psychotherapy. Greta has not been doing homework in her room; she has been carving her wrists with a pair of rusty scissors. When Sonya discovered this, she screamed, "Why are you doing that?" Greta stared at her desk; she didn't know why she was doing that. She had also written all over the walls of her room with ballpoint ink, the same walls that Sonya and Alex had spent two weekends painting. The markings made no sense; they looked like hieroglyphs. In desperation, Sonya turned to Alex. He said, "She's been through a lot. She needs help." Sonya feels this must mean she did something wrong; or at the very least, failed to do something right. She thought she had been so careful: only going to Alex's apartment on Friday nights after work; always phoning Greta in advance. Always, after the movies or dinner, setting the alarm for midnight, so Alex could drive her back to Berkeley; Greta always left a light burning. Alex only spends the night with Sonya when Greta is away for the weekend with a friend. Sonya and Alex are engaged; after much inner struggle, it has finally been decided by her, and by her remaining unmarried friends, that it is acceptable to sleep with someone if you are "in love" or engaged, both states being expected to lead directly to marriage. She has been discreet; she has exercised judgment. She has set firm rules for Greta, too, but allowed sufficient freedom within those rules. She has paid their bills on time and tried to set an example.

Some of Greta's friends have been caught stealing liquor from the liquor store. One ran away from home, another has become pregnant and dropped out of school. Sonya keeps in close communication with the parents of Greta's friends, even though they are twenty years older than she is; she doesn't want anything like that to happen to her sister. But it turns out they are just as much in the dark about raising adolescents as she is; she gets no answers from them. Greta comes home on time from parties, but often vomits in the hall. She blames it on the pizza at the party; she thinks maybe she is allergic to pizza.

The anonymous phone calls begin around this time. They always come in the middle of the night. It is always the same old woman; she never identifies herself. She asks for Ray, and Sonya tells her Ray doesn't live there. She is sure the woman is someone who is in love with Ray, or to whom he owes money, or both. No, she insists, she doesn't know where he can be reached. It makes her uncomfortable to protect him by lying, but it makes her more uncomfortable when she considers turning him in. Ray comes down from Reno once or twice a year and sleeps on the living room couch. He no longer complains about the apartment, and always buys special cuts of meat from the butcher in order to give his girls a treat. When Sonya tells him of the midnight calls, he scratches his head in a convincing facsimile of bewilderment and says he can't imagine who it could be.

He always stays two weeks, and on the day he leaves he always says the same thing: it breaks his heart that he has to spend so much time in the mountains, doing the backbreaking work involved in making a fortune, and can't be with his precious daughters more often. Once, just after he left, Sonya finds Greta curled up on her bed, crying. The scissors lie open on the bedside table and a bloody "G" sprouts on the inside of her wrist. "God damn it, why did you do that?" Sonya yells in panic. "It's my initial," Greta whispers.

Sonya begins falling asleep the first thing in the morning on the 8:11 bus, and again over her desk at work. During her coffee break she sits in the office waiting room tearing pictures of wedding dresses out of the magazines. She begins a scrapbook of pictures torn from magazines: women in stylish aprons smiling from the depths of sparkling kitchens; long tables set with seven-course meals; young mothers wheeling red-cheeked babies in plaid strollers. There is order and stability in these images; within that framework, she imagines, new families can be brought to life who will bear none of the scars of the past. She has visions of her future family: pure, undamaged, her own creation.

❧ Weekends with Alex ❧

Whenever Greta spent the weekend at a friend's house, I stayed in San Francisco with Alex. Climbing the narrow stairs to his apartment was like entering a new world. The nights were dense with fog, the stairs groaned under the weight of our groceries as we zigzagged our way to the top. On the back porch an old cat stood patiently by an empty saucer. "Well, hello! It's you again," Alex would say as he turned the key in the lock. It was a stray, but he always fed it when it was there. In time, we came to think of it as ours—the first living thing we cared for together. The smell of Italian cooking carried up from North Beach on the wind, and the foghorns echoed across the watery blackness of the Bay. The apartment was spare, and as yet without history. We burrowed there as explorers might, charting new routes to the underground. It was the first time I had ever felt free; I had been cautious so long, holding myself back when aroused, holding myself available to do the right thing if Greta needed me. There, the restrictions gave way as we followed the slow pursuit of impulse and sensation.

One morning, waking early, I studied the sleeping form that sprawled beside me. His hair rippled on the pillow, abundant as ripe wheat; his skin was smooth, and seemed to take on a glow after love that lasted for hours, sometimes for days. His movements were physical and proud, without embarrassment. His manner had so much of that grace and certainty that horses possess, I was overcome one day and wrote him a poem containing that image. He smiled uneasily, although he was touched, and said, "That's very nice." Staring at him now, I tried to make sense of our bond: he was fair, while I was dark; a realist, while I dreamed. He was impatient with illusions of any kind; science was his god, concrete his element. We were different in every way, and yet we adhered. It was hard to understand. I thought, we all make bargains; maybe ours was this: I would be his spirit, he my anchor.

I lifted the windowshade quietly and lay watching the sky. For the first time, I felt myself to be part of something that held possibilities, and dared to think that happiness was one of them. The fog was just breaking under the warmth of the morning sun; it raced across the sky with hypnotic speed. Alex stirred, then leaned over me. "Do you find answers there?" he wondered sleepily. "Always," I said. He moved so slowly into me, I caught my breath. And we slipped once more into that soft and violent heat, that loss of self, and rode those abrasive tides down.

After breakfast we watched the sun's light bouncing off white buildings, and listened to the bells from the church across the street. The sounds of Wanda Landowska filled the room as we spread the newspaper in sections across the floor. Only after we were engaged did it strike me: This man is the antithesis of my father. He is steady, reflective, and slow to act. I thought: He will be my protection against chaos.

Eventually, there were weekends when we fought. The argument would begin mysteriously, as arguments often do; and before long he would be shouting and I would be throwing things and crying. It proved beyond a doubt, as Alex was to say, that "we carry our chaos within us." It never crossed my mind then that I was on old, familiar ground. It never occurred to me that I had played those scenes before. I had been at war with Raymond Weiler for so long, I was prepared for combat, but not for love.

🦋 On the Switchboard 🦋

The year Greta turned seventeen, Daddy came to town and insisted on staying at the Travel-Lodge down the street. Sleeping on the couch at our place wasn't as appealing as it had been in previous years. He had developed an attachment to the Travel-Lodge chain; he brought us paper bags full of their mementos: hand soaps; bath soaps; paper shoeshine rags with "Courtesy Travel-Lodge" emblazoned on them; and a large white Travel-Lodge bath mat. "Daddy," I said, "the bath mat is going too far."

"Oh, Christ, honey! They can afford it. They *want* people to take their things. It's advertising!"

"It's stealing."

"Jesus, you can really be a killjoy."

He also brought us a set of eight tumblers, bearing gold trim and the initial "E." "Where did you get these?" I asked. " 'E' isn't our initial."

"I got them when I stopped for gas; what difference does it make what initial is on there? They were free—didn't cost me anything. Now you have a lovely set of glasses. Jesus, you're always carping! Why can't you just enjoy the things Daddy tries to do for you?"

During the week Daddy was in town, I went to work on the bus as usual and Greta went to classes at high school. After school she went to her part-time job in a pizza parlor. Her boyfriend owned the pizza parlor. She never brought him home when Daddy was there because any boyfriend of Greta's made Daddy go into his routine, and we had agreed to do everything possible to keep from provoking him during his visit.

One morning while working on the switchboard, I received a frantic call from Daddy. His voice was so high-pitched it was impossible to make out what he was trying to say.

"What? I can't hear you, Daddy. What's the matter?"

"I said: I-have-just-been-to-the-apartment-and-Greta-is-not-there. Her-bed-has-not-been-slept-in-and-she-was-not-there-at-eight-thirty-this-morning. Sonya-something-has-got-to-be - done!"

"What were you doing over there at eight-thirty in the morning?"

"God damn it, Sonya, that's not the point. The point is that Greta is off somewhere with someone! You can't pull the wool over my eyes any longer! *Where* is your sister?"

"Hold on; I have another call."

"What? What? Sonya, this is serious; something has to be . . ."

"I'll be back in a minute, Daddy," I said, as I answered the three incoming calls which had been urgently buzzing for the past two minutes. When I came back on the line he was steaming.

"What do you mean cutting me off like that! I said this was *serious.*"

"Daddy, this is a *job!* I *work* here! I can't discuss Greta with you now. We'll talk about it when I get home. She's seventeen now, she can take care of herself."

"Take-care-of-her*self*?! What the hell are you talking about? I should have known better than to let you raise her; you don't know what the hell she's doing, or where she is half the time. You're always busy somewhere else. She's a *child!* A child! Don't you forget that. She needs guidance!"

Later that evening Greta wasn't talking. I wasn't talking either, for a change, and Daddy left town convinced that he had lost his daughters as well as his fortunes. The knowledge changed him. I think it marked an end to something for him—an end to the pretense that we were still his babies and he could control, however remotely, what we did with our lives. He continued to maintain that he was seeking his fortune for us, though, even if it might eventually have to be shared with some son-of-a-bitch who owned a pizza parlor.

⚜

On the night of June 3, 1962, Sonya Weiler and Alex Greenberg sit in the audience, holding hands and bearing witness to Greta Weiler's graduation from high school. Ray has phoned his regrets from Reno: the biggest deal of his life was pending; it broke his heart that he would have to miss his precious baby's graduation. He knows she'll be disappointed now, but next month, when she's a millionaire's daughter, she'll understand.

Greta is not her child, but Sonya cries anyway, just as though she were. Alex sits beside her and understands. Greta has become partly his, through intervention. He has given advice and helped with homework, in addition to painting her room and finding her therapist. That summer, when the three of them drive to the Sierras to camp, it feels to Sonya just like a family. It is a peaceful two weeks, at the end of which, they all know, they must make the pilgrimage to Reno, Nevada, and pay their respects to Ray.

⚜ Wedding Present ⚜

The first time Daddy met Alex was when we were camping near Reno. "I think it's time to drop in on my father and tell him we're engaged," I had said.

"He'll flip when he finds out I'm Jewish," was Alex's reply.

"Let him flip," I said.

The three of us had lunch at a little restaurant overlooking the Truckee River. Daddy and Alex talked about baseball the whole time, until right at the end, when Daddy let Alex in on a little secret: "I don't mean to sound boastful," he began, but went on to intimate the wealth of uranium he had up there in the hills; he wanted to make sure any future son-in-law fully appreciated that he was marrying a potential fortune.

Later, when we were alone, Daddy let drop his first opinion of the inevitable new member of the family: " 'Still water runs deep,' " he said, which, translated, meant that underneath all the talk of baseball he hadn't been able to divine a goddamned thing. Still, he wasn't about to lose a daughter over it; there were situations which called for practicality and compromise.

"Some of the finest people on earth are Jewish," he whispered, as Alex returned from paying the check. "After all, look at Jesus Christ; no finer Jew ever lived." It was his wedding present to us.

❧ *The Wedding* ☙

I feel so unsure about marriage, about Alex, about life. But I know I'm tired of working. I want to settle down, like everyone else. I'm tired of being Greta's mother; I want a baby of my own. So this seems the right thing to do. Already I have learned to use "we" when presenting a collective front to the world. It has a cozy ring to it that makes me tingle and feel secure. It says: You will never be alone again.

We have been in the bedroom of a friend's apartment, drinking champagne and waiting for the guests to arrive. Now they are assembled in the living room; the hum of their voices can be heard through the wall. The friend signals that everything is ready, so we come out of the bedroom arm in arm and begin to walk through the crowd. The judge is over by the fireplace, so I guess that's the direction we should go. We haven't rehearsed anything, we wanted it informal. The living room is filled with people who represent all my past lives and former selves. Some know each other, some do not. Some know the "old" me, some the "new." I have become a new me in order to adjust to the people with whom I now live and work. Now that college and graduate school are a dream, a new self must be created to handle the demands of this situation. Some of these people know Alex, some do not. Some of his friends are in the same situation. We have been together for three years, so this shouldn't be so, but is.

We are walking together through the guests on our way to the judge. At the last minute, someone steps out of the crowd and takes my arm and in a peculiar but firm way begins to guide me. It is Daddy. It takes me completely by surprise. Fathers are supposed to give their daughters away in marriage. He knew that by instinct. I had forgotten that he was here. If we had not been related, I wouldn't have invited him at all. I never thought to include him in the ceremony. I am shamed and sorry at this moment; I am grateful that he has made the move. I don't need an escort, but he needs to be visible. It is a kind of final accounting, a last gesture that says: This is mine. I don't even protest. He hasn't spent a dime on this wedding, but he has the right to stand up and be recognized. He is a father. He is that much.

❦ Nona Dreams Her Death ❧

When people came up to Nona to offer congratulations to the grandmother of the bride, I think it made her uneasy, so she responded by saying, "She was perverse as a child," just to make sure they understood I wasn't perfect. It was her way of showing her love. She was eighty-three, with watery eyes and deep lines in her face, but she moved with energy and her mind was still sharp.

We postponed a honeymoon and tried to make Daddy and Nona comfortable in our apartment for the week they were staying. One afternoon, while Daddy puttered in the kitchen testing his old recipes, and Alex and I lay on the floor reading the Sunday paper, Nona suddenly looked up from her book and challenged Alex to explain the dream she'd had the night before. She was flirtatious with him, like a young girl; coy one minute, teasing the next: damning Freud, praising Jung, and dismissing any latent meaning in dreams, yet hungering to grasp some meaning in her own. Alex demurred at first; then, sensing the urgency in her voice, encouraged her to describe her dream. She began in a halting, apologetic way, denigrating the whole thing as ridiculous. "No, go on," Alex said, waiting. Nona blushed, then persisted. "Well, it was the strangest thing," she said, closing her eyes as though to see more clearly. "There was a shore, and on this shore were masses and masses of people, all facing a dark sea. As more waves of people approached from the land behind, those in front were forced into the water. They waded out in huge numbers, then disappeared. The process kept repeating itself. I thought I recognized my friends in front, friends who have died. I watched them go into the sea and drown. Now isn't that queer? What on earth do you think it all means?"

❧ *The Anniversary* ☙

By our first anniversary Greta had a full-time job and was more or less on her own. I had quit my secretarial tasks in order to devote my full attention to varnishing floors, washing Alex's socks by hand, and getting pregnant. I dug up the back lot behind the apartment and planted a large, complicated garden. One night when Alex had a meeting, I attended a concert on my old campus, and coming out of the auditorium I ran into Dr. Stedman. "Are you writing?" he asked, smiling broadly and taking my hand in a warm greeting. "Writing?" I asked blankly. "Oh!" I recovered, "no, I'm a homemaker now!" I said, as though that were a logical alternative to the old, forsaken wish. I glanced around quickly at the familiar paths and buildings; it seemed like a dream that I was ever there. Back on the freeway, I realized the full meaning of his question and cried all the way home.

On our anniversary night, we sat by the fire and opened a bottle of champagne. "I never thought we'd make it to this night," Alex said, joking. "Neither did I," I said, as the purring cat curled in my lap. We didn't need fancy celebrations; we had each other. In a matter of time we'd have more than that: children for the new family. Suddenly, the phone rang. Alex rose to answer it as I stretched in front of the fire.

Something in the low tone of his voice alerted me immediately; I had just sat up when he came back into the living room and said, "Nona's dead." I stared into the fire; it was hardly unexpected, but it shocked me all the same. Alex sat down beside me and waited. It took a while for my feelings to clarify. Her toughness and resilience had seemed like an eternal hedge against death; yet she, too, had been forced into that bottomless sea. It was hard to imagine her in that terrible void, suspended and invisible. It seemed only right that, at the end, she should be warmly enfolded, tucked in and rocked to sleep; eased into her journey and comforted in exactly those ways that she comforted me in my early child-void. The strains of "Kentucky Babe" swam in my head, and the impossibility of ever reaching out to her again swept through me like a great and sudden pain. Tears sprang to Alex's eyes, too, as he held me; we finished the champagne and sat until the fire went dead. It helped as we talked of Nona's perseverance and courage, even her idiosyncrasies; it helped dispel the image of ourselves as members of the crowd that pushed her off the beach.

I had no intention of attending her funeral; I couldn't see what good that did the dead at all. If I hadn't made the effort to attend her while she lived, what hypocrisy could persuade me to show up now? But Alex said, "You must," meaning, I must do it for myself; and he was right—although I didn't know that then. Her final little bungalow room at the end of a long row was saved from squalor by her individual touches: the carefully tended flower border outside, and her few, well-chosen and carefully arranged things inside. The walls of the tin shower stall in the bathroom were covered with her floral paintings, rendered in minute detail, even on its ceiling. I couldn't resolve in my own mind if all that lonely effort represented a tragic waste, or a crucial adaptation. Because it was early spring, only one flower was in bloom in the border outside: the forget-me-not. Hundreds of them had sprung from the hard earth to form a delicate memorial, her final admonition.

When Jack announced his intention to cremate her, no one protested; it seemed to make sense. But a few weeks later, when he wrote of her final placement, I was shocked: the ashes that were now her final form had been sealed inside a cement block and sunk in twenty fathoms of salt water off the shore of her beloved island. I had always thought of her as the one appropriate person, of all who lived, to be returned to earth. I had always seen her there: decomposing, spreading out, becoming one with the growth she tended so well.

⚇ Annette ⚇

I had been in labor fifteen hours when Alex pulled the cold pastrami sandwich from his pocket and sat down on the vacant bed in the now empty labor room and began to eat in front of me. I should have considered how long he had held off, but didn't. "Look, I'll leave the room if you want; I'm sorry you can't have some too, but you don't expect me to starve, do you?" He was getting jumpy. He had canceled all his appointments so he could witness the birth of his first child, and here was the mother screwing everything up. Nine other women had come, cooperated with nature, and left with new life in their arms. "Everyone is different," said the obstetrician with supreme indifference.

When little Annette was finally examined, wrapped, and placed between us ten hours later, the tension of the previous day and night dissolved. We admired her in disbelief. She was strange, yet familiar; ordinary, yet frightening; awesomely com-lex, and simplicity itself. Alex went home in a daze, and I fell into a tense and superficial sleep and immediately dreamed of Valery: She was on a strange street, walking away from me. She just kept going, farther into the distance, until she was just a pin at the junction of two lines. When I got home three days later and Greta, who had offered to cook and help with the baby, departed after one day, it was just like having that dream all over again. I cried bitter tears and blamed Greta for failing me, while she blamed me for being a mother to somebody else.

One morning while the baby slept, I read an article in the paper about the Chinese New Year, and scanning the Chinese calendar, was struck by an unusual feature: every sixty years, in the Year of the Horse, a rare phenomenon occurs, known as a Star Horse Year. I noted right away that my new daughter had been born in that year; as I smiled at that unique event I was shocked to see that Valery had been born in the Star Horse Year preceding that, sixty years before. I felt myself at that moment an agent in time, a link between two special people who would never know each other, but who both knew me. I couldn't decide what significance to attach to this strange coincidence, so I cried instead. Later, holding the baby, I tried hard to see something of Valery in her. I looked for a resemblance, but it wasn't there. Maybe it would appear in time, maybe it never would.

🐝 *Washing the Windows* 🐝

One year during his annual Christmas visit with us, Daddy de-cided to wash our apartment windows. They weren't really dirty, but he had exhausted all the other little chores which helped him feel useful: scrubbing the sink tiles; planting azalea bushes; put-ting up gates across the stairs for the baby.

He was determined to wash them; I couldn't talk him out of it. I bundled Annette up for her checkup with the doctor and as we left, Daddy could be seen rubbing away on the third floor, surrounded by Windex and rags.

Babies overflowed the waiting room; we were there for an hour and a half, and it was a full two hours before we got home. As we entered, there was Daddy, standing at the window, his face white with pain. It took me a minute to understand what happened. It was an old apartment; the window cords were rotten. Through tears, he explained that he had raised the window and was resting his hands on the sill while admiring the view, when it suddenly slammed down, trapping all his fingers on both hands. He had been imprisoned there for two hours. I wiped off the blood, but it required another trip to the doctor; his fingers were badly bruised.

That evening he went over it again and again, as though trying to rid himself of the horror. He couldn't get his mind off it: for two hours he had stood there, calling for help; no one had heard. I felt the horror myself; it was so similar to all the near-disasters and close escapes he had recounted in the past that I found myself doubting my own skepticism. What is there about him that invites these things, I thought, then felt bad for thinking he had had anything to do with it. It was my fault, leaving him there alone to wash our rotting windows.

After a quick discussion, Alex and I decided the time had come for a family conference. We would make it clear to Daddy that it was time to stop getting trapped in windows and plumbing dry mountains for slippery fortunes. We convinced ourselves we were ready to take him on no matter what the outcome might be. Phrases were rehearsed and discarded, as in a play, to determine the approach which would allow him a dignified way out of his obsession.

"My precious little family," Daddy intoned after two hours, "words are inadequate to express my gratitude for what you are trying to do. Please don't think Daddy doesn't appreciate it—I do, with all my heart. And I would love nothing better than to settle here for good with you precious loved ones. And I will, someday, I will. I know my work seems fruitless; but when I tell you of the opportunity I received in the mail just last week, you will understand why I must make one final trip to the mountains—not for me; hell, I'm over the hill! But for *you*!" With that, he produced a letter and handed it over to Alex. It spoke of the need to get some land out of escrow, listed the price as five hundred dollars, and looked authentic.

Alex studied it carefully—too carefully. I began to squirm. *Don't do it,* I signaled him from across the room. He didn't get the message. He seemed oblivious, preoccupied, even fascinated, in a way that seemed to say: You've handled your father long enough, and you've bungled it; now it's time for a professional to step in.

"Well, Ray, this looks pretty convincing," he said as the color sprang to Daddy's face. "I would be willing to stake you to the five hundred dollars, with the understanding that this is to be absolutely the last deal." It's hard to see your husband in the role of a sucker, but it was not unlike the cutting of wrists and mixing of blood: if this is what it takes to make him an undisputed member of the family, he's in. Daddy left town the very next morning, full of confidence and unparted from his dream.

ᨏ᪥ *Silver Strings* ᨏ᪥

We visited Daddy in Reno the following spring. It was almost as though nothing had happened, at least at first. Then, at dinner, the words plutonium and titanium began sifting into his conversation and little samples of ore began tumbling from his jacket pockets. I picked at my food and tried to adopt a philosophical mood. Nearby you could hear the music of Horace Hearn and his Silver Strings serenading the diners with his roving band of violinists. Horace Hearn was employed by the casino; he and his group were troubadours of the Wild West. He was very suave, and was partial to songs like "Flight of the Bumblebee" and "Fascination."

After dinner we went over to the slots to gamble. As he jingled

215

the coins in his pocket Daddy announced, "Honey, when he finishes this set, I want you to meet a very dear friend of mine. An upstanding citizen and a fine musician. We've had many long, wonderful talks together, and he and your daddy have become close friends." Oh God, I thought; he's going to do it to Horace Hearn. And sure enough, in time, he did.

⚜ Wally ⚜

Our next trip to Reno we met and had dinner at another casino; Horace Hearn was never mentioned again. With each visit the clubs became seamier, until we were down to the Silver Dollars and the Silver Slippers and the Losers' clubs. We always met and parted there; Daddy never asked us to his "room" and we never inquired. We did say from time to time, "You should come and live with us," but we knew he would always answer, "I appreciate your kind thoughts, but I have important work to finish here in the mountains, and I must be near my work. You'll see; someday things will be different for all of us." I wondered if that was why I felt free to ask. "Yes . . . you'll see," he repeated, his voice trailing off. He was in his early seventies, and had slowed down considerably. You were tempted to call him feeble, except that every Christmas he was still capable of blowing in the door when he visited, his overcoat wet with rain and smelling of mildew, scattering bills all over the table and announcing another "deal." The denominations were smaller, though, and he always gathered them up quickly and put them back in his pocket.

One Christmas Daddy began to speak of Wally. Wally was his new friend. Wally and his wife, Irma, lived on the outskirts of Reno. He didn't say where he had met him, or how. Just that they were "real people, fine people," who had begun to invite him to Sunday dinner on a regular basis. Did I give a sigh for Wally and Irma? By the time Christmas dinner was over I was thinking: What are Wally and Irma to me?

216

By the following year, it was clear that Daddy was hanging in with Wally; he declined our invitation for Thanksgiving. Wally and Irma would provide. We sent him small amounts of money from time to time, which he did not decline, and wrote him as seldom as possible care of his post office box in Reno. That Christmas he arrived driving Wally's car, which he tried to pass off as his. "Got me a fine little Chevy," he said, patting the hood. Did he think I was illiterate? The registration was right there in plain sight, saying, "Wally Venner, 153 Sage Street, Reno, Nevada." There were spent bullet shells in the glove compartment. I was determined to see the holidays through with as little hysteria as possible. I cooked turkey with all the trimmings, and Daddy passed out soon afterwards. He left town two days later, beeping the horn of his fine little Chevy, *toot toot!* I stood on the curb and waved for the shortest acceptable length of time.

Ding Dongs

The next year he arrived by Greyhound. I didn't ask about Wally until the next day. "How's Wally," I said, trying to be casual. There wasn't much left to talk to him about that wouldn't touch off some flurries about plutonium. In fact, you could never be sure anymore if any subject was neutral enough not to touch off plutonium. Mention that the cat was at the vet: "Oh, Jesus, those goddamned doctors—veterinarians, too—they'll get you coming and going. Someday I'll have enough plutonium to put them all out of business." Or remark at dinner, "Good roast beef." "Yes, Daddy knows his meats. But you have to start with the finest cattle. Take a man like Charles Steen, used to be a cattle rancher, one of the finest ... wait a minute; I think he was in cattle ... well, never mind. The point I want to make is this: Charlie Steen is a millionaire today, a *millionaire*. Discovered a fortune in uranium, right up there in the same mountains where your daddy is working his heart out, to get it out of the land, for you! The land, that's the only reality I know. You go in with your bare hands and you come out with . . ." His bourbon would be geting to him; he wasn't sure anymore whether you came out with uranium, pluto-nium, or jut a handful of dirt.

"Wally? Sure, he's fine. Irma, too. Just fine," he said, sitting down slowly at the kitchen table. He pulled a brown paper bag out of his jacket pocket and began arranging its contents in a row in front of him: one banana, with brown spots; one Snickers bar; and two Hostess Ding Dongs. They had been sitting in his jacket pocket since he got off the bus the day before.

"You're not going to eat that crap," I said. I had been fixing him lunch.

"Oh, honey, it's still food. Daddy doesn't like to waste good food; you know Daddy."

"There's no food value in it, except maybe for the banana." What was I doing feeling maternal toward him? Didn't he know that Ding Dongs and bourbon weren't a winning combination? Shortly after lunch I felt compelled to make my annual offer of room and board. I wasn't sure what I'd do if he accepted; but it didn't seem to matter that year. Something was very wrong when he couldn't distinguish between junk and nourishing food. He who had conned the grocer year after year in order to feed us well.

"Thank you all the same, honey; I appreciate your concern, but you know Daddy is working on the most important deal in his entire life. After putting in so many heartbreaking years, I wouldn't want to miss out on it now."

🐾 *Going Out* 🐾

One night during the holidays we went to visit friends and left Daddy to babysit. He sat on Annette's bed, obligingly reading the book she had chosen; but as we left the house I was sure I heard

218

the opening lines of Aunt Mary's stolen-apple-pie saga of years and years ago.

Over dinner we mentioned that Daddy was spending Christmas with us. "I remember your father," said our host. "We had a long talk at your wedding. I was tempted to invest in his venture; it sounded like a sure thing. But I never followed through on it. I probably lost a fortune, ha ha."

Driving home I said, "That's it. He goes." Doing it to others was one thing; hustling at his daughter's wedding, though, that was breaking a rule; some rule, somewhere.

I can't say it didn't hurt when Greta and I strong-armed him down to the Greyhound terminal the next morning; but it didn't hurt as much as I thought it would. He tried all the tricks, too: losing his ticket; buying a Snickers bar at the candy machine; making the snap break on his cheap suitcase. There was something about his presence there that caused all the children in the waiting room to shriek and wail, and the wino in the corner to vomit all over the bench. We held fast. "Happy new year!" we called after him, as the line shuffled onto the bus. I was sure we would sideswipe a truck or something on the way home, as punishment, but we didn't. I kept waiting, but as the weeks went by and nothing happened, I decided that maybe we are permitted some evil thoughts and heartless acts in this life, just so long as it isn't overdone.

❧ Timothy ❧

The day his son was born, Alex Greenberg peered into the tiny face and said, "He doesn't look like me." He was quiet for a minute, then added, "He doesn't look like you, either. He looks just like Ray." I listened with alarm but was careful not to show it. I knew it would please Daddy, and perhaps even please me to see him made happy in some significant way in his loneliness and

219

age; but it was not something I wanted for my son, to be like him in any way. "Leave him alone," I said, "he was just born."

The photo lady snapped him in his plastic bassinette and Alex sent Daddy a telegram that read: YOUR GRANDSON ARRIVED TODAY. PICTURE TO FOLLOW. In the months after his birth the resemblance faded and the issue was forgotten. At the age of four, however, he developed an intense preoccupation with rocks; he seemed mysteriously drawn to the glint and shine of the minerals that laced their surfaces. It was Alex's turn to tell me to leave him alone when he noted my anxiety. "He's a little boy, it's a normal interest." There was absolutely no logic in my fears; I couldn't explain them, even to myself.

❧ The Phone Call ❧

Since we only saw Daddy once a year now, at Christmas, we began to prepare for him mentally around November, which happened to be his birthday month. I picked out two birthday cards at the drugstore, one which read, "Happy Birthday, Grandpa" (Raccoon); the other "Happy Birthday, Dad" (Hunting Lodge). I wasn't wild about the lodge, since he didn't hunt; but the others all bore messages of the "You're Faithful and True/There's Never Been/A Father as Wonderful as You" genre. I signed them and sealed them and put them on the shelf. It was eight days early; I didn't want to send them too far ahead.

That night the phone rang.

"Is this Sonya?" the voice asked.

"Yes, who is this?"

"This is Wally Venner." I pulled the cord as far as it would go and just managed to reach my cigarettes. He's dead, I thought. "Yes, go ahead."

"It's about your dad. We went hunting with my brother-in-law Fred three days ago. I don't know if Ray ever mentioned Fred to you. We went up in the mountains to hunt deer and Ray got lost. We been trying to find him for three days now."

"Three days ago? Why didn't you call?"

"Well, I was up there the whole time, trying to find him. Fred, he came down the first night and notified the sheriff and they've had posses out there every day until today, when it started snowing up a blizzard. They had the Civil Air Patrol out too, but now they can't get in there on account of the snow."

Your last sky fades, larcenous eyes.

I asked for details; Wally sounded strange, panicky. I didn't know if it was exhaustion or something else.

"Did he have a gun?" I asked.

"Yeah, well, I gave him a gun, so he'd feel like the others, you know? But he don't shoot or hunt, so I left the bullets out. I thought it would be good for him to take him along with us; but he just sort of wandered off. I spent the whole first night up there shooting my gun off, hoping he'd hear it and find his way back to the camp."

It is the third day. Do you still dream of anything?

"How could he just wander off?" I asked. "Had he been drinking?"

"Well, you know, I worried about that myself, so before we left, I took his flask away and hid it in the trunk of the car."

I see my father wandering under the blackest stars. He is frightened and confused: he has no bullets to sound an alarm, no matches for a fire, Wally adds later, and no bourbon: his flask taken from him the way a bottle is taken from a baby. Was ever a man left to die so alone?

The phone was tied up for hours that night. It's amazing the way people can mobilize themselves, especially after a fact. Calls to relatives, long out of touch; calls to sheriffs who talk about finding bones in the spring.

"I have a letter from Ray right here in my hands," his withered sister in Topeka whispers over the long-distance wire. "It was written two days before he left on that trip. 'I have a foreboding,' " she quotes him as saying. "He must have known some-

221

thing," she sobs. His usual melodrama, I tell myself, to calm my renewed alarm. She must have a hundred letters of foreboding tucked in her scented drawers.

Late that night I found myself wondering if Wally was swarthy; I forced myself to take a sleeping pill and Alex said, "You're beginning to sound just like your father," but he said it gently. It wasn't the first time it had crossed my mind that night. Am I entering his world, or still functioning in my own?

"He could never have survived the first night out there in that weather, at his age," the man at Civil Air Patrol had said. Was it easier to think Wally swarthy than to think myself guilty of negligence?

"We usually find 'em in the spring," said the sheriff, eating potato chips; you could hear him crunching away all the way from Reno.

Dead is dead. There is no coming back from it.

ꙮ "Flue, Arthritis, and Longing for You" ꙮ

Two days later, Greta and Alex drove to Reno to pick up Daddy's "effects." I stayed home with the children and was grateful not to have to see what his last room looked like. I made a fire in the fireplace and ceremoniously burned the unmailed birthday cards. "Happy Birthday, Grandpa," said the raccoon as he went up in flames.

They returned at midnight with two cardboard boxes; that was all there was. You could see things like Ivory soap and a toothbrush on top, along with *Science and Health, With Key to the Scriptures,* by Mary Baker Eddy and a nude foldout from *Playboy.* Underneath were two packs of letters, wrapped in rubber bands. "The letters will have to wait until tomorrow." We all felt numb.

"The room was terrible," said Greta. "They didn't even wait

222

until we got his things out; another old man was moving his stuff in. It was in the basement and had liquor and urine all over the rug. It makes me sick to think of him living there; we should have forced him to come here."

"His pride . . ." I said, wondering how different things might have been if we had commandeered him here, the way we had commandeered him to Greyhound.

In the morning Greta and I started going through the letters. It is a duty the living perform for the dead—if they have any curiosity at all.

Hi My Sweet:
    I always say well if that is it then I have sure been played for a fool, and if that is my lot I will have to suffer the consequences. I am always in doubt about you and your deals.
    He has not tied into me again but I am expecting anything from them both. I tried to tell you last night not to mention me sending you money, but you rambled on and I could not say anything here. I am afraid he might have the wires tapped.

In the margin by this paragraph Daddy had made a notation in pencil: "He can't have the phone wires tapped. Only FBI can." That must have been very reassuring to her, I thought, as I passed the letter over to Greta.

"No!" was all she said. She had never wanted to believe anything negative about Daddy.

It was a confirmation. You're never really sure of anything until you see the evidence. And here it was, spread out in front of us halfway across the room. I wondered briefly whether this evidence covered as much square feet of floor space, here and now, as the Big Deal had, then and there. It was as though I had been doing everything, all my life, to keep the wolf from the door. And then, one day, here he is at my door, and I go up to him and say: Oh, there you are; I've been expecting you.

Hi My Sweet:
    Your news sounded wonderful but I am still not going to allow myself to get excited until I know for sure there is something to get excited about.

223

I never had anything, only what I worked for, and it seems always someone ready to take it from me. Well my Dear I don't know any more to say so will be waiting for your call Tues. or Wed. So Bye now Good Luck and Love & Kisses.

There is an enclosure with this one, a piece of paper in Daddy's writing:

Good news. Have to stay over another night; reason for staying: I got your 2 claims, that you bought, ready to clear the govt. regulations. Cost of papers, processing, etc.: $17.50

They are all from the same person, I think to myself. She appears to be an old woman. She doesn't even have a name. She is cautious, even terrified. Letter after letter she just says, "Bye."

Hi Honey,
   I don't know what you are going to do about your deal. I have told you not to ask me for any more. As it is now I do not have enough to even pay our rent.
   Have waited and hoped for so long that I am very doubtful. This promise for Friday is probably another stall.
   Call when you can because when I don't hear from you I just think well, this is the end. I want all you have said to be true so Jane can't be so sure she is right. She is so mad at me, say I have broke the hotel here and taken everything away from she and Mitch. So I am left alone and scared to do anything, only what she decides.
   Read between the lines and I just bet you that you have never destroyed any of my letters. Just like when you left here, she run across those & brought up 2 or 3 for me to read and she says I suppose from your Sweetie Pie after money, don't you send him one dime you know he's just pulling your leg as he has always done.
   Bye Bye—Love and call.

All the letters are written on Nash Hotel stationery.

100 Modern, Fireproof Rooms   *Daily Rates*

She lives in Seattle with Jane and Mitch and the three of them run the hotel. She works the switchboard nights, waiting for him to call. She lives in fear of Jane and Mitch; they have Daddy's number, but she has dreams. We sit on the floor trying to put the pieces together. The Nash Hotel was where he moved after he got out of jail. Here is a rough draft of a letter to her which Daddy had worked out on an airmail tablet:

Sorry I couldn't phone you last night. More good news than you can take: Spent 3 extra days in SLC with F. (He wants to be my best man at our wedding)! Also one night we had dinner together and the VP of Kennecott was with us!! Boy!! Now—F. wants all our claims (yours especially, he says). So I have three hard days work in the snow. I owe 2 months rent but he said let it go until our ship comes in. But I have to pay the other man 2 days wages. And the cost of setting up the other escrows is a few dollars more.

So, for the last time, I'll need $30 Wednesday. Last time you will ever have to send money *this* way. It will all be going back *that* way—soon.

Oh, you. You have lied for the last time.

Hi My Sweet:
I sent you another $15.00 yesterday making a total sent you $45.00 and another one today with $10.00.
Remember I am always thinking of you and being married in Reno is what I have always hoped for.
Remember what I told you the last time I seen you here, won't write it but expect you have forgotten, been so long ago.

Hi My Sweet:
Now I will be in hot water because I will be short of the $200 that I would have had and if I am trapped by either of them I will have a hard time explaining.
I have a pair of Finch birds, a parakeet and my pooch. Guess you think I am nuts, my parakeet have had him you know for

225

12 years. One of the guys here gave me the Finch birds and my poodle we all love her to pieces she is the queen of Sheba. She buries herself in the covers and she is so small that you have to feel all over the bed before you can find her. She is the smartest little rascal and can almost talk to me.

Well my Dear will ring off now and lots of love and kisses. Will hear good news I am hoping against hope.

Bye Bye.

Hi:

Well I wonder what has happened to you that you have not called.

It looks to me like this is it and I am just another one you have been fooling—you have disappeared like those who just drop out of sight and they never hear anything more of them.

After all you have said and promised, Ray, it just seems absolutely impossible for a person to be like that but who am I to say—only God above knows that. If I don't hear soon—then we will all know you have pulled up stakes.

No more to say now, everyone feeling bad, colds, Flue, Arthritis and longing for you.

The next letter is dated August 27, and comes to him in wavering script on Sacred Heart Hospital stationery:

Hi My Dear Sweet Heart:

I wonder if you can make out anything I am trying to write. It is awful hard. This just came like a flash a week ago tomorrow morning. I was dressing to go to work and I fell over on the bed back wards and that was it and I could not get up and the dog was trying so hard to help and barking to call attention but no use so I finally knocked the telephone off so Jane would hear me.

So God Bless you I need prayers from you if you really mean that you love me and all of the things you have said. So God Help me because my whole left side is paralized now. Sweet Heart I need to hear your voice.

I think I just need you by my side. Mabe now you will just say no.

Hi Dear:

Sweet Heart you can't imagine how bad I have been wanting to hear from you. That you are O.K. in every way. I do hope you are getting somewhere now and that it won't be the same old story.

I wonder if this will make any difference with you or does this give you a chance to get away. Was you always just fooling me? I wish you would please tell me the truth.

Now Bye Bye Dear and I hope to hear from you. Hope you got the $50 but do not mention it if you call please.

So Bye Bye my Love—hope you did pray for me and please keep on.

Fall, Reno snow, obliterate that sad, pale skin. Cover his sins.

Dear Honey:

Just received your letter. I cannot believe you did not get my letter and money, sent you $50. I just can't be sending you money and so many times you claiming you don't get it.

If this does not pan out as you say then I will be convinced that Jane and Mitch were right.

I hear lots of things and I think myself it is funny that after 6 years you would never show here so mabe I am the sucker after all.

Against all my good judgment I am sending you $50 more but no matter what I will not send any more.

Love and Kisses.

Hi,

I do not know how to start this but any way here goes & mabe for nothing.

I can't understand.

Are you sick or have you disappeared like you did before?

Mabe just because I did not continue to send you the amount of money like you wanted.

If that is the case and you were so near getting the money as you let on to me, then you have collected it all and flew away with it and Jane's advice has always been right and what a fool I have been all these years.

227

If there is nothing to it just be kind enough and honest enough so that I will know that you are O.K. and for me just say God Forgive.
Bye now.

This was the last letter Daddy received from her. Three days later he went hunting with Wally.

Bye baby bunting
Daddy's gone a-hunting
Gone to get a rabbit skin
To wrap his baby bunting in. Bye bye.

One by one we gather them up; all the letters go back in little piles in the box.

I am left with a terrible question. Is it my duty to write and tell her the news? What could I say?

Dear Bye Bye:
You were right all along.

Or should I let her die thinking he lost his life as a hero, putting her money to good use? Her good arm cradling the poodle, she would sink lightly into her covers and dream. I have considered the question carefully and have no idea what to do. No name, no name, who are you to me?

₴ Solving the Riddle ₴

There were still some papers and a few miscellaneous letters in the bottom of the carton, but lunchtime had long passed; we went into the kitchen to eat with the feeling of having finished most of a monumental task.

Over lunch Greta and I exhausted the dregs of all the remaining possibilities: Why did Wally let him go into such a desolate area without proper equipment? Did Daddy brag once too often of his fantastic treasures, and did someone decide to go after it themselves, after getting him out of the way? Did the sheriff really use the term "foul play"? Was his disappearance really an accident? Or had he invented it, like all the other times, only to have it become a bid for attention that backfired due to inclement weather? Was it still possible to care?

After lunch we attacked the remains, among which were two hundred pages of Daddy's private numbers system. He considered his system infallible. I guess if you aren't getting it out of the mountains you have the right to give the tables a try. As much as I wanted to burn them, these pages were haunting. They represented such precise calculations, such exact numbering, so much effort. It staggered me to think of the hours he had spent on it: two hundred pages of the neatest little rows of ballpointed numbers you have ever seen. It seemed a crime to destroy such meticulous work. I can't say it didn't cross my mind to hop up there with his system the next time I went to Reno; I felt a mild pull in that direction: the thought that I might fulfill one of his dreams— if not the big one, at least the subsidiary one.

All that remained was a 1929 valentine he had once sent to Mother, and a form letter from Wm. S. Rice, Inc., Adams, N.Y. Their stationery bore an explicit diagram of the male genital area.

Dear Mr. Weiler,

Today the postmaster at your office returned the C.O.D. shipment made you a short time ago. We are at a loss to understand why you did not accept the package, as it was sent C.O.D. upon special request from you. Possibly there was some mistake about the notice and you intended accepting the shipment later.

Now, we have been to considerable expense in making up this outfit for you, as it was assembled to your specifications, as shown by your description, and we do not feel you are doing the fair thing by not accepting the shipment. If you were unable to pay the C.O.D. charges just now, or for some other reason, you could not take the package, we will appreciate it if you write us just what that reason is.

We are confident your Rice Support, assembled to your individual described needs, will bring you comfort and security for which you have long searched. You can be assured of our every possible effort to assist you in overcoming your difficulties.

Kindly give this matter your careful consideration and we feel you will decide to give the Rice Comfort Support a trial. At least, write why you did not accept the package because we are holding it until we hear from you.

Very Truly Yours,
William Rice

I puzzled over their insistence that the addressee in question must write and give a reason why he has changed his mind. A possible response went through my mind:

Dear Mr. Rice:

I am in receipt of your letter of October 10, requesting an explanation for the refusal of Raymond Weiler to accept his C.O.D. shipment. I regret to inform you that Raymond Weiler will not be needing his Rice Support as he lies stiff and helpless under the driest stars, approximately thirty miles northwest of Gerlach, Nevada.

"Wait," Greta said, "there's something else stuck on the bottom." Sure enough there was. An airmail tablet and another letter. The letter contained a pamphlet describing sex aids, "as per request," and color illustrations of long penile sheaths studded with medieval rubber spikes. It was hard to bear, the thought of him at the age of seventy-five, in some filthy transient room, trying to get his sex aid on.

We flipped through the pages of the airmail tablet. "It's blank," I said; "there's nothing on it." At just that moment, out fell three bills, wilted and green, which floated to the floor. A ten and two twenties. It came as such a surprise, there at the end, such a paradox, that we were speechless for a moment. "He had fifty dollars hidden in there!" Visions of plutonium flickered briefly, then died. We did examine the pad carefully, just in case, and found that on the top of the first page of what appeared to be blank paper was written, in Daddy's script: "P.2. Would you want it any other way?"

"It must be the second page of a letter he started to someone," Greta said. We turned every blank page in the tablet, looking for P.1. There was something excruciating about seeing that fragment there, with nothing to attach it to. In the end, it turned out there was nothing else: neither money, nor message. We were left to take P.2. as the ultimate message, and did.

You go now, you fade into nightshades.

Well, this is the end, I thought. But not really a true end. That will probably come on the day, years from now, when they notify me that the bones have been found and they have every reason to believe (or no reason to disbelieve) that they are Daddy's. And we will all draw together one final time, like iron shavings to a magnet, and arrangements will be made because it is against some law to just leave bones out there, once they have been found. I don't know if the law requires you to view a skeleton as it does a corpse that is still intact; but with bones, it will be that much easier to wonder what any of it has to do with me.

Alex says we pay a price when we can't mourn. "Save it for your patients," I tell him. I knew he was waiting for me to cry so I could be free to spend my energy on the living, instead of squandering it on questions about the missing. He kept making himself available to me, in ways I couldn't use. There were times when I was sure he had more feeling for my father than I did. I was certain he could never understand my history with Daddy, or my lack of feeling now, because I had no understanding of it myself, just a conviction that feelings must be avoided at all cost. I wanted to reassure him, to cry for this loss the way I imagined he expected normal people would do. It was just like standing by Valery's coffin all those years ago, knowing what was expected, and not being able to do it.

✂ *The Benefit* ✂

Two months later a letter arrived from Social Security acknowledging the disappearance of Mr. Raymond Weiler. The letter added that, for the survivors, there was a benefit consisting of two hundred dollars toward the cost of burial, provided that the remains of the deceased were recovered within two years from the date of the presumed death.

"They'll find him the day after the two years are up," said Greta.

✂ *Mabel's Letter* ✂

Sister Mabel had to face reality, finally. She came through pretty well.

Dear Sonya,

Writing to you and Greta about your daddy is a task so difficult that I feel helpless before it. I collect my thoughts for something to say—then it is like gathering thoughts into emotions almost overpowering. I seem to be confronted with something waiting for an answer.

This is my answer: I still do and always will love my brother. I know—I think I know—about the accusations which may be brought against him. But the real person—the father, the brother, the friend—was as fine and as faithful and as true a person as anyone—born with such an intense desire to bring "gold" to his loved ones. We know that desire to this degree is liable to take the strangest forms. For him, there was no rest until his objective was reached. He never gave up hope.

Someone long ago said, "Only the dream is real." Could this be true? Then how wise the admonition: "Judge not." But this I believe: that in the design and the reason and all of life—your daddy will not now have to suffer in agony for mistakes or irresponsibilities while he lived upon this planet—because he already has. I have seen his agony of soul because he could not accomplish the things he wanted. This I know. The reason for everything I do not know.

Just a little verse, then I'll say I am thankful he left behind two such fine nieces.

> Yet, after brick and steel and stone are gone,
> And flesh and blood are dust,
> The dream lives on.

Maybe some dreams live on, I thought, but I didn't mind seeing this particular dream die. Of course I knew that it wouldn't die just because Daddy had. It would simply free-float for a respectable period of time, then embody itself in someone else.

There are still days when I expect to see him return, as he always did before. I imagine him ringing the bell some dark night, his shoulders covered with snow. He will enter, limping a little from frostbite, but otherwise unchanged. "Oh honey," he will begin, "you will never believe the story Daddy is about to tell you." Then the image fades, and I think: No. Never again. I ask myself: You wanted it this way, didn't you? No, not quite this way, although I can't say, now that it has happened, that it wasn't fitting; can't say it wasn't an absolutely clean, logical extension of everything that went before.

Every November, around the middle of the month, P.2. comes out to dance. "Would you want it any other way?" it says, circling downward through the brain like a falling leaf at year's end. There are moments when I am tempted to say: No. You're absolutely right; how astute of you to foresee it, and thanks for saving me the trouble. Sometimes I believe he planned it all, like a master spy, and left behind this one clue to pierce the heart.

233

*S*onya Weiler Greenberg sits on the floor with her son, Timothy, age five. He is looking through the picture album of her wedding. He has stayed home from kindergarten with a cold. The album is spread across his lap. He turns the page and asks the name of a face in the wedding crowd. Studying it, Sonya's eye wanders to another and then yet another. Old friends. Gone now; moved away, divorced. She names the departed guests for her son. He points to her sister, Greta. He knows her; she is his auntie. Greta is in India now, expanding her consciousness. Sonya is at home in California, watching hers shrink. She has little recollection of the years since her wedding: they seem a blur of giving birth, meeting crises, taking care of others. Time seems blind; the present is still, and without memory. The years flow into each other: the years of coping with Ray flow into the years of raising Greta, which flow into the years of raising Timmy and Annette. She rarely thinks of the past and she rarely thinks of her father, Raymond Weiler, who disappeared in the wilderness near Pyramid Lake, Nevada, five years ago. His legacy to her, the only trace of him to linger, is the terrors she now suffers in the middle of the night. She knows the spells are connected to him, but that knowledge doesn't help. She concentrates on giving her children what they need. It seems to take all her strength.

Timmy turns another page. He is absorbed in the celluloid drama. Other books litter the floor of his room: story books, albums, the children's baby books. It is raining outside. Sonya sits beside him on the floor as he stares at her wedding. She has an impulse to do something else, but suppresses it; children like company when they are sick. Absently, she leafs through the baby book. She hasn't seen it in years. Its images startle her: Who is the pregnant matron in that photograph? A deception, a masquerade; someone at a costume party, in disguise. *She is Mrs. Greenberg now. She carries his child. Her endometrium hums. Goodbye, old self! This persona is the best one yet: an altered shape, another name. No more Weiler shame.*

"Who's that?" Tim's voice breaks through her thoughts; he has spotted his grandfather in one of the wedding pictures, as she feared he might. Now she will have to talk about the dead grandfather, and she can think of no satisfactory explanation—not for a five-year-old child. Their minds never stop at one question. After he has asked, "Who is he?" he will want to know, "How did he die?"

"That's your grandfather," she says, rehearsing the rest in her mind: he went out in the woods one day and got (tired) (lost) (murdered) (   ) and never came back. To this day, his bones have not been found. If I tell you this version, you will end up like me: waiting for him to reappear. When there is no body, the mind tends to wait for a return. This is not something you can change by will.

She studies the photograph: Raymond Weiler is bending toward the judge; his cheekbones shine. His eyes are beginning to cloud, but they are still alert to possibilities. He is considering hustling the judge. He is going into the windup as the champagne flows; his German face is resigned behind its planes. He has accepted his daughter's marrying a Jew; it is time to move on to

236

more important things. He bends toward the judge, he is the father of the bride, no one would suspect, where does he get his nerve; you'd think he would remember the other judge in Seattle, the probation report, the files, the records, the black and white evidence of his guilt. He bends forward, the lamplight catching the height of his forehead, his high bones: the face has just begun to wither, but still shines. He leans into the situation, he makes a few suggestions, testing out the water, sniffing the climate. The judge inclines his ear. Sonya fingers the borders of the print and stares at Raymond Weiler: impounded, frozen, fixed forever at $f/8$ in December. There he is on Kodak paper, caught in the act, in his last pose.

Timmy doesn't ask, "How did he die?" Not this time. Sonya sighs with relief, and smoothes his thin blond hair. The grandson Ray always wanted. The one he never saw. Went out in the woods on the tenth of November and never came back. Didn't wait the four more weeks, it would have been Christmas, she could have shown off her new baby boy: Here he is, at last. You can instruct him in minerals and ores.

The rain slashes down over the window glass. In the next room the telephone rings. Slowly Sonya rises to answer it; her leg has gone to sleep. It is the call she has been expecting for five years. She has heard it ring in her sleep. Raymond Weiler has been found.

The sheriff offers details as she cups the receiver to her ear and stares out the window: a hunter discovered the body yesterday. Sonya's eyes jump to the calendar on the wall: yesterday, Halloween. The skeleton was fully clothed and leaning against a tree. It was remarkable, the sheriff insisted, that his position seemed to have been unchanged, even after five years. The items in his pockets were similarly well preserved. The name in his wallet is still visible. "Usually wild animals tear them apart and scatter the bones," he said. "In most cases." Sonya imagines the sheriff picking his teeth. The remains, as he calls Ray, are being held for examination. They are at the Washoe County Medical Center in Reno, Nevada, where they will undergo an autopsy. "How can they do an autopsy on a skeleton?" Sonya asks. Small currents race up and down her body. She is both numb and charged. "They examine the teeth to determine identity. They also look for skull fractures and bullet holes, as evidence of homicide." Sonya can't understand why they are raising the homicide issue again. Now that he is dead, and has been found, and will be buried, can't they let it go at that? "No, it ain't that simple," the sheriff insists. Wally Venner is being questioned. Again? "There have been inconsistencies in his story from the very beginning. Without a body, we couldn't do anything. Now we can." Sonya wonders how, if the name in the wallet is visible after five years, they could question his identity? "Do you have any idea how many murders take place in this county each year?" the sheriff asks rhetorically. "It's common to plant another person's identification on the body. It makes our job more difficult. We have to investigate every death as if it were a homicide. Mind if I ask you a question about your father's teeth?" Sonya jumps involuntarily. "No," she says. "Go ahead." The sheriff says, "Well, the body we have"—*there's a chance this thing, this pile of bones, is not Ray*— "has a tooth missing in front, and in order to establish the identity it would help if you remember who did his dental work, and what side of the mouth the missing tooth was on—left or right." Sonya closes her eyes. She tries to imagine Ray, smiling. *Find the missing tooth.* Find the faces hidden in the picture. Turn it upside down and usually you can make out the gnarled features of an old man's contorted face among the branches of a tree. She always hated finding the missing and hidden things in those dense, abnormal pictures. She sees Ray, he is smiling, but she can't remember the missing tooth, let alone the side of his mouth it might have been on. "I can't remember," she tells the sheriff. "His dental work was done twenty or thirty years ago, I have no idea where." She will call Ray's sister in Topeka; there is a remote chance that she would remember a detail like that. The sheriff says it's all right, she should call him if she remembers anything. She sees the skeleton lying on a slab in the examination room of the Washoe County Medical Center, grinning hideously. She sees Wally Venner sweating in a little room, reconstructing Ray's disappearance for perhaps the twentieth time. She doesn't know whether pity or fear would be an appropriate emotion for her to feel toward Wally Venner. The sheriff says they will be in touch with her when their investigation has been completed. Sonya thanks him and hangs up the phone. She must call Greta, but Greta is in India, Greta is nowhere. She lights a cigarette and inhales, trying to imagine the thing in the medical center—what it would say if it could speak.

Timmy comes into the room in his bare feet; Sonya lifts him onto her lap and rocks him absently. She can't cry after so much time. How can you cry for bones? Timmy turns in her lap and stares into her eyes; he senses her mood and asks, "What's the matter? Who was on the phone?" Absently she strokes his face with the back of her fingers. *Here it is at last,* she thinks, as she forms a quiet reply: "It was a man telling me that your grandfather, the one in the picture who got lost in the woods, has been found." "You mean he's OK?" He begins to smile. "No. He's dead. They found his bones." Involuntarily, she holds her son closer; mother and child blend together in the kitchen chair. And a strange thing happens: the son begins to cry. At first Sonya thinks she's misunderstood the sound she hears, but soon his body is heaving and he is wailing softly in her arms. Their bodies are close, as though it were one body. She can't understand how such a thing could be: he has never met or seen Ray; the word "grandfather" is an abstraction. He is only five years old! In fact, she now realizes, she has never even spoken of Ray to him. How could he be crying for Ray now? He is keening, it is a preternatural sound, nothing she has ever heard before—certainly not a child sound. It is as though everything she ever felt for Ray, but could not express, has passed in some mysterious way from her mute body into that of her son; and like a medium, he absorbs her loss and gives it voice. He has become an ancient, at the age of five. He has absorbed and transmuted a raw, profound obligation. He has met his grandfather at last. He is saying goodbye.

*   *   *

Sonya composes a letter to the director of the cemetery where Valery lies cold and forgotten. She twists the edges of Ray's cremation authorization form as she struggles with the wording of her inquiry. The issue of the tooth remains a mystery; his sister can't recall which side of the mouth, or even when the tooth became a missing one, or how. No bullet holes were found; no fractures of significance. The skeletal remains of Raymond Weiler are finally released by the Washoe County Medical Center into the hands of Foster's Funeral Home, on Sonya's telephoned authority. She does not know how he made the trip: in a box, in a van, in an ambulance, or in a plastic bag. The form before her is short:

AUTHORITY TO CREMATE

Arrangements for Permanent Memorialization of Cremated Remains must be made within one month from date of cremation.

The ideal way to perpetuate the memory of the deceased is to establish a suitable memorial at the Masonic Memorial Gardens.

Clothing: (check one)
save
destroy

The sheriff isn't satisfied, but you can't hold a body forever with no evidence. Wally Venner is reluctantly released. On Sonya's telephoned authority, the last personal effects of Raymond Weiler are released to the custody of Wally Venner. The sheriff asks her if she is sure this is how she wants to handle the matter of the personal effects; he, the sheriff, would be happy to mail them to her directly. No, she thanks him for all his help; she will authorize their release to Wally Venner. The sheriff sighs. "It's up to you," he says. Sonya doesn't know why she has made this choice. Her mind is a tangle of unplugged connections. If she breathes deeply, and focuses only on the matter at hand, she may be able to decide where to place the cremated remains of her father. The Masonic Memorial Gardens, outside Reno, having reduced Raymond Weiler to two kilograms of miscellaneous white

240

matter in the large incinerator out back, has graciously consented to "hold" those remains on a shelf for an indefinite period of time while Sonya decides their final placement. She circles the word "destroy." She signs the letter asking if it would be possible to inter her father's remains in the grave that her mother has occupied for the past twenty-seven years. She walks to the mailbox and drops both communications down the slot. She has been unable to sleep since the phone call. She doesn't know what Ray would want. She wants to cry, to float on air, to be rid of him forever, but he won't go away. He refuses to settle, he won't tell her what to do. His bones strain against the shelf in the Masonic Memorial crematorium as she tosses in her sleep. *You die as wolves do, leaving no clue.*

❧ *Ernest Goodman* ❧

Dr. Goodman has been the guardian of my history for the past five years. In the beginning, he heard mostly about the terror at night because that dominated everything; that got in the way of my living a normal life—whatever that is. There are times when I wonder. I wonder if it is possible to have one later, if you didn't have one before. I wonder if everything is a matter of degree, or a matter of courage, or a combination of both. Goodman would add insight to the list.

When those first months passed and Daddy was still missing, strange things began to happen in me. It seemed inconceivable that a person could disappear without a trace; I was suspended between two states of expectation: waiting for him to come back, and waiting for him to die. When he failed to do either, something inside me broke into a thousand pieces, and escaped. I imagined these parts of me rising, and continuing to rise, until they reached the outer limits of space. They would be annihilated in that void and there would be no witnesses. It seemed impossible that I would ever know myself again, or recover, or be whole.

Goodman has tried his best. He attempts to take me back in time, to examine old things. He reaches for something to connect the terror to, to give it shape and voice and substance. He tries to get me to cooperate in naming it, to define its origins and boundaries, so I can understand it and loosen its hold on me. I see the efforts he is making on my behalf, but I can't go with him; the threat seems too great. When he asks about Valery and Ray, I can't answer, because to speak of them is to enter the land of the dead. And that requires you to die, yourself.

"Where does that conviction come from?" he will ask, leaning forward in his chair. *Somewhere deep inside me; no one would understand, least of all you.* I tell him a dream from the night before.

"You were in it," I begin, and we laugh; an old joke. "We were in the country somewhere—no place I recognized, but beautiful, like a park. The sky was heavy with the strangest clouds, yet the atmosphere was soft. A sense of nature, as a force, was prominent.

"You seemed to be leading me somewhere; we were on an expedition, or a walk, I'm not sure. There was something you wanted to show me, a secret. You offered your hand and I went with you; we walked through fields. The feeling of expectation was sweet, as though you knew about something I did not, and were taking me there.

"There was a rise just ahead. I began to feel uneasy. I can't explain it, I just sensed something—the kind of tension you couldn't see, but feel. I hung back. 'Come on,' you urged, kindly. You seemed so reassuring, almost seductive, it was clear that I should trust you. We walked up the rise together, and then the earth seemed to change in texture, I could feel it under my feet, I couldn't believe you were doing this, I turned my head quickly so I wouldn't have to look, but I didn't do it in time: it was an open grave, freshly dug, black and inevitable. You stood there on its rim, as though to say: This is where all our inquiries and explorations are taking us; this is what you must look at; this is where it all ends. You were no longer my guide, but a betrayer, and I was alone, with the thing I fear most."

I was crying now, as I cried in the dream, but there was more

242

terror in it than sadness. I kept trying to catch my breath, while he tried to discuss the dream, but I heard nothing he said, the image was overwhelming: I knew everything led there, and nothing he said could temper that in any way.

※

Sonya is driving to Reno. Sheets of rain cascade across the windshield outside of Sacramento, and gusts of wind rock the car from lane to lane. The slick freeway stretches for miles; her hands grip the wheel. She has made the decision to sign a release for the placement of Raymond Weiler's remains in the Masonic Memorial columbarium. She will not investigate the charge of homicide. She thinks Wally Venner might be capable of that, and at the same time thinks the idea ridiculous. Fathers of four don't murder delusional old men. She has two children back home with the babysitter, wondering what is wrong with their mother. She must lay Raymond Weiler to rest and get on with her own life.

By the time she reaches Donner Pass, the storm has turned into a blizzard; cars litter the road—some fallen on their sides, some folded under the snow. She shifts slowly into second and keeps the car moving at a steady pace; she swallows a Librium along with some mints she finds in the glove compartment. The main thing is to stay on the road and keep a steady speed. Her foot feels the strain of maintaining just the right amount of pressure on the pedal; one false move and the car will slide off the world. It will be white, white, and again white. It will never end. She fights the sensation of being swallowed up. She is trapped in snow; all the visual lines of reference have disappeared: the center line; the roadside; the ditch; the vertical snow markers, most of which are bent or covered up. It is no longer a road, but a floating suspension where ground and air have merged. It is five o'clock and the dusk light is blind. She holds to the image of the cabin she will

243

spend the night in, of her friend waiting dinner, of her task in Reno the following day. If she can reach this destination, everything will fall into place. She will make Ray's decision for him, since he won't speak. She will bury him and he will never haunt her again.

She turns on the car lights and negotiates a curve ahead. It turns out to be an illusion; two leaning poles, the only visible guide, make the road appear to curve left when in fact it bears straight. She sees this just as the car begins to spin. The car rolls on its side and dies there, in the white ditch. She is leaning now, sucked by the force of gravity onto her side against the left front door. The little clock on the dashboard ticks; there is no other sound. She closes her eyes as her mind races. If she doesn't get out of the car it will quickly fill with snow and be buried. *Would you want it any other way?*

She pushes against the door facing the sky. It won't open; it doesn't even move. She is playing the final scene in a drama written by Raymond Weiler twenty-five years ago. Snow was his element. She is joining him. It was predicted. The dashboard clock ticks on. Lights from stray cars fade into the distance on the road above. Her children's faces suddenly appear in the air outside, squinting through the windshield, asking questions. She throws herself against the door with all the force she has. It opens a few inches and she struggles out. She climbs the embankment and stands on the frozen surface of the road and waits to flag down a car. Her hands and feet are numb; her face no longer exists. She is to die out here, fulfilling his awful prophecy.

By the time help comes and she is finally towed out of the ditch, an hour and a half has passed. It is now dark and she is trembling. She is in a trance, but she has a new determination, born of tasting the possibility of death. She navigates the blizzard; she is steel now, she has a single focus. She arrives at the cabin two hours late. She thaws, then shakes, then goes into convulsions. She vomits as chills grip her body. Toward the end of the long night, she sleeps. She is not herself now. She has passed through the other side, into something new.

In the morning, she drives over the mountains to Reno. She has

244

made an appointment to meet Wally Venner at eleven o'clock. She will take him to lunch and reclaim Ray's things, and perhaps learn the truth. She has allowed an hour to go to the library to read the newspaper accounts of Ray's disappearance for stray clues. She will bear witness to the account of his last hours.

MISSING HUNTER SOUGHT

Concern mounted Monday night following an unsuccessful air and ground search for a missing 65-year-old Reno man in Northern Washoe County.

She shakes her head as her mind leaps to the face bending in lamplight in his last photograph. Those luminous bones, those smooth planes. Yes, he could pass. Ten years off. His last lie.

The missing man, Raymond Weiler, a resident of the Depot Hotel in Reno, was last seen early Sunday morning about 45 miles northwest of Gerlach.

He had been in a hunting party of three persons, including Wally Venner, a longtime companion.

Meanwhile, three Civil Air Patrol planes flew a search pattern over the area Monday until darkness grounded them.

Lt. Bill Clark, public information officer for the Civil Air Patrol here, said last night that, weather permitting, six or seven planes will take off at 7 a.m. today to continue the search.

Col. John Stewart, of Reno, commanding the Civil Air Patrol's Washoe Jeep Squadron, said that perhaps a dozen or more four-wheel-drive vehicles with volunteer searchers will be participating in the ground search Tuesday if Weiler does not turn up.

The missing man's hunting companions said that Weiler had reported feeling tired as they hiked up a draw at about 9 a.m. Sunday. It was decided that he should return to the base camp alone and await the return of the others. That was the last seen of the missing man.

RENO HUNTER STILL SOUGHT

The search for a Reno man, missing since Sunday from a hunting party in northwestern Washoe County, will be continued today, weather permitting, by both ground and air units of the Civil Air Patrol.

Seven airplanes, a dozen or more vehicles, and some 63 persons were involved in the fruitless search Tuesday.

The missing man is Raymond Weiler, 65, last seen Sunday morning when he complained of being tired and dropped out of a hunting party.

Weiler, who resides at the Depot Hotel, had been retired for some years. Friends said Tuesday that he was "interested in mining ventures and apparently knew a great deal about such things."

Although he is believed to have been a resident in the Reno area for at least six or seven years, little else, apparently, was known about his background.

SEARCH HALTED
FOR MISSING RENO MAN

Hope for the survival of a missing Reno man faded Wednesday night as Civil Air Patrol air and ground search teams temporarily discontinued their search, as weather conditions limited visibility.

The missing man is Raymond Weiler, 65, of the Depot Hotel. He has been retired and living in this area for about six years. Two daughters are believed to be residing in California, and attempts are being made now to locate them.

Civil Air Patrol information officer Lt. Bill Clark said that arrangements for a massive ground search are being made for Saturday. Civil Air Patrol, Nevada Search and Rescue, Washoe County Sheriff's Mounted Posse, Job Corps members, and possibly some Boy Scouts are being prepared for a walk-through of the area around the base hunting camp from which Weiler disappeared.

One participant in the search said, "If he is still alive, he should have walked out by now, or at least have signaled his presence. I fear that the Saturday operation will be a task of recovering the body, rather than finding a missing person."

Sonya rewinds the microfilm and walks out into a blinding April sun; the slowly melting snow slides under her feet. She feels as though she has been reading an account of a tragedy that

246

happened to some stranger. Something in the wording, or something in the headlines, didn't fit. RENO MAN, for instance. She could have told them he wasn't Reno man, but she wasn't there when the accounts were being written. He was Reno man to them, but he was also Seattle man, Colville man, Sonora man, Buffalo man, depending on how far back you wanted to go, and from what angle you chose to view him. Buffalo, the winters were severe. His grandparents settled there after leaving Germany. Once, as a teenager, he drove someone's Ford across the surface of Lake Erie, slamming on the brakes to make the car spin out of control. Sonora was the search for silver; his brother Frederik joined him in that venture when they were young, and ended up in jail. Ray escaped, and the brothers never spoke again. Colville was where the gold was thought to be. Sonya was entering second grade as the trips to the mountains grew frequent and whispers of striking it rich were rolling off his tongue. Seattle represented the years between silver, gold and uranium. Reno became a simple failure to survive.

Sonya meets Wally Venner in the casino cafeteria, as planned. She feels a rolling apprehension in the pit of her stomach as she eyes him from across the room. His dark hair has been slicked back with a gel. As she approaches him and extends her hand, she sees the comb tracks. She steadies herself: Ray had delusions; she is determined not to share them. They slide into the red vinyl booth and place their orders. It feels strange to be sitting here with him. She fixes on him across the Formica table. She searches his eyes, observes his nervous fingers, folding and unfolding into themselves. His nails are black. She lights a cigarette and sips her coffee. Wally Venner's eyes jump around the cafeteria. It couldn't be easy for him, sitting here with her, thinking himself responsible for Ray's death. She says, "You did everything you could, you aren't to blame." He shifts position slightly, and wipes his nose on his sleeve. His half-smile is crooked. There are identical bodily gestures that describe both embarrassment and guilt. She mustn't let herself confuse the two.

Awkwardly, he tells the story again: how they fanned out, how it had been hours before Ray was missed. He gestures with his

247

hands and his speech accelerates; now there are details she has never heard before, not from Wally on the phone, not from the sheriff: strange allusions to another group of hunters Wally says were setting up camp the morning Ray disappeared, then mysteriously and inexplicably breaking up camp and roaring away in their van that afternoon. Sonya listens impassively. She stares straight into Wally Venner's eyes. They return her gaze. They have nothing to give away. They are fixed. He smiles. Her heart begins to race. Should she mention the inconsistency? How can she keep him from knowing she knows? Does she know? She finishes her coffee. She is not Nancy Drew. She is not Wonder Woman. By the end of this day, by the time the sun sets over the purple sage of this cow town, Raymond Weiler will be at rest. Deciding she will not pursue the matter has freed her to pursue it. She asks, "Why didn't you mention the hunters to the police?" Wally grins, then shrugs and says the questioning was so confusing he forgot that detail. Both times he was questioned? "Yeah," he says. "Why do you bring it up now?" She rummages in her purse for the money to pay the check. "Because they might have done it," Wally offers. What is the difference between ominous and stupid? Can you tell them apart? The air-conditioned coffee shop sucks all thought from her head. She is not a detective. She slides out of the booth. Wally says, "Thank you," meaning thank you for the lunch. She thinks that is what he means. She pays the bill and they exit through the revolving doors. The sidewalk swims under her feet. Wally says, "I have your father's things in my car."

They walk for blocks. Decaying rooming houses give way to Salvation Army warehouses and cheap casinos that no longer bother to sweep the hourly litter from their floors. Broken men weave and stumble down the streets. Turning onto a side street, Wally gestures toward the car: Sonya recognizes the black Chevy immediately from the Christmas Ray passed it off as his. She is aware of her heart turning in her chest as Wally gestures her into the car. She sees him slash her throat there on the outskirts of Reno; sees the way his lips move as he tells her: I can't afford to have you live. He slides in beside her on the driver's side and

248

reaches under the front seat and withdraws a transparent plastic bag. Sonya's heart is pounding but she doesn't get out of the car. She feels her destiny is fixed.

There, at the bottom of the plastic bag, lie Ray's wallet, comb, ballpoint pen, and his eyeglasses. Wally Venner withdraws the wallet and hands it to her. Its weight is cold on her palm; it has the chill of death. "Open it," Wally suggests. She glances through the windshield; there is no one walking on the side street. She is supposed to look at something she doesn't want to see. It is part of a ritual. It is one of the final steps in the process of burying Ray. She opens the billfold, and there is Valery's face shining through the fogged plastic picture slot. Her hair is filled with light; she is smiling, and continues to smile, and will smile there inside the wallet forever. Her image has survived five years of snowfalls and thaws. It has lain on top of Raymond Weiler's heart, on the dark mountain. Her features are untouched by melting ice. She has resisted the putrescence of decay. As Ray's body slowly melted off his bones, her face endured—behind clear plastic, imitation leather, the tattered hunting jacket.

Sonya puts the wallet in her purse and hands Wally the bag, saying, "I don't want the rest." Wally nods. She shakes his hand and gets out of the car. Halfway down the block, she turns and waves a half-wave. Wally starts up the motor, makes a U-turn, and disappears in traffic. Sonya walks back to her own car and drives in the direction of the Masonic Memorial Gardens. When she reaches the top of a steep dirt road, she bears right, as instructed by letter, toward a shed at the end of the cemetery. Inside is the incinerator where they cremate the dead. And somewhere on a shelf, in an aluminum can, waits the last of Raymond Weiler. The old man in khaki overalls who tends the crematorium hands it to her with a smile. "Here he is," he says.

She asks to see the slot in the columbarium where it has been suggested she place Ray's remains. The old man escorts her on a tour of the columbarium; his heart isn't in it. He points to a small compartment in the wall, just below the ceiling. "There it is," he says. Sonya squints up at the little compartment. It is slightly larger than a post office box. She casts her eyes over the rows of niches carved in the pale granite walls. They go on for miles. The old man finally says, "You know, it's legal to scatter in this state. When I go, my eldest child will take my bones and bury them up on the mountain." His voice echoes softly through the empty columbarium. When they return to the shed to sign the papers and negotiate the transfer of the bones inside the can from the crematorium shelf to Sonya's hands, the old man pauses beside the incinerator. It has a long metal trough running down from it like a chute. He points. The trough is filled with bones in every conceivable form of reduction: chips, powder, splinters, joints, fragments, knuckles, ash. Sonya inhales sharply and turns away. "Oh, it's just bones," the old man says kindly. A partial skull catches her eye. "That's someone I did yesterday; he was a large man," he explains. Suddenly, she realizes: the trough is never empty. All the people whose bones pass through this heat, and down this shaft, collide and mingle and eventually sift down upon each other until, in the end, they are one substance. She knows now that the bones inside the aluminum can with Raymond Weiler's name on it, whatever is in that can, is and is not Raymond Weiler. There is no method the crematorium can devise that would allow her to commit a whole person, in any form, to the earth. She stares at the aluminum can on the shelf. Will he burst through the lid, will he defy all laws this one last time?

"I will bury him on the mountain," she finally tells the old man. He smiles. It is a sudden decision, and she knows it is right. She hopes she can see it through. She takes a seat beside the desk; the old man hands her a piece of paper and she signs her name on the dotted line. She accepts full custody of Raymond Weiler. She shakes the old man's hand and lifts the can from the desk. It is both heavy and weightless, at the same time. She carries it like a baby in the circle of her arm.

Sonya clings tightly to the steering wheel as she drives the twisting road to the summit of Mt. Rose. Near the top, she stops the car and carries the aluminum can down the mountain until she finds a tree whose base is exposed by melting snow; there she kneels and parts the porous earth with her hands. Slowly she raises the lid of the can and faces the final evidence of her father's death. As she stares down at the twisted fragments, tears spring to her eyes. She wonders if it is possible that the wish to love is stronger than the need to hate. Her hand shakes as she holds the can over the shallow grave. The chalky pieces collide, then slide into the rich black hole. They tumble and fall and raise a fine dust; particles of Raymond Weiler rise in the hard April air. He has a life of his own, even in this form, a hunger for his elements. He slips inside Mother Nature's dark interior at last. He will burrow there, and dream. In time, he will harden into mineral and ore. He will become that thing he used to seek. Dust. Infinity. Bye bye.

🌿 *Rays Touthe* 🌿

Shortly after Daddy's sister in Topeka died, I received the strangest thing in the mail: an envelope within an envelope, sent on to me by her daughter. The contents were discovered in a dresser drawer, she writes. She doesn't know if I want it, but she thought it should be sent. I stare at the printed notation on the inner envelope: Rays Touthe. I pace the floor trying to imagine how his tooth got all the way to Kansas. And all my old suspicions rise up once more: the clue is right there on the envelope, in Wally Venner's illiterate scrawl. How did Wally get the tooth? I curse my father on his cool height: weightless, speechless, all my answers locked in his bones.

I try to trace things back, and I remember the night Alex and Greta drove to Reno to claim his things. I am not a detective. I remember the boxes of letters and the absence of clothing. They gave his clothes to Wally. I see the missing tooth inside a pocket. I see Wally Venner trying on Daddy's suit. He stands before his mirror, testing the fit. His hands go into the pockets where his finger senses a hard object. He is a simple man. He thinks Ray's

251

older sister might want that part of him. After all this time, I see it is in my best interests to come to a quick conclusion. There are explanations for everything; they are not all terrible.

I do not open the envelope, but I am unable to throw it away; in the end, I put it in the back of an unused drawer. It seems his body parts follow me everywhere. Pieces of him scatter, then regroup, like birds. I wonder if his anatomy will be coming home to roost in bitter fragments to the end of my days.

🦋 Ghosts 🦋

I had believed that seeing the evidence of Daddy's death, and laying it to rest, would settle everything, but it hasn't. I was sure I had done the right thing, but his ghost continues to walk the ridges above Reno as though something were not right. I hear him in the night, like a visitation. I imagine wolves, moons, sudden winds in the pines that surround his unmarked grave.

I hear Valery, too. She calls out in a thin, frail voice unused to asking things for itself. She has been silent all these years, but now she just won't be still. She is blaming me for something, I can tell by the tone, but the words are unclear. Maybe she feels Ray has received all the attention lately. It is as though the moment I placed him in the ground, his weight caused the balance of the earth to shift, so that as he sank, the signal went out for Valery to rise, one thousand miles to the north. Now that she is this close to the surface, she means to have her say. She visits me in dreams; she rises out of the dank, black earth just as they do in movies. I feel the chill of her presence for hours, sometimes days. I can't understand how someone, voiceless for decades, can remain alive in you, or how the invisible can wield such power. I have done everything possible to stay out of their territory, but they won't stay out of mine. I feel them moving inside me: ghosts, disguised as feelings. Valery has been missing so long, I have forgotten all the questions I ever wanted to ask. With Ray, it is different: the questions have to do with things like bones and teeth, and whether a con man is capable of genuine love.

Sometimes I feel I am getting stronger, and that is when their torment increases, as if my strength were a threat to their power. I can feel them inside me, twisting my intentions, making everything come out wrong. I envy my own children their privilege—having living parents and a stable life; I lock myself in the bathroom so they won't witness my decline. The ghosts absorb the energy I need to invent the mother in myself. How can I be to them what hasn't been to me? Invention requires a superhuman strength. I fall to the floor and beat on the tiles with my fists. The ghosts are all here, disguised as assumptions: *You are bad. You are alone.* I cry, but there are no tears, only sounds, dry and hollow and total. "I need you, I need you, I need you!" I scream. There is not a single picture in my mind; I no longer know who "you" is.

At night the terrors increase; strange and overwhelming seizures shake me like surprise attacks. I lie frozen on the bed and wait for it to pass. Alex lies beside me and tries to hold me, but holding doesn't reach it, nor can speech, or reason, or will. It is a panic so deep, it cannot be imagined—except as a force whose locus is not within, but the farthest reaches of a cold infinity. It invades in waves; and my heart races, and what I know as me dissolves in lunar chills. Sometimes it lasts all night.

In the morning I will try again to explain to Goodman a thing I don't understand myself. I feel so weak, like someone in a horror film after a visitation: drained of substance by an alien force, but still haunting its old habitations, an empty shell. When Goodman opens his door, it is all I can do to stand.

I have crossed this threshold a thousand times. I have descended here, and descended again, and he has borne witness and helped me to rise again. We sit down and I stare ahead, as in a trance.

"Try to say what it is you fear," he says quietly. A request so reasonable, it shocks me to hear myself screaming. "Loss, loss, loss!" I wail, as I begin to rock. He is quiet as I reflect on this. I can feel my control slipping away, I know how much safer it is to stare into space, to freeze the mind over, to stay with an old, a

253

known and familiar death and yearn for what is already lost, than re-enter the world and risk it all over again. But my naming the fear has loosened something; I feel it going, I close my eyes.

I am back in that time again, fading, slipping; I try to stop it but it is like a destiny, it carries me forward. I feel emotions that are so strong, they are like rivers surging. They have lain buried through time, underneath the world; now they are surfacing with a force that no one could stay or undo. There is no choice but to flatten myself on their surface, and ride; to stretch out, as a victim might, or a supplicant, and offer myself to them. I am filled to the limits with fear, yet I unbend. Wherever they're going, and whatever their substance, I will be that thing. And then I feel it. I feel that old tragedy as though it were yesterday. And I go down, down.

I have crossed this threshold a thousand times, and taken my grief to him. It assumes an actual shape, and occupies the center of the room. We turn it this way and that, measuring its dimensions, testing its depth. Sometimes it lodges in the corner, where it is easy to observe; at other times it fills the room, expanding with each breath, until there is no air left, no space, or light, and everything goes black and is lost to it. He sits very still, as always. He has stood by me in ways that didn't look at all like standing by at the time, but seemed more like indifference, and sometimes like death. He has never lost me to the weight of the grief, at least not yet; he has always drawn me back with the thread of his voice. He makes himself visible in the center, displacing the grief to the edges. He has always brought me back; everything depends on remembering this now.

It is getting harder to breathe; it isn't symbolic, it is actual. I am gasping for air, trying to get enough. It crosses my mind that dying is what I deserve. And at that moment they suddenly appear before me and hover there, near the ceiling. They have even invaded this room. He doesn't seem to notice. I'd point them out, but I can't move. Valery is in the foreground. I don't even recognize her as my mother; she is just someone with that name from the past. I try to speak, but nothing comes out. I communicate by thinking. Was it Ray? I say. Was it his fraudulent swindles and drunken nights that finally lodged in your body and festered there? So that all his loving care, all the Christian Science and Kotex in the world were not enough to heal the wounds? Or was it I? Nona said it, that's the part I didn't remember at the burial, just before she tried to throw herself in with you, she said, *You killed your mother*. What did she mean by that? Was I that bad, that powerful? Or was she that overwhelmed with despair? What kind of grandmother would say such a thing? She loved me once, I was her Kentucky Babe. I look to the ceiling, but she isn't here to explain herself or tell me she is sorry. She is at the bottom of the sea, beating her fists against her cement-block tomb, enduring the unendurable silence that collects at fathoms. Small fish surround her and hover, unmoving. Their bubbles are all that moves in that dark light. She has no smart comments for them; they are silver, indifferent, deaf.

Now Daddy comes forward, he's trying to fit himself in above my head. I have to confess it to him, even though he knows already. *I killed you*, I whisper as loudly as I can, but he doesn't seem to hear. It wasn't Wally, or even if it was, he did it after the fact. A crime after the crime. You don't need me to say this, you've always known it, that's why you're here. I killed you with my refusal to love. With my Greyhound ticket. Waving goodbye to your overcoat as the doors sucked closed behind you with a hiss. A very modern killing, neat, invisible; no one in the station noticed.

There isn't enough oxygen in this room, there is not enough air to fill me up. I am going down, this is the last time. I no longer know the difference between hunger and grief; maybe they are the same thing. I have tried to imagine going home again: I dream of a door opening, and someone inside. And then I see it is just the imaginary family; there is nothing there but empty houses, and the reliving of old shames. I open my mouth, as though to cry out, but it seems like Goodman's voice, not mine. I hear it as though at the end of a long tunnel, straining against the distance between us; and then it is drowned by the silence of that gulf.

255

The room swells with the pain of going back and finding no one there; it is too small to hold all that was longed for and lost. It bursts, and then evaporates. It becomes the void itself. If I can get through the door, if I can cross the threshold, there will be air on the other side. I am taking the first steps when I hear the voice clearly as his. He is beside me, taking my hand.

His pressure is firm; he holds on until I respond. "Look at me," he says, trying to close the gulf. It is like coming to after fainting: the blackness fades slowly, first from the center, then from the edges, then altogether. Consciousness is strange; I step back into it in stages and it hurts—like pins, pricking. But his hand is warm; there is a current there, bridging the distance. It is solid. It waits. It seeks to convince me I am not alone, not entirely. If that is true, it might be possible to survive.

My vision clears and the room gradually comes into focus. We sit down again and I agree to see if there is some way I can, through thought and speech, explain. All I have inside now is a powerful intuition that I must go back to the source, the original scene, and test, after all the years of sadness and fear, the depth of my strength. To take its measure, a sounding: how deep? Goodman wonders why I feel I have to go back, and I can't explain. He probably thinks the symbolic journey would be sufficient, if only I'd cooperate with him in pursuing that. But that's part of the problem; there are some things you have to do alone.

As I talk, the rest of the answer takes shape: the alternative is to remain forever in that narrow space between living and dying, trapped in the limbo of the half-lived life. The alternative is to remain the child of old ghosts, instead of becoming a woman of my own: staying within the boundaries they impose, joining them in their cold places before my time.

He doesn't speak. I don't know if he approves or disapproves; it isn't his decision, they aren't his ghosts. He is there, though; I see him standing by. All these years I have cast myself against that still and faithful form, and discovered my own. I have raged at him, loved him, and mourned. I have discovered my shape and substance by throwing myself on the constancy of his love. I see it clearly for the first time: a rare and special kind, like some metal that was missing from my alchemy; it joins the others now, and slowly blends. He completes the job that Ray and Valery began.

It rains the day before Sonya leaves. As she is stooping to clear some of the children's books from the floor, an album slides out of her hand and snapshots slip from their moorings and fall onto the floor. She puts them back into place and returns the books to the trunk; as she starts to lower the lid some notebooks at the bottom catch her eye. They have lain there fifteen years, and contain the poetry she wrote in college. She lifts them out cautiously and spends the rest of the afternoon going back in time, recovering this lost part. There is a comment on one of the notebooks in Dr. Stedman's hand and seeing it again, after all these years, shakes her to the core. He wrote: "You have the capacity to do things of importance."

🐾 *Going Back* 🐾

I am on this train again, going north, suspended at the center between the old, ghost family up ahead and the new, living family left behind. I have imagined myself back in that place: calling their names, loosening their stones, confronting their bone weight. It seems my last hope to be whole. Someone, it wasn't Goodman, said: Do the thing you fear. As the engine parts the unseen space ahead, I see that all motion is renunciation; and that moving or not, all things eventually end. Through the window I can see a thin horizon of lights, the dense stars, the black night, and suddenly a phrase of Goodman's comes to me: *It doesn't have to end before the end.* He has said it many times; it means, live while you still live. It hasn't always been possible to put it into practice, but I hold to it as a vision. I lean my head against the window and wonder if it is possible that a future self is forming, even now, within the confines of this air-conditioned train: suspended in space and time, its tiny embryo splitting its beads, dividing, and dividing, and dividing.

As this strange destiny moves closer, I begin to recognize the signs: the visionary mountains, dark forests, pale skies and thin, mysterious vapors that ring the far horizons. I suddenly remember leaning out the window of the red brick house, watching that sky and thinking: Someday I will leave this place, and find others to love. I wonder if that is what strength is: waiting out difficult times, holding to a possibility.

The train is entering the old King Street Station now, and I see that nothing has changed. It is all here: the crumbling brick, the darkening sky, rain falling over everything, as it always has. The platform shines with an old and absolute blackness. I walk its length and pass back through the doors that delivered me out twenty years ago. I become unborn again.

I have chosen this motel deliberately. It is anonymous, even obscene. There is no one here who knows my name. It is a fortress, without history; nothing is familiar. It will serve as a protection against memory and longing, and I will go out from it a day at a time. I don't know which will be harder: the one-room basement apartment on Capitol Hill, or the dream house on 51st Avenue South.

Stepping out of the rented car and taking my first step in the ancient, original neighborhood, I felt the pavement resonate under my feet. I was sure I saw a crack in the sidewalk, filled with tar, that was there when I was a child. Nothing here has changed. The old apartment building rises before me, and my heart jumps: there, in the window of the basement unit, is Valery's pale begonia! I stare into the darkness beyond, my old darkness; it belongs to someone else now. Someone else's plant soaks the meager sun from that sill.

Here is the street where Daddy and I bucked the wind in winter. I lean into it, instinctively. He takes off his scarf and wraps it around me, and gently rubs my cheeks with the backs of his fingers for extra warmth. It is blowing so hard, it brings tears to our eyes. As I retrace our steps, I come to the corner where Valery scanned the sky for war planes, and eventually, the Capitola comes into view: its courtyard overflows with decaying ferns. Sidney's ghost is in the doorway, his mouth stopped with dirt. Walking back to the basement apartment, I consider knocking on the door. "I lived here once," I'd say.

I am slowly connecting with my earliest self, that old child: Valery has me by the hand, and together we are walking to the park. The morning air is humid, sweet. So it is true, I think; this is where I began. And I hear something familiar, but recent; new sounds are drifting from my old building: The Rolling Stones have replaced The Sons of the Pioneers. As I drive away, I know I have recovered a lost part. It was important to feel Valery's presence, however slight. It will help me now. I am on my way to the dream house on 51st Avenue South, where she disappeared for good.

I feel the chill the minute the car enters the neighborhood. I park it two blocks from the house so I can feel my way, and take this one step at a time. My body is weightless; it doesn't want to touch down. Not here, not on this sidewalk, the scene of that terrible loss, all my shames, Ray's drunken sleeps, the empty holidays, Greta's hollow ears, the housekeepers, the arrivals and departures.

*   *   *

I am approaching it, I am sliding by the porch. I have entered it in dreams. I will not go to the door.

I wonder if Valery's spirit is here, and not in my head; does it haunt the owners now? Does it beat frail hands on the bedroom walls? Does it frighten their children at night?

My feet are anchored to the sidewalk; they have settled, I no longer levitate. I see the maple tree is gone. The house is a different color. It is undistinguished.

I stare hard at the back bedroom window where Valery breathed her last breath. On the lawn, a child's tricycle lies on its side.

This is where something terrible happened, many years ago. Here I am, walking by, trying to make peace with it. I am grounded, not weightless. I can hold my own in this place.

A light wind is blowing up 51st Avenue South from the lake. I sense Valery once again.

She is preparing to speak. I can't make out the words, the voice is so frail. *Live the rest yourself.* Is that it? That's what I want it to be.

That's what I want from you, Mother. I want you to say: *No more suffering for imaginary crimes.* I want you to let me off the hook.

51st Avenue South is quiet; the dream house is still. *Live the rest yourself.* It is not a blessing; it was not Valery's voice, but my own. I have acquitted myself. It comes as a kind of shock: I acknowledge the cold truth of her death for perhaps the first time. She is truly gone, forever out of reach, and I have become my own judge. Everything else is voices in the head, memories.

I drive back across the city, with its bricks the color of blood, with its hundred shades of green. Water surrounds it, its pavement is dark with years. Its trees belong, lawns abide. It is at peace with its history. I feel the city inside me, its geography is my home.

If any one soul of us is all the world,
this world and the next, to any other soul,
then whoever it may be that thus loves us,
the inadequacy of our return, the hopeless debt of us,
must strike us to our knees with an utter humility.

Seeing Marian Linden was a shock, because it seemed she hadn't changed in twenty years. It felt so right to be in her warm apartment once again, but awkward, too, because I couldn't quickly bridge the gulf of all those years. It was painfully clear that letters are only tokens; reminders, rather than a true connection. I knew exactly what was wrong, but I couldn't give it voice: I

261

remembered these exact feelings had been stated once, long ago, at the end of an important book that Berta Nordstrom gave me. It occurred to me that if I could somehow show Miss Linden that statement, and Berta Nordstrom, too, they would understand. It said what I could not; it gave my narrow fears a universal frame and helped me to forgive myself.

Over lunch, I continued to grope for some explanation that might make sense of my confusion, but my feelings weren't yet comprehensible to me. The odyssey was too new, the vision hadn't clarified, but I knew it would in time, and so did she. The years accommodated, shrinking the distance and allowing a fragile bridge between us again. "I couldn't tell you then how much you meant to me," I finally said. There were tears in her eyes, hearing this; and I knew she loved me then, and always would.

Berta Nordstrom is eighty-four years old. Over tea in her apartment, she, too, declares her love. I stare at her and see how absolutely she has shaped my destiny. She has pictures of my children on her desk. I tell her why I'm here, and explain that there are things I cannot say, but someday will. She takes my hand and says, "Dear child, there is no need for explanations. I know. I know." I know she knows, I always have, but this time I must explain, if only to clarify for myself. I know it won't change a thing for her, but having an explanation will change me.

As the light fades outside, she points to some objects in the room. She puts it delicately, but the message is clear: they are meant for me after her death. I admire them all, but refuse to select or respond. I already have the important objects inside me, she must know that. She and Marian Linden loved me when no one else did. Together, they were the rest of my Valery.

I am standing in front of the one-room basement apartment for the last time. I'm glad the building is still here, because if they had torn down the evidence, these physical memories would be lost to me for all time. Because it is here, I will be able to let it go.

It is my visible past, confirming something in me; and as I reclaim it, I feel my lost parts reassembling. I am the last missing person.

I still have trouble with it, the fear of dying before my time. *Like mother, like daughter.* I know we will all be lost to each other eventually, and that loss will be final. In the meantime, we must find our places; we must live our lives.

IN THE SUPERIOR COURT OF THE STATE OF WASHINGTON
FOR KING COUNTY

STATE OF WASHINGTON,)
PLAINTIFF,)
vs.)
RAYMOND D. WEILLER,)
DEFENDANT)

INFORMATION

I, John A. Burgess, Prosecuting Attorney in and for the County of King, State of Washington, come now here in the name and by the authority of the State of Washington, and by this Information do accuse RAYMOND D. WEILER of the crime of GRAND LARCENY, committed as follows:

He, the said RAYMOND D. WEILER, in the County of King, State of Washington, on or about the 20th day of September, 1955, with intent to deprive and defraud the owner thereof, did wilfully, unlawfully and feloniously obtain from the owner, Wilbur F. Johnson, the possession or title to certain property, to wit: lawful money of the United States in the sum of $10,000 by color or aid of fraudulent or false representations and by trick, device and bunco;

Contrary to the statute in such case made and provided and against the place and dignity of the State of Washington.

JOHN A. BURGESS
Prosecuting Attorney

My hand is trembling on the handle of the microfilm projector. My heart jumped only twice: when I saw my father's name in bold letters, and when I saw the word "crime." After twenty years, it is still an embarrassment, a statement in a public place. I had to speak his name aloud to the clerk when I requested his file.

263

I dragged the heavy ledger from its shelf and ran my finger down the inked-in names of all the old, forgotten felons until I came to Ray's. I have finally exercised my right to see the evidence. If I now belong to this place, and if I am separate from him, then I have the right to look. The crime was his, not mine. He paid his price. The State of Washington endures.

It is a hard thing to face, but it doesn't overwhelm. I allow it to sink into me and then, walking out into the afternoon rain, I let it all lift out. The evidence, once dense, now thins. It rises on the air and is borne on westerly winds where gulls navigate the currents. It lifts far over the city of Seattle, where it no longer harms any living thing.

Walking through the doors of the King Street Station is hard. It is like leaving all over again, in 1954. I see Ray standing over by the jewelry counter, buying the pair of earrings he plans to surprise me with on the train. I can't suppress the old feelings, maybe they never die. I call to his ghost:

Did you really love me? Or was that a con job, too?

He is still. It's hard to tell if he is stunned, or thinking fast. I don't let him get the upper hand, I hurl every doubt I've ever had at him; they echo for miles across the filthy station floor.

Larcenous! Fraudulent! False! Trick! Device! Bunco!

He doesn't even blink. I try a different angle. This is hard.

When I was sick and you sat with me all night, when you stroked my face, when we bucked the wind, was it real?

No response. He really means to have it his way this time. The train is about to leave.

WHERE IS MY PROOF? I scream at him.

It's inside you! he finally shouts. A trick.

Why weren't you a better parent? I cry.

Why aren't you? he yells back.

I do my best!

Yes, well, that's the way it goes. So did I.

And then I see. And then I forgive.

*   *   *

Leaning against the train window, I take a last look: the city rises behind me, a garden of buildings—the new coexisting alongside the old, as things do inside us. It strikes me how aspects of people we love attach to the geography of a place and become forever afterwards a part of that place—long after the events, the people, the feelings themselves, have passed. This landscape is the screen on which I projected all my longings, losses and desires. It will resonate forever with those parts of me. When I embrace this place, I am embracing Valery, Ray, my own past self.

The train isn't moving, just sits here, steam rising from the platform. There is something stirring in the aisle, imperceptible, sensed. Not again! *Relax, honey, we still have three minutes left.* The angle of the gray morning light casts a faint shine along the bones, thin now, just a suggestion. He reaches out his hand and strokes my cheek with the back of his fingers, the lightest touch, in exactly the way I stroke my children's faces. So that gesture is his final gift; no cheap earrings this time—just a memory. A habit that has been imprinted in the cells, and is passed on, and will endure. Such a small thing, I don't know if it is important enough to cancel out and transcend larceny. That particular sweetness in him—it was there all the time, and is in me, too; a kind of blueprint. I recognize it in others; I am able to love. Slowly the train begins to move, and Raymond Weiler evaporates with the steam—silent, and perhaps at peace.

I press my forehead against the window and smile: Farewell, beginnings. I feel the pull, then the slow acceleration, as the buildings grow small, the multiple greens recede, and the infinite pale sky over all remains, vaporous and everlasting. I feel myself alive, and separate, and moving on.